2ND HOLY WARRIOR

THE HUNT FOR HITLER

Book 2 of the Visions series

V. RAY

CONXM PUBLISHING
Lakewood Ranch, Florida
www.CONXM.com

Illustration credits:
1. Cover artwork licensed from CanStockPhoto, Artist Jetrel, and edited by V. Ray.
2. Back cover images from the public domain by unknown photographers and edited by V. Ray.
3. All chalkboard drawings created by V. Ray.

While several historical figures and events are incorporated into this work, it is a work of fiction. All historical figures and events incorporated into this work are done so fictitiously. All other names and characters are fictitious, and any resemblance to actual persons, living or dead, is purely coincidental.

CONTENTS

Main Characters

Abraham Toch: Fictional German physicist.

Adolf Hitler: Historical figure; German dictator.

Albert Einstein: Historical figure. Scientist most known for his Theory of Relativity.

Sir Archie: Beta Knight of the First Order.

Bernie: One of the Boys training with young Max.

Dave Roth aka Sergeant Smith: Top combat trainer for Project Spear in Princeton.

Dieter: One of the Men training with young Max.

Erik: One of the Men training with young Max.

Gregory Rutledge: CIA Director and Max's closest friend in the present day.

Hagan Ister: Director of the Thule Society in Germany.

Helen Tyson: Retired high school teacher who raised Trey Tyson and his siblings. Max's cousin.

Dr. Jessica (O'Neal) Tyson: Doctor of Gerontology. Married to Trey Tyson.

Johnny Fox: Max's mentor. Sebastian's uncle. Samantha's great uncle. Shawnee descendent of Chicf Tecumseh.

Karl: Deceased Alpha Knight of the First Order.

Kirk: One of the Men training with young Max.

Maximo "Max" Medici: Retired director of Advance Intelligence division of Secret Service in present day. Descendent of Nostradamus. Young spy training with Albert Einstein in 1945.

Michel De Nostradame (Nostradamus): Historical figure. Prophet, alchemist, and visionary.

Dr. Niels Bohr: Historical figure. Danish physicist known as one of the leading proponents of quantum mechanics.

Nora Cohen aka Nurse Jones: Army nurse. Administrator of Project Spear in Princeton.

Samantha "Sam" Fox: Deceased member of Advance Intelligence division of the Secret Service. Shawnee descendent of Chief Tecumseh. Trey's best friend.

Sebastian Weinhardt: Max's best friend and fellow young spy in Project Spear.

Trey Tyson: Promising visionary descending from two family lines with historic prophetic abilities.

Ulrich Von Becker: German SS and Bodyguard to Hagan Ister.

Victoria "Tori" Cromwell: Associate Director of Science with the Smithsonian's National Museum of Natural History.

Zelda: Stray Sister of the Oracle family line, advising and assisting Hagan Ister.

Chapter 1

ALBERT EINSTEIN
PRINCETON, NJ, USA
MARCH 20, 1945

A traitor?

The mere possibility terrifies me. My stomach convulses, causing bile to rise to the point where I can taste it. My hand trembles uncontrollably and I almost crumple the coded letter. I want to be wrong. I want to believe I made a mistake in decoding the message, but I do not make mistakes like that. With my hand still shaking, I reach for the black telephone on the corner of my cluttered desk and press the red button below the rotary dial.

Less than two hours after my call, Dr. Conant arrived, along with these three other men across from my desk. Standing. Staring. Waiting.

It is a warm late morning in New Jersey, considering we are still in March. The poorly insulated walls of the log cabin that serves as the project's administration building often let in a chill from the outside. Today, however, the chill emanates from within.

Dr. Conant, with his pungent cologne overpowering the typically dingy smell of the cabin, slowly tilts his head down to peer at me over his black-rimmed glasses. He exhales through clenched teeth before saying, "Professor Einstein, we're a mere seven days from sending your first group of young spies into Germany and you discover you have a *traitor* on your campgrounds. Who is it?"

No introductions – just right to the point.

Beads of sweat roll down my forehead, and at 66 years of age, my back throbs. The pain in my stomach piques for a moment, yet I manage to maintain eye contact with Dr. Conant. Common courtesy would have me stand when these men barged into my office, but I fear if I do, I will topple over in pain. People say my name as though it is synonymous with genius; that odd-looking professor with the wildly frayed white hair who comes up with even wilder theories. The man with all the answers. Well, I do not have *this* one.

"I am afraid ... I do not know," I finally respond.

Dr. James Conant is not only the President of Harvard University; he is Chairman of America's National Defense Research Committee. The project ... the campgrounds ... my involvement ... they are all part of his elaborate plan.

He is accompanied by a tall thin man in his late forties with neatly combed brown hair and wire rimmed glasses, wearing a dark gray suit. They could be brothers.

The other two men are built like tanks in black suits.

When I first came to America, Conant recruited me heavily to take a teaching position at Harvard, and I am beginning to think that he never forgave me for choosing Princeton instead.

As though he could read my thoughts, Conant seethes, "I should have known that letting you keep your job at Princeton was a mistake. You understand that President Roosevelt is going to be here for your first team's graduation? You've been at this for nearly a year, and now, *seven days* from sending your first three spies into action, you discover you have a traitor. We need to figure this out, and figure it out now."

I find him to be so irritating and it hardly helps that he is pointing out what I already know. "I may not know who, but *someone* is about to betray us. *Ze* consequences ... well, it is not going too far to say *ze* entire world and all its people are at risk."

Conant nods to one of the three men – the one who looks like his brother. "Professor Albert Einstein, this is Dr. Vannevar Bush. Dr. Bush is the Director of the Office of Scientific Research and Development. Congress moved my committee under his purview. So, now I report to him and he is the Chief Science Advisor to President Roosevelt. Under the circumstances, we had best bring Dr. Bush up to speed with the situation."

"Even under the circumstances," Dr. Bush says as he sets down his briefcase and reaches to shake my hand, "it is an honor to meet you, Professor Einstein." Bush is a little taller than Conant and a bit more distinguished.

"Dr. Bush, your achievements are *well* known. *Ze* honor is mine."

"The two gentlemen who have accompanied us are agents here on behalf of the Secret Service and need to evaluate the camp prior to the president's arrival," says Bush, who exudes competence, without being obnoxious or overly confident. "Perhaps they can do so while we talk?"

"Of course."

"Floyd, what questions do you have for the professor before you look around?" Bush asks the larger of the two agents.

"Well, Professor Einstein," starts Floyd, "I only saw two guards at the gate. How have you kept the camp secure?"

"Because we are so close to Princeton University, we keep a small security force of twelve men with four on duty at all times. Ze theory has always been ze fewer people who know about our camp – ze more out of sight and out of mind – ze better. Two secure ze gate at all times and two more patrol ze camp. We only keep a few guns, both American and German, to train our young men. When they are not in use on ze shooting range, we store them in ze instructor's cabin."

"Can you give us a general layout of the camp?" asks Floyd, taking notes on a small pad he pulled from his inner jacket pocket.

"I can help with that," says Dr. Conant before I can begin to answer. "We have a large stretch of property that borders the northwest shore of Lake Carnegie here in Princeton." He points out the small window in my office. "You can see the gymnasium and the path to the shooting range. Other than being so close to the university, the camp is ideal for our needs. Located deep in the woods, five small cabins were already on the property. The construction of the gym, science lab, and mess hall was completed well before Professor Einstein identified the first team of trainees. The Army Corps of Engineers shaped long, natural-looking berms to hide the camp from any potential prying eyes. They used thick rows of evergreens and more berms to section off the shooting range."

"What about visitors – who comes and goes?" asks Floyd.

The pain in my gut subsides a little and I decide to answer that one. "We keep a jeep and a truck on site, but I am ze only person who regularly comes and goes, and that is usually on foot. Ze camp is so close to my home that I can easily walk ze distance. Nurse Jones goes out for supplies once a week. Oh, and one of ze trainees, Maximo Medici, occasionally sits in on my evening lectures at ze university."

"That would seem to be outside of protocol – why does this one trainee leave the camp?" asks Bush, obviously uneasy with my decision regarding Max.

"*Ze* Medici boy has a remarkable understanding of physics and I encourage him to learn more from my lectures. As you know, Project Spear was conceptualized by Dr. Conant, and –"

"Yes," Conant cuts me off in a harsh tone. "We are in a race with Nazi Germany to build the first atomic bomb. We all know the Manhattan Project was launched to build the atomic bomb – that's our offense. Project Spear is our defense. These six young men are being trained to infiltrate Germany and sabotage the Nazi efforts to build the bomb."

How was it that Conant described Project Spear when he first approached me to lead the project? He had been trying to decide between the names Spear and Shield. *When defending yourself against a powerful enemy,* he said, *I would rather have a spear than a shield. The long reach allows you to keep your enemy at bay, and the sharp tip allows for a pointed counterattack, or, even better, a first strike.* The man may be pompous and surly, but it is difficult to find fault with his reasoning.

I am finally feeling well enough to stand. "*Ze* young men have to train for both *ze* physical and intellectual challenges they will face in Germany. Sergeant Smith is teaching them to use American and German weapons, as well as his techniques in hand-to-hand combat. I am teaching them *ze* physics behind an atomic bomb, and to recognize materials and equipment needed to produce one. Most of *ze* trainees show much more enthusiasm for weapons or combat training than science lab, but not *ze* Medici boy. Maximo – he goes by Max – has shown a real aptitude for physics. *Ze* more he learns about it, *ze* better he will be able to accomplish his mission."

Bush nods, seeming satisfied with our answers.

"Okay," Floyd says, after waiting to see if Bush had any additional questions for me, "can someone show us around?"

"Nurse Jones!" I attempt to say her name loud enough for her to hear from her office, but my weakened voice does not carry far.

Still, she hears me and steps into my office quicker than she should have been able to if she had been sitting at her desk in her office. Now that I think of it, I remember seeing her hover outside my office door a few times recently.

A plain and often stoic 34-year-old woman, somewhat shorter than average, but with an athletic build. Bright, but far from genius, her real strength – what she adds most to the project – is her attention to detail. Jones not only treats the many scrapes and other minor injuries the trainees sustain, but also manages the supplies, mess hall, and most of the paperwork needed for the project. She stands in the doorway, looking quizzically at the visitors to our camp. She has met Dr. Conant before today, but none of the others.

"Nurse Jones, these two men are Secret Service agents. They are here to make sure it is safe for *ze* president to visit. Please show them around *ze* camp."

"Of course, Professor," she says in her typically professional voice, and noticeably without any signs of surprise on her part. "Please follow me."

Once Jones and the agents have left the administration building, Conant and Bush take the two chairs opposite my desk.

I am still clutching the letter that started all of this, but reluctantly place it on my desk as I sit.

"Let's start with this letter you received," says Conant, pointing to the paper. "What, exactly, does it say?"

"Wait," says Bush. "First, who sent it?"

"Abraham Toch, a dear friend and former colleague. He sent it from Germany. *Ze* Kaiser Wilhelm Institute in Berlin, to be specific. He is a physicist and is being forced by *ze* Nazis to work on Germany's atomic bomb development." Both men raise their eyebrows, instantly suspicious, but let me continue. "It is a short, coded letter that simply says his superiors have been discussing Project Spear. *Ze* Nazis are aware of our project."

Bush and Conant exchange a glance before turning their attention back to me.

"Someone, who knows about Project Spear, must also be in contact with someone in Berlin. They are passing on information, but we do not know what they have passed on yet."

"I agree with your assessment, Professor," says Bush. He stands, and paces twice across my office. I have seen that look before in other scientists – deep in thought – and have been there often myself. I know I would not want to be interrupted mid-stream. Sitting again, he continues, "That leaves us the difficult decision of how to move forward from here, knowing we have a traitor in our midst. What's your recommended course of action, Dr. Conant?"

"That the Germans are even aware of the name of Project Spear concerns me. Then you add the fact that it comes out a week before graduation and President Roosevelt is planning to attend …. I don't think we have any choice but to scrap the entire operation," Conant smirks. "I'll take full responsibility for the failure … for putting the wrong leadership team in place."

This spikes my ire instantly.

"No!" I pound my fist on the desk. "There is too much at stake to give up now. This is about Adolf Hitler! Neither of you is a Jew. You do not know *what* it is like. Here in America, we face mistrust … dislike … sometimes even hatred. But, our history in ze rest of ze world has been nothing short of brutal. From ze beginning, we have had to fight for our freedom … for a land to call our own … for our very survival. Now, under Hitler, it is far worse. *Ze extermination of all Jews in Europe.* How did we come to this … this … genocide? If Hitler builds ze atomic bomb, do you really think he will stop once he kills all ze Jews? With ze bomb, he will be able to kill anyone – and in massive numbers."

"No," Dr. Bush shakes his head assertively. "Letting Hitler build the bomb is not an option. We don't know what the Germans know about Project Spear. And, we cannot simply scrap the program – it's too late in the game. We're better off to root out this traitor before they can truly hurt the project. I want details about everyone who knows anything about it. Let's start at the top. How did you become involved with the project in the first place, Professor Einstein?"

Conant's smirk is gone. This did not take the direction he anticipated. That does not matter, though. We still have a traitor in our camp. My head drops and my eyes fall upon the letter again. "It is possible this is entirely my fault – this race to build ze most destructive weapon in ze his … ze his … ze his … ze *history* of ze world." Dear God, I have not stuttered like that since I was a child.

"What do you mean?" asks Bush, gracefully ignoring my stutter.

"Science is so simple. It only gets complicated when you factor in personalities, borders, politics, or religions … *especially* religions."

"You see," I continue, "1905 was ze year I published much of what I had been working on during my youth … four papers, actually. Ze first, called ze Production and Transformation of Light, is considered by many to be ze foundation of all quantum theory. Ze second paper, ze Motion of Small Particles, explained ze empirical evidence of atomic theory. Special Relativity was ze third and –"

"Professor," interrupts Conant, "we are both aware of your accomplishments. There's no –"

"Indeed," Dr. Bush similarly interrupts Conant, but with a much kinder tone. "Those three papers, along with the fourth, transformed the way we think of the universe. The name *Einstein* will one day be said with the same reverence as *Copernicus, Galileo,* and *Newton.* Please continue."

Dr. Conant's hand finds its way onto my desk and his fingers begin to tap out some sort of pattern. Maybe a song? There is so much more I could say about the difficulty I faced in starting my career and I am certain it was anti-Semitism ... but these men have never had to experience any of that. They both have American accents to their English ... both born here in America ... isolated from the troubles in Europe.

"In 1908, I finally secured my first teaching job at the University of Bern as a Lecturer. I had gained a reputation as a world leader in science, and by 1914, I could choose to move to most any university or institution. I went back home to Germany as a Professor at *ze* Humboldt University and *ze* Director of *ze* Kaiser Wilhelm Institute for Physics in Berlin."

"The same institute where the Germans are now building the atomic bomb," Conant points out.

"Yes," I shrug off the comment. "My family, friends, and colleagues were all in Germany. I was happy and successful. But, *ze* prosperity I was experiencing at *ze* time was not common. *Ze* German people were suffering greatly from a lack of resources and out of control inflation due to *ze* loss in *ze* First World War. A new political party came into power, represented by a charismatic leader. To hear him talk was something very special. He grasped *ze* attention of *ze* people with his message of German superiority. Then, he rallied *ze* population around a common enemy – *ze* supposed cause of all *ze* problems – *ze* Jews. *That* was *ze* message that worked for Hitler and *ze* Nazis, inspiring *ze* German people. And, that was how World War II and *ze* genocide of all Jews began."

"You could easily be there next to your friend Toch, being forced by the Nazis to work on their bomb," says Bush, again with a kind tone.

"I was fortunate. I could move my family to Switzerland before moving myself to America. Others did not have *ze* same options. Most of my former colleagues have been forced to work on what *ze* German people know only as *ze wonder weapons.*"

"We sometimes forget that it's not just the atomic bomb they're working on," Conant's tone has softened to match Bush's.

"True, but the atomic bomb is the game changer," says Bush, who faces me squarely. "There was, of course, your fourth and last paper of

1905, on Matter-Energy Equivalence. From it, came your most famous equation: E=mc^2. It's the basis of nuclear energy."

"*E=mc²,*" I am barely able to whisper the equation. "It is my theory and my equation, so it could easily be argued that this is entirely my fault. Without it, would Adolf Hitler still be in power? Would we *still* be fighting this war? Nuclear energy is at *ze* very heart of *ze* matter."

"We are trying to build an atomic bomb here in America. The Germans are also trying to build an atomic bomb, the most potent of wonder weapons. The future of the world depends upon which country finishes first," Dr. Bush states, resolute to our victory, as the alternative is unfathomable.

Bush directs his next question to Dr. Conant, "When did you start the project?"

"I had long known Professor Einstein while he was considering offers from many universities in America," Conant begins, "and it was the professor's letter to President Roosevelt – 1939, I believe – that got both the Manhattan Project and Project Spear launched."

"Really? How did that come to be?" asks Bush, turning back to face me.

"I was quite content as a simple Professor here at Princeton, until a fateful meeting six years ago with physicist Leo Szilard – another Jewish scientist who had to leave Germany and make his way to America. *What would happen if we were to split uranium atoms?* It all began with this simple question from Szilard. My equation for *ze* relationship between energy and mass has sparked more interest than anything else I have ever published. *E=mc².* Energy is equal to mass multiplied by *ze* square of *ze* velocity of light. Simply put, a very small amount of mass can be converted into a *very* large amount of energy."

Conant is still tapping his fingers on my desk impatiently, but does not interrupt me.

"Then, by 1939, atom-splitting nuclear fission experiments were already verifying my theory. And that was when Szilard arrived at my summer home. He had been splitting atoms of beryllium, indium, and graphite. He asked if I ever considered what would happen if we were to split uranium atoms."

"Yes," says Dr. Conant. "The three of us are all scientists. We now know that the dense nature of uranium, when subjected to neutron bombardment, creates a chain reaction of neutron collisions. The end result of this chain reaction is a loss of mass –"

"No," I counter. "It is a *conversion* of mass to energy. $E=mc^2$. This chain reaction could be almost endless, bounded only by *ze* amount of uranium used. *Ze* energy released from this chain reaction will be *staggering* and nearly instantaneous. Szilard implored me to understand *ze* implications … someone might be able to convert this massive release of energy into a bomb. And, what if such a bomb were in *ze* hands of Adolf Hitler?"

Conant stops tapping his fingers and leans back in his chair. "Explain to Dr. Bush how you found out the Germans were working on building the bomb."

I have to pause for a moment to consider what Dr. Conant is really trying to discover. Am I the focus of their investigation? I certainly would not blame them for considering me. Others might refuse to say any more. There might be risks in telling the full truth. On the other hand, we must find the underlying cause of this as quickly as possible.

"Once I realized *ze* potential threat, I immediately wrote to my friend Toch in Germany. He confirmed that *ze* Germans were, in fact, stockpiling uranium. I then wrote urgent letters to President Roosevelt, describing *ze* threat of *ze* atomic bomb. *Ze* president quickly acted to get America's atomic energy program started."

Dr. Conant nods impatiently, "And here we are today. I wanted Professor Einstein to lead the Manhattan Project. However, building the first atomic bomb was something he ardently refused to do."

"It was my theory and my equation that started all of this and I would contribute no more to building an atomic bomb. I felt compelled to turn down your offer."

Conant shrugs as though my second rejection never bothered him, yet I am certain it did. "Then, in 1943, we received further intelligence that the Germans were progressing with their atomic bomb efforts. I approached the professor in person. Asking … no, more like *insisting* that he help stop the Germans from being first to build the bomb."

"I have always considered myself to be a pacifist – especially after seeing *ze* massive number of deaths from *ze* First World War. I wanted *nothing* to do with building *ze* atomic bomb, but *defending* against *ze* Germans building one … that was a project I felt comfortable I could lead."

Dr. Bush carefully picks up the letter from my desktop and places it into his briefcase. "I am completely confident, Professor Einstein, that you are not the traitor implicated by this letter. Let's talk about the rest of your team, though, starting with the security guards."

Conant flashes an angry look at Bush and says, "The security team is mine. I personally vetted each of them. First, they don't even know the details of Project Spear and, second, they are under strict orders to have no interaction with any of the trainees. We'll find the traitor on Professor Einstein's team." Turning to me, he says, "Where do you keep your personnel files?"

"Follow me." On unsteady legs, I walk out of my office and into the next office, which belongs to Nurse Jones.

It is a reality. There is a traitor in our camp. Someone is revealing our secrets to the Germans.

But who?

As I ease myself into the chair behind the desk, looking up to the ceiling, I find it difficult to swallow. My abdomen is aflame, and the pain feels as though it extends from my bowels all the way to my throat. Is this what a heart attack feels like? I have not been able to keep any food down for a couple of days and my doctor tells me this ailment is life threatening. He says I need to take it easy. Avoid stress. Maybe even consider retirement.

Retirement? With Adolf Hitler building an atomic bomb? Of course, I cannot explain that to my doctor.

While unlocking and opening the file drawer, I cough and some of the acid from my stomach splashes on my esophagus. The *burning*.

"I suppose we should start with David Roth," I mutter through the pain while handing David's file to Dr. Bush. "For *ze* sake of secrecy, he is known only as Sergeant Smith to *ze* trainees. We brought him in from Fort Bragg, where Roth had been teaching new army recruits hand-to-hand combat techniques. His service record is impeccable. He pushes *ze* trainees hard, but with *ze* nearly impossible mission we are facing, Roth's techniques are necessary."

"Any changes in Roth's emotional state or his daily habits lately?" Bush questions.

"No, he is a rock. David is 53 and still keeps himself in perfect shape. His routines have routines. It is *ze* same every day with David."

"What about this Nurse Jones?" asks Bush.

I leaf through the files to find hers and then briefly wonder about the wisdom of having her keep a copy of her own personnel file. Too late to worry about that now.

"Her real name is Norah Cohen and she comes from Pearl Harbor. Cohen survived Japan's surprise attack and was one of *ze* few nurses on base who kept her wits about her. She saved many lives and ended up receiving a commendation from ze Navy. In addition, she is Jewish. Both Roth and Cohen were chosen because they are exceptional at what they do, and because both are Jewish. With ze atrocities against our fellow Jews in Germany, I cannot believe either would *ever* help ze Nazi cause."

"Could the traitor be one of the trainees?" asks Dr. Conant. He helped choose and recruit Roth and Cohen, so is probably more inclined to believe they are not the traitors.

"God, I hope not. These six young men are too important to our cause. *Men?* With ages from 15 to 21, it is difficult to think of them as men. Some of them are still just boys."

"Why so young?" There is more than a hint of concern in Dr. Bush's voice.

"That is a function of our mission. *Ze* trainees must fit in with ze German soldiers inside German borders. They have lost most of their men of fighting ages to ze war. *Ze* soldiers left standing in Germany are either young boys or very old men."

"So, to fit in, the trainees are all young and all German?" asks Bush. "And, while the instructors, Roth and Cohen, are both Jewish, they both may have family in Germany. Is that right?"

"Yes," I admit, realizing his point. "Can ze atrocities in Germany against Jews be enough to guarantee ze loyalty of *all* Jews? What if ze Germans are holding someone they know and love as a hostage? Could either betray our project to save a member of their family? It is a fair question .... I barely escaped Germany in time myself and I made certain my family was safe. But, to be honest, Roth and Cohen may not have been able to do ze same."

"The question may no longer be whom *can't* we trust?" proffers Bush.

"But," I finish his point, "whom *can* we trust?"

Glancing at each trainee's personnel file, I can feel my chest tightening. Another wave of pain grips me. We have to consider them all. They are all German. They all have family in Germany. *Except one* ....

Just then, a loud grunt outside the cabin grabs our attention and two of the trainees sprint past the window, side by side and stride for stride. I recognize them instantly. Sebastian and Max. Two or three seconds pass, then Bernie runs past the window.

With the commotion over as quickly as it began, I quickly review each of the trainee's files as I hand them over to Dr. Bush. The last file lingers in my hand a bit longer than I intend and Bush has to reach for it.

"Maximo Medici," he reads on the file tab.

"He is *ze* youngest of our trainees, at 15."

"Actually," says Bush, reading from Max's file, "today's his birthday. He's now the ripe old age of 16 .... Is he one of the boys that just ran by?"

"He is."

"The one who *doesn't* look German?" Bush asks with raised eyebrows.

"Yes. I have a different plan in mind with Max."

"I'm guessing you do," says Bush, as he places the personnel files in his briefcase, shuts it, and spins the combination lock mechanism.

The administration building's outer door creaks open and slams shut quickly. Then I hear the light, fast-paced footsteps of Nurse Jones. It sounds like she is alone.

"Professor?" She forces herself to smile when she enters her office … to be courteous even though we are in her territory. I wonder how many of her relatives are caught in the holocaust in Germany. "The agents are finished with the tour of the camp and are waiting outside."

Dr. Bush stands and offers his hand. "We're finished here, too, Professor Einstein. We have seven days to figure this problem out." He reminds me of our timeline, without giving away too many details to Jones. "I'll return these files once we've had an opportunity to review them thoroughly. Just part of the process prior to the president's visit. It was truly a pleasure to meet you."

"I want to thank you for your assistance."

The two men both nod to Nurse Jones before leaving.

"What was that all about – what's the problem he mentioned?" she probes, once the men are out of earshot.

She has always been a little too curious. What can I say? What does she already know? The breeze kicks up outside and the air pushing into her office whistles as it passes through the gap between the logs of the outer wall. It is not enough to get rid of the stench of Conant's cologne, but does give me an idea.

"Nurse Jones. I … I am hoping you can help me?"

"Of course, Professor." She glances around her office and then looks back at me, her heel tapping the tile persistently.

"Would you kindly find Max and ask him to meet me at *ze* pier?"

"The pier?" Her forehead scrunches as she tilts her head to the side.

"Yes. I will be waiting for him." Ignoring my pain, I stand and briskly walk out the door before she can question my purpose.

Chapter 2

MAX MEDICI

PRINCETON, NJ, USA
MARCH 20, 1945

My heart pounds and my breathing more like panting. My feet feel leaden against the heavily wooded trail we run *every* morning. Rain, wind, even snow – we run no matter what the conditions are. At least it's a nice day, a warm and breezy first day of spring, with the sun shining brightly through the breaks in the trees. Under my feet, the ground is mostly solid, but has many large roots and marshy patches to navigate. Sebastian sprints next to me, almost every step in sync with mine. I can hear Bernie – roughly fifty yards behind – whenever he runs through leaves or snaps a twig.

Starting at our cabin, the five-mile run begins east around the shooting range and then northeast along the shoreline of Lake Carnegie. Sebastian rounded the halfway tree about ten yards ahead of me, but I've closed the gap.

Between breaths, I glance at Sebastian. We're both nearly six feet tall, but his thin build and long legs are better suited for a marathon. With my broad shoulders and thick legs, I'm much better at sprints. This five-mile distance favors him and he consistently wins the race. I'm just trying to keep up with him until we get near the finish line. He looks just as tired as I feel.

"When we get back, it's a hundred push-ups for you!" I yell.

"No way, Max!" Sebastian yells back, laughing.

Rolling my eyes, I refocus on the race and try not to let his laugh get to me – that hefty laugh all these Germans seem to have. Sebastian is a mix though. He gets his German looks from his father, but his mother is Native American.

I, on the other hand, am not German and I'm reminded of it every day. I'm the only one with dark hair, dark eyes, and dark skin, just like the Italian side of my heritage points to. I don't let the scowls and insults from the others get to me. I'm just as capable for our mission as any of them.

Sebastian has been my best friend for years. He's the closest thing I have to family, actually, but there's been a constant pull by the other trainees to separate us. No one knows about our past, except Professor Einstein, and he told us we need to keep it a secret from the others. The only chance we ever get to truly talk is at night after Bernie's asleep in the cabin the three of us share.

Sebastian looks back and then yells, "Don't think I'm going to let you win today just because it's your birthday."

"Don't you dare use that excuse when I win!" I yell back.

At the start of the race, Sebastian took off a split second before Sergeant Smith yelled "Go." He got a 20-yard head start while Bernie and I waited for Smith to stop him. If that had been me, Smith would have made me come back and do tons of push-ups before I started the race again. But not with Sebastian. Bernie figured it out before I did and started to run. I gave Smith a quick glare then took off after them.

It's not who starts first that matters, but who finishes first. They're Smith's words echoing in my head. Of course, Smith is an asshole and Smith isn't even his real name.

Training for Project Spear takes place on a large campground just a short walk from Princeton University. The last time I went to one of Professor Einstein's lectures, I saw the university had posted signs about celebrating their bicentennial next year. It's been here in New Jersey for two hundred years and I don't think anyone from the university realizes campground is even here, just south of campus. Einstein does, of course, but he's the head administrator for the project.

There are two classes of trainees here at Project Spear, each consisting of three young men. The older class, known simply as the Men, has been training for almost a year. Sebastian, Bernie, and I are collectively known as the Boys and we've been training for three months.

I don't know how the Men were chosen, but the arduous selection process for the Boys began with about ninety teenagers. I heard that many of them had tried to join the military to fight in the war, but were too young. Others, like myself and Sebastian, had been found by recruiters for the project. We've been drilled on secrecy from the start. We're not supposed to share any personal details about ourselves with anyone else in the camp, not even our last names. Secret or not, I couldn't help but notice that each and every one of the potential recruits was German – except for me.

First, they tested us on physical endurance and that weeded out over half of the recruits. Then came intelligence testing and that knocked the group down to fifteen. Psychological profiling brought us down to nine and that's when they opened up about the fact the project would be highly dangerous. Not too many details at that point, but enough for two boys to decide it wasn't for them. Even when we were down to only seven potential recruits and we knew they would select three of us, I still never felt like I had a chance.

Selection day came and when Professor Einstein chose me for the project, I nearly fell over in shock. Sebastian took it in stride, but Bernie looked like he was about to puke.

During the recruiting and selection process, the administrators of Project Spear shared very few details. They only told us we'd be doing our country a great service in a time of great need. The conventional war is being fought on two primary fronts – in the Pacific against Japan, and in Europe against Germany and Italy.

Project Spear, as we learned once we were accepted into it, isn't concerned with the conventional war. We're part of a race to develop the first atomic bomb. Others might be playing on offense. We haven't been told anything about that. Our part in this race is on defense. My heart skips a beat whenever I think of the Germans possessing the atomic bomb. The loser of this race will be forced to truly fear the winner's every whim. If the Nazis win, anyone left alive will be speaking German soon.

Germany, we were told during our first briefing after being chosen, has renowned scientists, the world's best engineers, a stockpile of uranium, and a head start of at least a couple years. That was the first time I heard Sergeant Smith say, *"It's not who starts first that matters, but who finishes first."*

As we pass the shooting range, I notice a strange car near the administration building. One of our security guards stands next to the car, relaxed, as though there's nothing strange about this rare visit to our camp. I'm about to yell this to Sebastian, but he lengthens his strides a bit and pulls ahead of me. It's the same every race, like he uses the shooting range as a marker to start tapping into his reserves.

Doubt creeps into my mind. Doubt about catching up. Doubt about ever winning one of these races. Bigger than that, though, I still have trouble understanding why the professor chose me for this mission. It's just like when I was a kid at home and my dad always told me there was something wrong with me, that I didn't fit in. He was in the concrete business and spent his days working with his hands. His dad was in the concrete business and so was his grandfather.

I never wanted anything to do with concrete. Every day I spent hours at the library or reading at home. Some books were fiction, some were about science, and others about history, but the books would take me to a place far away from my reality.

My dad always said I'd be a failure at whatever I did and he had me believing it. Everything changed when they accepted me into Project Spear. It gave me a purpose and a reason to believe in myself.

With the war going so well, Sebastian thinks it will all be over before we ever get the green light to go to Germany, but I find myself hoping I do go ... hoping to make a difference. Sergeant Smith doesn't think I can fit in. Like my dad, he thinks I'm destined to fail. I'll show him ... I'll show them *all*.

Sebastian and I fly by the last few trees before reaching the clearing of the main camp, and I'm still trailing him. Sergeant Smith stands near the flagpole staring at his stopwatch. The sunshine reflecting off his head is nearly blinding as I draw near. He seems to be sweating even more than I am.

That's not too surprising, because Smith trains with the Men, keeping his posture remarkably straight for a man in his fifties. When he yells at us, which is most of the time, his face turns varying shades of red. I couldn't help but let out a laugh the first time I saw Smith's face turn pink and it cost me two hundred push-ups.

As we approach the flagpole, I pump my arms and legs quicker. In spite of my efforts, Sebastian is still ahead and I can hear Bernie closing the gap. I have to dig deeper.

A hundred yards to go and I reach for my last reserves of energy. Losing is not an option. Suddenly, I hear the crash of Bernie taking a tumble from only ten yards behind. He always finishes last in our morning runs and today is no different. Fifty yards to go and I'm still a step behind Sebastian. Damn, he's fast!

With twenty yards to go, we're neck and neck again.

Push! Sebastian reaches for the flagpole with ten yards still to go. Too soon! A split second later, and I reach for it, too.

Ping-Ping! The sounds of our hands clanging against the metal pole were nearly simultaneous. I crossed on the right an instant before Sebastian on the left. Then, a full ten seconds pass – giving Sebastian and me a glorious opportunity to catch our breath – before the last ping on the pole when Bernie reaches it.

Immediately after touching the pole, Bernie hunches over with his hands on his knees for support, gasping for breath. In between gasps, he starts vomiting. I look at Sebastian to see his reaction and his raised eyebrows say enough. I know all of Sebastian's looks by now.

"You're all worthless and weak!" belts Sergeant Smith. "God help us if we have to rely on you Boys to save us." He glares at Bernie, shaking his head in disgust.

Sometimes, when the sergeant speaks, he reminds me of my dad. The thought sends a shiver up my spine.

"Bernie," Smith bellows, "You're the last one up every morning, the last one to finish every meal, last on your science exams, and last in every race. You'll be late to yer own fuckin' funeral, boy. That's two hundred push-ups for ya."

To avoid his breakfast in liquid form, Bernie steps briskly to the side, then drops and starts doing his push-ups.

"Max," Smith looks at his stopwatch, "31 minutes and 56 seconds. It's a full minute behind the time the Men posted this mornin'. That's not good enough, boy. You're gonna have to run a hell of a lot faster 'n that if you Boys ever wanna be Men. Ya owe me a hundred push-ups .... Sebastian, I'll have 50 push-ups from ya."

I blink, hardly believing my ears. He *has* to be kidding. "Sir?"

"What are ya waitin' for, Max – a written invitation?"

"I won that race." The son of a bitch is either blind or he's messing with me. "I hit the pole first."

I look to Sebastian for support, but his only response is a quick wink and a barely audible snicker.

"That's not how I saw it, Max. Give me two hundred push-ups."

"But –"

"That'll be two hundred sit-ups, too," Smith cuts me off, his face turning its first shade of pink. "Got anything else to say?"

Sebastian drops and starts doing his push-ups. I'm not going to win this argument, but I'm not giving up.

"*There* you are, Max." It's Nurse Jones, coming from the direction of the administration building. "The professor would like to see you ... he wants you to meet him at the pier."

I look at Sergeant Smith, who now wears a deep shade of red that's approaching purple.

"On the double, boy! The professor don't have all day," Smith grunts. He's angry, even more than usual, which means I'm going to be doing hundreds of push-ups, sit-ups, and pull-ups the next few days.

Looking to Jones, her only reaction is a quick tilt of her head in the direction of the pier. She turns and heads back toward the administration building without another word.

The pier is only about a two-minute jog from the main camp, but I spend the entire time agonizing over why I'm being singled out. Over the past three months of training, the Boys have always trained as a unit. The Men always train together as well. The only variable is that sometimes our two groups have classes together ... science lab, demolition, shooting, or hand-to-hand combat. Meeting with the professor, individually, breaks all precedent.

The trees are sparser as I approach the pier and I spot Professor Einstein standing next to his little blue sailboat with the yellow sail. Carnegie Lake spans a great length, north to south, but is comparatively short from east to west. The pier is on the west side of the lake, and I can easily see the eastern shore past the professor and his boat. The breeze causes his wild hair to tilt to the side and this image makes me smile. The rickety old pier creaks as step onto it. Looking down to make sure I have safe footing allows me to hide my smile now that the professor can see me clearly.

"Ah, Max, finally here." Professor Albert Einstein always insists the Boys and the Men speak German around him. Immersion, he calls it, and he always does the same. Yet he just spoke to me in English. *Why?*

The professor is about the same age as my dad would be if still alive, but his demeanor is so different. Einstein is calm and he thinks before he speaks. When he does speak in English, it's at a very deliberate pace, with a strong German accent and a surprisingly high pitch.

"Hello Professor *Ein*-stein." My voice just cracked. *Unbelievable ...* try to calm down. Maybe the professor won't notice.

Professor Einstein extends his hand. "Happy birthday, Max. I thought we could spend some time sailing today."

I cautiously shake the professor's hand, finding it hard to believe anyone other than Sebastian would acknowledge my birthday. We're all sworn to secrecy. The Boys and the Men aren't allowed to disclose anything about our pasts – and certainly not our birthdays. Of the three administrators, only Professor Einstein uses his real name and only because he's famous.

"I, um ... well, thank you, Professor."

"You turned 16 today." The professor tries to smile, but it evaporates almost immediately. "I fear we are asking you Boys to grow up too soon. You are not even eligible for *ze* draft for another 4 years."

"I might not be eligible, but I would have lied about my age if I had to. I'd have found a way to join." I don't know where this meeting is going, but the start sure makes me feel uneasy.

"I suspect that is true," Professor Einstein agrees. "Come aboard, Max."

As we board the small, single mast sailboat, I notice the name on the back. "What does the name Tinef mean?"

The professor shrugs and smiles. "It is *tiny* – almost worthless."

I don't know anything about sailing and, as far as I can tell, Professor Einstein is far from an expert. He's wobbly enough on land and even more so on a boat. I often wonder how the professor doesn't trip over himself.

We sail for nearly five minutes without a word spoken. The silence seems to suit the professor quite well, but it makes me uncomfortable. I have to say something and finally blurt, "Have you been sailing long, Professor Einstein?"

"Indeed, Max. Most of my life." There's a glint of light reflecting off the professor's eyes as he looks east. A small gust fills Tinef's sail and pushes us gently to the north. The wind is much stronger and colder here on the lake than it was at the main camp. From the west, I can smell leaves burning, but don't see a flame.

Another awkward silence follows. It leaves me wondering, again, why I'm here alone with him. Maybe Sergeant Smith convinced the professor to kick me out of the program.

When he finally speaks again, it startles me. "I would like to learn more about you, young Maximo."

First my birthday and now my full name? He's been viewing my file. *Why?* I study him closely and he notices my hesitation.

"A situation has come up … unexpectedly," he continues. "I will be having these conversations with each of you trainees over *ze* next few days. I need to ask you about your family, starting with your parents … as much family history as you can provide. Where were they born? What was your relationship like with them? As you well know, none of you trainees are supposed to know anything about each other. Secrecy is of *ze utmost* importance, if we are to be successful. But you and Sebastian came here together. You are very close and there is no secrecy between you. When did you meet and what can you tell me about Sebastian's family?"

I blink, overwhelmed with his questions. I hardly registered *family history* before I was thinking about my dad ... and my mom. The professor is studying me, evaluating my reactions as if I'm some sort of experiment of his. Is this a test? Is he trying to see if I'll talk too easily? Sergeant Smith just started to teach us what we're supposed to say if we ever get captured in Germany. Do I follow that line, or is this more of a test of loyalty?

"I ... I'm not sure what to say." If this was my dad and I didn't answer his question immediately, I'd have been slapped across the face by now, or worse. I even flinch a bit, but there's no such aggression from Professor Einstein. The professor looks concerned ... not angry in the least.

"Please, relax," he says. "I know you have been sworn to secrecy. This is different. It is me. And we are on a boat in *ze* middle of a lake with no one around us. For *ze* sake of *ze* project, I need to know your family history and how you met Sebastian."

"Where should I begin, Professor?"

"I do not want you to spare any details, Max. It is important and, as you can see, we have *ze* time."

The *last* thing I want to do is relive the horrific memories of my dad and mom. Do I tell the truth or make up a story? Something safe and easy?

I clear my throat before beginning my story, "I was eight when I met Seba ... Seba ..." *Really?* The stuttering has to hit me now? I've never been able to say Sebastian's full name without stuttering, so I've always called him Ian. Taking a deep breath, I decide to start over. "I was eight when I met Ian – Sunday, December 19, 1937 – it's a day I'll never forget."

Suddenly, I just stop talking. I'm looking at the sail, then beyond the sail and at the sky, but my mind is in another place. Another time.

> *"Stu, stu, stupido! You're wasting your time with that book. You'll never fit in!"* I was all of six years old the first time my dad gave me a black eye. At school the next day, my teacher asked if I had been in a fight, and that was the first of many times I lied and said I tripped.

I shiver, recalling my dad's berating voice.

"Max?" says Professor Einstein gently. "Are you alright?"

"My parents," I blurt out, trying to separate the present from the past. "I was very close to my mother, Irene. She was born in France."

"Do you know much about her parents and grandparents? Is there anyone in *ze* family line from Germany?"

"I don't know her family line past my grandparents, but they were all French. I know they moved from Paris to Montreal, initially, before moving to Detroit. My mom was still very young when they came to America."

"And, from your mother, you learned to speak French?"

"Yes, but my French is far from perfect. My dad didn't like it when my mom and I spoke in any language other than Italian."

"Your father. His name was Alessandro? He came from Italy?"

"Yes, he moved to Detroit with my grandparents and my aunt when he was a teenager."

"And, from him, you learned to speak Italian?"

> *"Stupido!"* My father would scream. *"I told you – you'll speak Italian in my house, or you'll leave it!"*

"I, uh … yes, from him."

"Tell me more about your father, Max," he continues. "What about his family line?"

I recall my dad's way of teaching me about our family line when he caught me with a book from the library.

> *"A history book? Stupido! Our family history is the only history you need to know. My grandfather taught it to my father. My father taught it to me. I teach it to you. Someday, if you can ever get a girl to like you, you may have a son and you need to teach him this …"*

"My father taught me about the Medici family line, all the way back to Duke Alessandro de' Medici, who ruled Florence briefly in the 16th Century. The Duke's father wasn't known for certain, so that's as far back as I know, but I was taught that they've always lived in Italy. Never Germany."

"*Ze* Medici family line is quite well known, and has always supported both artists and scientists," Einstein says in an appreciative tone, as if I had something to do with it.

"My mother told me that, but I don't have any ties with my dad's family in Italy." Not all Medici men are like your father, my mother had once said, or your grandfather. There was trepidation in her voice. Fear. But, she wanted me to know some of the positive from our family history and that I didn't have to be like my dad. My mom first took me to the library … first introduced me to a world outside of our existence in Detroit.

"How did you meet Sebastian?" asks the professor, seemingly satisfied that my family isn't a threat to our mission.

"I remember being sent by my father to ask our neighbors to borrow something …."

"I'm out of whiskey, Putanna." My dad wrapped his thick, calloused hands around my mom's throat and squeezed.

"Please," I remember pleading, *"st … st … st …."* I wanted to say *stop*, but the word wouldn't come out. I always have trouble saying the ST sound without stuttering.

"St, st, stupido!" My dad mocked my stuttering and backhanded me across the face, but at least he released my mom. *"I told you to speak Italian in my house. Now make yourself useful and go find me some whiskey."*

He lifted by my shirt off the floor and threw me out the front door into three feet of snow. No coat. No shoes. I didn't know what to do. I remember wondering if it was safe to leave my mom with him.

I soon decided it was best to get him whiskey and fast.

Trudging through the snow and slush, I knocked on one door at a time. Every house in the neighborhood was a red brick bungalow. Some had white siding on the top level, but most were completely brick. The only way any of the houses differed – the one spark of creativity – was the paint color chosen for the front door. I knocked on black doors, red doors, white doors … gray, blue, gold … none of our neighbors answered.

Three blocks away, a different world for an eight-year-old, I found the one and only green painted door. I knocked, and to my surprise, the door opened almost immediately. A dark featured woman with a chubby, friendly face let me in. She took pity on me and wrapped me in blankets so I could warm up.

"… Just a few blocks from my house, I met Ian's mom. She said they had just moved to Detroit and her son was my age. She thought I might be a good friend for Sebas … Sebas … " I try to keep my frustration in check. "Sorry Professor. I sometimes have trouble with getting words out."

"I had a similar problem with stuttering when I was young, Max. I know how difficult … how frustrating it can be …. If you recall, it was through Johnny Fox that we found both you and Sebastian. How did you meet Johnny?"

"Ian and I quickly became best friends. I spent more and more time with his family. We'd spend our entire summers together at their cabin in Canada. And I met Johnny there."

"Sebastian's father is German, but his mother is not. She is an American Indian?" the professor asks.

"Um, yes. Johnny is Ian's uncle and he says they prefer to be called Native Americans – even better by their tribe, the Shawnee."

"Yes, of course," he smiles. "Tell me about your time with Johnny. I understand you did some training with him?"

"Ian told me his Uncle Johnny worked for the Canadian military, training their army recruits in hand-to-hand combat. He liked taking us fishing and hunting, and we were spending most of our summers with him. One day, without even asking me about it, Ian asked his uncle to teach us to fight. Johnny was hesitant at first, but Ian convinced him we may be going to war someday and it could only help us to learn to take care of ourselves."

"Our own Sergeant Smith had come to fight alongside Johnny Fox during *ze* last Great War; said Johnny was *ze* best fighter he has ever seen. So, we sent a recruiter to find him. We were looking for trainees like yourself …. I am curious. What did he teach you?"

"He did his best to teach us Nileča, a martial art that he invented and taught to the Canadian Special Forces. Nileča is a form of close quarter, hand-to-hand combat training that's defense and counterstrike oriented. We would train with Johnny for hours every day, then he'd try to get us to meditate at night."

"Meditation?" Einstein asks. "Why did he teach you meditation?"

"Johnny often said that an angry warrior is rarely a wise warrior. We had to learn to master our emotions. To control them, so they wouldn't control us."

"Now I am curious if we should be teaching meditation to all of our recruits – maybe right before your plastic explosives classes?"

We make eye contact and I realize Professor Einstein is joking. We both laugh and I think it's the first time I've ever seen him lighten up.

The professor notices that we're closing in on the northern end of the lake, and turns the boat around using the rudder and tying the sail – something Johnny once told me was called the main sheet – to the opposite side of the small boat. I move to the other side of the boat to keep it stable.

Comfortably sitting at the rudder, the professor takes on a serious tone again, "How was Johnny able to get two energetic young boys like you and Sebastian to calm down and meditate?"

"He explained the importance of meditation to Shawnee warriors and the connection it can provide to the spirit world. Johnny said his family line went all the way back to Chief Tecumseh and his brother who the Shawnee called the Prophet. Some people, like the Prophet, could use meditation to talk to the Great Spirit and even to see the future. That's all Ian and I needed to hear for us to want to try it. Then, one night, when Ian and I were both twelve, he demonstrated the power of it to us. He lit a fire and then lit a peace pipe. He explained that we had to clear our minds ... to focus on nothing but our breathing and the flickering flame."

"Very intriguing," the professor says. "Logic can point you from A to B to C, but *imagination* can take you anywhere. Max, I have always believed *ze* human mind is capable of so much more than we currently know. And there are reports throughout history of accurate prophecies that seem difficult to dispute .... Did it work?"

"This memory is so clear .... Johnny smoked from the peace pipe first, then Ian, and then it was my turn. I inhaled deeply, just like they did. The first puff made me cough so violently, my eyes watered. Ian just laughed. After my third turn with the pipe, I became light-headed. Letting my mind relax and my eyes focus on the flame, I think I fell into a deep trance state. At first, the flame was all I could see. It was burning brightly, but it was diminishing before my eyes. Darkness encompassed the flame, seeming to force it in on itself. There was a voice in the darkness – someone crying out ... pleading. The voice was familiar, but I couldn't place it at first. After a few moments, I realized it was my mom. The flame in my dream shrunk ever smaller, flickered once more, and then went out. I snapped out of the trance state instantly."

The professor's expression is a mix of shock and concern as I continue, "I absolutely panicked, told Johnny and Ian what I had seen, and his family took me back to Detroit. There … well … it was a madhouse. Police cars everywhere … lights flashing …." My voice suddenly gives out.

This time, Professor Einstein fills the awkward silence. "Max, I read about *ze* murder-suicide in your file. You don't need to elaborate."

"My dad was a monster and I wasn't there to protect my mom, Professor. I'll never forgive myself for that. And, do you know that I never shed a tear for her? How is that possible? What's wrong with me? My anger for my dad completely overshadowed the loss of my mom. If he hadn't killed himself, I would have … I would have …."

The professor sits silently for a moment, looking at me with a sadness his eyes are able to convey better than anyone I know. When he finally speaks, it's just above a whisper. "You became an orphan. What happened to you after that?"

My overpowering feeling was simply anger and I held onto it as if it was the last torch in a long, dark tunnel. But that's not a feeling I want to share with the professor. *Breathe*, just like Johnny taught me during our summers together.

"I had *no* idea what to do or where to go. But, Ian's family opened their doors to me. They've been so kind. Over the last three years, Ian and I spent our school-months in Detroit and our summers in Canada with Johnny. I taught Ian some Italian and he taught me some German."

"And, so that explains how you learned to speak some German before getting here," Professor Einstein nods slowly, with raised eyebrows.

"It was during this past summer with Johnny that your recruiter came knocking."

"Yes," the professor says softly, still absorbing my story. "As you now know, we needed to find young men who were highly intelligent and well trained in hand-to-hand combat for this … assignment. I remember what our Sergeant Smith said to *ze* recruiters he sent out. He said I want a PhD who can win a bar fight."

"*And* you were looking for men who looked German." I touch on a point that has been bothering me since I first stepped foot in Princeton.

"That is true, Max," the professor admits. "Johnny Fox has developed a nice reputation for himself when it comes to training Canadian forces and we hoped he could lead us to recruits who could fit our requirements. When we found Johnny, his nephew Sebastian was a perfect fit for *ze* program. I understand Johnny was rather insistent that we consider you as well, even though you do not have *ze* appearance we sought."

"Then, *why* am I here?"

Professor Einstein, after thinking about it for a few moments, finally admits, "Accepting you into Project Spear was *not* a unanimous decision."

I remember how Sergeant Smith refused to make eye contact with me when the administrators told me I'd been accepted. It was so ... uncomfortable. It was obvious he didn't think I fit in ... that he didn't want me in the project. I didn't know why at the time, but now that I know our mission, I understand. I *don't* fit in.

"However," the professor continues, "*ze* decision was ultimately mine to make, Max. You excelled in every area we tested, but more than that, you are a survivor. *Ze* horrors of your childhood made you *ze* young man you are today. Sometimes, when your enemies can easily overpower you, survival is *ze* only goal you can hope to achieve. There is a saying I hear sometimes from my Jewish friends in Germany, in Israel, and even here .... *Live*, to fight another day. And, that is *ze* trait I see in you ... a trait that cannot be taught in this camp."

Thinking of what Hitler is doing to the Jews is infuriating. The professor has had to live with it, knowing so many people he cares about are in concentration camps ... or dead.

"Why?" he asks.

"Professor?"

"You now know why I chose you. But, you were never forced into this assignment. You volunteered for it. So, why?"

"I've seen, too often, when someone *hurts* someone else ... because they're angry ... because they're bigger and stronger ... sometimes for no other reason than because they can. I hate bullies and Adolf Hitler is the worst bully of all."

A gust of wind sends the sailboat tilting to the side, so I deftly move to the high side of the boat.

"Can I ask you a question?"

"Of course, Max."

"If we're training to sabotage the German atomic weapons program, am I right to guess that we're also trying to build our own atomic weapons before the Germans can?"

The professor looks curiously at me for a moment before answering, "You are *very* bright, young Maximo. However, if there were such a project, it would have *ze* same Top Secret classification as Project Spear."

"I'm curious, though," I press on. "Assuming we have our own atomic weapons program here in America, why aren't you leading that project instead of this one?"

"Would you get rid of me so easily?" The professor laughs.

"No. Of course not."

"Have you ever heard of *ze* Nobel Peace Prize?" Einstein asks.

"Sure, I have."

"Alfred Nobel was a brilliant chemical engineer, made famous and enormously wealthy for inventing dynamite and manufacturing armaments. When he invented dynamite, it was *ze* most destructive force on *ze* planet. There is no guessing at *ze* number of deaths throughout history that have been caused by his dynamite and other armaments."

Professor Einstein shakes his head, seeming for a moment to guess at the number, before continuing, "It has been said by people who knew Nobel that he felt, and carried with him, a great guilt that he could never let go. He set aside much of his fortune to establish and fund *ze* Nobel Prizes, including *ze* Nobel *Peace* Prize. I believe he did this to appease that great guilt he felt."

"Well, Max," the professor looks down for a moment and then returns his gaze to me. "A single atomic bomb, should it ever be built and used, will release *ze* same amount of destructive energy as *30 million pounds* of dynamite. One atomic bomb could wipe out a city and its inhabitants in nearly an instant. Even if detonating just one of these bombs could end this war – end *ze* German death camps and all *ze* atrocities committed against my fellow Jews – that is *far* more guilt than this old man could bear."

I respect Einstein more than anyone I've ever met, but I'm not so sure I could maintain the same moral scale he has. If I could wipe out Hitler and the Nazis with an atomic bomb – put an end to the war and all the atrocities – I wouldn't hesitate.

"What do the Germans do to the Jews in these death camps we hear about? Sebastian told me some of the stories he heard from the Men. The stories are terrifying ... despicable."

The professor pauses, reading me, thinking of his response, then says, "There is little likelihood that you will need to be concerned about German death camps. First, *ze* war in Europe is nearing an end. *Ze* Germans know this. They made a drastic mistake when they attacked *ze* Russians, and now they are facing enemies from both *ze* east and *ze* west. Only one chance exists for *ze* Germans to be victorious. If they can build an atomic bomb *before* we can stop them .... Well, we simply cannot let that happen. *Ze* Men will go first, and they may well succeed in finding and destroying *ze* German atomic weapons program before your training is even completed. Or," he says hopefully, "*ze* German people may rise up against Hitler and force a surrender. Maybe, even, *ze* Allied forces can get there before *ze* Germans can build *ze* bomb. And even if they do build it before we can stop them, there is still *ze* matter of delivering *ze* bomb. *Ze* British have devastated *ze* German air forces."

I don't think he understands. He keeps trying to convince me that I probably won't have to go to Germany ... like that's what I want, and he's helping to calm my fears. But, my real fear is that I won't be able to go ... that I won't be able to make a difference.

"You've already explained to us in our science classes that the Germans have been successfully building and launching rockets. What if they're able to attach an atomic bomb to the nose of a rocket?" The professor frowns at my question ... It's silly of me to ask – he must have thought of this already.

"It is conceivable," the professor says. "But *ze* range of these rockets is limited. There would be a massive threat to Europe. However, *ze* rest of *ze* world would be safe from such an attack."

"What if ... what *if* the Germans can launch an atomic rocket from one of their U-boats?"

Professor Einstein suddenly looks off into the distance. He sits silently for a few minutes. I know he's not being rude. He often takes breaks like this in the middle of a science class to simply think. German U-boats are far more advanced than American submarines. They can hide deep underwater to evade Allied ships and then pop up anywhere, completely undetected. Sebastian heard a rumor that a U-boat had been spotted once in the Hudson – after passing right near the Statue of Liberty. They have sunk almost three thousand Allied warships and merchant vessels. The U-boats effectively own the Atlantic. Nothing in the American fleet can defend against their torpedoes.

The professor faces me and says, "If Hitler's scientists can figure out how to build an atomic weapon, attach it to a rocket, and launch it from a U-boat … well … then none of us are safe."

"That's why we have to stop the Nazis. I get what we're up against. I just wish I could fit in easily in Germany like the others. I'm not afraid. I want to make a difference."

Professor Einstein stares for a minute – first at me, then past me – before saying, "*Ze* world is a dangerous place to live; not only because of people who are evil, but because of people who do nothing to stop them. You Boys are supposed to be a contingency plan, Max, but you may just get your opportunity."

The professor, with the wind making his hair stand up even straighter, looks me squarely in the eyes for a long time before continuing, "I have to tell you something …. It is something you cannot repeat to anyone else, not even Sebastian. Are you able to commit to this?"

I knew there was more to this day, sailing alone with Albert Einstein, than just my birthday. "I am."

"I have several contacts among German physicists. Some, I know I can trust. There are others that I know I cannot." Even though we're on the only boat on the lake, the professor still looks in all directions, trying to confirm no one can hear us. "From a former colleague, whom I trust completely, I have learned that someone within Project Spear has been in communication with high-ranking German officials."

My jaw drops open. *Who?* I want to scream, but the professor continues before I can ask.

"*Ze* reason you and I are having this conversation, Max, is simply that you are *ze* only person involved in our project with no ties to anyone in Germany." Einstein takes a deep breath. "So, you are *ze only* person here I know I can trust."

I'm not sure if I should feel proud or afraid, knowing this. "I can personally vouch for Ian. There is *no* way he's involved with the Germans!"

"Before I received this information, I thought I could personally vouch for *everyone* here." The professor shrugs sadly. "But, it appears, we can trust no one else with certainty. Is that understood?"

I nod slowly, but don't waver in my belief in Ian. "Yes, but I still don't understand why you're telling me this. What can I do to help?"

"Nothing …. At least nothing right now. If, however, we do send you to Germany, I want to give you *ze* name of one person you can trust should you need to." He pauses a moment. "Abraham Toch is a physicist in Germany. During your search for *ze* facilities they would use to build an atomic bomb, you may well encounter German scientists. Toch is a friend."

"Toch is a friend," I repeat. "Anyone I should particularly watch out for?"

"Yes," the professor answers immediately. "Werner Heisenberg. He heads up Germany's atomic weapons research. Toch says that he and many other scientists are trying to stall research and development, but Heisenberg has *enthusiastically* led *ze* German project and supported our enemies."

"Where can I find them?"

"*If*," the professor emphasizes, "you get deployed and *if* you need to find them, I believe they will be most likely working at Kaiser Wilhelm Institute in Berlin …. Let us both hope you never need to know this."

I nod in agreement, but hope I *will*, in fact, be able to put this to use.

Smiling his knowing and gentle smile, Professor Einstein abruptly changes the topic, "You know, Max … I have noticed that you do not stutter when you speak in German. Not once that I can recall. Why do you suppose that is?"

"I have no idea. But I'm guessing that –" I stand and leap for the professor.

Suddenly, a large wind gust causes the main sheet to come untied and the boom to go flying across the rear of the vessel. The boom crashes solidly into the professor's shoulder and he's heading over the side of the boat. I catch Einstein's arm just before he falls in. First, I gently help the professor to his seat and then I tie down the main sheet.

"Thank you, Max." Professor Einstein takes a moment to calm himself before he speaks again. "You reacted *before ze* wind gust hit us. It should have been impossible for you to catch me just then."

He smiles while gently shaking his head. "There is something unique about you that I do not fully understand. All of you young men recruited for this mission are truly amazing physical specimens. And, dare I say, some of you test out with genius level intelligence. Yet, *you* are still very different. That dream about a flame before your mother's death?" It sounds like a question, yet the professor moves on. "Your

31

reaction times are so far ahead of *ze* others that you appear to be *prescient*. I saw you moving toward me before that gust hit *ze* sail. You would have never been able to reach me in time otherwise. How do you think that is possible?"

"To be honest, Professor Einstein, I don't think I'm any better than any of the others in the project. As a matter of fact, I still can't figure out why I was even considered for it."

"Do not ever lack faith in yourself, Max. *Ze* human brain is largely a mystery to us and we have no idea what its limitations are. You appear to be an example of that. There is something special about you. You sensed that gust before it hit. You steadied yourself first and you were on your way to me before I could take a tumble into *ze* lake. Somehow, you *saw* it coming. Your mind is quicker than *ze* others as well." The professor takes a deep breath as he reaches the point he wants to make. "And *that*, young Max, is *ze* cause of your stuttering."

"I'm not sure I understand," I reply before really thinking it through.

"You do not stutter in German because you think in English and you have to convert each word before you say it. *Ze* problem is still there in Italian because, I imagine, you can also think in Italian. But, as of now, you cannot think in German. You require more time before you speak and this slows things down. This way, your mouth can keep up with your thoughts."

I sense the truth in this. It's amazing that the world's most famous and gifted genius has taken the time to consider and try to solve so basic a problem as my stuttering. Not knowing what to say, all I can come up with is "Thank you, Professor. With everything else going on, how do you have the time to worry about my speech problem?"

"You are not *ze* first person with a quick mind to have a problem getting words out," Einstein winks. "You have been coming to more and more of my university lectures, I have noticed. Tonight, there will be a very special lecture – mostly with other physicists in attendance. I believe you would benefit greatly by attending."

Chapter 3

Ulrich Von Becker
Atlantic Ocean
March 20, 1945

I've never considered myself to be claustrophobic, but being cooped up in a U-boat – even one as large as U-797 – leaves me craving the open air and firm footing I left in Berlin.

U-797 is our newest design, with two complete cylindrical hulls joined together, side by side. They say it's extremely stable this way, and we have more than twice the space of a standard U-boat, twice the engines and batteries, and a second conning tower that no one seems to use. U-797 is one of two experimental U-boats that we built by doubling up the type XVIII Walter plans. Along with the double hulls and being much larger, the feature that really stands out about these experimental U-boats is that they have a large enclosed hump in the middle.

When I first heard of these underwater boats – what the Americans call submarines – I swore I would never step into one. Yet, here I am.

I had no say in the matter. I was second in command of Adolf Hitler's personal guard – a risky position, to be sure, but at least a prestigious one. The Fuhrer always told me I did a good job and I would have been content to stay at his side. But, then came along Hagan Ister, about six months ago. Herr Hitler knew Herr Ister quite well and Hitler put him in charge of the Thule Society.

Hitler also let Ister choose two of his personal guards, and he chose Rolf Barbie and me.

I fear no man, but Herr Ister's erratic behavior makes me uneasy. A week ago, he suddenly decided he wanted to go to America. U-796 was the first of these experimental designs to be built and is Adolf Hitler's personal U-boat. U-797 has been assigned to take Hagan Ister wherever and whenever he wants to go. Where he wants to go is New York City and he ordered a wolfpack of four additional U-boats to accompany us.

This leaves me confined to the tight quarters of U-797. More difficult than the tight quarters, though, it's having *this many people* in tight quarters.

Because we can only run on batteries when submerged and the batteries need a steady flow of fresh water to function, we are always conserving water. The chief engineer has rationed our coffee and issued orders that the crew can't shower. This many men, in the constant stress of war, never knowing when an American battleship might drop a depth charge on us, tend to sweat … a lot. No showers. The odor is beyond belief.

I've explored this vessel from end to end and there's only one place where I can get a break from it all – up here in the second conning tower. It's a small oval room perched above the main hull with a bunch of panels, switches, and gauges. The only way to get to the conning tower is by going up a steel ladder from the control room, and the ladder continues up to an escape port at the top of the tower and the observation deck outside.

Since the captain is usually in the control room and the crew tends to avoid the captain, no one but me ever comes up here.

As soon as I have myself convinced the crew and Herr Ister will leave me alone, I hear the scuffling of leather boots on metal flooring, then someone climbing the ladder that rises from the control room below. Almost every part of the U-boat is made of metal and in the shape of a tube, so even the slightest, mouse-like sound travels from one end to the other.

"Herr Von Becker, *what*, precisely, are we planning to do once we get to New York?" Everyone has been asking me the same damn question since we left Hamburg a week ago. This is different though. This time, the question comes directly from Captain Otto Saltzwedel as he emerges into the tower. The captain's appearance commands respect. He's tall and lean, with short white hair, steely gray eyes, and a perfectly groomed beard. His service record is so impeccable it only enhances the aura he projects. He's sunk more enemy ships than any other captain in the German fleet. And it earned him the command of U-797.

"Even if I knew, I wouldn't be able to answer you. Herr Ister is very private when it comes to his plans."

"Where did he come from?" the captain presses. "The first time I heard Hagan Ister's name was when he handed me papers from the Fuhrer telling me that U-797 is his to command. *His!*"

I never imagined Captain Saltzwedel would be happy with the new assignment. Even though he's captain of one of the two largest and most advanced U-boats in the German fleet, he's not truly in charge of his own vessel – not so long as Herr Ister is aboard. And, I have to admit – to myself – that I've wondered where Ister came from ever since I was assigned to lead his personal guard. I'm not so stupid as to ask the question, though. Having served as one of Hitler's personal SS guards before this assignment, I've seen how many people the Fuhrer has had killed for questioning his orders.

At first, I was eager to finally get out of the Fuhrerbunker. With the war taking a turn for the worse, the British bombing our cities, and the Russians closing in, the Fuhrer took to spending much of his time in his bunker, leaving me and his other guards stuck underground with him. If we weren't in the Fuhrerbunker in Berlin, we were in another bunker in Austria. I thought this assignment would lead to more space, maybe some fresh air, but this U-boat feels even smaller and more confining than a bunker. With Ister in his private stateroom, and none of Saltzwedel's underlings able to get an answer, the captain finally decided to ask me directly. I can answer this question from the captain, but it won't be an answer he likes. Ister warned me this moment would come and specifically told me what to say when it did.

"Herr Ister is an advisor to the Fuhrer. He heads the Thule Society."

The Thule Society is well known to be where Adolf Hitler learned about politics and leading people – where he was molded into the Fuhrer he is today. The Thules believe in – and actively practice – the occult. They collect mysterious antiquities, preaching that true Germans descend from some ancient, yet highly advanced race known as the Aryans. As a member of the SS guard, I know what it's like to have people fear me. There is one group to be feared far more than the SS, though – *the Thule Society*.

The SS may beat you … we may even kill you. However, if you become an enemy of the Thules, you *and your family* disappear without a trace. One day you're here, and the next day your neighbors are wondering where you went and arguing over your possessions.

"The Thule Society has been wiped out. The people are gone, probably in a concentration camp. Hitler, himself, saw to it." Saltzwedel speaks confidently, using his steely glare to test my resolve. I imagine he would intimidate lesser men.

"No, not wiped out." I watch the captain's reaction as I fold my arms across my chest. I may not have the steely stare or impeccable record like the captain, but being nearly seven feet tall and flaunting the size of my chest and arms is usually enough to intimidate anyone. I stay quiet for a moment, waiting for the captain's response. I can see his confidence in his own knowledge is dropping like a lead weight in a shallow pool of water. He's suddenly less sure of himself, perhaps wondering if he should just accept his orders without questioning them. Mentioning the Thules – and perhaps the arm flexing – has achieved the desired effect. Now to drive home the point. "While the Fuhrer did remove the leadership of the Thules, the group still flourishes. They are now being led by Herr Ister."

The captain nods slowly. "It was unwise of Ister to bring the woman with him."

"Hagan Ister is the Fuhrer's advisor, and Lady Zelda is Herr Ister's secretary and advisor. She travels with him, wherever he goes."

"Is she *advising* Herr Ister in his stateroom right now? *That's* what she's doing?"

He's trying to provoke me into telling him what he wants to know. I should just let it go, but he's talking about *Zelda*, and the sarcasm is so thick in the captain's voice that he leaves me no choice but to address the issue. "What threat does she pose to you?"

"She poses no threat. But, she's a beautiful young woman at sea with a crew full of men. These men haven't seen a woman for weeks. For some of them, it's been months. She prances around – with her hair – and it's …" the captain takes a moment, apparently to choose the right word, "*unsettling* for the men."

"Lady Zelda does not prance!" I cannot allow him to broach this subject without reprise. Although her hair, golden blonde and stretching out behind her in one long ponytail that nearly reaches the floor, has always been mesmerizing to me as well. When she speaks, her beautifully small mouth barely moves. Her hair flows with waves that seem to crest with each of her soft words. There's something about Zelda that I can't figure out. Very petite, she can't be older than her late twenties. Yet Hagan Ister, a man who seems to take great pleasure in the fact that he terrifies everyone he meets, treats Zelda very differently from anyone else. He refers to her as Lady Zelda, when everyone else is known to him by their surnames only. Ister has never called me anything else but Von Becker. I'm not even sure he knows my given name is Ulrich. I think it's part of the way Ister likes to control the people and situations around him. Now … what would Ister do in this situation? He'd turn the tables.

"What is the real problem, Captain, are your men not disciplined?"

The captain bristles at the question, refusing to address it, "Herr Ister travels with a very strange entourage. You – pardon my frankness – are a hulk of a man, barely able to stand up straight in most of the U-boat …."

He pauses for a second, as if I'm supposed to explain *why* I am so big. I'm not taking the bait.

The captain continues, "Lady Zelda is rumored to be able to see the future …."

This, I do answer, "If Lady Zelda can see the future, that would be of great benefit – especially since she advises the most powerful person in the Reich … other than Adolf Hitler, of course."

He rolls his eyes, jaw jutting out, "Your counterpart, another personal guard to Ister, this Rolf Barbie carries that baton with him everywhere. He hit one of my men with it … just because he thought the man was chewing his breakfast too loudly!"

I explain, "Yes, Herr Ister has two personal guards. That's hardly surprising for a man of his importance. And, it's true – Rolf does have a temper." I've seen him do far worse than hit a man with that baton of his.

"And then there's Dr. Brandt. Have you heard that he performs *experiments* on humans?" he asks.

"Not humans. He only experiments on the Jews."

"Oh … well … only the Jews," the captain says facetiously. "There are no Jews on my U-boat. Just whom will he be doing his experiments on now?"

"Dr. Brandt is Herr Ister's personal doctor now. He hasn't been experimenting on anyone for quite some time. You can see … Herr Ister needs the doctor."

The captain nods, finally something we can agree on, "Yes, with all those scars, he must have seen some action in the last war … Look, Von Becker, we are only two days away from reaching New York. *When* will I be notified of our purpose there?"

I glare at the captain just long enough to make my point without overly provoking the proud man. "Precisely when Herr Ister sees fit to tell you."

He turns in anger. The captain outranks me and he's accustomed to having his orders obeyed without question. The problem is that it's the same with Ister, and Ister is his superior.

"Be careful in here," he cautions after a moment to regain his composure. "These are the targeting and launch controls. The last thing we need is for you to launch the rocket with the bay door still closed."

Chapter 4

MAX MEDICI
LONGBOAT KEY, FL, USA
MARCH 19, 2014

This is the third … no, perhaps the fourth time Trey has been in my office since he built this … this … he calls it home, but it's more like a compound. He only visits me here when there's something troubling him.

Even at this old age, I like to stay fit, so I alternate between hikes on the beach and swimming laps in the pool every morning. I already finished my hike and had just settled into my favorite chair to read when there was a knock on my door. Considering I get visitors about once a month at the most, the knock took me by surprise. Trey didn't wait for me to answer the door, just following his knock by coming right in and walking into my office.

I'm fortunate to have an office, let alone one of the two guesthouses Trey built next to his main house here in Florida on the barrier island of Longboat Key. A decent pension, a few good friends, a tiny sailboat, and my collection of books and trinkets are all I have after a long career in the US Secret Service as the head of Advance Intelligence.

This guesthouse is larger than any of the apartments I've ever rented and I have a western view of the blue-green waters of the Gulf of Mexico from both my bedroom and the second bedroom I use as an office and library. Looking out the window, I see the Gulf is unusually choppy today, with eight-foot swells. Surfers, who rarely visit these typically calm waters, are out in force.

It's easy to get lost in that view. I imagine where my life would be if Trey hadn't invited me to live in this guesthouse on his property … probably still living alone in an apartment in DC. The last apartment I had was small, yet still barely affordable. I had books everywhere. Trey, knowing my love of books, had every wall in this office built out with shelving and every shelf is now full of books … and trinkets … memories from my travels and adventures. I have a large safe built into the wall behind a painting of Albert Einstein on the wall opposite the window. It hides the few trinkets I have that I need to keep hidden.

"March 20, 2014 – your calendar is a day off," says Trey.

"What's wrong with my calendar?"

"Other than being amazed you can even find it with all the clutter on your desk?"

"I'm a visual person, Trey. I have to see all the things I'm working on, or I might forget one of them."

"Well today's the 19th and your daily Sudoku calendar sitting here on the one bare spot on your desk says it's the 20th." He points to my calendar, then without thinking, removes his wedding ring, and rolls it around the palm of his hand with his index finger.

"Oh. I already completed today's puzzle …. My dear boy, quit fiddling with your ring and sit down." He's been married to Jessica for eight months, and he's constantly twirling and removing his wedding ring, then putting it back on. "That's what happens when you wait till you're 48 to get married. Is it really that uncomfortable?"

"No. It's fine, Max. It's just that –"

"You're worried about her," I finish for him.

"Wouldn't you be?"

Trey may be my son, but I didn't raise him. In some ways, he and I are so much alike, but in our connections to family, we're so very different. I lost my parents – traumatically – at the age of twelve, leaving me with only an aunt and a cousin that I knew. Unfortunately, I wasn't very close to either of them. A very loving, close-knit family raised Trey.

I never thought he would learn that I'm his father. When Trey was born, I had to hide him from his mother. Katarina, the one true love of my life, was anything but true. As a Russian spy, her only goal when she met me was to use me to get to President Kennedy. She played her part well … all too well. I was in love. The one … the only time in my long, lonely life that I allowed myself to trust someone, to get that close to someone, to be that vulnerable … and she used me … she betrayed me. She would have used Trey, too. I had to hide him from her. She would have used him or killed him.

I came up with a plan involving my cousin, Helen Tyson – to have her raise Trey as her own baby. She had given birth to twins a few hours before Katarina went into labor. One of the twins was stillborn. Tragic as it was, it gave me an idea – to switch Trey with the stillborn twin –

an opportunity for my son to part of a real family, away from all the turmoil that living with me would have brought. Helen's only condition … that we never tell Trey the truth. He grew up with two normal parents, a twin brother, and two sisters in a normal family and a normal community.

From Trey's point of view, I was just his mother's cousin … involved with his family … sometimes a mentor … close, but not too close. Trey didn't know I was in the Secret Service, or that I headed up the Advance Intelligence division of the Service, but he knew I worked for the government, and that much of what I did was classified.

When Helen's husband, Thomas – the man Trey thought was his father – died in a car accident, it left a great void in Trey's life. I can only hope I was able to fill some of that void … to be the father I always wanted to be … the one he always needed. I wasn't Thomas, but I always tried my best.

Trey went on to be wildly successful. A star college football player for the University of Michigan, a spectacular career in professional football with the Tampa Bay Bucs, he later founded his own company, and is now extremely wealthy. He may have grown up with some awareness of his abilities, but did not – could not – know his true heritage.

It was during our quest against the third Antichrist in 2012 that we learned so much … lost so much … and were still left with so many unanswered questions.

The events of the 2012 crisis forced me to reveal the truth to Trey … to break my vow to Helen. There was no way around it. We were following clues left by my great ancestor from the 16th Century, Nostradamus. A visionary and prophet, Nostradamus had foreseen the coming of three Antichrists … three men of such great evil as to be the polar opposite – the antithesis – of the pure good represented by Christ.

The only daughter of Nostradamus married into the Medici line, and that prophetic bloodline carried through the centuries and into me. Katarina, on the other hand, descended directly from the line of the Oracle of Delphi, a line of women with even more powerful prophetic abilities than the Nostradamus line. In Trey, the two lines cross for the first time in history. No one – not even Nostradamus – knows the extent of his abilities.

They say family traits can skip a generation, even many generations. I've had to face two of the three Antichrists using limited abilities that must seem almost childlike to Nostradamus and even to Trey.

I can't do what they can do ... something quite amazing really ... Nostradamus, from his lifetime in the 16th Century, somehow found a way to communicate with Trey in our time now.

Nostradamus possesses the power to cross the great divide of time to be in contact with Trey while they are both in trance states.

I was there when it first happened – the HOLY SHIT moment when Trey put on his amulet, stared into a flame, fell into a trance state, and then heard a voice ... not any voice, but the voice of Nostradamus.

Now, they make the connection almost every night, and use this connection so that Nostradamus can train Trey to be a prophet, and something much more ... a *guide* for the future.

If only I had this gift. I have no desire to take it away from Trey, but why couldn't we both have it? To be able to talk with Nostradamus ... to find out what he saw in his prophetic visions in his own words. To be trained to be a prophet ... to guide the future of humankind ....

God never had that path in mind for me. I'm stuck with abilities that look like cheap parlor tricks when compared to what Nostradamus and Trey can do.

Trey – my son – is the chosen one. I've always known it. He's the holder of the keys of fate ... the one Nostradamus can connect with ... the one who will be trained to see the future.

Before he can look to the future, Trey is training by looking into the past – a much easier journey according to Nostradamus. The training started with trance-state visions of his own past, led by Nostradamus. Then, Trey tells me he will visit further back in time through visions of my past, then my father's past, and so on. The more recent the event, the closer the family connection and location, the easier it is to visit in a vision. The further back in time Trey goes, the more difficult the journey.

To understand the future, one must first understand the past.

It's the past – in our battle against the third Antichrist – where Trey lost his birth mother, his sister, and his best friend. The losses hurt him so deeply. Now he knows the risks involved ... what's at stake. This path in life is not one he would have chosen, but sometimes destiny gets in the way of the choices we would make.

Still, the way he internalizes the losses ... the way he blames himself ... I worry how that will affect the choices he makes going forward.

He's been training with Nostradamus nearly every night, sleeping less and less. The sessions require Trey to be in a trance state in pitch black, except for a flame in a brass tripod. The duration of the sessions has been growing and they're taking a toll on Trey. At a little over six feet tall, Trey looks very much like my son, with my bronze complexion and dark hair. What he has from his mother – his eyes – the same piercing blue eyes Katarina had – look unusually tired.

"Why don't you take a couple nights off from training," I urge him. "My old friend, Greg Rutledge, is in Tampa for a week and I'm meeting him there tonight for dinner. I'd feel better if you took the night off and spent it with Jessica. I'm sure she'd appreciate it as well."

"Is that your copy of *The Prophecies* by Nostradamus?" asks Trey, pointing at the book in my hand and blatantly changing the subject.

"Yes. Nostradamus originally wrote *The Prophecies* in Latin. My copy is dated 1565, the year before he died and I believe this is from the first edition printed in Old French." The leather cover is so worn and tattered, it's hardly recognizable as leather anymore and the book is littered with holes from bookworms. Yellow plastic bookmarks protrude from the top of several pages, and I have quite a few orange bookmarks protruding from the side. Along the bottom are only three red bookmarks.

I delicately hand Trey the book.

"This has to be worth a small fortune. Tomorrow is your birthday – why am I getting a present?" He's always had a way of making me smile, or even laugh, during the most serious situations.

"I never said I was giving it to you, Trey. I turn 85 tomorrow and I won't be around forever. I want you to be able to find it *and* understand what it means should you need it."

He picks one of the orange bookmarks, and opens the book to that page. The book contains prophetic poems written by Nostradamus to chronicle his visions of the future. Each poem is four lines, or a quatrain. He quickly locates the quatrain the pointed end of the bookmark designates. Translating the Old French to English, Trey reads it aloud:

"Century 6, Quatrain 37
The ancient work will be accomplished.
From the roof, evil ruin will fall upon the great man.
They will accuse an innocent, in death, of the deed.
The guilty one is hidden in the misty copse."

"Is this an event that took place in the 6th Century?" he asks.

Looking to the heavens, I find it difficult to believe that selection was just random. That day was the worst day of my life … Katarina's betrayal … Kennedy's assassination … the day of the greatest failure I've known.

"No," is the only answer I have.

"Then how are these ordered?"

"There are one thousand quatrains in total … ten groups of a hundred. Nostradamus called each group a century. As far as the order … I think it's simply the order in which he saw his visions of the future."

"So, the centuries are not chronological centuries?" he asks, still having trouble understanding the labels Nostradamus used.

"I'm not able to communicate with him, like you do," I try to keep the envy out of my voice. "But, if my interpretation of these quatrains is correct, then they are *not* written in chronological centuries."

"Okay, then what makes this quatrain so special? Why have you marked it?"

"Quatrain 37 of Century 6, I believe, is a prophetic vision Nostradamus had of November 22, 1963 – the assassination of President John F. Kennedy."

"Misty copse," he says. "Sounds like a grassy knoll. I should have guessed. Max … you weren't one of the Secret Service agents on duty that day, were you?"

"I'm afraid that's classified."

"You know," he says, "I'll most likely be seeing all of these classified events from your past. Sooner or later, you might as well talk about them."

"That may well be true. But, we'll cross that bridge when we get there."

Trey points to the book, and asks, "What makes you think the quatrains were written in the order in which Nostradamus had his visions?"

"Go to the first yellow bookmark."

The first yellow bookmark is near the front of the book. It points to the first quatrain and Trey proceeds to read it:

"Century 1, Quatrain 1
Sitting alone at night in a secret study.
Emanating from a seat of brass,

a small flame comes out of the emptiness,
utterings which one would be vain to believe."

"Sound like anyone you know?"

"The brass tripod," says Trey. "A small flame ... and a voice."

"Read the second."

"Quatrain 2

The gripped branch ... no, that's not right ... *The stick in the hand is between*
the legs.

The water he sprinkles on the limb and foot.

A voice. Fear. Trembling in his robes.

Divine splendor. A presence sits nearby."

"Because of your connection, Trey, you are probably closer to Nostradamus than any other person in history, except maybe his son .... What do you think when you read that?"

"It sounds like he lit the flame in the tripod, heard a voice, and then pissed his pants in fear," he says with a mischievous smile.

"Yes," I laugh. "But he was wearing a robe, not pants. Imagine what he must have felt – especially reading those first two quatrains – to be in a trance state and to suddenly have someone start talking with him ... someone who wasn't physically there."

"Yeah. That would freak me out ... and it did the first time Nostradamus communicated with me."

"Trey, we have to realize that Nostradamus has been training you to look into the past and he will eventually train you to look into the future. He's being your guide. *Someone* had to be his guide. Someone from his past. It's obvious, though, that he thought his guide was ... divine. Perhaps even God."

Trey and I have differing views on religion. We don't broach the subject often.

"Anyone who could cross into the future and speak to you would seem divine," he says. "But, what about these two quatrains makes you think this book is written in *any* order?"

"These two quatrains describe how Nostradamus began to receive his visions ... or his guidance. They are the beginning to his vision story. The order of the events from his visions doesn't seem to follow any other chronological order, so I believe they are in the order his guide intended for him to see them."

"And you think Nostradamus is revealing things to me in a specific order for a reason?"

"Yes. I do."

"What are the red ones for?" he asks. Flipping to a red bookmark near the center of the book, Trey turns to the page and reads:

"Century 10, Quatrain 72
The year one thousand nine hundred ninety nine, seven months.
From the sky will come a great King of Terror.
Resurrect the great King of Mongolia,
Before and after Mars to reign by good luck."

"That's odd," he says.

"What?"

"The date. Nostradamus is famous for his obscurity. Here, he actually published a date for one of his prophecies."

"Yes, this one obviously points directly to the emergence of the third Antichrist, Luis Khan, and his shuttle incident in 1999. My guess is that Karl used his aerospace company to orchestrate the whole thing to make Khan look like a hero. A great way to launch his political career."

"And it worked," Trey says.

"It sure would have helped, *prior* to our encounter with Karl in 2012, if we had known what we were up against. The lives we could have saved … Samantha … Katarina … maybe even Judith. If there's one thing I'd ask you to ask Nostradamus —"

"Why was he so obscure?" Trey finishes my question. "Why didn't Nostradamus tell us, in plain language, when something really bad was about to happen? That's the same question you answered for me back in 2012. He saw the future. A prophet living in the 16th Century. There were three inquisitions going on during his lifetime. The Christians were torturing and killing anyone who claimed to see the future. He couldn't be too direct or obvious. He had to deny having visions and being a prophet. Yet, he had to give enough hints to the truth so that his prophecies would remain in publication long enough for …." Trey stops. Staring at me, a question bubbling to the surface, perhaps not fully formed yet.

"Have you asked him about Karl?"

"Of course," he says.

"And ...."

"And, he doesn't know any more than we do .... Karl didn't seem to have a last name .... He came from a secret group known as the First Order .... The surviving descendants of the Oracle of Delphi are either part of or working with the First Order .... The First Order wants to control or destroy the world .... Where they are, and why they do what they do, none of us know. They're able to hide from his visions ... and mine."

"It never seems to get easy for us, does it?"

"If it were easy, we'd all be prophets and fighting Antichrists," he jokes.

I gently take the book back from him and place it on the shelf behind me. I've lined up most of my books, side by side, like in a library. Not *The Prophecies* by Nostradamus. This book has its own stand and a tinted glass cover to keep dust and sunlight from damaging it. Next to it on the right is a nearly life-size crystal skull. On the left are three more books displayed individually on stands – *The Bible,* Homer's *The Iliad* and Einstein's *Relativity: The Special and General Theory.*

"The red notes," I confide, "are the quatrains I believe most directly point to the three Antichrists."

"*When* and *how* did you find this book?" he asks the question that finally took shape in his head.

"Nostradamus is showing you things in a specific order for a reason. I'm sure of it. Let the tale unfold as he intends it."

"You may be more right than you know," Trey says. "Guided by Nostradamus, I've already seen visions of much of my own past. During my last training session, Nostradamus told me that I would soon be visiting 1945 to see my father's past ... *your* past. Think about it."

"About what?"

"Max ... what if you could have known about the Kennedy assassination *before* it happened." Trey's history of success in his life has been his source of confidence, and perhaps even overconfidence. He acts without thinking things through sometimes. He needs to temper his bravado with caution.

"Don't you think I've thought about this myself? You can't change the past. And, let's just say for a moment that you could – how do you know things would turn out better in the long run?"

My hope to get him off this track of thinking only forces him to become more resolute, "The Germans were defeated in World War II, but only after millions of lives were lost, and mostly due to the ambitions of one evil man. The second Antichrist. Adolf Hitler."

"I lived it, Trey. I know."

"I've seen documentaries that detail the end of the war. It's my understanding that the Americans from the west and Russian forces from the east raced against each other to reach Berlin first. They both wanted to be the ones to capture Hitler. To put him on trial, very publicly."

"Yes, and?"

"No one," Trey shakes his head vigorously, "wanted Hitler to be able to get away with all that he did. Not the Americans. Not the Russians. Not the British, Not the French ... *no one* .... There had to be an example set. A *reckoning*. A public trial and a public execution. Yet, the public trial never happened. The Russians reached the bunker first. They reported that Hitler committed suicide before they got there. But his body was burned by his security guards."

"That is my ... understanding of the situation as well."

"So, how do we know that burned body was really Adolf Hitler?"

Trey is fiddling with his ring again, waiting for my reply, but it's another question I can't answer. All I can do is shrug, "There must be a reason Nostradamus is showing you events in the order he's choosing. Let the history play out as he intends it."

Chapter 5

TREY TYSON

Longboat Key, FL, USA
March 20, 2014

Yawning, I try to rub some of the sleepiness out of my eyes. Seagulls squawk, and the smell of salt water and beach wafts in through the open sliding doors to the bedroom. Soap, perfume, and cologne makers have been trying to copy this smell for decades, and still don't have it right.

Opening my eyes, I'm thankful for the view. It never gets old, that's for sure. I designed the house for this moment … waking up to the sight of the Gulf of Mexico … every morning. The back of the main house faces west, and the bedroom wall consists entirely of a huge glass sliding door that opens to the patio.

Combined, the main house and two guesthouses form a U shape that surrounds our patio and pool. A sparse line of tall palm trees acts as the last and western border for the patio. Beyond the palms stretches a long private beach of fine white sand and then the warm green-blue waters of the Gulf. Waking up to palm trees, white sand and the gentle sound of gulf waves every morning is incredible, but I built the place with views facing west more for the sunsets, and they're nothing short of glorious.

Jessica's already out, probably in the pool, or taking a power walk on the beach.

I change into swim trunks and head out, not bothering to close the sliding door.

Checking the pool first, I don't find my wife, but I do find my father, Max, swimming laps like he does most mornings.

"How many laps is that – three?" I yell to make sure Max can hear me while he's swimming.

Max reaches the end of the pool closest to me with four quick strokes before he stops, stands, and smiles broadly. "More like 33!"

He's in remarkable shape for his age. "Not too bad for an old man on his 85th birthday."

"Old man? Listen here – you're no spring chicken, my boy. As a matter of fact, why did you even bother to crawl out of bed? You look exhausted. Did you spend half your night with *him* again?"

With Max's hair wet and pulled straight back, the scar above his left eye comes into view. I asked him once how he got it, but he told me – like so much of his past – that it was classified information. That naturally makes the scar even more intriguing.

"Yes," I admit. Max had suggested I take the night off and he hates when I do my sessions when he's not around to stand guard over me. Nostradamus, however, keeps pushing me to have more sessions … longer sessions. It's part of the training to build up my endurance.

"Your wife is eight months pregnant and she needs you now more than ever."

Reproach? I just got up and I despise being reproached, especially after I just wake up. "The training is important. *You* know that better than anyone. And Jessica has me as much as she needs …. Is she on the beach?"

Max nods, noncommittally, and then returns to swimming laps.

It takes me about five minutes of running on the beach to catch up to Jessica, who is power-walking near the water's edge. From the back, she barely looks pregnant, as she carries our baby high and straight out in her womb. Some of the doctors and nurses tell us to expect a boy, based on the way she's carrying the baby. However, Jessica insists she wants to be surprised at the birth and doesn't want anyone telling us the baby's sex, or even to have any ultrasounds done. I know she wants a girl and my instincts suggest she'll get her wish.

Jessica cut her long red hair recently and now it's very short with a few carefully untouched longer wisps. Even though she's tall and pregnant, the cut makes her look quite sprite-like. *Utterly adorable*, I remember thinking the first time I saw it, *her first mommy cut*. Her long, thin legs are still pumping as I approach her.

"If you slow down a bit, young lady, perhaps we can get to know each other? How about over a nice glass of wine?"

"Aye … maybe … in about seven or eight months. Once this little one is born, and done breastfeeding." She doesn't look back or even slow down a bit. Her slight Irish accent comes out when she's upset, tired, or just spent time talking with her mother, whose accent is much stronger. She went to bed early last night, so I'm hoping she just had a conversation with her mom, but doubt it.

I increase my pace to catch up beside her. "You haven't heard the rest of the offer though." I smile as her glimmering green eyes finally meet mine. "We can take the next flight to Paris and enjoy the wine with dinner on the Eiffel Tower."

"The last time we tried that, we almost died *and* the world nearly ended." She shakes her head and points to her protruding belly. "And besides, I'm in no condition to fly anywhere right now *or* have a glass of wine."

"That's fair, I suppose. But, it would be nice to try that trip again … someday … *without* all the drama."

"It's going to be a while before we can do that on our own, you know. But it's a pleasant enough thought." Finally, she slows her pace. "We used to run the beach together every morning."

My second reproach today and I've only been awake a half an hour! "Look, I'd love to be able to get up early and come with you. But, if I don't sleep in then I don't sleep. I can only do the training after dark and the days are getting longer now … as are the training sessions. We've talked about this. I've been very open about what's involved. You know the stakes and you've supported me from the start. At least until now."

Jessica stops walking and faces me. She starts to say something, catches herself, and then does finally speak. "I never thought it would take up *this* much of your time."

I want to tell her it will get better. I want to tell her everything will be fine in time. But I know it will be getting worse – much worse – and soon. *The truth.* She should know it sooner than later. "We went through hell in 2012 to stop Karl and the terrorist attack, and we couldn't have done it without being guided by Nostra –"

"Aye, true enough," she cuts me off, "When I first found out that Max is your father and you're both descendants of Nostradamus … and that you have these amazing abilities … I was impressed. Truly. If you ask me, though, it's turned out to be more of a curse than a blessing. If Nostradamus was so powerful, then why does he need you? Why this disruption to our lives?"

"We've been through this." I reach out and hold both of her hands in mine. "Nostradamus foresaw the three Antichrists, who were destined to live well after his own time. He knew he had to find a way to stop them and he needed to get help from someone in his family line who would be alive when each of the Antichrists came to power. He can't communicate with Max and Max's fate – I don't know if it's destiny or doom – but Max's life has spanned the last two Antichrists. *I'm* the next in line. It's my fate – *destiny* or *doom* …"

"I'm afraid it's more doom than destiny," she says softly.

"That may be, but Nostradamus couldn't communicate with me until I was ready … too late for the 2012 crisis. He had to leave the clues during the 16th Century for us to find in 2012. It was the only way we could stop the third Antichrist. While he had amazing abilities, Nostradamus was only one man with one lifetime. He could only reach so far. Now he's training me to be a guide. It's not an easy or a quick task. When you and I discussed it, we had an idea of what it would be like."

"But we're about to have a baby," she says as her eyes fill with tears.

"That only makes my responsibility more personal, sweetheart. You became a doctor for a reason. You studied for years. You worked countless late nights in the emergency room in Detroit. You built a practice here in Florida to take care of seniors … Jess, you did all of this to *help* people. I saw how you helped my mom when other doctors didn't seem to care. I've seen you sacrifice so much of your personal life for people who are complete strangers to you. That's one of the reasons I fell in love with you. Using my abilities is the way *I* can help people. If I don't do this, who will?"

A wave comes in that soaks her from the knees down. She hangs her head low and I'm not sure if it's because of the wave or if she's unable to look me in the eyes anymore.

"Trey … I'm sorry. I know you've been supportive to me since the day I met you and you never once complained about the hours I kept. You never once made my life as an ER doctor any harder." She looks up at me again. "I may not have said it, but I always appreciated that. Now, here I am doing exactly what I wouldn't want you to do to me. I wish I could just accept it. Accept your responsibility … I just don't know, though. I don't have your ability to see the future. I'm afraid."

"Afraid of what?"

"Of losing you … of being alone … of raising this baby on my own."

"I'm not going anywhere."

"You don't know that! I've worked the ER for too many years … seen too many families lose someone …. They don't expect it. They don't ever see it coming."

"Look, Jess. I can't say this doesn't have risks. It does. But, my abilities are growing every day and Nostradamus is looking out for me. Looking out for us. Think about what's at stake .... Nostradamus foresaw and left the clues needed to stop three Antichrists. If I can somehow learn how he did it ... learn to see and maybe even prevent someone like Napoleon, Hitler, or Khan from doing all that damage ... killing all those –"

"Aye," she blurts out, but then her tone quickly softens. "If the worst thing that can be said of you is that you're trying too hard to help people ... well ... well, I think that says more than enough about you. That you're more than just a dumb jock who got lucky in the stock market."

Raising my eyebrows, I feign taking offense at that comment and she finally smiles.

She wipes her tears and continues, "I guess the problem I'm having is that I know I have to share you. Sometimes it seems unfair ... but, I do understand how important this is ... and I'll do everything I can to support you." She smiles again, stands on her toes, and kisses me.

"I do miss our runs together on the beach," I say, relieved that she's coming around.

"I'll make you a deal," she winks. "If you can slow down to a power walk for the next month or two, I'll wait till you're up in the morning so we can still go together. Fair enough?"

"Deal!" We kiss again, and then walk the beach, hand in hand ... *together*.

Chapter 6

ULRICH VON BECKER
ATLANTIC OCEAN
MARCH 21, 1945

So much free time!

I allow myself to relax. While the remnants of body odor in this underwater tin can still rise from the control room into the conning tower, the crew has left me alone all day. Ister and Zelda have been meeting in his stateroom almost the entire voyage from Germany with Rolf standing guard outside his door. They only come out for communications with Berlin, and even then, they don't say much to anyone. The situation leaves me, for the first time in months, with time on my hands.

I've been up here for nearly two hours, reading my book and smoking my cigarettes. Taking a long drag and slowly exhaling, I'm feeling at ease for the first time in a long time. There are no chairs in the conning tower and very little space. I found a large panel with quite a few gauges that I have absolutely no interest in trying to understand. The important part of the panel is that it has no switches or levers I can accidentally hit. It's perfect to lean against.

Sitting with my back against the panel, I finish my cigarette. Then, I allow my eyes to close, letting my book rest against my chest.

I never heard someone climbing the stairs from the control room – not even the footsteps across the floor of the conning tower. I was fast asleep … until the sudden and insistent tap on my arm.

Startled, I let my book drop. Then, I need to blink a few times before my eyes can focus on the tiny figure of Zelda staring down at me.

"Lady Zelda?" She's wearing a white blouse, form-fitting gray wool skirt, and long black boots that cling to her calves. She pulled her long wavy blonde hair back and tightly tied it into a single knot before allowing it to flow freely to just above the floor.

"Ulrich, what are you doing up here?" Her high-pitched voice has such clarity; it reminds me of when I accompanied Hitler to a symphony orchestra in Nuremberg. There were many instruments of all types booming out in harmony, yet there was a single flute that started to play. One by one, the other instruments faded. The booming quieted and eventually all that was left was the single flute ... crystal clear ... rising ... pitches bouncing off the ceiling and every wall ... permeating my very soul. That is what I hear when Lady Zelda speaks.

I take in her beauty. The smell of her hair ... the hint of sadness in her eyes ... the small cleft in her chin ... the shape her mouth ... I've been fighting the urge to kiss her – to at least touch her – from the first moment I saw Zelda. Yet, I know even the most innocuous touch would lead to yearnings and a kiss would lead to death. Standing a little too quickly, I bang my head against the top of the conning tower and then try to compose myself.

"Am I needed by Herr Ister?"

She takes a step closer, now only inches away. My jaw clenches.

Then she reaches up, gently and gracefully, and places her hand on my cheek. "It is not Herr Ister who needs you at the moment."

Nooo! I want to scream. She's stirring up feelings deep inside, feelings I can't control. This is beyond dangerous ... it's utterly reckless. Sound travels through the U-boat from end to end. The entire vessel is made of metal. Every noise reverberates. *Someone will hear.* There are at least several men in the control room right below here at all times. Any one of them might need to see one of the gauges behind me and could be in the conning tower in a matter of seconds.

I put my hand on hers, not wanting to, but firmly removing it from my face. I try to keep my voice steady and just above a whisper. "What are you doing?"

"I see the way you look at me, Ulrich. Don't deny it." A seductive smile forms on her face.

"You're being too loud."

"The captain and his officers have just left for dinner in his stateroom. The control room was empty when I came up."

I place my index finger on her lips, trying to keep her quiet, but it backfires. First, she kisses it. Then, she pulls it into her mouth, rolling her tongue around it. *Madness, weakness, and stupidity!* I don't pull away. "We can't ...."

Her hands move to my chest, squeezing my pectoral muscles, and my free hand – almost involuntarily – moves to her breast. I haven't touched a woman in almost a year. Her breast is small but firm. The currents building in me are too strong to hold back. I've already crossed the line. If I'm going to die, it might as well be with a smile. I pull my finger from her mouth. Standing a half-meter taller, I place my hands around her tiny waist and lift her off the ground. Drawing her higher and closer, I kiss her. A powerful kiss, rough, seizing control. My mouth, twice the size of hers, feels awkward at first. Then her tongue darts between my lips. Thoughts of stopping vanish.

The kiss seems to last forever, yet ends too quickly.

Her hands gently push against my chest, trying to pull away. *Why?* Did she hear someone? I don't want it to end – not yet – not ever. She's still pushing, so I set her down, reluctantly and as quietly as possible. She turns to the stairs and I prepare to watch her leave the way she came. However, she only glances into the control room to confirm it is still empty. Then, she turns back to me, her hands moving to my breeches before I can react. She opens them quickly and silently. Before I can think of any words to say in protest, she hikes up her skirt and leaps back into my arms. Slowly she slides down, grabs, and steers me with one of her hands, and … *I'm inside.*

Warm and wet, are my only thoughts as I look down. Her hair is hanging nearly down to the floor, her eyes intense. Wrapping her legs around me tightly, she alternates releasing then squeezing her legs slowly. The in and out effect, one centimeter at a time, is maddening. We kiss again, deeply. My tongue pulses into her moist mouth to the beat of pounding heart. With every pulse, she draws me in deeper and her pace quickens. She releases a slow, silent, and warm breath that makes the hairs on my neck stand up. I turn us around and push her against a control panel, praying it's the one with no switches or levers. Against the panel, she has no choice but to take all of me. I kiss her again and her tongue lashes out into my mouth. I'm pumping quietly, but firmly, just about to explode. Then I hear her exhale in an audible moan. She bites down on her tongue and her eyes roll back as her legs quiver. I can't hold back a moment longer and bite my tongue as well. It's the only way to stay silent as my orgasm causes my legs to convulse. Her eyes meet mine and she holds my gaze as we both climax.

The release … and the relief … are like nothing I've ever known. I allow myself a moment to cherish it, yet I know, deep down, that this changes everything. My life is now in her hands. One word of this to

Ister and my face will never be able to deny what happened convincingly.

Zelda efficiently has her skirt in place and helps get me clothed in moments. She then picks up my book and hands it to me, turns and starts walking to the ladder.

"I ..." Hell, I don't know what to say.

She is two steps down the ladder, still visible from the waist up, when she faces me again. The sounds of activity in the control room mean the officers have finished their meal and the crew will eat now.

Zelda speaks in a steady voice, as if none of this just happened, "Herr Ister would like to speak with you in his stateroom after dinner."

Bloody hell.

Chapter 7

TREY TYSON
LONGBOAT KEY, FL, USA
MARCH 21, 2014

I pull the thin silver chain attached to my amulet over my head and let it rest around my neck. What Nostradamus told me the first time I discovered we could communicate turned out to be true. The more I wear it, the more the amulet amplifies my mental abilities. Much like twirling my wedding ring has become a habit, I find myself running my fingers over the amulet, caressing the indentation where the bullet meant to kill me had struck in 2012.

If the bullet had struck a mere two inches in any other direction, it would have killed me and our efforts to save the world would have failed.

In all the world, three of these amulets exist. Nostradamus found a meteor while wandering the countryside back in the 16th Century. Touching it, he discovered it caused him to undergo a metaphysical transformation. He felt an enhanced clarity to his abilities. The strange extraterrestrial metal was extremely difficult to forge and shape, but Nostradamus was an alchemist and eventually figured out how. One amulet he kept for himself. All three were destined to be part of his plans to stop the three Antichrists.

Nostradamus hid mine well, yet meant for me to find in 2012. Without the amulet, we would have never stopped the third Antichrist. Max found his during his mission against the second Antichrist, Adolf Hitler, but I don't know how he found it. Where Nostradamus hid the one he possessed … how he ensured it would be found … who found it … what clues it possessed … I don't know any of that – at least not yet.

"Was it good to see your friend last night, Max?"

"Yes," he replies. "Greg is one of the few people in my life I can talk to."

"Because he has Top Secret clearance?"

Max laughs, "That's true. But, I meant because he's a great friend and has been for quite some time."

We're sitting on lounge chairs on the patio, facing the Gulf. Max has taken to smoking his old peace pipe during my training sessions. It's the same peace pipe carved in the 18th Century by the Prophet, brother of the great Shawnee Chief Tecumseh, originator of the Presidential Curse, and ancestor of my best friend, Samantha Fox. Max had Samantha smoke this very pipe when he was using her abilities to break the Presidential Curse in 1983.

Sam! Her death is the biggest regret of my life. She died trying to stop the third Antichrist, but she didn't have to die. Nostradamus warned me she was in danger – at least the best way he could at the time – but I didn't understand. I ended up handing her to the wolves of hell. Her death was completely my fault.

"Do you ever wish you could go back and fix the past?" I can't seem to let go of this thought.

"Only every single day of my life, Trey ... but it's just not possible. Nostradamus is showing you how to perceive the past, but you have no way to influence it. He's training you so you can build up your abilities. So you can someday perceive the future ... that's what you'll be fixing, what you can influence ... the future, not the past."

Just as it had once helped Sam, the smell of the pipe smoke seems to ease my transition into a trance state. Max looks relaxed. No, not relaxed – he's tired. "You know, you don't need to stand guard over me every night."

"You're essentially dead to the world while you're in this state. It leaves you very vulnerable. I wish you wouldn't do it when I'm not around, as you did last night. You're the chosen one, and I need to make sure you stay safe," he says.

"I'm pretty sure Nostradamus or I would know if something terrible was about to happen while I was training."

"I have to admit that sometimes I'm a little envious of the connection you have with Nostradamus."

I meet my father's gaze. "I'm surprised you never tried to communicate with him like this."

"Oh, it's not that I never tried. Let's not forget that you get half of your abilities from your mother. Katarina's abilities greatly surpassed mine …. You have her eyes." The intensity of Max's gaze grows, and I quickly surmise that he means more than the round eye shape and blue color Katarina and I shared. It's more about our vision abilities.

"At least you had Albert Einstein on your side."

"How on Earth do you know anything about that?" Max seems truly surprised by my revelation. It takes me a moment to realize that while Max was often reading books written by or about Einstein, he has never actually told me anything about the great scientist. My knowledge comes from my training with Nostradamus.

"Nostradamus has prepped me. Visiting your past is the next step in my training."

"I didn't know you were finished exploring your own past yet."

Nostradamus had started my guide training by taking me back to events in my own past. Every event I observed brought a flashback to that time, and I soon came to the realization that my younger self was feeling our presence.

"At least I discovered why I had all those migraines. Every time this me showed up in my past, the younger me had to pay the price with a migraine and sometimes even a bloody nose. You know the way of it. My own past is easiest to visit, then the past of my parents, grandparents, great grandparents and so on. It will take some time before I'm prepared to look forward."

Max suddenly takes on a very serious look. "You understand that you're going to observe some highly classified historical events?"

"Yes, and I'm not to discuss them with *anyone*. I get it." Nodding, I attempt to at least appear to be taking the classified bit seriously. "Try not to worry."

"I can't make that promise. In fact, I wish *you* would try to worry more. These are some of the most important events in human history. Nostradamus wouldn't be guiding you there unless your involvement was critical." As complete darkness settles over us, Max leans forward and lights the candle.

I sit back, forcing my breathing to slow. Staring at the flickering flame, I focus on relaxing. "I'll try …." The words trail off in my voice and in my mind. I'm not even sure I said them aloud. Clearing my mind, I allow only one word to stream across my consciousness. "*Nostradamus … Nostradamus … Nostradamus …*"

The flame is all I can see. I know the smoke from Max's peace pipe surrounds us, but the aroma from the tobacco is barely noticeable. There are no sounds, and the feeling of the chair underneath me is starting to fade. I'm reaching out with my essence, summoning, "*Nostradamus …*"

"*I am here, my son of many sons.*" Nostradamus' voice, if I can call it that, has grown slightly weaker in our most recent training sessions. I don't know how much longer my great ancestor can go on with our training from his own time.

The flame is shrinking as the extent of my awareness grows. Smaller. A pinpoint. Then … it's gone.

"*Are you still there?*" It's not exactly my voice reaching out, but it feels more like talking than any other description I can imagine. Extended thoughts? A projection of will? I've often tried to define our communication to Max, but there isn't a clear explanation for it. He speaks Old French mixed with some Italian and even Latin, but I hear it in English. I speak English and I think he hears it in French. I don't know how … maybe thoughts transcend language … it just works.

"*I am. Are you ready to take the next step?*" The projection of Nostradamus says.

"*To visit the past of my father? I believe so.*" I have so many questions, but there's an important one I've been asking since my first contact with Nostradamus. "*You've explained how my training will go, to some extent. You've guided me to events in my past. Now, we're going to observe events in my father's past. When will I be looking forward? The past is the past. You've said we can't change it, so what's the point?*"

"*We have to build up your strength of will and your concentration level. And you must understand the past to have any hope of understanding the future.*" Nostradamus always gives the same response.

"*But you were able to look so far forward from your time. Centuries! You've been able to influence the future, guiding it along your grand design. I understand that I must train to be able to do the same. I'm just concerned that we're spending so much time training that I'm going to miss some critical event in the future.*"

"*Your wife is soon to give birth in your time, Trey. It is natural for you to be concerned about the future. However, the time for you to look forward has not yet come. Looking forward is infinitely more complicated than looking back. There are no reference points that you know. Time, itself, must be understood by you.*"

"*I think I'm ready and I want to understand it.*"

"*There's a critical event in your father's history. It's where we'll begin. I expect it will help you even more than it helped him or me. Focus on your father. Focus on the Princeton University professor and scientist, Albert Einstein. March 21, 1945. Focus and we shall go there.*"

Okay, this is new. *Clear my thoughts … Max Medici … Princeton University … March 21, 1945 … Max Medici … Einstein … Princeton University … March 21, 1945 … Max Medici … Einstein … Princeton University … March 21, 1945 …*

A swirl of space suddenly forms around me. Stars emerge, and they start to circle counterclockwise above me. No, all around me. The movement of stars gains enough speed as to blur into a long, circling spiral of light with an electric blue hue. I'm suddenly flying through space-time, or maybe space-time is flying around me. I can't tell the difference. It stretches beyond my vision, ever moving. Nausea threatens. Nothing is stationary. No focal point – except my own position. Take a deep breath. I mean *relax!* I keep forgetting that I don't need to breathe here. Still, the thought of a deep breath helps.

Max Medici … Einstein … Princeton University … March 21, 1945 …

The spiral of light begins to slow. My nausea subsides. I can once again make out individual stars as the universe starts to come into focus. Slower still, the stars fade and go dark. Total blackness again for just a moment before a blur of bright light strikes me.

"Are we there yet?" It's a joke that I know Nostradamus won't understand, because it's a reference to a kid on a long car ride. Cars weren't invented until four centuries after he died …. Dies? Died? Past, present, and future tenses are starting to make less sense.

"For once, Trey, you must have patience, and I must insist upon your silence. Your father, even at his young age in 1945, may perceive us if we communicate. He must stay focused on his situation. Everything depends upon it."

Admonished. It's just as bad as being reproached … maybe worse.

The blurred light begins to sharpen. We're in an auditorium. My essence is floating near the back of the room. As I gain my bearings, I can tell the room is filled with people. They're stationary, making no sound at all. Around 30 people, almost all men, seem to be watching and listening. I scan right, then left, and then behind. A young man – no, more like a teen – catches my attention.

Can it be? *No way!* I've never seen any pictures of Max at a young age, but the young man is indeed my father. His hair has a little salt with the pepper in my time, but here it's all dark brown. I have to fight back the urge to laugh. Wearing tan slacks, a crisp white t-shirt, and a tan casual jacket, Max is the only person in the room not wearing a dark wool suit. He's also the only one under the age of 35 by my estimation. What's he doing here? He's so out of place.

Sound? I think my ears are starting to work again. First, I hear Max's breathing. Then come the sounds of the people near me. Someone shuffling in his or her seat. The unmistakable sound of cracking knuckles toward the middle of the room. Finally, a voice from the front of the auditorium breaks through. Ah, there are a couple of figures seated. Everyone here is watching and listening to …. My vision and hearing both continue to sharpen. I can now see one of the seated men. His wildly flowing white hair, the bushy mustache, the quiet confidence he exudes – all uniquely Albert Einstein. Not in a suit, same as Max, but Einstein wears a frayed brown sweater and loose trousers. Function over form. Comfortable, and not caring what anyone else thinks. Awesome!

I don't recognize the other man. What an odd setup for a lecture or debate – two men sitting on lounge chairs … a small table with two glasses of water between them.

"… and that is *ze* foundation of Relativity. *Ze* speed of light is *ze* only true constant in *ze* universe." Einstein's voice – methodical, high-pitched, and laden with a thick German accent – is almost entertaining. It reminds me of some of the movies I've seen with Einstein as a character, even cartoons of him from when I was a kid. What the movies never captured is the charisma of the man. He doesn't need to speak loudly, because when he speaks, people naturally listen. They hang on his every word as if they're waiting for a religious revelation. He's the scientific equivalent of a rock star.

Einstein seems to be finishing a point he was making when he says, "It's not the knowledge or wisdom we lack, but the imagination required to bridge the gap between the Theories of Relativity and Quantum Physics."

A man in the audience raises his hand.

"Yes?" Einstein asks.

"Your theory states that time is relative – that the pace of time varies depending on speed. How can that be? I've travelled on airplanes, and time still kept moving at the same pace."

"You were *ze* observer in your scenario, and your pace of time will not change from your point of view at any velocity," answers Einstein. "However, time dilation holds true in Relativity. *Ze* faster an object is moving *relative* to *ze* observer, *ze* slower time moves for that object from *ze* observer's point of view …. So, let us assume you and a friend are at an airport wearing watches set to *ze* exact same time. Your friend stays at *ze* airport. You board an airplane, fly around *ze* world, and land back at *ze* airport. When you compare watches, yours will be slightly behind your friend's. From your point of view, it is your friend who experienced time a little faster than you did. From your friend's point of view, it is you who experienced time a little slower."

"That seems impossible …" The man shakes his head, trying to grasp the concept. "How much will the time differ?"

"At *ze* speed of an airplane and *ze* distance around our planet … approximately a few billionths of a second. Unfortunately, it is beyond our capabilities at present to accurately measure this difference. However, at significantly higher velocities – those approaching *ze* speed of light – *ze* difference in pace of time also becomes quite significant."

This is incredible! Most scientific advances throughout history have come from observing and experimenting, then finding theories that matched the results. Einstein took a different approach. He used thought experiments and imagination to create theories that couldn't be experimentally verified until decades later. Time dilation from his theory of Relativity was a great example. Scientists in my time have used atomic clocks on space shuttles, and have accurately measured the time difference compared to clocks that stayed on Earth – verifying that portion of Relativity.

Okay, buddy, whoever you are, why don't you ask Einstein about time travel?

As if I could influence the man's thoughts, he does just that.

"So, was author H. G. Wells truly writing fiction when he wrote *The Time Machine*? Does your theory allow for the possibility of time travel?"

Einstein smiles. "What a vonderful mind Mr. Wells has – so full of *imagination*. Let us change our example just a bit. Now, you and your friend are at a spaceport instead of an airport. Again, you both wear watches reading *ze* same time. You board a spaceship and travel at 90% of *ze* speed of light for one day. Then, you turn around and come back to Earth, again traveling at 90% of *ze* speed of light. For you, two days would have passed. For your friend, who waited ever so patiently for you, over four and a half days would have passed."

Einstein takes a sip of water before continuing. "So, you would have experienced two days, and everyone on Earth would have experienced over four days. You would have *physically* travelled forward in time from your point of view back on Earth."

The man stands before posing the next logical question. "Professor Einstein … How, then, would someone travel back in time?"

"*Physically*, it is not possible, but!" Einstein lets that word sit for a moment while he takes another sip of water. "But, *perception* of *ze* past may be another story."

The man looks around to see if anyone else understands, and seems to gather solace in the vacant stares from most of the people there. I look to Max and see something different. Not confusion … more like contemplation. Max is excited about this topic, intently trying to take in as much as he can.

"Allow me to explain. *Ze* closer proximities of three-dimensional space are easily within our perception," Einstein continues. "I can see all of you within this room. However, perception can stretch beyond these walls. How far, would you say, can *ze* average person see?"

The man, still standing, seems comfortable enough to take on the other end of the conversation Einstein is having with the group. "Twenty miles? On a clear day, maybe thirty."

"Have you ever seen a star?" Again, the wry smile from Einstein. "There are stars that are millions of light-years away, and yet we can perceive them."

There are three huge chalkboards on the wall behind Einstein and the other man. The left chalkboard is a few inches higher than the other two, revealing that the chalkboards are each on a slider mechanism, and there are three additional chalkboards behind the front three. Einstein moves to the left chalkboard, and briskly draws X, Y, and Z axes, each with arrows at the end.

Facing back to the audience, he says, "*Ze* axes of three-dimensional space are infinite, but just because we are not able to see most of *ze* universe does not mean it does not exist. *Ze* same is true for time. Time is *ze* fourth dimension and *ze* space-time continuum is also infinite. Even though we physically reside at a single point in space-time, all of time has played out. So, like seeing *ze* distant stars in space, who is to say that we cannot *perceive* distant points in time."

He places the chalk down and walks back to his lounge chair. "Relativity theorizes that we may someday be able to *physically* travel measurably forward in time. However, traveling perceptually would be very different – *in theory*. We may be able to perceive events from both *ze* distant future and distant past. *Ze* human brain is an amazing thing. We do not have *ze* first clue about what we are truly capable of doing with it."

There was a buzz in the air … the entire room thinking about relativity and time travel … space-time and perception.

Einstein seizes the break in questions, "That will conclude *ze* Relativity portion of our discussion tonight. Now we can move on to quantum mechanics. Dr. Bohr, from Denmark, is one of *ze* leading physicists focusing on quantum mechanics, and he has most kindly agreed to visit us here in Princeton. Perhaps, Dr. Bohr, you would give our guests a brief introduction to *ze* topic?"

Bohr? This must be Niels Bohr.

"Thank you, Professor Einstein, and I thank you all for taking the time to learn more about this topic. The math behind quantum mechanics is fairly straight forward, but the concepts can be challenging." Bohr waits for a moment, and the group seems to sense it was so they could provide a round of applause. It is soft and polite, but they oblige. Bohr is a stark contrast to the unkempt Einstein. He wears a tailored gray suit and is clean-shaven. What little hair he has left is neatly slicked back.

"Professor Einstein, as you know, gave us the theory of Relativity." Bohr nods to the professor. "But what you may not know is that the very same year, in 1905, he also gave us one of the first ever workable theories into the way light works. His work provided the basis of understanding that light exhibits properties of both waves and particles."

Einstein jumps in, "Are you blaming me for quantum mechanics?" Almost everyone in the auditorium laughs. Even the stoic Bohr cracks a smile.

"I'm thanking you, not blaming you!" He rebuts and gets more laughs.

Who knew physicists could have a sense of humor?

"Quantum mechanics," Bohr continues, "is a branch of physics that helps explain the nature of light and other sources of energy. Its foundation was built by German physicist Max Planck and our own Professor Einstein, who first showed that the speed of light is constant in Relativity and then showed that light could be conceived in the form of quanta at the particle level with his theory of the photoelectric effect. The nature of light is that it can be viewed *either* as a wave, *or* as particles known as photons." He pauses to let the group digest this.

"Once more, I am being blamed," Einstein quips again. "I never thought it would take *ze* direction it has taken." He shakes his head in a mix of humor and some genuine dismay.

"The direction it has taken is to explain the universe where Relativity has gaps," Bohr counters.

"Oh, I know that quantum mechanics has its place in physics. I believe it is *incomplete*, though. There has to be a better way to model *ze* universe … a way to unify Relativity and Quantum theory."

It's so odd to see this live … as it's happening. Einstein and Bohr had a series of these debates about quantum mechanics and Relativity. And in my past, Einstein had died, still trying to unify the two branches of physics. I read once that Einstein's unfinished unification manuscript was found on the table next to the bed when he died. This is too weird. The man with perhaps the greatest intellect in human history is alive and kicking *right here*.

"There is no reason the two theories can't coexist," Bohr replies. "Relativity does an amazing job of explaining the macroscopic. At the microscopic level, Quantum theory explains energy and the existence of parallel universes."

"That is only conjecture!" Einstein is suddenly agitated.

"It is with thought experiments and conjecture that you came up with the theory of Relativity," Bohr counters calmly. "What is your favorite saying again? *Time is a dimension and all of time has played out.* I trust that you'll allow me the *time* to demonstrate what I mean?"

"Of course," Einstein smiles, seeming to regain his composure quickly.

Dr. Bohr stands and walks over to the middle chalkboard. It takes him a moment to find a piece of chalk that he likes.

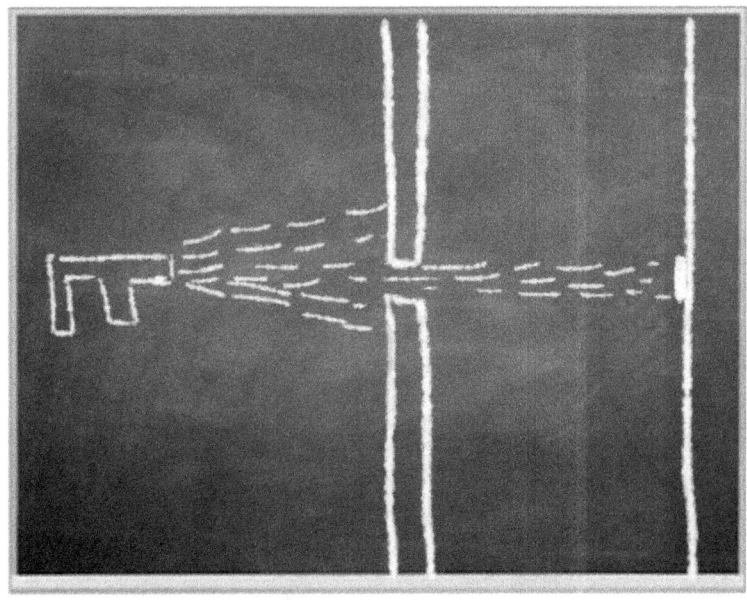

Bohr draws a submachine gun on the left, a vertical line with a gap in the middle, a solid vertical line to the right, and a bullet spray pattern from the submachine gun.

"This one experiment can tell you all you need to know about quantum mechanics. It's called the double slit experiment. We take a submachine gun, which sprays bullets from here," Bohr says as he points to the gun. "The bullets spray in a random pattern at this metal wall with the slit opening here," and he points to the vertical line in the middle of the drawing. "And, on the back wall we end up seeing a bullet hole pattern in the same shape as the slit opening."

That seems obvious, I think, and a few people in the crowd gently nod their agreement.

"Now, I'll need a volunteer," Bohr says to the crowd.

"I am not standing in front of your submachine gun," jokes Einstein.

After a quick burst of laughter, one of the two women in the crowd stands.

"Thank you, young lady. What's your name?" asks Bohr.

"Ingrid," she replies.

"Now, Ingrid, if I were to use a source of light instead of the gun, what would you expect to see on the back wall?"

She seems a bit hesitant, but soon answers, "A projection of light in the shape of the slit?"

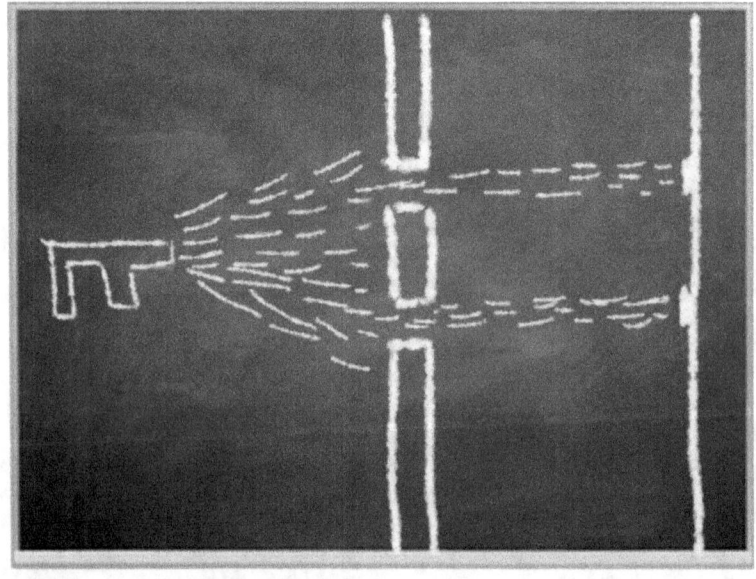

"Quite right!" Bohr says excitedly. He locates an eraser, and removes the middle wall in the drawing. Then, he redraws the wall with two parallel slits. "Now we have two parallel slits in our middle wall. We'll use the submachine gun first. It sprays bullets at the first wall. So, what would you expect to see on the back wall?"

Ingrid doesn't hesitate this time. "Bullet holes in the shapes of the two slits?"

"Correct again!" Bohr erases the submachine gun, and draws a crude looking light bulb, using blue chalk to draw the filament. "And, so we switch to the light. What will we see on the back wall?"

Full of confidence now, she replies, "light projected in two slit shapes."

Bohr shakes his head. "*This* is where the properties of quantum mechanics start to show …. On the back wall, we will see a pattern of *many stripes of light.*" Using the blue chalk, he draws a series of stripes on the back wall to illustrate his point. "Ingrid, do you know why we see stripes?"

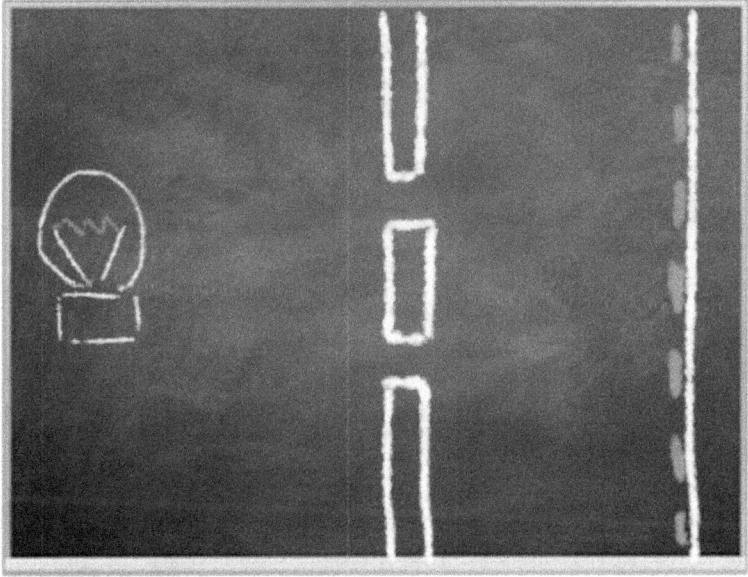

She shakes her head.

"Anyone else?" asks Bohr.

Einstein looks to see if anyone else will answer, then he raises his hand.

Bohr smiles. "By all means, Professor Einstein." He holds out the chalk while Einstein stands and walks to the board.

"When *ze* bullets are shot from a submachine gun, they are moving like *particles*. However, when light is used, stripes occur because light is moving from *ze* source in *waves*." Einstein draws ever-larger semicircles from the light bulb to the middle wall. Then, from each of the two slits he draws ever-larger semicircles that crisscross until they hit the back wall. "Each of *ze* light stripes is where two separate light waves combine, and each of *ze* dark stripes is where waves interfere with each other."

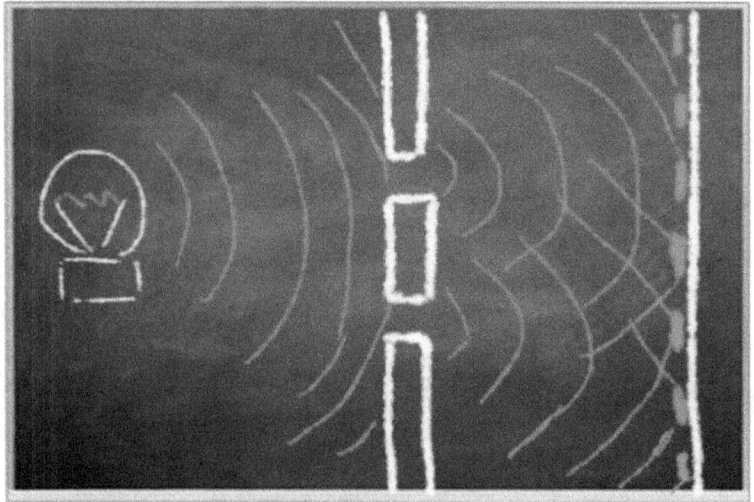

"Thus, proving that light moves in waves and that separate waves can interfere with each other," postures Bohr.

"I can concur with that," agrees Einstein.

Bohr moves to the right chalkboard and draws another light bulb, middle wall with one slit, and a back wall. "Now, let's go back to one slit and reduce the light so it only emits *one photon particle of light at a time*. The spray pattern is random and we'll spray a thousand photons at the middle wall. Ingrid – let's assume the back wall is made of film and will record each photon hit. What are we going to see on the back wall?"

She had taken her seat while Einstein was drawing, but now stands again. "A similar pattern to the submachine gun?"

"You're very good at this, Ingrid. Yes. We'll see a spray of light dots in the shape of the slit."

Bohr erases this middle wall and draws another with two slits again. "And, now, shooting *one* photon at a time with *two* slits, what do we see on the back wall?"

"With only one photon at a time, there won't be any interference, so we'll see two slits of photon light dots on the back wall," Ingrid deduces.

Bohr shakes his head slowly and emphatically. "That is, *most certainly*, what I would expect as well. But, sorry Ingrid, that's not the way it works when we do this experiment." He quickly draws the stripe pattern on the back wall. "What we get on the back wall shows groupings of light dots that form the *same stripes* as when we used a steady stream of light."

"But, how can a single particle show an interference pattern?" Ingrid looks troubled by this.

"*That*, dear Ingrid, is the basis of quantum mechanics." Bohr is truly excited now. "For each photon that makes it through the first wall, there is a 50% chance it went through the left slit and a 50% chance it went through the right slit. *Both* possibilities occur at the same time and the photon interferes with … itself!"

Bohr smirks, taking in the astonished faces in the crowd with a bit of amusement. Then, he looks right at me, or at least he seems to. Spooky!

"You have a question back there?" Bohr appears to be posing the question to me, but I know that's impossible. Then I hear Max's young voice and realize that he must have raised his hand.

"This is why you believe in parallel universes?" Max asks. "Because the photon is moving through the right slit in one reality and the left slit in another reality. And, thus, the interference pattern on the back wall is observed?"

Dr. Bohr looks at Einstein in amazement. Einstein only smiles.

"Why ... *yes,*" Bohr finally replies. He's smiling, too, looking quite impressed with Max. "One of the laws of quantum physics is that every possible outcome of every event spawns a new reality where that outcome is what actually happens. How intuitive of you, young man." The entire audience turns to look at Max.

Max appears to be both intrigued by this concept and troubled by the possibilities it represents. While his face hints at many questions in his mind, he speaks confidently. "But, there's a problem with your explanation. It's not quite ... complete."

Einstein nods excitedly.

Bohr physically takes a step back, caught off-guard by this teenager in the back row. "What do you think is ... *missing?*" He then leans forward and seems to be gathering his thoughts, preparing to squash this little bug who is questioning him.

"Well, if the two realities exist separately – the fa ... fa ... *first* universe where the photon went through the right slit and the second universe where the photon went through the left slit – why is the interference showing up? Aren't these two separate universes? Separate realities? Each with only *one* photon?"

"They ... they ..." Bohr stammers and starts to rub his chin. Turning to Einstein, he says, "How old is this boy and what is he doing here?"

Einstein raises an eyebrow and says, "He is a student of mine, quite gifted, actually. I think it would be *enlightening* for you to answer him."

Bohr turns back to Max. "There have been some thoughts on the subject. It's possible that light is able to cross the reality divide."

Max stands. "With all due respect, sir, that doesn't seem very plausible. If light could cross the reality divide, we'd see things from alternate realities all around us all the time. The light from all sources in all realities would be so intense; there would never be a night sky."

I've never seen my father like this. He's so young and full of vigor!

Einstein jumps in, "*Exactly!* Max, what do you think this means?"

"I believe," Max pauses for just a moment. "I believe it means there *are* in fact parallel universes."

"Then, what do you believe could be the cause of the interference?" Einstein's focus is squarely on Max, as is Bohr's and everyone else in the auditorium. Every person in the room, who had been facing the scientists, now turns completely around to face Max. I can't believe Albert Einstein, Niels Bohr, and all these people are taking the opinion of this this younger version of my father so seriously.

"This is just speculation based on your ta ... ta ... ta ... *test* results, but is it possible that each potential outcome of an event does, in fact, spawn a separate parallel universe, but these universes converge into one when the differences between them are small? Maybe there's some force, similar to gravity, pulling them together – some sort of quantum gravity?"

Bohr's face suddenly glows like a light bulb has just turned on. His expression toward Max evolves from defiance to looking at Max now as though he's some sort of royalty. "Yes! Why ... *quantum gravity* ... that makes *perfect* sense! However, what constitutes a small difference? When are the differences large enough to truly spawn realities that remain separate?"

Einstein answers that one, "*That* is for God to decide."

Suddenly, I feel a vortex opening. I don't want to leave yet, but I'm being drawn away from this time. This must be the end of what Nostradamus wants me to see. "*It's time to go back ...*"

The electric blue spiral of light forms – moving clockwise this time. The spiral slows and eventually stops.

I wake slowly from my trance. It usually takes a few seconds to gain my bearings ... to figure out which year I'm actually in. At least my senses come back almost immediately upon waking, and that helps me figure out I'm in my own time. Max is still sitting in the lounge chair next to me, staring at the tiniest glint of light that bounces off the many peaks of the Gulf waves.

"Wow," is the first word that escapes my mouth. "I had no idea you were such a science geek. You were right there with Albert Einstein and I think you actually had a better understanding of quantum physics than Niels Bohr."

Max blinks a couple of times before saying, "So, you went back to 1945 ... to the debate I attended between Einstein and Bohr. I'm certain Nostradamus has a reason for taking you there, but I can't imagine what it is."

"I can."

"I'm not sure I want to hear this," says Max, and for a moment, I can't decide if he is serious.

"Don't you get it?" I'm fully awake now and turn to face Max. "Einstein explained through science exactly what we're doing – what Nostradamus has done and is teaching me – our *perception* of different times. You were there, and back in 1945, you *did* get it! You grasped the concept of parallel universes. What was the term you used ... quantum gravity? Don't you see what it means?"

"Trey, you're still thinking about trying to fix things in the past that didn't turn out the way you wanted and Nostradamus told you it *can't* be done. Now, you've been through the same debate with Einstein and Bohr that I experienced back in 1945. You have heard it from two of the most brilliant physicists in history. You can't physically go back in time."

"I get that, yes .... I can't *physically* go back in time."

Chapter 8

ULRICH VON BECKER

ATLANTIC OCEAN
MARCH 21, 1945

I'm in a precarious position. I don't like it … not in the least.

What happened with Lady Zelda was a mistake and I know I'm going to have to pay a price. Even if I could, I wouldn't change what happened. I've longed for Zelda from the first time I saw her. I have no idea why she did what she did, but in her hands, she has my heart now … my devotion … and my life.

Dinner with the crew was torturous. They were all looking at me as if I was on the menu – as if they all knew what had happened in the conning tower. If anyone knows, how long will it be before Ister finds out? Then, how long before I face a firing squad? Who knows? Maybe in a U-boat, they just shoot you out of a torpedo tube to execute you.

The crewman who just cleared the dinner plates from Ister's stateroom walks up to me and I swear he's more nervous than I am. He mumbles, "Herr Ister is expecting you." The little man shuffles away before I can respond, not that I have a response.

As I make my way down the narrow passage to Ister's stateroom, I can't help feeling that I've had my last meal and I'm essentially walking the plank right now. Without even realizing it, my pace slows, and the busy crewmen struggle to pass me. Don't they know that this is it? That this is my walk of death? I'll take as much damn time with it as I please.

My legs carry me to the door of the stateroom sooner than I had hoped. *It's time.* I lift my hand and knock. The first two knocks of my fist are too soft … *pitiful.* I'm so embarrassed that the next two knocks are nearly slams of my fist against the door. It's an agonizing five full seconds before the door opens from the inside and Lady Zelda is looking up at me. She holds my gaze for just a moment and then turns to the side.

"Von Becker, come in. Herr Ister is ready to speak with you." Her voice is enchanting. I'd follow her anywhere ... even into the stateroom of Hagan Ister, head of the Thule Society ... the man I'm here to protect ... the man who will most likely be the death of me.

"Von Becker, close that door behind you!" Ister speaks with a quick pace and very loudly, on the verge of yelling. It's almost as if he's hard of hearing and that could well be the case. He's obviously been in action, possibly a prisoner of war ... tortured at some point. His face is horribly scarred, especially around his ears. It appears someone cut his throat, with more scarring there, and his voice was affected. While he's always on the verge of yelling, his voice is scratchy, almost tinny. Whatever cut up his face, must have also torn through half of his vocal chords. I'd put his age at around fifty, and he's about average height and weight. While I tower over him physically, the man carries himself like he's the biggest man on the planet. His eyes are what stand out most, though. Clear and blue, they're always alert, darting around, taking in his environment.

"You wanted to see me, Herr Ister?"

The stateroom is small, but considering we're on a U-boat, it seems palatial. The bed where Ister sleeps folds up and into the back wall. Along one side wall there's a storage closet and dropdown desk, and along the other is a dropdown table with three chairs.

"Sit down ..." Ister sounds almost friendly, as if he's happy to see me. My heart is pounding nearly out of my chest. I've seen Ister kill people. He's ordered me to kill people. Almost every time, he's as calm as can be. As though he just calculates it is better if that person is dead, and then he makes it so.

I expected Lady Zelda to leave, but instead she sits in the middle seat. With this, my heart slows a bit. I find it hard to believe he'd kill me in front of her. Taking a deep breath, I sit in the chair closest to the door. My legs don't fit under the table, so I need to sit further back.

Before Ister sits, in the seat facing the door as he always does, he removes his gun from his jacket pocket and emphatically places it on the table. My heart races again for a moment, but I quickly realize he wouldn't let the gun out of his hand if he were going to kill me. The gun is the only advantage he has against me. He would be stupid to let it go if he wanted me dead and Hagan Ister is not stupid.

The gun is a Smith and Wesson revolver, which has always baffled me. Why carry a revolver, and an American revolver, no less? Our German Lugers are automatics and considered far superior. Yet Ister carries the revolver. I've heard several Nazi leaders choose them over Lugers … even Hitler carries one. I have always wondered if there's an advantage to the revolver I haven't heard about.

"Have the crewmen been asking about our mission in New York?" Ister asks politely, as if we are just sitting down socially to have a couple of beers.

"Yes."

"And, what have you said in reply?"

"Nothing … just as you said I should."

"Good, Von Becker. That's very good. And, Captain Saltzwedel?"

"He was more patient, but yesterday he also asked."

"The captain is a more *willful* man. What did you tell him?" Ister's tone is suddenly more serious.

"The same, uh, nothing. But, I don't even know why we're going to America, so in truth, what can I say to them?"

"Precisely." Ister grins, which causes his puffy face to scrunch oddly. "Now, we must be prepared for anything. When we reach America, we're going to do something the captain may not agree with."

"It might help if I know what we're going to do first?"

"You don't need to know … not yet. The reason I'm telling you this much now, is that Lady Zelda has foreseen a potential problem with the captain. She believes he will obey orders, but she has seen that there's a chance that he won't."

Zelda sits still and expressionless, giving away nothing.

Ister continues, "I don't like chances. I prefer certainty. So, you will carry your gun on you in your jacket pocket the way I do."

Part of me wants to point out that the captain asked us to not wear our guns on the U-boat, that maybe it isn't safe to be shooting a gun in this tin can, but I know what Ister's reaction to that would be. So, I simply say, "Yes, Herr Ister. But … I had to hand over my gun when we boarded."

"I will make sure you get it back before we arrive. When we reach America and I announce my plan, I want you right next to the captain. Should he or anyone else seem like they won't obey my orders, you're to seize the captain. Don't kill him, though. We'll need to use him to control the crew. Understand?"

"Perfectly, Herr Ister."

"Good …. The Fuhrer told me you are a good man, Von Becker, and a pure German. Someone I can trust to do whatever is necessary for the Reich." He produces a sinister grin, stands, and pats my shoulder firmly.

"You can trust me, sir." Out of the corner of my eye, I notice Zelda blink twice as I profess my loyalty.

"Good," says Ister, not noticing Zelda. "Go now. Tell the captain it is time for an update with Berlin."

We have a relay system set up to maintain communications with Berlin, and we surface to send and receive updates almost daily. Each time we do so is a risk though, especially so close to America. Again, my only response is, "Yes, Herr Ister."

Chapter 9

MAX MEDICI

PRINCETON, NJ, USA
MARCH 22, 1945

Ow!

Geez, everything hurts. You know it's bad when just rolling to my side in bed is difficult. Of course, this is more of a cot than a bed. My shoulders, probably more than anything else, ache from the hundreds of push-ups and pull-ups Smith made me do today. He tried to get me to admit that I lost yesterday's race to Sebastian. I refused. He said I didn't have to do any sit-ups if I just told the truth. I stuck to my guns and ended up doing sit-ups, too. My abs burn, but it still doesn't compare to the pain in my shoulders.

I don't care that Bernie is snoring again. I don't care that it's a bit too chilly in our cabin. I'm so exhausted that sleep is quickly taking over, even with the pain.

The transition to deep sleep is nearly instantaneous and I begin to dream. Some nights there are dreams that mean nothing. Tonight, this dream is *vivid* and *alive*. This is real happening, or at least had really happened at one time.

The sun is high in my dream and it's a clear day. Looking at the landscape, there's a great clearing surrounded by a dense jungle. Around the edges of the clearing are several large stone structures. One structure commands my attention – a hundred-foot-tall pyramid near the center of the clearing. It's not one of the great pyramids of Egypt – I know the difference. This pyramid has columns of steps at the center of all four sides. It doesn't end with a point on top like the Egyptian pyramids. Instead, there's a flat stone plateau with a large four-sided stone temple perched on top. This must be the Mayan pyramid temple of Chichen Itza. I remember seeing a picture of it in a book once – a book that my mom brought home from the library for me one day.

This is the same start to my dream for the third night in a row. Floating toward the top of the pyramid, I wonder if it would end here again as it has the previous two nights. No. Not tonight – tonight, I can hear voices emanating from within the stone temple. They are speaking a language I don't recognize, yet the words flow easily and understandably through my mind.

"Votan, you cannot do this!" the first voice commands.

"It is necessary, Kukulkan, my king."

As they emerge from the temple, I can see that both men are tall, with copper-toned skin. The king, heavily muscled, wears a bejeweled gold crown that funnels a mass of long feathers and braided hair up through the crown opening. Atop the crown sits a life-size, clear crystal skull. It makes him appear at least a foot taller than Votan, even though they are about the same height.

Votan and King Kukulkan walk out of the temple to the northern edge of the plateau topping the pyramid. Eight Mayan warriors follow them closely, each dressed in only a hanging loincloth and feathered headdress. The warriors carry long spears with obsidian tips. Votan carries a wooden club that resembles a four-foot long baseball bat. It has a round handle just like a bat, but the other end is flat like an oar. The oar end has obsidian blades on both sides that run half the club's length.

The king walks gracefully with long strides, but appears to have his hands bound behind his back. Thousands of people surround the base of the pyramid. Their attention is affixed to the top of the pyramid where King Kukulkan, Votan, and the warriors have stopped walking. Scanning the crowd, I see the people are emaciated, with dark circles under their eyes. Most have matted hair and hollow cheeks. Some wear loin clothes, while others are naked. They stand in stark contrast to the healthy, robust physiques of Votan and the king.

"People, you *must* hear me!" Votan yells and then waits impatiently for the crowd to be silent. "As your high priest, I have meditated many times to see the future of our people. For 4000 years, our priests have looked to the future. Not one of us has ever seen past the end of our long count. Today, this shortest of days, we are precisely 1000 years from the day the long count ends."

I can't help thinking back to another book my mom got from the library – this one about the Spanish explorer by the name of Fernando Cortez, who conquered much of what is now Mexico. By the time Cortez arrived in the 16th Century, the Maya had all but disappeared.

This dream, or vision, obviously takes place before Cortez and the Spanish arrive … probably the 10th or 11th Century AD. The shortest of days must mean the winter solstice, the 21st of December on our modern calendars.

Votan looks to the skies briefly and then back to the crowd. "We have suffered the wrath of the gods for many years now. There is little fresh water and our crops fail. We have sacrificed many of our enemies and we have sacrificed many of our own. But the gods are very angry, more than ever before!" Votan's voice is deep and rich, and it projects clearly to everyone in the crowd. "We must *appease* the gods. If nothing changes, I see that we will not survive to the next shortest of days. The gods demand something more from us!"

A voice from the crowd below yells, "Sacrifice!" Another voice follows with, "Yes, sacrifice!" The first man starts chanting, "Sacrifice … Sacrifice …" At first, a few people join in, then a few hundred. After the fifth chant, they all join in, "Sacrifice … Sacrifice!"

A chill runs down my spine as the crowd continues chanting louder and louder. Then, Votan raises his free hand and the chant suddenly becomes softer – but doesn't stop.

"Yes!" Votan's voice rises above the crowd's noise and his eyes dart to the king. "The gods demand a sacrifice greater than ever before! They demand a sacrifice of *royal* blood!"

Again, almost in unison, the crowd shouts, "Sacrifice! Sacrifice!"

Votan raises his bladed club as high as his arms can reach and waits. The crowd falls silent.

"Do you, King Kukulkan, have anything to say to your people?"

The king leans forward, to the point where I think he might flee down the pyramid steps. Yet he holds his ground. Facing east, he turns slowly to the north and then the west, glaring at the crowd gathered to see today's sacrifice – his sacrifice.

"I *do* have something to say to *my* people!" he shouts in the most savage voice I've ever heard. "Votan is our priest and our prophet, but he cannot see beyond our long count! Not one of our priests or prophets has *ever* been able to see beyond our long count. *I* have seen. I have had a vision! You can sacrifice me to the gods. It matters not, as I am already one of them. If you do this, I shall return. I will appear as a *flame* crossing the sky!"

The king makes an exaggerated turn of his head to the northwest sky. The entire crowd follows his gaze, along with Votan and the warriors. A comet makes its way slowly across the sky, its tail visible even in the bright mid-day, and blazing a fiery trail toward the ocean. Several gasps can be heard, then utter silence.

Kukulkan returns his gaze to the people below. "Your king shall return as the prince of princes! Great famine will be known by all! Great sacrifice will be made by all! When the long count ends, I shall rule all! I am Ku – Kul – Kaaaaaan!"

The king's vehement screaming of his name ends abruptly – silenced, as the blade of Votan's club, swung with enormous force, hits the back of Kukulkan's neck and lops off his head. The crystal skull that had been perched on the king's crown tumbles to the side, bouncing twice before settling next to Votan's feet. The king's severed head flies halfway down the pyramid before making contact with the stone steps. Mimicking the crystal skull, it also bounces a few times and lands almost perfectly centered between the two serpent head statues at the base of the northern pyramid steps. The king's body, spraying blood from the headless neck, falls forward and slides slowly down the steps. It gradually picks up speed and soon hits the bottom of the pyramid, near its lost head.

The crowd cheers in mass hysteria. Do they believe that sacrificing their king is their best chance at appeasing their gods? Seeing it only makes me feel ill.

This seems so real, like it actually happened sometime in the distant past. Why am I dreaming this?

Votan reaches down and touches the crystal skull. His eyes close, and his body visibly shivers at the touch of it. Slowly lifting the skull, he stands motionless for several minutes before addressing the crowd again. "I have sacrificed so many people, but I have never before sacrificed royalty. This club, stained by the god king's blood, will never be used again." He slowly turns his back to the cheering crowd and walks toward the temple chamber.

My essence follows Votan, as the warriors wait outside the entrance. The outer chamber is empty – nothing but stone walls and a passage to an inner chamber. Votan moves to the inner chamber, which is also empty, except for the deceased king's throne. I stay close as Votan walks over to the throne – a red stone jaguar, cut in the shape of a bench sitting atop a rectangular stone base.

Votan stares at it for a moment and then turns around, scanning the room to make sure he's alone. He presses in on the jaguar's green left eye until he hears a loud *click*. He then pushes on the front of the jaguar and it slowly slides back, revealing a compartment below that is just smaller than the base of the throne. Votan proceeds to slide the blade of the club over the face of the skull – smearing Kukulkan's blood on the skull's perfectly shaped teeth as though he were trying to feed it. He then places his club into the compartment, quickly concealing it by moving to the back of the jaguar and pushing the throne closed. As he does this, the pushed-in eye slides back out to normal position with another audible click.

He places the bloodstained crystal skull on the throne facing the entrance to the inner chamber and I swear it seems to be grinning … a red, bloody grin of a predator that has just ripped the throat out of its prey.

The vision blurs momentarily, then regains clarity. Votan is gone, but I'm still in the stone temple atop the pyramid. The room is darker. Dark brown dirt and light green moss canvas the walls. The jaguar throne remains, but no crystal skull. I turn, and an image painted on the wall seizes my attention. Adorning the wall in blood red paint, or possibly in real blood, is a large swastika. My throat tightens and the red in the swastika forces me to relive the vision of Votan beheading Kukulkan.

I wake abruptly and sit up in my cot. Sweat drips down my temples and my heart races. Both of my hands reflexively spring to my neck so I can make sure it's still holding my head in place.

Later in the morning, I could barely keep my eyes open during breakfast with the Boys and I have no motivation for our run. There's a traitor in our camp, and beating Sebastian and Bernie in a race has lost its meaning. Having just cleared the last cluster of trees, I wipe the sweat from my brow as I approach the flagpole. Because my mind has been swimming with thoughts of crazy dreams, time travel, and parallel universes the entire five miles, I'm about to finish last today, well behind the other Boys. Hell, with the amount of push-ups and sit-ups Smith is going to make me do, it doesn't even matter. Wait … where is he?

Sebastian and Bernie are both sitting on the ground, catching their breath – but no Smith.

Slowing to a jog for the last 50 yards, out of habit, I still slap the pole as I pass it.

"Where's Smith?" I plop down between Sebastian and Bernie.

"We haven't seen him," replies Bernie.

"Really?" This is like a vacation. Smith hasn't missed a day since we've been here and he couldn't have picked a better day to be gone. I can't begin to contain my smile.

"Don't go thinking you've escaped your push-ups and sit-ups. Smith will probably treat us all like we lost the race." Sebastian's speaking in English. He must think we're on vacation, too.

"Should we still head to the gym?" asks Bernie … in English.

"Yes," I say, switching to English myself. "He's probably waiting for us there."

We start walking the short path from the flagpole to the gym. A light rain begins to fall, so we increase our pace to a jog, quickly reaching the gym entrance. The gym is the largest building here at the camp, with free weights, pull-up bars, punching bags, ropes for climbing, ropes for jump-roping, and ropes for learning to tie up your enemy. There's plenty of floor space for jumping jacks, running in place, and practicing combat moves. In the center of the gym, we have an elevated boxing ring, surrounded by a few metal folding chairs. The gym smells as though some sort of mold has taken over, and is usually dusty – I think because Jones doesn't want to clean it when any of us are in it, and there's usually at least one of us in the gym.

"That's the first time I've ever beaten you in a race, Max." Bernie is still breathing heavily as he holds the door open. "You okay?"

"I st … I st …" Thanks to Professor Einstein, I know more about my problem, but still don't know how to stop stuttering in English. I want to say that I *stopped* caring about the race, and insist on trying to blurt it out before anyone can cut me off and try to finish my sentence for me. "St … St … St …"

Not only do Bernie and Sebastian have to endure my stuttering, but the Men are in the gym, waiting for Smith, and they hear me as we walk in. It's not the first time they've heard me stutter. It doesn't help that I'm the only Italian among them and the youngest, but my stuttering makes me an easy target. Fortunately, most of them ignore the issue. Kirk, however, is different.

Kirk is the largest, strongest, and as far as I'm concerned, the toughest of the six of us training for our mission into Germany. He's a tall brute and all muscle. One of the few personal details Kirk has shared with us is that his father had been a professional boxer in Germany. Kirk has been weightlifting and boxing most of his life, and often leads our hand-to-hand combat training at Sergeant Smith's direction. Because he's the oldest of the Men and Boys and a natural leader, Kirk's opinion carries a lot of weight with everyone. He often points out that we're supposed to blend in with the German troops, and I don't look the part, even arguing with the administrators that I'm a threat to our operation. Kirk once went so far as to say my stuttering would draw unwanted attention in Germany. As much as I don't like Kirk, I find it difficult to disagree with his points.

"St … St … Stupid!" Kirk only stands ten feet from our position near the door, but still chooses to yell while making fun of me. He glares at me, taking the few steps necessary to confront me directly, and then he unexpectedly shoves me to the ground. "You are utterly *stupid!*"

Lying flat on the floor, staring up, I see Kirk glowering at me. *You are stupid.* They were Kirk's words, but they were also my dad's words. My growing rage threatens to cause me to lose control, but I try to remember Johnny's training. I stand slowly. This is more than an immature attempt to embarrass me; this is a direct challenge. We've long established that we settle these things in the boxing ring and I'm determined to make sure that's how we'll settle this as well.

"You should have stayed down, Boy." Kirk says this with anticipation, even a hint of excitement in his voice.

"I'm no coward, Kirk … Why don't we settle this in the ring?" I've trained with Kirk and know I can never beat him using the Combative hand-to-hand method we've been taught. Nor would boxing or wrestling be of any use. Kirk has mastered each of those. Yet, I have to fight Kirk, or forever be labeled a coward by the rest of the team. If I back down now, I'll never gain the team's respect. It might mean taking a beating, but so be it.

"Sure, Ma … Ma … Max," he teases further, "Let's take this in the ring."

Kirk climbs eagerly and effortlessly into the boxing ring. I try to match his enthusiasm as I follow, but nearly trip as I struggle to get through the ropes. The other Boys and Men quickly surround the ring.

"Who wants to bet on how many minutes Max will last before Kirk beats him?" It's Erik, trying to make light of a tense situation. Or, maybe, just trying to make a few bucks.

Dieter follows Kirk and me into the ring, taking on the role of referee. He's talking to Kirk first in his corner.

After a minute of arguing about bets, with no one really wanting to bet on me, Sebastian surprises everyone, "I'll take all bets that Max lasts at least three minutes." The others all jump at this opportunity and that ends the betting.

Dieter now comes over to my corner. He's almost as big and strong as Kirk, but is more likely to use his mind than his muscles to solve a problem. Speaking just above a whisper so only I can hear him, he says,

"Look, Max, stepping in here with Kirk was brave but stupid. Now it's time to be smart. Try to avoid getting yourself killed. I'm not going to let this go very long, so stay safe as long as you can."

"Stay safe … good advice, thanks." There must be an unreasonable calmness to me, because I notice I just said the word *stay* without stuttering. Maybe I am stupid. Maybe I don't fully understand the beating I'm about to get.

Dieter moves to the middle of the ring. "Gentlemen …" I walk to the middle and Kirk meets me there, salivating. "There will be no pokes to the eye, no biting, and no kicks to the balls. Understood?"

Kirk and I each nod our understanding of the sparse rules of engagement.

Dieter continues, "Erik will work the bell. Rounds will be three minutes, and if there's more than one round, there will be a one-minute break between rounds. When I say it's over, then it's over. Is that understood?" This, he directed to Kirk, but we both nod our acceptance. "Okay, go to your corners and wait for the bell."

While waiting for the bell to ring, I quickly think about what Kirk will do. The Combative method we've been taught is very offense-oriented. The theory is simply to disable your opponent as quickly as possible. The Combative method teaches us to deliver explosive first strikes to vital targets. A punch or elbow to the throat or a kick to the inner part of the knee are examples of first-strike attempts we've been taught.

Nileča, however, is the exact opposite. Johnny Fox taught me to allow my opponent to make the first move. Nileča is defense-oriented, teaching blocks, counters, throws, and holds. It was specifically designed to allow a smaller person to use leverage in such a way as to turn a larger opponent's size against them. Sebastian and I haven't had a reason yet to use our Nileča training, but I have one now.

The bell rings. I take two steps toward the center of the ring and wait, trying to anticipate how Kirk will attack. I've seen Kirk spar and he usually goes for a quick first strike. Now, with the other trainees betting on how long I can last, there's no way he'll be able to resist trying to end it quickly.

Nearly running across the ring, Kirk has a somewhat crazed look to him. I assume a defensive position.

Bernie yells, "Get out of the corner, Max! He'll trap you there!"

At full speed when he reaches me, Kirk propels his right fist right for my throat. Sensing it was coming, though, I block Kirk's punch to the side. His momentum has him still lunging forward. I grab Kirk's shirt and start falling backward, pulling Kirk with me. Curving my back to allow myself to roll when I land, I jab my feet into Kirk's abdomen and kick up with all my might. I've turned Kirk's momentum against him and send him flying, easily clearing the ropes of the ring behind me, and crashing on the cement floor with a loud thud.

The other young men stand silent, astonished.

Kirk sprawls back to his feet, now with a look of utter fury. He leaps back into the ring and immediately shifts back into attack mode. This time, however, he doesn't run toward me. He slowly stalks, having learned something from his first attack. Now, face to face, a mere two feet apart, Kirk keeps his balance and starts a three-punch combination attack.

Quickly and efficiently, I block each punch while maintaining my defensive position.

Kirk then tries a two-punch combination, followed by a kick aimed at my knee.

Again, I'm able to block the punches. I could see the kick coming and perform a perfect leg sweep maneuver that lands Kirk on his back once more.

This is when I make my first offensive move, leaping to elbow Kirk's midsection. Kirk anticipates it and rolls out of the way.

Kirk immediately counters, throwing himself on top of me and putting me into a wrestling hold. It wasn't the beating he had hoped to inflict on me, but I'm sure he thinks I can't escape the hold.

Thanks to Johnny's training, I'm able to squirm my right arm free. I deliver an elbow to Kirk's midsection at full force, and he lets out a yelp. Then, I grab Kirk's arm, spin around, and gain the top position. I keep my weight on Kirk's left arm while putting a chokehold around Kirk's neck and right arm. The only move I leave him is a roll that would require him to dislocate his left shoulder. I'm not letting go, and start applying more force to the chokehold. Even though Kirk must be on the verge of blacking out, he doesn't submit.

Dieter reluctantly comes to our side. "It's over! Max, let him go!"

I'm not ready to let go just yet, though. I don't intend to kill Kirk, but I want him to think about this every time he decides to make fun of me.

"Do you submit?" I relax my chokehold just enough for Kirk to get a single gasp of air.

"Never," is the only word Kirk utters before I tighten my hold again.

Amazing … Kirk would apparently rather die than submit.

He's on the verge of blacking out, when I feel Dieter's hand on my shoulder. "Let him go, Max. It's over. Let him go."

I finally do release him and Kirk starts convulsively gasping. To his credit, it only took him a few moments to gain his feet and stomp out of the ring.

As I stand, Dieter whispers in my ear, "That was a hell of a fight, Max, but it's over now. It's time to let it go and remember we're on the same team. Do you understand?"

Even though I'm breathing hard, my nerves are remarkably calm. "I think someone better remind Kirk of that at some –"

"Max!" Sebastian suddenly yells from my left and I'm about to turn that way when I hear "MAX!" from a different voice on my right. I turn to my right just in time to see the leg of a chair fly into view and smash into my forehead. I black out an instant before crashing to the floor.

Chapter 10

TREY TYSON
LONGBOAT KEY, FL, USA
MARCH 22, 2014

The training session with Nostradamus didn't last as long as they usually do. I went back to 1945 to see the next installment of the Max Medici show and it was a doozy.

It's so strange to see him living events in his 1945 life, with no clue that a son he won't even conceive for another 20 years is watching him during these amazing experiences from so long ago.

Seeing Max in a fight was intense. The old man – when he was a teenager – actually beat the much bigger trainee named Kirk. I couldn't help myself when I saw that chair heading for him, so I yelled out his name. I instantly lost my concentration, along with my connection to the past. It was one burst that caused a blip in space-time, severing the connection, and forcing me abruptly back to now.

When I fully wake from tonight's trance, my first thought is about Max's forehead.

I stand up and face him where he lay comfortably on his lounge chair. A small trail of smoke still floats from the peace pipe and Max looks truly relaxed. He barely moves as I lean over and shift the hair over his left eyebrow to find that his scar is … *gone*. He indulges my search patiently as I slide my hand over and find the scar is there, after all, but now it's over his *right* eye.

I did it – I just changed the past! A small change, to be sure. I may not have rid history of Adolf Hitler's existence. Moving Max's scar is no big deal, but it happened. It worked. The change stayed in our universe, just as Max thought it would. Quantum gravity – the old man is absolutely brilliant!

Do I tell Max? How will he react if I do? There's one thing I need to know and it requires that I *do* tell him.

"Max?"

He smiles, still indulging what must appear to be extremely odd behavior on my part. "Yes, Trey?"

"Will you tell me how you got your scar?" I turn my chair to face him and sit again.

"I told you, that's —"

"I know … it's classified, but I'm going to see this entire classified Hitler-era stuff anyway. You know that, right? I'll respect your secrecy, but I need to know the story from your point of view."

"Well, I suppose you're right. The scar …" I watch as Max reaches above his *left* eye, "is here because of a fight I had. After the fight, the young man I fought against hit me over the head with a chair."

"This is important, Max. Can you touch your scar?"

"Why?" He looks confused.

"Please, just indulge me on this."

"I'm lucky my friend warned me about the chair. It ended up being less of a direct blow to the head. The scar is here, over my left eye."

"Leave your finger right there." I pull out my iPhone, turn on the camera on the front of the phone, and hand it to Max so he can see himself like it's a mirror. "Take a look."

Max does as I ask. The dumbfounded look on his face is priceless. "I … I remember the chair hitting me here, but I also remember it hitting me here over my right eye. And … a *second* voice yelling my name, warning me … could that have been *you*, Trey?"

I nod slowly, "Yes. That was me."

"I remember both blows to the head … both histories."

"It's hard to believe, isn't it? I didn't go back with the intention to change anything, but when I saw the chair hurled at your head, I just … well, I just reacted. Do you know what this means?"

"That next time you can go back and warn me *before* Kirk hits me over the head with a chair?"

"Ha Ha!" I can't help but laugh. "No, Max. It means you were right about quantum gravity! Small changes in history can be kept in *this* space-time continuum … in *this* version of reality."

"Trey," Max suddenly looks very serious. "Just because you *can* do a thing, doesn't mean that you *should* do a thing. You have no idea how much this change that you think is meaningless will affect the bigger picture in our reality. I think there must be a gravity-type effect between alternate realities. It's not inconceivable that a small change you cause brings about a merger with another reality where much larger changes take place. Don't forget that we won the war. We beat the Germans in building the first atomic bomb. Your small change could affect all of that."

"You know me – I'll be careful." I wink at him.

"I know you, yes …. You best keep me involved, because you don't exactly have a history of being careful."

Chapter 11

ALBERT EINSTEIN
PRINCETON, NJ, USA
MARCH 25, 1945

"Professor Einstein?" Nurse Jones has an annoying habit of walking right into my office without ever knocking. I have spoken to her about this several times, but she still does it. It was the same way with my ex-wife, Mileva, when we were married. No respect for a man deep in thought. Of course, with Mileva, I was able to divorce her.

"Yes?"

She's about to say something, stops, looks at my desk, and then asks, "Would you like some help organizing your work?"

Admittedly, my desk is cluttered ... perhaps more than cluttered. Stacks of documents and project notes take up every possible square inch.

"If a cluttered desk indicates a cluttered mind, what, then, does an empty desk indicate?"

"Sorry, Professor."

"Why did you want to see me?"

"I believe the president is here."

"Dodds? He does not even know about this place. What are you talking about?"

"No," she says while rolling her eyes at me, "not the president of *Princeton University*, the president of the *United States*. He's being helped out of his car now."

"*Ze* Men's graduation is not scheduled until tomorrow. Why is he here today?"

"I don't know, Professor. I just saw a shiny green and black limousine drive into the camp, and then several men began fumbling with a wheelchair."

"Very well, there must be a good reason. Would you please ensure we have some time to talk?"

"I'll go to the gym and make sure everyone stays clear." Jones heads toward the door at her usual quick pace.

"Thank you ... wait a moment." She does a military-style about face. "Keep everyone else away, but ask Max to join us."

She looks at me for a long moment before finally saying, "Yes, Professor."

The door to the administration building had closed for no more than a few seconds after Nurse Jones departed when a quick, firm rap announces the president's arrival. I make my way to the door and open it. My God, the man is not doing well. So thin ... held upright by two men, but one could easily do the job. Near death's door most likely. "President Roosevelt, are you ... please, come in."

I hold the door open as a Secret Service agent enters, eyeing the administration building with distrust. An aide and another agent assist the president through the door. A fourth agent follows with his wheelchair and as soon as the chair is in position, they ease the president into it. Following them, are Dr. Conant and Dr. Bush. Today, they are both wearing navy blue suits.

"Professor Einstein," Roosevelt holds out his hand with as much energy as he can muster and I gently shake it. His hand is clammy, probably from a combination of his illness and the effort it took to get from the car to the building. "What's this news about a traitor in your camp?"

The taller of the Secret Service agents begins walking through the entire administration building, another goes outside to stand post in front of the only entrance to the building, while the third stands at attention behind the president. The aide stays at the president's side.

"Mr. President, thank you for making the trip, but we can handle things until you are –"

"I'm fine. Please sit down, Professor. I'm not going to stand and it gets damned tiring constantly looking up at people. Now tell me what's going on around here." Some color was starting to show on his mostly gray cheeks.

The administration building is nothing more than a log cabin with a lobby area, a hallway, and three rooms that serve as offices. The wood floors are bare and nothing hangs from the walls. Only a door, a single window, and a hallway ... otherwise, the lobby would be a box – not exactly inspirational for a thinking man.

We've always had several chairs in the lobby area of the administration building, but this is the first time I can remember having a need for them. Conant, with a stern look, takes one of the chairs. Bush has a professional and friendly look as he comes over and shakes my hand, then without a word takes another chair. I sit after angling my seat to face the president.

"I received a letter from a former colleague of mine in Germany ... someone I trust. Somehow, knowledge of Project Spear has made it to German leadership. This former colleague, a true friend who is being forced to aid Hitler's efforts to build *ze* atomic bomb, says that *ze* Germans are aware of our efforts. I do not know how ... or who it could be, but someone here is relaying information back to *ze* Germans. We have a *traitor* in our camp."

Roosevelt looks to Bush, who opens his mouth, but says nothing as the president quickly turns back to me and says, "We're two days away from sending your first three men to Germany and you find out *now* that we have a traitor. Don't you find the timing to be suspicious?"

"*Ze* note from my friend was written over a month ago. It took that long to reach me."

"Did your friend give you any indication ..." the president has to pause for a coughing attack. His aide produces some medicine, but Roosevelt waves it away. "How far along are the Germans?"

"He was not specific, but did say that we should *hurry*."

Roosevelt leans forward and says, "What do you recommend we do, Professor?"

"We do not know whom *ze* traitor is, so I am afraid to send *ze* men on their mission."

"*Fear*, Professor, is the real problem. Fear is exactly what Hitler wants us to feel. I was elected during the Great Depression and fear was the first thing I had to conquer. America didn't want this war, but this war is upon us. If we do nothing ... if we don't send your men to Germany, it could be the greatest mistake in the history of man. So, don't tell me about fear. Tell me how we best proceed with the mission."

I wonder why Roosevelt is so set on proceeding with the mission. It seems like too high of a risk for potentially no gain. "It is my understanding that we have almost won the war."

"Almost winning a war is the same as almost surviving. Either we win, or we don't. *Survive* ... or don't. Your team may have the final say in the matter. Yes, as of this moment we are winning the war in Europe.

The Russians are advancing from the east and we're coming at the Germans hard from the west. We're pushing them out of the rest of Europe. Squeezing them back into Germany, and cornering them back into their homeland."

"Then why *ze* urgency to send my men?"

"Have you ever hunted? Ever seen a cornered animal? That's when they're most dangerous .... The Germans are on the defensive, but we have a major concern. Captured German soldiers keep talking about the *wonder weapons* coming soon. It's the only reason they keep fighting to defend their country. They're trying to hold out long enough for these wonder weapons to be completed."

President Roosevelt is struck by a coughing attack again, much more severe than before. Conant ignores it. Bush looks concerned, but doesn't interrupt. The president waves off the help of his aide before continuing, "If Hitler gains the ability to build an atomic bomb, then everything changes. What seems like certain victory today becomes a tragic defeat. He won't be afraid to use it. He won't hesitate to blackmail the Allies into backing off." Roosevelt looks so frail and may not be around long enough to see this war through to the end, but for the moment, his color is returning to his face. "At least ... at least America is out of his range."

"Are we?" Before I can explain, there's a quick knock on the door and one of the agents enters.

"Mr. President, one of the, um, boys, is here to see Professor Einstein. He says the professor sent word for him to come."

"Thanks, Floyd," Roosevelt says to the agent and I recognize Floyd as one of the agents that came to scout our camp.

"Mr. President," I want Roosevelt to meet Max, but am not sure he will allow it. "The boy is *ze* only one of our trainees I know we can trust. He's *ze* only one we can rule out as a traitor. I would like you to meet him."

Roosevelt turns to Floyd, "He's okay. You can let him in."

"Yes, sir." Floyd holds the door for Max, who is wearing a bandage over his right eye.

"Professor Einstein, sie wollten mich sehen?"

"English, Max," I tell him.

"Of course, Professor. You wanted to see me?" Max is a very bright young man, saying the phrase the same way in English so the president would understand what he had said in German.

"Max, President Roosevelt was supposed to be here tomorrow for *ze* graduation of *ze* Men, but he is here today and I want you to join our discussion."

The president extends his hand to Max and says, "I prefer English, but understood what you said in German. Max, what's your family name?"

Max shakes his hand while looking to me before answering. I nod my approval.

"Medici, sir."

"Sit down, Max," and he does. "Medici is an Italian name, correct?"

"Yes," replies Max with some trepidation in his voice. He takes a good look at the president and the concern in his eyes is readily apparent.

As Max is taking in the look of the president, Roosevelt is likewise evaluating Max.

"Professor, it's my understanding that your trainees are all supposed to be able to blend in with the German troops," says Roosevelt.

"Max does not fit that mold, to be sure," I respond. "But, *ze* Italians under Mussolini are allied with *ze* Germans. Max speaks both German and Italian fluently, plus some French as well. My plan is to portray him as a messenger from Mussolini."

"A messenger from the Italian dictator to the German dictator who speaks both languages fluently … I like it … that might just work," the president admits while nodding. "And, because Max isn't German, you feel you can trust him?"

"He has no ties to Germany whatsoever. *Ze* traitor must have connections in Germany. It rules Max out."

"If you say so, Professor," says the president, still studying Max. "Now, why did you want me to meet with him?"

"He has expressed a concern about *ze* Germans and how they might use *ze* technological advantages they possess. Tell *ze* president about your theory, Max."

The boy clears his throat before speaking. "From what we've been learning in our training, we know the Germans have two advanced technologies in place already – the V2 rocket and the U-boat. If they do finish the atomic bomb, well I don't see why they couldn't attach it to the nose of a rocket and launch it from a U-boat."

The president's cheeks turn fully gray again, but he doesn't hesitate long. "Professor, do you think this is a viable possibility?"

"*Ze* Germans have been launching rockets at Great Britain with regularity. Their V2 rocket appears to have a range up to at least fifteen hundred kilometers. Now, launching a rocket from a U-boat would require some modifications ... a launch tube and hatch on top ... a rather dramatic design change to add to its stability. To enclose *ze* rocket would require a large metal hump on *ze* top middle of a U-boat. All of that is possible today. So, it would just be a matter of building an atomic bomb that fits in *ze* nose of a rocket ... If you assume Hitler wants to rule *ze* whole world and not just Europe, then it is logical for him to pursue this."

"I think it's safe to assume there are no bounds to Hitler's ambitions." Roosevelt sits quietly for a moment before continuing, "Professor, I won't be able to attend tomorrow's graduation for your first group of men, but it's critical that we get these men deployed immediately. Is Max in your first group or your second?"

"*Ze* second."

"Well, he's in your first group now." The president faces Max directly. "Son, if you're the only person on this team we know we can trust, I have a *special* mission for you."

Conant and Bush look at each other in surprise, but still don't speak. They seem to respect the fact that President Roosevelt is running the meeting.

Max sits up even straighter, even more attentive, "Sir?"

"The rest of your team will be focused on finding and destroying the German atomic program and that's your top priority, too. Nevertheless, I like the prospect of this *messenger of Mussolini* ploy. The northern half of Italy is under German control, while the southern half is independent. It's tumultuous for the Germans and Italians alike, and Mussolini's position in the north is at risk. I can see a time, very soon, when he might actually have to send a personal messenger to Hitler, asking for more Nazi support. A message like that could get you into Berlin. And, this is the kind of thing that might just get you face to face with Adolf Hitler."

Roosevelt motions for Bush to come to him and whispers something into his ear. Bush considers what the president has said, nods, and returns to his seat.

The president faces Max again, "I want you to understand, son, there is no way we can allow Hitler to escape Germany. He has proven to be a very influential orator and if we let him get established somewhere else, we may well end up with another World War on our hands. Some people are simply … *evil*. So evil that the world is better off *without them in it* …. Do I make myself clear, Max?"

To his credit, Max gives the president's request serious thought before replying, "I under … understu … understu … under*stand* perfectly, Mr. President."

Roosevelt glances at me, eyebrows raised, seemingly to ask if this stuttering teenage boy with a bandage over his eye is really up to the task of infiltrating Germany, destroying their atomic weapons program, *and* assassinating Adolf Hitler. Really, though, who *would* be up to those tasks? Yet … there is something special about this boy … something unique.

"Mr. President," I start as confidently as I can. "It is my opinion that Max is as ready for this assignment as anyone can be."

The president looks to Bush and says, "Do you concur?"

Conant stands before Bush can respond and says, "Mr. President, I don't think we should be moving forward with this for a second. Look at this boy. You're going to put the hopes … the security of the American people in *his* hands?"

Bush doesn't stand, noticing how the president has to crane his neck to look at Conant. He simply says, "Please wait outside Dr. Conant."

Conant looks to Bush, then the president, and sees he's not in the majority. He's about to sit, when Bush says more firmly, "Jim … *outside*."

Floyd holds the door open and Dr. Conant – very reluctantly – does leave the building.

"Thanks, Vannevar," says the president, "I've had enough of that cologne of his, anyway."

Max looks to me with a hint of a smile on his face, as if he knows I'm glad Dr. Conant and his cologne have left the building as well.

Dr. Bush opens his briefcase and returns our personnel files to me. He then looks from me to the president and says, "Sir. I have complete confidence in Professor Einstein and if he believes Max, here, can do the job, then I support him fully."

"Remember this, Max," says the president, "It's not the critic who counts … not the man who points out how the strong man stumbles, or where the doer of deeds could have done them better. The credit belongs to the man who is actually in the arena, whose face is marred by dust and sweat and blood … who strives valiantly to do the deeds … who knows great enthusiasms, the great devotions … who spends himself in a worthy cause … who at the best knows in the end the triumph of high achievement and who at the worst, if he fails, at least fails while daring greatly, so that his place shall never be with those cold and timid souls who neither know victory nor defeat."

Max bows his head solemnly for a moment and then lifts it up again, nodding. Softly, yet confidently, he says, "Thank you, Mr. President … I'll remember."

"Very well, Professor," the president turns to me again. "The deployment team will be here the day after tomorrow and I want Max to join your first group of men."

"Our team will make *ze* proper arrangements, Mr. President."

The president's aide, perhaps assuming the meeting is over, tries to wrap a blanket around the president.

Roosevelt waves the aide off again, turns to Max and says, "You need to know something, young man. We've gotten close to Hitler before. We even thought we got him once, but it was a double. Hitler has two headquarters. One is in Berlin, the other is somewhere in Austria. He will be in one or the other, but my bet is that he can't give up control … that he's in Berlin. Another thing – something the British intelligence has shared with us – the real Hitler has a twitch in his left hand, and he never goes anywhere without his valet and bodyguard, Heinz Linge. If you get close to him, try to observe him … to make sure it's not a double."

"I won't let you down, sir," Max says.

"Vannevar, show the photographs we have of Hitler to Max," says the president.

Dr. Bush reaches back into his briefcase and removes another file. He produces a stack of photographs from the file and hands them to Max.

"See this man?" Bush asks Max. "He's standing right behind Hitler in every photo. Usually in his black SS uniform, Linge is tall, with thinning hair and often has a lugubrious expression."

"I'll be able to recognize Linge when I see him," Max says confidently.

"Good!" says President Roosevelt. "All the luck in the world to you, Max. You do your best to stay safe."

Max stands, shakes the president's hand, and states, "Thank you, President Roosevelt. You stay safe, too."

The president's aide and the Secret Service agents help him back into the limousine. Dr. Bush shakes my hand and then Max's before he departs, leaving Max and me alone in the administration building.

"Max, it is important that you do not discuss this conversation with anyone, even Sebastian. In fact, it is probably best if you do not talk to anyone about anything for *ze* next two days. Do you understand?"

"Of course, Professor."

"One more thing, Max."

"Yes?"

"I just observed something during your interaction with *ze* president. It seems to me that your stuttering has always been with *ze* ST sound, but did you notice when you told *ze* president to *stay* safe, you did not stutter?"

"Huh?" he replies, almost absently. "I guess you're right, Professor."

"You may have stumbled upon a phrase that will help you overcome your difficulties. Incorporating *stay safe* into your conversations in English will get your mouth accustomed to using *ze* ST sound, and should help when you use *ze* sound in other words."

Max contemplates what I just told him, or maybe he is thinking about leaving for Germany in two days … probably the latter.

"Thanks, Professor … for everything. And, *stay safe.*" He winks before heading back to his cabin.

Chapter 12

TREY TYSON
LONGBOAT KEY, FL, USA
MARCH 23, 2014

"What's on your agenda tonight, Trey?" Usually Max is relaxed when I'm about to go into a trance state and train with Nostradamus. However, much like the gusts of wind and choppy evening seas on the Gulf, Max seems somewhat unsettled. He probably guesses at what I'm planning. While I'm certain there's part of him that wants to stop me, I bet there's another part that hopes I succeed.

"More training." It's not a lie, but it feels like one. Nostradamus is not training me tonight. Tonight, I intend to train myself.

Max lights the candle in the tripod, then lights his peace pipe. He either accepts my answer, or is willing to trust me and see how my next attempt to change the past works out. If this works, it'll make moving his scar seem like child's play.

We both take our usual seats, facing the tripod with the Gulf in the background, I inhale deeply as the aroma of the peace pipe wafts over me. I'm excited, yet so at ease with my decision that I quickly relax physically. Entering a trance state is getting easier all the time and only takes moments now.

I'm going to save Sam.

When Max and I were trying to save the world from terrorists in 2012, the cost … it's been more than I can bear. I lost my birth mother, my sister, and my best friend. As much as I'd like to save them all, I know that's not possible. In the end, we succeeded, and even with the losses we suffered, I know I can't risk changing that. There's too much at stake. Samantha is the only one I think I can save without overly affecting the course of history. Her death was my fault. She was my best friend and it was my idiotic decision that killed her. Max had set a trap because he thought she might be a rogue agent, spying for the opposition. The trap worked and Italian police captured her. Max came up with a way to take her out of the equation and to keep her from being a threat if she was the rogue, without hurting her. Looking back, it was brilliant. The old man never ceases to amaze me. I was the one who insisted on getting her out of custody and I set in motion the course of events that led to her death.

I can imagine two possible ways to save her by going back in time. The most obvious answer is to somehow change history such that she remains in police custody until after we stop the terrorists. The only way I see to accomplish that, though, is to communicate with my younger self. In all my training with Nostradamus, that's never been possible. Every time I visited my own past, my younger self suffered a debilitating migraine. No words nor message could get through, only pain. I believe I *can* communicate with the younger Max, especially considering how it went with his scar. But, Max had already been convinced Sam should remain in custody and I was too passionate about getting her released to listen to him.

There is another option, though …

Staring at the flame in the tripod, I try to clear all thoughts. Jessica is safe in the house, resting comfortably and most likely watching CNN. Good – clear it. Max, like always, has my back. Good – clear it. Anything else will take care of itself.

Me … October 31, 2012 … Florence, Italy … Basilica of Saint Mary of the Flower … Me … October 31, 2012 … Florence, Italy … Basilica of Saint Mary of the Flower …

Having gone through the electric blue spiral of stars effect again, the memories come flooding back as my vision clears.

I see our rental car from 2012 stopped in Florence near the cathedral. It's the middle of the night and the streets appear to be empty. Max sits in the driver's seat, repeatedly looking in all directions, and Samantha is riding shotgun. Jessica and my younger self are in the back seat.

Sam is about to get out of the car, walk toward Florence's cathedral, and be captured by Italian authorities. It had been an elaborate trap set by Max to ferret out the rogue agent in AI – or the Advance Intelligence division of the Secret Service. Max had founded AI and led the division for decades before retiring and handing off leadership to my sister Judith. We were up against a terrorist group that was being controlled by a secretive organization we only now know as the First Order. Max's trap was ingenious. He had the Italian police and the First Order convinced we were headed to Florence's cathedral, but it was a decoy. The only problem was that Max had wrongly snagged Sam in his trap. We learned later – too late for Sam – that she wasn't the rogue agent.

Based on how it went when I moved Max's scar, I know I'll only be able to communicate a word or two. My changing the past must create a warble in space-time as two separate realities form and then merge into one. The effect on me is dramatic. Last time, I was only able to say a single word before being forcibly drawn away from the past and back to my present. At best, I can only hope to get out a couple of words. *What* words, though? What message to accomplish my goal?

I can hear the conversation we had in the past and it goes just as I remember it. Max had us all thinking we were about to find a clue from Nostradamus at the Basilica of Saint Mary of the Flower. But, we knew a rogue may have revealed our plans. He told us his plan to split up and approach the cathedral from different directions, and Samantha was to be the first to go.

"Are we looking for another T3 on the wall?" Sam asks Max, because our previous clue in 2012 had been a stone with 'T3' engraved on it. She looks unsure of the situation and must suspect that Max doesn't trust her. That's probably why she went along with his plan without hesitating … an attempt to rebuild his trust in her.

"That wouldn't surprise me, but we have to be open to other clues as well. Stay safe," the 2012 version of Max replies.

He told Sam to stay safe and I'm sure Max really meant it. What I didn't know then, but I do know now is that Samantha Fox was very important to Max. Just as important as she was to me.

I see the younger me cringing in pain from the migraine my presence is causing, and I remember how suddenly and ferociously it hit me back at this very moment in 2012.

"*Max!*" I yell with all my being. He whips around to see the 2012 me in the back seat. Max looks confused. The sound he just heard came from outside the car, but he unmistakably heard *my* voice. Yet my younger self only sits there silently with eyes closed from the pain I was feeling. A drop of blood trickles from my younger self's nose.

My essence shudders and the forces trying to pull me from the past become suddenly intense. I fight with every ounce of concentration I can muster to stay in 2012.

"Okay, see you shortly," Sam says as she exits the car and then starts walking toward the cathedral – where she is about to be captured by Italian police.

"Trust Sam!" My essence … my spirit … I'm not sure which it is, but I yell as though my life depends on it. In a way it does. I haven't been myself since Sam's death. If I can *change* this …. If I can bring Sam back somehow … maybe, just maybe, I can be me again.

The spiral of stars forms instantly, spinning clockwise, which I have come to realize means I'm moving forward in time. Odd … there's a thin red stripe blurred into the electric blue spiral.

Did I get both words fully out before being sucked into the vortex of space-time? Was it the right message to get Max to stop Sam? I sure as hell hope so.

Chapter 13

ULRICH VON BECKER

ATLANTIC OCEAN
MARCH 28, 1945

I wake to a sudden tap on my arm. *Bloody hell!* It's Zelda again. Here in the conning tower … again. Beautiful as ever, today her hair has no ponytail. It's just flowing freely like her spirit. She belongs to Ister, but doesn't. Somehow, she carries herself with an air of independence that transcends the usual command structure of the Reich. In her hands is a half loaf of bread wrapped in a cloth napkin.

Blinking a few times, I stand and try to shake off my sleepiness. There's a lot of movement in the control room below us.

"Zelda," I say with all the firmness I can muster. "We can't do this any –"

"Hush," she interrupts. "He will hear you."

I can hear Herr Ister's voice, loud as ever, in the control room below. There are several voices involved in a conversation with him, but I can't make out whom the others might be.

"It's the middle of the night. What are you doing here?" I whisper to her.

"Ister will soon be ready to reveal his plan. He wanted me to bring you this." She hands me the bread.

"He wanted you to bring me a sandwich?"

"No, Ulrich, look inside the bread," she rolls her eyes at me, but the smile with the expression is more caring than mocking.

I see the loaf is in two parts and separate them. Within, I see the grip of my gun. I had to surrender it to the crew of the U-boat when we boarded and I haven't seen it since. There's a small armaments locker near the engine room, but they have someone stationed there at all times.

"How did you get this?"

"Oh, I have my ways," she says with a smile and a wink. A sudden flicker of jealousy rises within me. My imagination runs wild, thinking of Zelda using her womanly ways on the crew to achieve Ister's goals.

"Are you with him?" The volume of my voice is louder than I had intended. Zelda quickly places a finger to her lips to remind me.

"With whom?" she asks.

Can she really be that naive?

"Are you *with* Ister?" Again, my voice is a little too loud.

She smiles and shakes her head slowly. "I am my own person, Ulrich. The question is ... are you?"

"Am I what?"

"Your own person. Are you able to make your own decisions ... or will you follow orders to the bitter end?"

"What are you talking about?"

"This war, Ulrich. It won't last forever. As a matter of fact, I don't think it will last much longer at all."

"And?"

"*And*, where will your decisions take you. Will you follow Ister, be his bodyguard, and help him do what he's doing? Without question? No matter the consequences?"

I don't know what to say to this. Nazi leaders test us like this all the time. Someone you think you can trust asks you to betray your command ... betray the Reich. It's invariably a test, though, and answering incorrectly has led many to their deaths.

"Me?" I decide to turn this around. "What about you? You're at his side day and *night.*"

"Ulrich, it's not like that," she places a hand on my arm. The physical contact is warm, reassuring.

"Then, what is it like?"

"I do what –"

Before she can finish her sentence, the captain's voice barks from below, "Take us to periscope depth."

The activity level in the control room intensifies. Someone is climbing the ladder to the tower.

"It's time," Zelda tells me and she heads to the ladder. I put the gun in my pocket like Ister commanded and follow, but her question lingers in my mind. Will I make my own decisions, or am I going to follow Ister into whatever doom he's planning? I don't have an answer ... at least not yet.

A couple crewmen come up the ladder into the tower before we are able to descend. Changing depths is one of the times when the conning tower has some activity.

When we make it down to the control room, Herr Ister is already there, along with the captain, one of his officers, and five crewmen working the various controls. Rolf Barbie, my counterpart, stands ready at Ister's side.

Zelda takes her place next to Ister, opposite of Rolf, and I position myself next to the captain as casually as I'm able.

The U-boat ascends quickly and then levels off.

"Periscope depth," one of the crewmen announces.

The captain raises the periscope and peers through it. He slowly rotates, scanning the horizon, then suddenly stops.

"This is what you wanted to see, Herr Ister," the captain motions to the periscope and steps to the other side of the control room. I'm at a bit of a loss as to what to do. If I now cross to the other side of the room to be next to the captain, it will look extremely suspicious. If I don't, I'll be failing to follow Herr Ister's orders.

Ister walks to the periscope, looks, rotates it a few degrees to the right, and then turns back to where the captain had been viewing.

"Ha! Yes, that is it, Captain." Ister's scarred face twists with his high-pitched laugh. "Von Becker … come see this." Ah, Ister is quite clever! If I go to look through the periscope, I can also move to the same side of the room as the captain without raising any suspicion.

I've never before looked through a periscope, so I'm intrigued both by how it works and by what I will see. Raising the level of the eyepiece as high as it will go, I still have to bend down to look. In the night sky, I don't expect that I'll be able to see much. However, what I see is so close and so well lit, it almost causes me to jump back. I've heard of this and have seen a picture before, it never imagined the size. The Statue of Liberty! Bathed in electric lights, she has a green hue and stands majestically high into the dark sky.

Curiosity takes hold. I scan in a full circle and see something even more astonishing. We have left the ocean and are now in a river. Land … lit up buildings and American land! They nearly surround us. Rotating back to the view of the statue, I then scan over a few degrees to the right, just as Ister had done. There, with more tall buildings and bright lights than I've ever seen, is what must be New York City.

"Impressive," is all I say as I take position next to the captain.

"We need to get closer," Ister directs to the captain.

"We're already too close. Someone will see us," Captain Saltzwedel replies.

"Another kilometer will do, Captain. That's an order." Ister isn't budging.

I reach into my pocket and grip my gun. It's a luger and I trust it more than any revolver.

The captain doesn't move or say anything for several seconds. I'm ready to spring at him should the need arise. He looks nervous, eyes shifting in all directions, with each new angle appearing to be a new direction in thought for him – and this has me thinking he's going to do something stupid. Ister, on the other hand, is as cool as they come, although it's hard to gauge anything with the level of scarring on his face.

"I would feel much more … *comfortable* … with your order if I knew your plan," the captain finally says.

Now it's Ister's turn to act or talk. One signal from him and I know what I have to do. But, he simply grins again, twisted as it is.

"I will tell you this much, Captain, to make sure you are *comfortable*. My plan – and the Fuhrer's plan – is to get one kilometer closer. We will then launch the rocket we've been carrying into the middle of Manhattan."

The captain still doesn't move, but looks at me briefly before saying, "And then what?"

"And then," Ister says, "we will move on to our next target, while one of the other U-boats will stay here to give the Americans something to chase."

My hand is now sweaty and I move my finger to the trigger.

Ister adds, "This moment will live in history. You, Captain Saltzwedel, will be the *first* German to strike a blow to the Americans on their own soil."

The captain starts to nod, slowly at first, then with more conviction. He belts out an order, "One kilometer, to the northeast!"

His officer repeats the command into a microphone to notify the crew to execute it.

It's not long for the U-boat to cover the distance, but I keep my gun at the ready.

Even when the control room officer announces, "In position, Captain," I'm concerned that the captain has something up his sleeve.

But, the crew is simply following his orders and he's following Ister's.

The captain yells, "All stop." He then moves to the periscope and performs a slow full-circle scan of our surroundings. "Herr Ister?"

Ister moves to the periscope and does his own scan before saying, "Perfect, Captain. You may fire, when ready, at the center of the city."

"Surface!" the captain orders and his officer repeats.

"Would you like to see this from up top?" the captain directs to Ister.

"I can imagine nothing, Captain Saltzwedel, that I would like more. Barbie, Von Becker, Lady Zelda, why don't you join us." Ister is nearly giddy. What I thought was sweat oozing down the side of his face, may actually be a bloody mucous coming from a scar on his hairline. He seems to notice it finally, and pulls a large handkerchief from his pocket to dab at it.

We make our way up the ladder to the top of the conning tower and outside the U-boat. Taking a deep breath of clean air, I feel an intense relief at being outside the tin can. All the tall American buildings could be intimidating, but they provide a physical bearing that I haven't seen in so long. An engineer has joined us topside, and hands the captain and Ister binoculars while he works some sort of optic device he has aimed at the city. A sprawling metropolis, the city has rows of buildings in all directions and on every shore, but there is clearly a center to it all – an island with tall buildings – Manhattan Island.

Meanwhile, I hear the sound of latches opening and then loud hydraulics. The hump in the middle of U-boat slowly slides to the rear, exposing the first part of the tube opening that runs through the middle of this modified U-boat. A few seconds later, and I can see the tip of a rocket. The hump reaches the back of its track, and then stops with the sound of metal clanging metal.

The engineer belts out some coordinates, but I barely notice because while Ister and the captain are staring through the binoculars at the city, Lady Zelda has secretly clasped my hand. My other hand still holds my gun in my pocket, but I'm starting to believe I won't need it.

"Ready to fire," the engineer says.

The captain takes a deep breath, glances at Ister, and then says, "Fire!"

"Fire the rocket," the engineer yells to the officer stationed in the conning tower. The command seems to echo through the U-boat, but I know several crewmen are simply repeating it down the line.

The wind calms and everyone goes silent at once. There's the sound of an ignition, a red glow from the launch tube, then the nose starts to lift slowly. The propulsion sound seems to go from a low gear to top gear in one step, and the rocket suddenly leaps from the U-boat and streams toward the city. The fiery tail of the rocket looks almost like a comet in the night sky. At what appears to be halfway to the tallest buildings in the middle of the island, the rocket starts to angle back slowly downward.

It's only moments before it strikes its target – one of the tallest buildings.

The plume of smoke rises from the center of the city – visible without the need of binoculars – seconds before we hear the echoing sound of the explosion.

Chapter 14

Trey Tyson
Longboat Key, FL, USA
March 24, 2014

Last night's vision took a lot out of me. As drained as I was, all I could do was say goodnight to Max and head off to bed. Jessica had been long asleep by the time I got here. Thank God her alarm didn't go off at 5:30am when she usually starts her day. It's nice to wake up and have her still sleeping next to me. Rolling to my side, I press my body against hers, stroke her cheek gently, and kiss the back of her neck.

"Mmmm," she moans. "Now that's a nice way to start the day."

As she stretches, I suddenly realize just how aroused I am. I fondle her nipple for a moment, noticing just how much bigger her breasts have become. I can't help but squeeze one.

"Ouch!" she says, shoving my hand away. "Don't do that. It hurts."

"Sorry."

"And, quit pressing that, that … *that* into my back."

"I was just trying to hold you," I roll to my back, frustrated.

"Sure enough, that may be how it starts, but that's not all you want. I'm over eight months pregnant, as big as a house, and permanently nauseous. Making love, or anything else … it's just not happening right now."

"It's been over two months." I try not to sound like I'm complaining, but I am.

"Aye, and it's going to be a wee bit longer. Hang in there. You'll have to handle this problem on your own."

The doorbell rings.

"Can you get that?" she asks. "I have to go to the bathroom."

Pouting, I throw on my robe and jog to the front door. "Who shows up at this hour in the morning?" I yell back to her.

I open the door and my jaw drops. The front door faces east, and with the sun just above the horizon, the blazing light forces me to squint. Still, the person I see is more than just a silhouette.

"Samantha!" She's actually standing here ... *alive!*

New memories flood into my mind .... In 2012, Sam didn't walk all the way to the cathedral in Florence. Max chased her down and had her rejoin us. We stayed together on our quest to stop the Somali terrorists, at least until ... until just about the end when the president called Sam back to DC before we got to Viktor's headquarters. I couldn't change everything. My sister still died. My birth mother still died. Yet, somehow, Sam is alive! I dig through both sets of memories, remembering that we still stopped the terrorists. It worked!

I throw my arms around her and lift her off the ground with a sudden embrace that surprises even me. She embraces me right back, and I realize – too late – that I am still quite aroused. Samantha's face is only inches from mine. Her black eyes are smoldering hot. She shifts her body to grind against me and I think I feel a slight quiver emanate from her. Neither one of us seems to want to let go, but as I slowly lower her back down, I'm reminded just how remarkable her athletic figure is. Sam and Jess are about the same height, but while Jessica is naturally lean, Sam has defined muscles and no body fat whatsoever – a copper-toned panther with the ability to pounce at any moment.

"Sorry." I don't know what else to say for a situation like this.

"So happy to see me! I like that," Samantha says, as she glances down below before giving me a different look with raised eyebrows – and somehow her eyes are still smoldering.

"Holy fuck, Sam."

"You know," she smiles – and Sam has always smiled with just her right half, kind of a wink and smile together, "Sex that one time was great ... but, a *religious* experience?"

"We were teenagers in the bathroom in high school."

"We should have fucked like that more often."

"It would have made staying friends hard."

"Hard," She murmurs as she glances down again and sees that I'm still rock hard. Raising one eyebrow, she says, "I've caught you checking out my ass a few –"

"*Sam* .... Enough. Come in. I need to know what's been happening with you since ... well ... lately."

"Fuck it. *Fine.* I need to talk to you and Max together. Is he around?"

"He should be out back swimming laps. It's through the –"

"I know where the fucking pool is, idiot. It's not like this is my first time here."

"Oh … right. I'll get dressed and meet you out there."

"If you insist." Sam swinks as she heads to the pool. That's what I used to call it when we were kids and she did her smile-wink. I'd call it a swink and she would laugh every time I said the word.

As I'm walking back into the bedroom, feeling on top of the world, I see Jessica is wearing her running gear. Normally she'd be in some colorful spandex, but around the fifth month of her pregnancy, she switched to dark gray loose-fitting fleece.

"You ready to go?" she asks. "Remember … just a power walk, right?"

"Power walk?" My mind is swimming with new memories about Samantha, a new past swirling around with the past I experienced before the change – a change in the past that I made happen.

"Yes, power walk," Jessica is instantly irritated. "You have to be kidding me. You don't remember? Trey, what the hell is going on? Just *yesterday* we figured out a way to make our relationship better. And *today* you forget about it?"

"I … um … sorry, but it was Samantha at the door. She needs to talk … to Max and me. Can we do the power walk a bit later?"

"Oh, this just keeps getting better. You're missing our power walk because *she* showed up? Fine enough – don't worry about it. I'll just go on my own."

"Sweetheart, wait," but before I can get my arms around her, she storms out of the room. The way she slammed the glass sliding door, I'm pretty sure it would have shattered if it weren't designed to withstand hurricane force winds. Jessica stomps down our balcony stairs, and past Sam and Max without a word to either. As soon as she hits the beach, she transitions from stomping to power walk mode.

I quickly change into some running clothes and head out to catch her.

"Trey, wait," Max is wet, and was sitting to talk with Sam, but now stands to block my path.

"I have to catch up with Jess. I'll be back in a little while."

"No, you've got to hear this," he insists.

"What can't wait a few minutes?"

"The Germans bombed New York." Sam says as she stands to join Max in blocking my path to the beach. After a statement like that –

especially from someone who isn't even supposed to be alive – I don't need either of them blocking me anymore to keep me here.

"What the hell are you talking about? Germany is one of our closest allies. Why would they bomb New York?" I remember a line from the movie, *Animal House*. The college fraternity kids are all trying to rally to a cause and they're talking about not giving up. Bluto, played by the hilarious John Belushi, says something like, "Did we give up when the Germans bombed Pearl Harbor?" The joke is naturally that the Germans didn't bomb Pearl Harbor. It was the Japanese. Things have changed …. Now, I can't remember if the movie even exists anymore.

"No, you fucking idiot," Sam never has been one to hold back her true feelings. "Not today. In *1945*. The Germans launched a rocket into the middle of Manhattan in 1945. The blast killed 249 people."

"Oh my god!" These new memories start to fill my head now. I was so focused on Sam being alive that nothing else mattered, but now I can remember. Again, there are two sets of memories. The Germans did hit New York with a rocket, and 249 people died from the explosion and fire that followed. With my new memories of history, I now know that the Germans were about to complete the first atomic bomb. Their rocket that hit New York was a test … or a warning … or maybe both. It wasn't atomic, but still packed a big wallop.

"What have I done?" In saving Sam, I just killed 249 innocent people from the past. Not just them … but their kids … their grandkids … three generations already and every day there are people who would have been born that never will … because of me.

Max takes hold of my shoulders and his grip is remarkably firm for his age. "What do you mean by that? What *have* you done?"

"I … I decided to save Sam."

"Save me?" Sam looks completely confused and she should be. "Save me from what?"

"Trey," Max shakes me once before letting go, "you better explain. This could by why Sam is here in the first place."

"Let's start there," I say, needing a minute to collect myself. I motion for us all to sit. "What brought you here, Sam?"

"A fucked up call from Bruce last night," she begins.

Bruce Cullens is the head of AI … no, wait … Bruce was the head of AI in the old reality. Sam is the head of AI in this version of history. Bruce and Sam both have some psychic abilities – as do the other agents in AI. Bruce is one of her agents now.

"Bruce started rambling about the Germans bombing New York and that it was all wrong. It took me a while to figure out what he was talking about. I mean, we all know the Germans launched a rocket at New York in World War II. They were trying to send a message that if our troops got too close to Berlin they would make us pay."

"The message," Max jumps in, "was taken the exact opposite way. The Allies knew they had to make a massive push to get into the capital before the Germans could build and attach an atomic warhead to their rockets."

"True," says Sam, "but that's not the point. Bruce kept insisting the attack never should have happened. He said he had two very different sets memories and the mind-fuck was kicking his ass. He said the first, where the Germans never attacked New York is the way it was supposed to have gone. Then he said *I* was new, too."

"New?" asks Max.

"Yeah, *new* was how he put it. Like I wasn't supposed to be here. He had vague memories of me dying. Back in 2012, he said ... while we were on our mission to stop the terrorists. I didn't know if I could believe him, but he was so sure of it. So, what's a girl to do when she's told she's *new* ... that she's not supposed to be alive? How messed up is that? So, I came to the sources for answers. To you two."

"Trey," Max says after a few seconds of silence. "What the hell happened last night?"

"Like I said, I decided to save Sam. Well, actually, I decided to try to get you to save Sam. Obviously, it worked."

"Save me from what?" Sam's still hoping I can provide some answers.

Sam needs to know the truth. The true history of how she died. From walking to the cathedral ... the trap set by Italian police ... to an Italian jail cell ... to my arranging for Judith to get her released ... when she and Judith confronted Karl ... and her death. As I went through the story, Max kept nodding and interjecting with questions. Apparently, he was experiencing some level of dual memories as well.

"So, my training with Nostradamus," I say, catching up with the present day, "led me to believe I may be able to do something about you ... about your death. I was able to get a two-word message through to the 2012 version of Max. It was –"

"Trust Sam!" Max exclaims. "I remember now. It was your voice after all. I was testing her loyalty ... err, your loyalty," he turns to face Sam. "I couldn't tell if the voice was just in my head, but I felt compelled to stop you from going to the cathedral in the first place. I suspected the Italian police would be waiting for you there and apparently they were."

"Yes, but I knew you would never betray us, Sam," I reassure her. "It was *my* idea then to try to rescue you and that ended up being what got you killed."

Sam abruptly stands and walks away from us, pacing next to the pool. Then she turns back, her black eyes smoldering a different kind of heat. "Holy shit, it's true. I'm supposed to be dead. And you, Trey? You *changed history* to bring me back?" Tears were starting to form in Sam's eyes and as long as I've known her, I've never seen her cry. I spent a lot of time with her family growing up. Maybe it's because of their Native American heritage, or maybe it's just something within their family, but her parents tried to instill in Sam that she should always portray herself as being physically and emotionally strong – no matter what she's going through. Crying, to Sam, is a weakness, and I swear I can see her shake off the urge.

"Samantha," Max gestures for her to join us again and she does, "I'm certain Trey had the best intentions when he saved you. But at what cost?"

"You're not suggesting I go back and figure out a way to let her die again?" I say this while wondering if I could even do it. Then, the thought hits me that if I could, *would* I? If the scale of fate has 249 innocent strangers and the generations that would have followed them on one side, the other side has my one best friend.

"No," Max replies, "I'm not suggesting that at all. Remember the Einstein debate?" He turns and faces Sam. "Samantha ... Trey and I were able to take part in a debate with Albert Einstein in the past. The topic of multiple realities came up. The theory is that for every possible outcome of any event, a new reality is spawned for each outcome. We went on to theorize that there's a sort of *quantum gravity* between the realities and that realities with small changes between them are drawn to each other to merge into one. I believe these theories have proven to be true over the events of the last two nights."

Sam likes to take things in for a minute before asking questions, pacing with too much energy, and she's doing that now.

Max continues, "There's simply no way to correlate a change in *2012* where you're now alive in our time to a new rocket strike on New York from *1945*. The *only* possibility is that the seemingly small change in history that Trey made caused our reality to merge with another reality where the Germans shot a rocket at Manhattan from a U-boat. Those 249 deaths in New York did happen in another reality, and now, that's *our* reality."

"So, what do we do about it?" I ask, thankful Max is here … that he always seems to keep his cool in any situation.

"Nothing," he shakes his head emphatically. "The simple truth is that any other change we might try to make may force a new reality on us where things get far, far worse. Imagine if Hitler did have an atomic warhead on the rocket that hit New York."

I'm busy nodding my head, but Sam looks concerned. "What is it, Sam?"

"This is a complete mind-fuck. I can't say I understand much about quantum gravity or different realities, but I do believe a change has happened. I have no memory of the changes, because, as Bruce pointed out, I'm *new* to this reality. I think I get that part of it, but you two are aware of it. Bruce is aware of it. It only makes sense that other psychics will be aware of it, too. Who's to say that another psychic – maybe one in the First Order – can't figure out how to do this, too? Can you imagine the shit-storm of problems we'll be facing if the First Order can go back and change history?"

"*This*," Max's jaw clenches as he points squarely at me, "is why Nostradamus told you this kind of thing is impossible. Because the ramifications are massive. You've opened a door and we have no idea *who* is going to walk through it."

"What," I close my eyes to gather myself for a second. "What can I do to make this right?"

"There's no quick solution to this, Trey," says Max. "We have to figure out, first, how we'll know if anything in the past changes. And, second, we have to figure out if and how we can fix it, or even better if we can prevent it before it happens …. Sam, we're going to need the full resources of AI."

"When I tell the president what's going on, I'm sure we'll get her buy in," she says.

"The way I see it," says Max, "is that you, Samantha, will be critical to knowing about any changes. You won't be able to see two histories, so if Trey or Bruce thinks there is a change, they just need to ask about your memories for verification of which one came from the old reality and which one belongs with the new reality. Bruce seems to be more aware of the change than either Trey or me. It may be that he's extra sensitive to changes in history – so he's on the team. Trey, you'll need some guidance from Nostradamus. He may have seen this coming in this reality and maybe he knows how to help. You two will need to start working together with Bruce quite a bit more than just a consulting relationship. Trey, you're going to have to start working with AI full-time."

Max is focused on me, so he doesn't see Sam swink. He's right. I did this and I need to fix it. But, *damn*, this is going to be a strain on my marriage.

"I'll consult with Nostradamus tonight and do whatever I need to do to make this right. Maybe in this reality, he knows more about the First Order."

Chapter 15

SIR ARCHIE
PYTHO ISLAND
MARCH 24, 2014

There are only two ways to get to Pytho Island – by boat through a hidden port, or by helicopter from Bermuda. The most secretive location on the planet, Pytho Island is completely isolated, located on the Atlantic Ocean a few hundred kilometers south of the Bermuda Islands. Our First Order ancestors from Ancient Greece chose the location carefully. First, for the secrecy it provides, but also because it's fertile and able to sustain our growing population that is now over ten thousand people.

Formed from what must have been a massive volcano, the tall and barren outer rim of the island has nearly vertical walls. Completely hidden from the surrounding ocean, the inside is in the general shape of a huge crater with multiple tiers of lush green lands. A snake-like network of dangerous reefs serves to block the passage of any ships that don't know the safe path to our single port. The port – tunneled with a turn through the volcano wall – serves to hide our bay and piers from passing ships. Because the land within the volcano ranges from the main plateau at 30 meters above sea level to hills and smaller plateaus all the way up to the top of the outer volcano walls at 650 meters above sea level, mists and clouds often form above the island, shielding the city from the rare plane that flies over the area.

Our island-wide defense system is able to take out those few ships or planes that do see any trace of our civilization. It's a series of ancient weapons that can rotate to most any angle and project a beam that we here on the island call the death ray. Whatever the death ray is pointed at – if it has water in it, like a person – is instantly disrupted ... melted ... nearly disintegrated. The death ray doesn't harm a plane or a boat, just the occupants. Being one of the very few of our people who ever visits the outside world, I believe it's a form of intensified microwaves. Our council leaders never talk about the origin of the weapons, but the technology is beyond our abilities to invent.

We do have the ability to utilize the death rays, however. Our small, but vigilant security forces have been able to take out every stray ship or plane that has seen our civilization so far, which has fed the dangerous reputation of the Bermuda Triangle. This has worked to our advantage, dissuading most from even entering the area.

It was the Russian launch of Sputnik, the advent of satellite technology in 1957 – more than 20 years before I was even born – that created a new problem for our hidden city. Stray planes and ships we could handle. Satellites with cameras presented an entirely different level of problem.

Sir Karl, my mentor, came up with the solution. He was a young and brilliant Knight of the First Order back then and he suggested we throw our vast financial resources into American satellite development. Knowing that controlling just the American satellites wouldn't be enough, Karl came up with an ingenious answer to the global problem – GPS software written in hexadecimal coding. The hex code is so fast and accurate that all American satellites began to use it. Then, he *let* the Russians, Chinese, and eventually every other space capable country license the code to use with their own satellites. Hex code is extremely difficult to make any sense of if you didn't write it, and this hex code has a secret subroutine that modifies any satellite imagery taken to make sure Pytho Island *always* has a thick cloud hiding us from prying eyes.

Coming to Pytho by boat requires a rather dangerous approach to our hidden port and that's only part of the problem. Once in our harbor, people still have to climb the equivalent of ten stories of heavily guarded steps – just to reach the inner base of the volcano and our main plateau. It's a winding stairway and path called Via Sacra, and along the sides of it are hundreds of replicas of the votive statues that stood at the side of the original Via Sacra in Delphi. The main plateau serves as the hub of Pytho, with most of our people housed there and most of their jobs, schools, and leisure activities are there, too.

Traveling by helicopter isn't much safer. The distance from Bermuda to Pytho is just barely within the range of a helicopter. If one of our pilots faces an emergency – such as a plane or ship they want to avoid – they sometimes don't make it all the way. Even when they do make it, climbing to the altitude necessary to clear the volcano wall becomes a challenge with the intense Bermuda Triangle winds that swirl around the island. Then, there's the landing, usually in clouded skies and mists swirling around and hindering the pilot's view. Only one, maybe two days a month, the skies are clear above Pytho.

Lucky me. Today is a clear sky day. A rare day to be at the highest level of the volcano wall on a clear sky day. From here, I have the one and only position on Pytho where I can look down on the Temple of Apollo. It sits atop a four-sided pyramid, which sits atop a small plateau near the top of the volcano wall. The temple is a little more than half enclosed in walls, with the open part best known for its six columns facing the main plateau of Pytho. The side of the temple is visible from here and has fifteen columns – a simple fact that many of our people don't know because most have no access to these heights and this viewing angle.

Someone must have carefully calculated the height of the temple, as it sits perfectly within the clouds that normally hover over the island. This, naturally, lends to the godlike aura of the Oracle and her sisterhood, who all reside in the chambers within the temple and pyramid.

A benefit of a helicopter approach is that I can reach the entire city by walking downhill from the helipad. I've never landed on a clear sky day befor and the views from here are spectacular. There are elevators carved into the inside of the volcano walls and I would normally take one. Not today. The steps leading down to the city may be ancient and they may be many, but I'll take them nonetheless.

Off in the distance, I can see the descending semicircle of the teatro, or theatre. With thousands of seats carved into the hillside, the teatro can host our entire population – even if it doubles.

Near silence settles, as the helicopter rotor finally stops.

The midmorning sun reflects beautifully off the dew that covers much of the tall grasses and flowers on the steep downward slope between here and the city. A hummingbird darts between the violet buddleias that encircle half of the helipad. Maybe it's because of the rare enduring sunlight, but the flowers are putting out a sweet fragrance that screams the arrival of spring is finally here.

"No luggage, Sir Archie?" asks the security guard at the helipad.

"I prefer my full name – Archimedes." Not that Archimedes is my real name. We have to give up all traces of our identity when we become a Knight of the First Order. Karl was an Alpha and he chose me as his Beta Knight. We all work in pairs, a more senior Alpha who mentors a Beta. Karl didn't choose me for my strength, my speed, or my ability to fight. Those aren't attributes I possess. Where I excelled was in the intelligence testing done with knight candidates.

Karl wasn't going into the world to fight a physical fight ... he was going to fight business, scientific, and financial fights. He didn't need a grunt. He needed me.

Alphas get to choose the new name for their Beta Knight. We give up our past, never see our family again, and take on a new name. Then, the First Order sends us into the world to do their bidding.

Seeing the level of my intelligence, Karl chose for me the name of the most gifted mind from Ancient Greece ... Archimedes. What he really liked about the name was that there was a short version – Archie – that would work well in America.

What I didn't know then, but learned through several hard lessons, was that the name Archie – in America – is a famous comic book character. This hardly helped me in the many business dealings I undertook on Karl's behalf.

"Forgive me ... Sir Archimedes," he tries again. "Do you have any luggage I can carry for you?"

"No. I don't plan on staying long."

"Sir Karl is not with you?" asks the elderly guard. He's the same guard who worked at the helipad the last time I came home.

"What's your name, again, Pedasus?"

"Know thyself .... My name is Pedaeus," he says.

I don't know anything about his background. Unlike knights, security guards get to keep their names and their families. He's much older than most of our security forces, nearly 70 I would guess.

"Pedaeus ... my turn to be sorry ... I've always been much better with numbers than names. Sir Karl has passed." With Karl as my Alpha, I traveled with him every trip prior to this, so the question is natural. The fact that Karl died well over a year ago, and this guard has no idea, reminds me just *how* isolated our society is. The inner council never shares news from the outside with the people of Pytho.

"Sir Karl is no longer with us? The gods can be cruel." The emotions from Pedaeus seem sincere. "That explains why the council wants to see you immediately and why they have an ascension ceremony scheduled. They must have some new Beta choices for you."

"You have to be kidding. My ascension ceremony ... today?" I guess I should have anticipated this. I've been flying solo for so long that I've grown accustomed to it. Back to using the elevator, after all. Pedaeus and I turn and head toward the volcano wall.

I'm to ascend to an Alpha … *finally*. Karl was an incredible mentor, but eighteen years is excessive to be a Beta. Most of our knights ascend after five, maybe ten years. Karl didn't want to let me go. He constantly praised my value to him and the building of Starr Aerospace – the primary company we used to build both satellites and the software to run them. He said I was too important to his plans – ambitious plans to destroy the world's oceans and much of its human population.

The First Order has been isolated … hiding … for nearly two thousand years. In one grand act, he would have restored our people to our proper place in the world. Leading all. Not just seeing, but also controlling the fate of all.

Karl may not have been psychic, but he had a vision. Moreover, he had the guts to pursue his vision, at any cost … even his life.

I remember being a simple citizen of Pytho. My selection to join the First Order's knighthood. My initiation and assessment, along with the grueling mental and physical testing. Council leaders assign new knights into one of four groups. Knights of War are the strong arm of the First Order and most candidates aim for this group. Knights of Leadership are typically our most savvy candidates. They must be cunning, and able to get close to and influence politicians of the outside world. Knights of Science head out into the world to discover the latest advancements in science and technology, and bring them back to our inner council.

With my complete disdain for violence, I had no interest in being a Knight of War. My consistent fainting at the sight of blood led to the quick assessment that I wouldn't be a good fit for that group … to my great relief.

While I scored really well on the cunning tests, I lack the ability to influence others, and that's a minimum requirement to be a Knight of Leadership. In science, I have some inclination and ability. My real strength, however, is in finance … a Knight of Economics. Working the numbers. Avoiding taxes. Growing revenues. Reducing expenses. Finding synergies. Backing the right ventures. Making deals. Karl saw my raw ability when I was one of the Beta choices he had. He could have put his three Beta options through more physical testing, but he really didn't care about that. Karl focused on our math skills, our business savvy, and the way we interviewed. I outscored the other Betas and did especially well in questions of finance, so Karl chose me.

Finance is also the true strength behind the First Order. Our military relies mostly on stealth. We are so far behind the outside world in science, that our people don't even know what a microwave oven is.

We only make advancements by stealing technology rather than inventing it, and most of the time, the inner council hides new technology from our people instead of sharing it. Our Knights of Leadership are rather successful in many parts of the outer world, but that often stems from the vast financial resources we've accumulated over the millennia.

Money equals influence.

Economics … Finance … We came before the Knights Templar, before the Teutonic Knights, before them all. We are the Knights of the First Order, originating in Ancient Greece. We built the first banks, and – even today – you can find a branch of our First International Bank in every major city in the world. Over two thousand years of investing and backing enterprise, and our resources are far greater than anyone can imagine. That history of success is what drew me in. Wanting to continue it. Wanting to take it to new levels.

The council chambers are only ten minutes from the helipad if we're taking the elevator. It will have to be a little longer before I get to revisit the architecture of Pytho. It's the ancient Greek city-state of Delphi reincarnated. The wood, brick, steel, glass, and stucco of modern buildings in the outside world don't have the same appeal as do stone, arches, and columns.

"Perhaps, Sir Archimedes, you would like a few minutes to change your attire before meeting with the council?" suggests Pedaeus.

The inner council has housing at the highest levels of the inner volcano walls. We knights are at the next level down – so it would be a quick side trip to stop and change. I just don't want to.

One of my new habits since I've been spending so much time outside of Pytho – I like my business suits. *Dressed to the nines* they say on the outside. Our Knights of War might wield guns, but as a Knight of Economics, the pen is my weapon of choice and a custom tailored three-piece suit is my armor.

Clothing here in Pytho is as much a reminder of Ancient Greece as is our architecture. Everyone wears a chiton or peplos, each a simple square of cloth wrapped around the body and held with a clasp. Our people rarely need the outer chlamys, or thin cloak, with our tropical climate.

Our ancestors loved brightly colored fabrics, but with our isolation, we lack access to many dyes. So, most of our people wear white, with clasps of color. This guard's clasp is black, the color of order. Most of our people wear green or yellow clasps. Our council leaders wear blue clasps ... the color of the gods. Alpha Knights of the First Order wear red clasps – the color of war ... also the color of love. Very odd and perhaps highly insightful of the gods to mix those two concepts together.

"No," I say, "I'll just wear my himation." It's the one item of clothing that crosses over from Pytho to the modern outside world. A large gray cloak and it matches my charcoal suit perfectly. I wrap it around me and use my white clasp – the color of a Beta Knight – for the last time today.

The council will elevate me to an Alpha and I'll choose a new Beta. With all these layers, it'll be a bit warm, but the formal attire should set the right tone for the first meeting with my new Beta. Eighteen long years I was Karl's Beta. I remember being so impressed when he chose me. Karl always had an air about him ... like there was something, very important, that only he knew. Often that was true, I learned over the years. I want my Beta to feel the same way about me. With my years of experience in the outside world, it should come naturally. Yet, people never look at me the way they looked at Karl. Maybe the suit will help.

Karl was the most famous knight in our history, with more years in the outside world than any of our other knights. His fame derived from his vision and his boldness, and his penchant for making sure news of his deeds somehow made it past council censorship and spread among our people. He bent or broke most every First Order rule, but he got things done. As much as he loved his own autonomy, he tried to monitor and control everything I did. Still, he was the best Alpha I could have hoped for, teaching me a great number of things about the First Order and about the outside world. Karl showed me how to blend into society outside of the Order, how to set aside some money should I ever need it, and how to work the leadership within the First Order.

It's been my job to pick up the pieces after Karl's failure. He took a bold risk, and *almost* accomplished what the First Order has been unable to do for nearly two thousand years. He was on the verge of setting the world back to where we could lead it. Where we could rule from a position of strength. It was a matter of seconds. Success or failure came down to the last few seconds of a timer on a network of explosives that would have changed the world.

Now, I have to salvage what I can. The financial assets we lost were a significant setback, to be sure. The land Karl, under his assumed name of Roy Starr, had acquired was rooted out and seized by the US government. They also seized the Starr companies and divisions. Almost $200 billion in total was lost in Karl's great gamble.

I was able to get some of the liquid assets secured into our financial institutions, but probably not nearly enough to satisfy Zeus, the head of the inner council.

Two guards, each with their black clasp prominently visible, stand outside the entrance to the council chambers.

"Sir Archie is here for the ascension ceremony," Pedaeus says to the other guards. I was beginning to like him. Using the short version of my name – after I specifically asked him to use my full name – is nothing short of disrespectful. I'm not going to let him know it bothers me, but once I'm an Alpha, I'll find a way to pay him back.

"They're waiting for him," the shorter, more muscular guard replies.

The two guards step aside to allow me to enter the outer chamber to the great hall.

From the outside, the council chambers look much like many of our other buildings. White stone blocks, columns, and a single entrance. The chambers are one of the few structures on Pytho to have a stone door that closes and locks. Behind the chambers and built right into the volcano wall, carved out offices and tunnels seem to stretch for kilometers. Inside, the ceiling is ten meters high, and all the windows are closer to the ceiling than to the ground.

The great hall is quiet, as sound seems unable to escape the inner council chamber when the doors are closed.

The inner council chamber is the largest of the rooms I've seen carved into the volcano. It's a massive cavern with no windows. The main entrance faces the great hall and the only other entrance leads into private volcano tunnels. Only the Oracle, the council leaders, and their personal guards have access to these tunnels.

Guided by the visions of the Oracle, the council of fourteen men and women rule the First Order and the city of Pytho. Our society deems the fourteen council offices to be immortal even though mortals occupy them. Each office represents one of the immortal Greek gods, and when someone joins the council, they lose their birth identity and take on the identity of the office. Meaning, the man who is currently the head of the council no longer goes by his given name. He is Zeus.

The responsibilities for governance of Pytho are separated by office, and are designed to reflect the abilities of the immortals they represent. Zeus is the king of the gods, known for ruling the skies and the weather. The First Order air forces, as well as all matters of law, order, and fate are under his purview.

Poseidon rules our naval forces and Hades rules our land forces. With our greatest threat coming in the form of pirates, our combined military forces are modest, designed primarily to keep our civilization hidden. Stealth is our greatest strength and secrecy our greatest asset.

The entire inner council convenes for an ascension ceremony and the leaders are all here – sitting atop the dais – centered by Zeus.

To the right of Zeus sit the Oracle, Poseidon, Athena, Ares, Apollo, Hephaestus, and Hermes. To the left of Zeus sit Hera, Hades, Aphrodite, Hestia, Demeter, Dionysus, and Artemis.

I've never seen *this* Oracle, although she looks very much like a younger version of the previous one. We're told that looking into the future is physically demanding and a young woman is best able to bear it, so as the current Oracle ages, she selects her own replacement – often one of her younger sisters. The departing Oracle then spends her years advising her replacement and mothering the next generation of Oracle candidates.

Very little is known outside of the temple about how the Oracle sees the future, or how they are bred or chosen. The council procedures are much more transparent.

A man or woman chosen from our population represents the office of each god and goddess, and sometimes they choose one of the more senior Alpha Knights of the First Order. The inner council consists of eight men and six women, each of the same sex and as nearly as possible the same traits of the represented god or goddess. The council member sits for life and, upon death, a replacement is determined by a vote of the remaining council members.

The Oracle is usually present for council meetings and her voice carries great weight.

Below the dais are two chairs. In one, sits a young man. Seeing me enter, he stands. I've never seen him before. Tall and athletic, black hair cropped short in a military style cut. Hmmm. He's wearing a white clasp. He's the only other person in the chamber, so they must have already chosen him to be my new Beta. He seems to take note of my suit and tie, only partially visible under my himation.

After bowing to the council leaders, I take the seat next to my Beta, peering at him as he also sits.

Zeus stands. He isn't a particularly imposing figure, but his mind is quick, and his glare can be intimidating.

"Glad you could finally join us, Sir Archie." Zeus directs that glare of his at me now.

I'm about to stand and address the council, but seeing or sensing this, Zeus lifts his hand and says, "No explanation necessary. We know you've been quite busy on the outside. You're long overdue to be paired with another knight and we've chosen Sir Nicanor as a good complement to your abilities."

They've already chosen a name for him, too! I can't let this go on. When I was a chosen to be a Knight of Economics, Karl had his choice of several new knights as his Beta. And, *he* chose my name.

Standing, I say, "Are there no other options? I'd like to interview several new knights and choose my own Beta."

Zeus smiles. "I'm afraid, Sir Archie, something has happened … something we never knew could happen. We have a mission for you that will require the skills of a Knight of Economics, such as yourself, along with a Knight of War. Sir Nicanor. Have a seat while I explain."

I've never heard of such a thing happening. Slowly, I sit, trying to understand. I'm to have a Knight of War – *already chosen and named* – as my Beta. Why?

"Before the ascension … before the red clasp is presented … you must both know what you're getting into," Zeus begins, sometimes addressing us directly and sometimes addressing the room. "As you know, the Knights of the First Order have served as our bridge to the outside world for Pytho for over two thousand years. Knights of War, like Sir Nicanor, keep our society secret and safe. Knights of Leadership strive to advance our causes with the politicians of the outside world. These two branches of our knighthood have been with us since the beginning … since our great ancestors were forced to flee Greece and formed the First Order. Within the third branch, Knights of Economics were originally dubbed Knights of Commerce. Our ancestors formed that branch with the mission of collecting tolls and fees for protecting trade routes.

"Later, we formed some of the first banks in the world, and today, you can find a First International Bank in every major city in the world. The success of the Commerce branch has been the catalyst for the success of Pytho. We had to expand the concept of the branch, changing the name to Knights of Economics, which better represents our financial strength. Change may come slowly to our society, but it does come. Knights of Science, our fourth branch, did not even exist until the Italian Renaissance. The inner council of the 15th Century saw the rapid advancements of the outside world, and knew we needed to adapt … to add this fourth branch of knighthood to face that challenge."

Zeus glances down to the Oracle, seated to his immediate right, before continuing, "Something has happened and now we need to adapt further. The Oracle has seen something … something that … well, I'll let her explain." He motions to the Oracle.

A young girl, about sixteen, the Oracle's long auburn hair hangs to her waist. She stands and her large, expressive eyes pierce me as though she's probing my inner thoughts. Looking right *through* me. What does she seek? What does she see?

It's a full ten seconds before she speaks.

"This one is the right one," she says, more to the council leaders. The Oracle takes a deep breath, eyes again focused on me. "There has been a breach in time."

"A what?" I ask.

"A breach in time," she repeats. "The past has changed."

"That's not possible," says Nicanor. His voice is deep and cold, almost robotic.

The Oracle nods. "That is as we always thought as well … throughout the entire lineage of the Oracle. We have seen the past. Seen the distant. We have seen the future. We have used this vision – especially of the future – to aid Pytho. To keep us safe in troubled times. We saw the Christian uprising and our society fled to Germania. We saw the Inquisitions and we found this island. We were able to avoid threats to our society by acting on our visions of the future. The past, however, is not malleable … or so we thought. *Someone* has changed the past. The breach is clear. Someone has found a way."

The Oracle sits. She's so fragile looking, yet exudes wisdom and confidence.

Before anyone can ask her a question, she sits and Zeus stands.

"You've had a long time out there on your own, Sir Archie," says Zeus. "Where do we stand in the wake of Karl's debacle?"

Zeus isn't asking about Karl, even though they were friends. It is now – as it always has been – about the money. "I've been able to secure $37 billion in assets." We've been trading in US dollars ever since Karl set up shop in America. "In total, there was $198 billion in land and the companies within Starr holdings that have been seized by the United States."

We knights report directly to Athena. This is the first time I've ever met with Zeus or others in the council without Karl at my side. Zeus had always been cordial with Karl, but he and Karl were friends long before Zeus came to power.

Zeus sits. No words. Just glaring at me for a full minute while the council waits.

He looks down for just a moment, before addressing me directly, jaw jutting out, "Which of those two figures – the amount you say you secured, or the amount you say has been seized – includes the $15 million you deposited into your personal account in Zurich?"

"I …" He knows about that? A drop of sweat glides down from my temple and I wipe it off with my charcoal gray sleeve.

"*You what?*" Zeus seems to chew his words when he's mad.

"I … I will return that, sir."

"*No need.*" He chews those words as well. "I already have it back. That happened to be one of our own institutions. Not all of our banks are named First International, in case you didn't know."

"Karl had, well, he told me I should always have a … um … a backup plan."

"Just because Karl was your Alpha, doesn't mean the privileges I extended to him somehow transfer to you." He glares at me for a long moment. "Is that understood?"

"Yes, sir … Thank you, sir."

He looks at me quizzically before saying, "For what?"

"For reminding me of my place. A Knight of the First Order should never have made such a mistake."

Zeus smiles, genuinely. His usually sharp hazel eyes are less so. A little more relaxed. "There is hope for you yet, Sir Archie. You've been a Beta, on your own for quite some time. For you, this is long overdue. Let the ascension ceremony begin."

Athena stands. Representing the goddess of wisdom, warfare, and heroes, one of her primary responsibilities is the leadership of the Knights of the First Order. In theory, at least. I've always reported directly to her, but Zeus seems to make all the important decisions.

Holding a red clasp in her hands, Athena's eyes go from me to Nicanor, and back to me.

"The ascension from Beta to Alpha," Athena begins, "is perhaps the most important day in the life of a Knight of the First Order, and the day where my pride in your achievements comes to fruition in the awarding of this red clasp."

I wish my parents were here to see this – and my sister – but knights are required to give up all of the relationships from our past. I don't know how they're doing … if they're healthy … even if they're alive or dead. All these long years under Karl's leadership. I may not have the opportunity to choose my Beta, but I'll finally *have* a Beta. Nothing can take away from this. Not today. Not even the fact that I'll be paired with a grunt like Nicanor.

Athena extends the red clasp and says, "You have served us well as a Beta. This council expects even greater deeds and service in your future. Rise, sir Knight."

I stand, trying to keep my composure. Looking down, I see my slacks are wrinkled, and out of habit, I brush them with my hands, hoping to get rid of the wrinkles and maybe even some of the sweat in my palms.

I look back to Athena and her eyes open wide. It's not a look of pride on her face. Nor is it warmth, or even the camaraderie I expected to see. I've known her for years and I've seen variations of these types of looks from her, mostly for Karl. No. This is more of a look of surprise. Maybe even shock.

"Sir … Sir Archie," she lowers the red clasp.

A hand touches my arm and then grasps it firmly. I don't really register whose hand it is or why it might be trying to hold me back.

Zeus stands, shaking his head. "Sit down, Sir Archie. This is Nicanor's ascension to Alpha. Not *yours*."

Nicanor's ascension … not mine.

My legs won't move. I know I should sit down, but my body resolves to stay standing. Then, my mind catches up to my body.

"Nicanor's ascension? Not mine?" The questions come out more nasally … whinier than I would have hoped.

"Yes," says Zeus. "Now, sit down!"

I still refuse. "But … but, he's a grunt."

"Sit down, Sir Archie!" Athena glances at Zeus and matches his fury. The grip on my arm tightens to the point where it feels more like a tourniquet. "Sir Nicanor is a Knight of War and this council has determined that this mission is best led by a Knight of War."

I try to pull my arm free; now realizing the hand holding me back belongs to Nicanor – the young, stupid grunt who is to be my Alpha. His grip is stronger than I could ever muster, but I won't let him deter me so quickly. I can't rip free of him, but I'm not sitting down.

"Why should a grunt be in charge?" My voice is less whiney now, but the inner voice in me that has been screaming to sit down and shut up thinks it still sounds like I'm pleading and unreasonable.

"Grunt?" says Athena.

"Knights of War," I say. "Grunts think that brute force can solve any problem. If it doesn't work, they think they just need *more* brute force. What kind of leadership is that?"

Athena suddenly takes on a look I haven't seen from her before. It's anger and it's raw. "*I* was a Knight of War before being chosen for this council. Choose your next words more carefully, Sir Archie."

That was stupid. I should have thought that through a bit more before speaking. My inner voice is gaining some traction. Somehow, the grip on my arm becomes even tighter. Blood has stopped flowing past my bicep and I know there will be a hand-shaped bruise that I'll have to keep covered up for a week. Nicanor's hand is forcing me back to my seat. I stop fighting.

I'm not ascending to an Alpha. It starts to settle into my consciousness. I'm still a Beta. This stupid grunt is my Alpha. How did it come to this?

The ceremony continues, but I'm in a different place in my mind. Nicanor replaces his white clasp with his new red one and I barely notice.

Wondering if I can get out of this, I start to calculate my chances on my own ... outside of Pytho. No one I can trust. The First Order hunting me down. I had a stash of cash for this exact type of situation, but Zeus found it and took it.

I'd have nothing.

I'd be nothing. And, I'd be on the run.

Zeus is explaining the mission. Something about a crystal skull that we're going to retrieve. It's important to the Oracle. Yada, yada, yada. These backward idiots wouldn't even know that *yada, yada, yada* comes from a television show called Seinfeld. Fuck Zeus. Fuck Athena. Fuck the Oracle. Fuck them all. The stupid grunt is the Alpha. He can pay attention to the mission details.

Chapter 16

TREY TYSON
LONGBOAT KEY, FL, USA
MARCH 24, 2014

As I'm staring at the flame tonight, about to summon Nostradamus, I feel like I'm a kid back in school and walking down to the principal's office. I'm about to be told just how wrong I was to do what I did. I really hate that ... but, like in school, I know I crossed a line. I got caught, and whatever is about to happen ... to be said ... I have it coming.

Max is watching over me tonight as I enter a trance state. My natural father ... Max. When I was a kid, I had no idea he was my father. I just thought he was my mom's cousin and sometimes a mentor. In truth, he's been watching over me my whole life. Protecting me. That's what he intended when he had Thomas and Helen Tyson raise me as their own. Helen, the woman I've only known as Mom, gave birth to twin boys the same day I was born. One of the twins was stillborn. Max wanted to hide me from my birth mother and Helen offered to raise me. They were the only two people in on the secret.

The man I always thought of as *Dad*, Thomas, always thought I was one of the twins born to Helen in 1964. He died never knowing the truth. My three siblings all thought I was really their brother. I don't think Max would have ever told me that I'm his son if it hadn't been necessary during our chase of the Somali terrorists in 2012. He never would have told me that we're descendants of Nostradamus and I'm certain he never would have told me that Katarina Krostov was my birth mother. I only knew Katarina for an hour before she died. The loss hurt ... not from what I knew of her, but from not having an opportunity to get to know her.

As hard as it was for me, I think Katarina's death absolutely devastated Max. He loved her more than he'll ever admit and he's never had another love interest since Katarina.

It's comforting knowing Max is here. It's not about protecting me. I do think Nostradamus would be aware of a threat to me and warn me somehow. I'm more worried about Max protecting Jessica and our unborn baby while I'm in this state.

Protecting. It's what Max has always done. A Secret Service agent for decades, protecting a line of presidents. The founder of the Advance Intelligence division of the Service, or AI, Max recruited and trained a group of agents with psychic abilities that secretly protect our country from espionage and terrorists. In 2012, he protected the whole world from destruction. Now, retired, he's protecting my family. Even Mom, when she stays with us in the winter months. Max dotes over her. Helps her into and out of her wheelchair. A history teacher for her entire career, Mom would be happy spending the rest of her life reading her history books that take up half of her guesthouse. Max finds a way to motivate her to do something else every day … anything … as long as it's outside and with our family.

Max settles into the chair next to me and I start to fade. He lights the peace pipe, but the aroma isn't nearly as sweet as it was last night.

Oh well. Time to face the music.

Nostradamus … Nostradamus … Nostradamus …

When I connect with Nostradamus, he usually calls me his son of many sons. I think he says it to remind me that he's my ancestor. His daughter married one of the Medici royals back in the 16th Century and his abilities carried on through the Medici line – sometimes skipping several generations – all the way through to Max.

My choosing to keep the Tyson name after I discovered Max is my father has never sat well with Nostradamus. During my second training session with him, he asked when I would start using my father's family name, Medici. I may be a Medici by bloodline, but I'm a member of the Tyson family. I've always bee and always will be Trey Tyson, I told him.

"Trey! What have you done!"

The psychic form of yelling from Nostradamus causes a sharp pain in the upper right quadrant of my brain. I had held out some hope that with the merging of the two realities maybe Nostradamus wouldn't notice that I changed history. No such luck. *"This was a door that was meant to stay closed. The consequences … I don't think you have any idea what they are. Why did you do this?"* His voice, usually methodical and resonant, sounds tired. His pace is much faster due to his obvious anger.

"Nostradamus … Have you seen what has happened from your time?"

"Of course, Trey. You are only looking back, thus far. And looking back, there is always only one direction … one path to take. When we start looking into your future, you will see just how easy it is to identify a branch in time. This merger you caused is easy to see … to me and other visionaries. What you did was foolish and irresponsible – this is a door that should never have been opened!"

"You told me that changing the past is impossible. I thought it might work and, well, I had to try."

"You made a choice without considering the consequences and they will be far greater than you could have imagined … if you had ever taken a moment to even consider them."

"You're Nostradamus. If the consequences are so bad, I thought you would have stopped me … at least warned me once you saw what I intended to do."

"I can't clearly see your future. You have the gift and the curse of possessing a psychic cloak that comes from your mother's side. It's the same as the Oracle sisterhood. And you can be sure they will have noticed this new open door to changing the past."

"The Oracle and the First Order? What will they do?"

"That is difficult to see. The psychic family lineage within the First Order descends from the Oracle of Delphi. The movements of that line have always been impossible for other psychics to follow. We can only see the wake from their path and the damage they cause."

Nostradamus is being open with me for the very first time. He's never given any details of the First Order before. Max and I only know of it because Katarina told us in her dying breath. Maybe, just maybe, I can finally get some answers.

"Can you tell me anything about the First Order, and why they want to mess with the past?"

"We should not be having this conversation yet, but you have never been one to be patient. I suppose … because of what you have done, you will now need to train and prepare even faster. There are some things you need to understand. However, the First Order originates from long before my time, so much of what I know I only know from my guide."

Nostradamus is my guide and he's training me to be a guide through these visions. I suppose it's only natural that he went through similar training in his time from some guide in his past. I once asked Nostradamus who his guide is and all he would say is that it's better if I don't know that … yet.

135

"Maybe you can start with explaining the difference between the Oracle of Delphi and the First Order?"

"Yes," he says, *"that is a good place to start. The Oracle of Delphi is represented by a lineage of young women with prophetic abilities said to be granted by Apollo. Their influence spans the last six centuries of ancient Greece through the first four centuries of the Roman Empire. When the Romans adopted Christianity, they went on to disband all pagan religions – including the Oracle – in the 4th Century. The Romans sent their armies throughout their empire searching for and destroying any traces of the pagan religions they considered a plague to Christianity, and the Oracle of Delphi was at the top of their list of targets. When they reached Delphi, however, the Romans found that much of the sisterhood and many of the priests had evacuated Greece – just before they got there. Thus was formed the nomadic tribe of the First Order. And, they are willing to take extreme measures to regain the position of prominence they enjoyed for a millennium in which kings and emperors bowed to them, seeking their prophetic guidance, and where they were paid quite handsomely for their services."*

"Do you know where they went when they left Greece?"

If I opened a door that should have remained closed, then who is going to go through it? Where are they now?

"As I said, it is not possible to see their exact movements. They had to veil themselves in secrecy, but I believe they initially went to Germania."

"Germania? What makes you think that?"

"The wake of their path, Trey. The First Order considers Roman Christianity to be the reason for their downfall. They will do anything in their power to strike back … to take down the Roman Empire then … to rid the world of Christianity. The wake was clear back in Roman times. It was a century of attacks by the barbarian hordes, originating from Germania, which finally ended the Roman Empire in the 5th Century. What the First Order most likely failed to see at the time, however, was that Christianity had spread far beyond the Roman Empire … and it has endured."

"And I'm sure it will continue to endure. What I don't get is how my bringing Samantha back is so terrible? Or how it can affect Christianity?"

"Much like the Oracle, you are leaving great damage from the wake of your path. I've often said to you, Trey, that I don't know the extent of your abilities. You are the cross of both family lines – the Oracle's and mine. I always thought changing the past was impossible. You've shown that it is not. It may be extremely difficult, but not impossible. The door is open and the First Order will see it. They will attempt to do what you have done. They will attempt to change the past."

I think of the lives in New York taken by the Germans in 1945 ... the generations of lives that are now gone ... erased from history ... the damage from the wake of MY path.

"What can I do to make this right?"

"I'm afraid, Trey, that you may be spending the rest of your days trying to make this right. We knew you were going to have to defend against the First Order in your time and your future. And now that this door is open, you're going to have to defend the past as well."

"That's all? Just the past, present, and future?"

"This is the door that you opened and these are the consequences."

"Yes ... I know. At least I have your help to see the breaches in time that are in your future."

"The sisterhood of the Oracle has very different abilities than other psychics and visionaries. How they will be able to use the doorway that you have opened, I do not know. However, you must keep training if you are to defend against them. You must find them to stop them."

"Where do I begin?"

"It seems to me that you should start by looking for signs of the First Order in Germania ... or Germany of your time. I believe, continuing your training sessions will provide the best opportunity to do so."

"Okay, so we're going to follow Max as he gets deployed to Germany?"

"Yes. We are going to follow your father, but you need to see his graduation in America first. March 28, 1945 in Princeton, New Jersey ... And, Trey?"

"Yes?"

"Now, at least, you understand the consequences of changing history. I trust that you will not interfere with it again?"

"Changing history was wrong. I get that. Yet, knowing that I saved Samantha — even with the consequences — doesn't feel wrong. I get the sense that there's a greater good that will emerge in the future because she's alive."

"I can't argue against what you say." His resonant tone and energy are returning to his voice. *"There is more we must discuss and we need to include your father."*

"You want to speak with Max?"

"Max is your father," Nostradamus points out the obvious.

"There's nothing Max would enjoy more, I'm sure, but both of you have said it's not possible."

"I have seen a vision of him next to you in your time. There's a flickering flame in the brass tripod. Smoke drifts from that strange pipe of his. You are both in a trance state. And, you are both touching a crystal skull."

"The crystal skull? Max has one in his office. It's nearly the size of a real skull and clear."

There's a slight pause before Nostradamus says, *"Sorry, Trey, but the crystal skull from my vision was not clear. It was white."*

Chapter 17

MAX MEDICI

PRINCETON, NJ, USA
MARCH 28, 1945

"Max, why are they getting us up so early?" Ian asks in the middle of a yawn. "Sun's not even up yet."

"I, uh, I suppose it's for graduation. Since the president couldn't be here for it, they pushed it off to this morning. Deployment is later today."

"I don't know about you, but I won't be missing Kirk after he's gone."

"Yeah ... I guess not." Sebastian and Bernie don't know yet ... they have no idea that I'm deploying today ... or how much I'll really miss them.

"What's up with you, Max?" Bernie asks.

"Huh? What do you mean?"

Ian gives Bernie a quick look and then explains, "You had some sort of a nightmare last night. Something you were dreaming about made you sit up and start yelling. You woke me and Bernie up."

"Yelling? I don't remember ... What was I yelling?"

"It's a chicken," says Bernie. "Weirdest thing. You said it like ten times. It's a chicken ... It's a chicken ... over and over. Maybe you were hungry?"

"Sorry, guys. I ... well, I guess I just have a lot on my mind right now."

"You Boys keep yer mouths shut!" Sergeant Smith is pleasant as ever. "This is a big day for the Men. Best if you shut up and listen. You might just learn somethin' important. Now, let's get to the gym ... on the double."

Smith's cabin is next to ours and he came storming in here to wake us. Jones has her own cabin near the Men's, so I imagine she's getting them up and to the gym.

"What time is it anyway?" I can't tell, but it's before dawn.

Smith ignores the question, pacing back and forth, and is starting to turn pink. He instructed us to wear clean uniforms and he brought new combat boots for us. The boots stretch above our calves, and lace all the way to the top. Ian and I are ready, but Bernie is still trying to lace his boots.

"Goddammit, Bernie! Last again. You'll be late to yer own funeral, Boy. Let's go, let's go, let's go!"

Bernie gives up tying his second boot and just leaves the long laces hanging. He has to walk funny to keep from tripping over himself, but at least he got Smith to stop yelling.

We line up behind Smith outside of our cabin and start the quick jog to the gym. No hint yet how far off sunrise might be. Bernie is in front of me and he's hopping every few steps to avoid tripping. Smith always yells at us if we talk without permission, and I wouldn't put it past him to make us drop and do a hundred push-ups, even if it delays graduation. I'm not saying a word, and Bernie and Ian seem to have come to the same conclusion.

Entering the gym, I see Jones and the Men are already here. Kirk, Dieter, and Erik are talking quietly, and Jones is busy placing some packs on a table. The packs are dark brown leather, have a shoulder strap, and there are *four* of them. I've seen these army packs before, and they usually have a large US marked on the flap. Three of the packs are unmarked. The fourth has a flag embroidered on the flap. Three vertical stripes – green, white and red – the *Italian* flag.

It's really happening. I'm about to deploy to Germany. First, we'll go to an American base, I'm sure, but Germany won't be far behind.

The enormity of our mission starts to hit me.

Find the German physicists who are working on their atomic bomb.

Stop the Germans from building an atomic bomb.

Find Adolf Hitler

Make sure he's the real Adolf Hitler.

Kill him.

All on my own.

What have I gotten myself into? This is complete lunacy.

After placing the four packs on the table, Jones sees us by the door. She waves her hand. "Come in, Boys, and have a seat. Professor Einstein would like to begin immediately."

There are six chairs facing the table, so it's not hard to figure out where to go.

As I pass by Jones, she places a hand on my shoulder and asks, "How is your head, Max?"

"I'm fine, thanks." My forehead never really bled much, but a scar formed all the same and it looks permanent. Erik joked at dinner last night that I wouldn't need a costume on Halloween anymore – that I can pass as Frankenstein's monster, just the way I am. We all laughed, and it seemed to put an end to the tension between everyone ... even Kirk and me.

Just as Ian, Bernie, and I take our seats, the door is pushes open and the professor bursts into the gym. He's sweating and looks panicked.

"Please, please, everyone take a seat. I must speak with you all at once."

The Men don't hesitate, sitting without a word spoken. Jones and Smith stay standing on the left side of the table with the packs.

Einstein hurriedly moves to the right side of the table. He looks pale, almost matching Smith's color ... even the pink tone when he's upset.

"There has been a change in plans. *Ze* Germans ... they ... " Einstein puts his hand on the table, trying to support himself. Jones takes a step in his direction, but Einstein waves her off. "*Ze* Germans have launched a rocket at New York City ... downtown Manhattan to be precise."

"What!" Erik leaps to his feet, "What happened? How'd they get so close? You said we were out of their range!" Now that we're all speaking in English, I can hear the distinct New York accent in his voice. Maybe his family is in the city. Erik always goes about his business as if this is just another job, almost like we're all training to be plumbers or something. This is the first time he's ever shown any emotions since I've been here.

Einstein seems to take the outburst like a physical blow to the gut. He bends over in pain for a moment, then rights himself.

"It appears that *ze* rocket was launched from a U-boat." The professor looks at me and raises his eyebrows before continuing, "One was spotted near *ze* Statue of Liberty just after *ze* explosion. It stayed on *ze* surface and was heading north along our coastline, possibly heading for Boston next. I spoke with ze president. All available ships are chasing after it right now."

Erik is still frantic. "Was it an atomic bomb?"

"No," Einstein shakes his head, still sweating profusely, "but there were quite a few casualties, nonetheless."

"Let's go! We can help," Erik turns to face Sergeant Smith with a pleading expression.

"We are gonna help, son," Smith stands tall, using a commanding voice with just a hint of compassion. "But, New York is not where yer off to. There's a transport on the way. It'll be here in a couple hours. Yer off to Norfolk. You'll get yer deployment orders there. You Men, and … *Max*."

Ian stands, just as vehemently as Erik had. "Max?"

The others all stand. They all face me … even Smith and Jones are staring at me. It's suddenly silent. But the silence is broken by a crumpling thud we all hear.

The professor has fallen over and is on the ground in a fetal position, embracing his abdomen.

Jones reaches him an instant before I do. We're both kneeling at his side. She cradles his head.

"Professor Einstein?" she says.

"Take care of them," the professor's voice is weak. "Keep them safe."

"Yes, Professor, don't worry about them. They will be okay." Jones looks up to Smith. "We have to get him to a hospital, now!"

"Wait," the professor says with a little more energy. "Max … remember everything I told you. *Everything*."

"I will, Professor. We'll see you when we get back. Stay safe." I wipe his feverish forehead with me sleeve. "Please … stay safe."

Smith leans over and scoops up the professor as if he's a small child. Heading for the door, he turns and faces Kirk. "Stay here."

"Yes, sir," Kirk stands a little taller as he replies.

Jones holds the door as Smith carries the professor outside. It's only a moment before we hear the camp Jeep start up … and then we hear it leave.

"Did they all go?" Ian asks, directing the question to Kirk.

As if in answer, the gym door springs open and Smith strides back in.

"Why didn't you go with him?" There's an angry undertone in my voice that surprises even me as I approach Smith.

"He'll be alright. It ain't the first time the professor's had problems with his insides. One of the security guards went with them. He and Nurse Jones can handle it. Besides, the professor told me to stay to get you ready for deployment. Now I don't know how long it's gonna be before the transport truck gets here, so all of ya ... take a seat."

The Men don't hesitate, but Bernie and Ian are behind me, waiting to see what I'm going to do. Do they look at me as some sort of a leader, ready to back me if I decide to go help Professor Einstein? The day of deployment is not the day to break the chain of command. As much as I want to run outside and take the truck to follow the professor, I know it's best if I just take a seat and listen to what Smith has to say. Reluctantly, I do, and the others join me.

Smith is standing where the professor stood before his fall.

"Professor Einstein insisted we continue on without him. Today, he would have told ya how proud we all are. You've taken everything we've thrown yer way – the combat, the weapons, the languages, even the science – and you've learned ... you've *grown*. Four of you will be deploying, but ... as of today ... yer *all* men in my book. There's no certificate for ya. There's no new stripes for yer shirts. What you've earned is an *opportunity* to make a difference in this war. To make a difference in this world. Kirk."

Kirk stands and approaches Smith, and Smith smiles a genuine smile before placing his hand on Kirk's shoulder.

"Kirk, you were our first recruit. The first accepted into Project Spear. You've done good and led the others by example. It's only right that yer the first to graduate. Congratulations." They shake hands and Kirk turns quickly and returns to his seat.

Before sitting, Kirk turns back to Smith, "Permission to speak freely, sir?"

"Say what ya gotta say," Smith seems more patient than usual. He's not even pink.

"Why is *Max* graduating with the Men?"

"It seems that the Professor has had somethin' *different* in mind since the day Max was recruited. Just like you, I don't know any more 'n that. 'Cept," Smith faces me now, "you'll be getting *different* deployment orders when ya get to Norfolk ... somethin' the professor worked out with the president in private."

I only nod, not knowing what to expect. The professor is gone, but what he said is in my thoughts almost every moment. Remember *everything*, he said. What he couldn't say, not with everyone else in earshot, was that someone here is a *traitor*. Now, I'm the only one left who even knows there is a traitor. We'll be vulnerable. Everything we're about to do can be blown by one person giving us away once we're in Europe. I find myself hoping Smith is the traitor. Our chances would be better; at least once we're away from here.

Smith bellows, "Dieter," breaking my chain of thought.

As Kirk sits, Dieter stands and approaches Smith. Before Smith can say anything, there's a rumbling sound outside.

"That'll be yer transport, men. There's nothin' else I can teach ya at this point." Smith pats Dieter on the shoulder. "Good luck on yer … *assignments.*"

The sound of the transport grows louder – two, maybe three trucks are approaching. They stop at the gate, but it's only a moment before the guard lets them in. The trucks come to a stop just outside the gym.

"Ya best grab yer packs 'n get –" Smith never finishes the sentence, as the gym door bursts open.

First two soldiers rush in, then another two. They're in US army uniforms, but there's no designation as to their division. Most likely in some sort of covert group like ours. They're waving submachine guns around and moving in our direction.

"Gehen," one of them yells. It means proceed, in *German*. Why are *they* speaking in German?

Four more soldiers rush through the door and fan out along the sides of the gym.

They now have eight soldiers with submachine guns in a semicircle around us.

"Behind me," Smith yells.

Kirk is the first to react, leaping to his feet and heading for the back of the gym. Dieter and Erik are right behind him. Before they can reach the back door, someone kicks it in from the outside. The door pops off its hinges and slams to the floor. Flying through the door is the bloodied body of one of the security guards, his head bashed nearly flat on top, having been used as a battering ram on the door.

In walks the largest man I've ever seen. He's also wearing a US army uniform, but it doesn't come close to fitting him. The bottom of his pants is at least six inches above his ankles. His biceps are stretching the seams of the shirtsleeves to the limit of their strength. It may have happened when the man kicked in the door, or long before, but the top few buttons of his shirt stood no chance to stop his chest muscles from popping them off. He has a menacing presence and yet the way his clothes fit is almost comical. No submachine gun, just a German Luger in his hand, and he aims up and shoots once into the ceiling.

The Men stop dead in their tracks.

I stood when the soldiers first came in, but never ran for the back door. Flanking me are Bernie to my left and Ian to my right. Smith never intended to flee, either. He looks angry, assessing the situation, and I think he came to the same conclusion I did. Fleeing isn't an option. They have us surrounded.

The massive man motions with his gun for the Men to step back and rejoin us. They do so slowly and never turn their backs on the man with the Luger.

From the back door, two more soldiers emerge with submachine guns, followed by two men wearing officer uniforms and then a petite young woman in civilian clothing.

The tall, lean officer with the white beard steps forward as though he's in charge.

"Sehr gut," he says, nodding to his men.

"Captain," the other officer says as he steps forward. "In English, so these young men can understand us." This one is of average height and build, wearing a hat with an unusually large brim. As he removes his hat, I see why. He has a hideously scarred face. Stretching his neck a bit, he reveals a scar that runs all the way across his throat. There's an eerie screech to his voice and I imagine this man has seen battle. Someone tried to kill him. They nearly cut his head off, and yet he survived.

Their captain seems to defer to him, so he must be their leader. One of the soldiers – this one stands out with his black hair – shadows the leader's every move.

Outside the gym, I hear several sets of running steps. Doors opening and shutting in every direction. They're searching our camp. For what?

"We can keep our visit to your little camp brief and pleasant," the leader says, "but that will require some … *cooperation* … on your part." He walks slowly around the room, making eye contact with each of us. His blue eyes are so different from the rest of his appearance. They're clear, assessing … aware. He lingers a little longer on me, but when he gets to Sergeant Smith, he stops.

Smith is already pink, on the verge of turning red. His arm muscles are flexed, his stance coiled, ready to strike. The man with the Luger sees this also, and steps between the scarred man and Smith.

"Captain," the scarred leader says, "did you ever hear of an American soldier from the last war who could change colors like this?"

"Das rosa spion," the captain answers at once.

"Remember what the Americans called him, Captain?"

"*Ze* pink slink," the captain says in a heavy German accent.

"Yes, the pink slink," the leader repeats with less of an accent. "This man … this *pink slink* killed *many* of our German soldiers in the last war. So many that he became somewhat of a legend among the Americans and the British. Germany even had a bounty on his pink head. Do you know, Captain, that we questioned American prisoners, trying to find out more about this devil … this pink slink?"

The captain doesn't answer, but shakes his head.

"We never captured him. No one ever claimed the bounty, but eventually we learned his name. He is David Roth. The pink slink, who killed so many Germans … he is a *Jew*."

Smith uncoils and hurls himself in an attack at the leader that catches everyone off guard … except the massive man with the Luger. The gun looks almost like a toy in his huge hand, but he uses it to hit Smith on the side of his neck, knocking him to the ground.

He then aims the gun down at Smith and is about to fire.

"Don't shoot," the leader rasps. He takes a step back, methodically looks at our boxing ring, then back to the captain. "It seems, Captain, that the Jew would like to fight us. I am quite certain it would make the Fuhrer pleased to know that one of our German soldiers could beat him in a fair fight. Perhaps you have a man among your crew who is up to the challenge?"

Again, the captain answers immediately, sure of himself. "Heinrich!"

He's one of the first two soldiers who stormed through the gym's front door. Tall and athletic, he doesn't hesitate to place his submachine gun on the ground and climb into the ring. Once in, he starts performing combination punches, gliding around the ring like a seasoned professional boxer.

"Ya may know who I am," Smith says as he cautiously climbs to his feet, "but I don't know you at all, and I think I'd remember a face as messed up as yers. If it was me that gave you that scar, ya wouldn't be here right now. What's yer name and why are ya here?"

"Those are questions that I would be asking you, should our positions be reversed. My name is Hagan Ister. It is my understanding that Albert Einstein is here at your little camp. Now, perhaps you can save us all a lot of time and be so kind as to tell me where I might find the professor?"

Smith rubs his neck, glaring at Ister, before he says, "I don't know any professors. This is just a training camp for boys learning to box. Ya know, for the Olympics."

"Is that so?" Ister folds his arms across his chest, his eyes probing Smith. "Well then, it is fortunate that our Heinrich here has come with us to your training camp for boxers. We have some time to kill while my men are searching your camp. Why don't you step into the ring? Perhaps the activity will jar your memory."

Smith starts walking, somewhat gingerly, to the ring. He climbs up the platform and through the ropes. The man they call Heinrich is still shuffling his legs, throwing combination punches at the air, and he looks both quick and strong.

"Who's gonna ref?" Smith asks, never taking his eyes off Heinrich.

"A referee will not be necessary," Ister replies, "because there are no rules."

Heinrich is still shadow boxing. He looks at the captain, maybe to make sure he's watching.

"How will we know who wins?" Smith asks.

"The man who survives. Captain, would you mind ringing the bell?"

The captain is still several steps from the bell, when Smith hurls himself at Heinrich. We've all trained with him, and I knew he was fast, but the speed of the attack is astonishing. It's a vivid demonstration of Smith's strike first and fast training and he catches Heinrich completely off guard.

The first blow is a front kick to Heinrich's groin. As his legs begin to buckle, Smith delivers a cross-hook combination to the man's head that works to keep him standing and dazed. As Heinrich struggles to get his arms in front of his face, Smith deals him a nasty right cross to the lower abdomen. This causes Heinrich to drop his arms and curl his body in, and that was Smith's intention all along.

Smith grabs Heinrich by the hair as he's falling forward, pushes his head down as he brings his knee up in a crunching blow to the nose. The break sounds far worse than just a nose busting. Smith lets Heinrich drop like a sack of potatoes, and the soldier makes no attempt to break his fall. Lying prone and motionless on the ground, blood pours from Heinrich's nose ... or the flat area where his nose once was.

The captain draws his gun from his side holster, but Ister holds up his hand to stop him.

"He did not wait for *ze* bell!" The captain looks pissed off, still waving his gun in Smith's direction.

"We have to give the Jew some credit for ingenuity," says Ister. "It is a trait that we sometimes forget they possess … I did say there were no rules."

Two German soldiers enter the ring. One checks on Heinrich while the other aims his gun at Smith.

"Tot," says the kneeling soldier. He's *dead*. Smith killed him. That fast, and a man is dead. Welcome to the reality of war. Holy shit.

"Pull him out of there," Ister orders, and the two soldiers oblige by dragging Heinrich to the edge of the ring where two other soldiers take hold of the body and carry it toward the door.

Pausing before the door, one of the soldiers turns back and asks, "In die lastwagen?"

The captain shakes his head, "Nein. Verlassen den korper auberhalb." They're going to leave the body outside.

Smith, still standing in the ring, turns and laughs at Ister. "How 'bout you, kraut? Wanna take a turn?"

Ister sneers at him. "While I am unable to accept your invitation, I can send someone in my place … Von Becker."

"Let me," says the soldier with black hair. Visually, he stands out among all his German colleagues as much as I stand out among all the trainees.

"No, I would prefer that you keep an eye on our hosts. This," Ister says to us, "is Rolf Barbie. He is not a man that you want to anger."

Barbie walks over to us, pulls a leather bound rod from his belt, and whips it across the side of my neck. The pain is instant and excruciating.

"Hello, little brother," he says to me in perfect English.

My neck stings. I can't tell if the skin broke where the rod lashed me, but I'm not going to touch it … not going to give Barbie the pleasure of acknowledging the pain.

The massive man, Von Becker, hands his Luger to Ister and carefully climbs into the ring – never once taking his eyes off Smith.

"No rules and no bell," says Ister. "Let us see if you can handle *this* German."

Smith glances for a moment at Kirk and says, "No matter what happens here, Men, I'm proud of each of ya."

Even before finishing his sentence, Smith launches himself at Von Becker, and it appears to be the same attack as with Heinrich. It's a front kick with his right foot aimed at Von Becker's groin. At the last moment, though, Smith leaps, swinging his left foot from the ground with a round kick aimed at Von Becker's head.

This move, I imagine, would strike a fight-ending blow to any opponent Smith might face ... except Von Becker.

Von Becker deftly steps back and blocks the sergeant with a sweep of his arm that sends him sprawling to the side. Smith springs back to his feet and bull rushes toward Von Becker, screaming a guttural battle cry. Like a linebacker facing a runningback in the open field, Von Becker lowers into a crouch and lunges forward to tackle Smith. Smith delivers a downward chop of a punch to the back of Von Becker's head, as he tries to sidestep the lunging giant.

Von Becker doesn't seem to notice the chop, his long arms easily wrapping around Smith's torso. He lifts the sergeant high over his head, turns him over, then drives Smith, head first, into the floor of the ring.

Smith is stunned, but he isn't finished. He still struggles to break free of Von Becker's hold. Squirming, twisting, and pounding with his fists, he seems to free himself partially. Not from his effort – it's more that Von Becker needed one of his arms to deliver his own strike.

It's only one blow. An elbow, with all of Von Becker's force behind it, to Smith's chest. There's a crunching noise, followed by a wheezy, inhaling gasp from Smith. His eyes bulge and his shade turns quickly from pink to a deep violet. Smith audibly releases the breath from the gasp. It's his last breath.

Von Becker stands, straightens his shirt that has lost another two buttons, then climbs back out of the ring.

I'm stunned and horrified. As much as I think I hated Smith – or David Roth, as Ister claims is his real name – the man stood up for us. He faced death with bravery, still trying to teach us one last lesson.

Ister claps Von Becker on the back, then hands him the Luger to hold. "Now *that* is how a German handles a Jew properly." He turns and faces Kirk directly, perhaps assuming that leadership has now passed on to him. "Can any of you young German men explain why you are here training with the Americans? Under a *Jew*, no less?"

Kirk says nothing.

Ister moves to Dieter, then to Erik, Ian, and Bernie, looking each in the eyes one at a time. None of them talks. None of them even budges.

"Hmmph," Ister grunts as he walks past me and to the table. "I don't suppose any of you care to tell me what these packs are for?"

He doesn't wait for an answer, opening the first unmarked pack. "Well now. These don't look like Olympic boxing uniforms, do they?"

Ister holds up what is unmistakably a German army uniform. He places it back on the table and digs through the other two unmarked packs. "There are two uniforms and unit identification papers in each of these packs. Captain, can you imagine why Olympic boxers would need German army uniforms and papers?"

The captain just nods.

"Yes," Ister hisses, "so can I."

Ister reaches for the pack with the Italian flag on it. The woman, who had been standing behind one of the German soldiers, takes a few steps in my direction. She's ignoring the others, just staring at me. Her eyes are somewhat glazed, as if she's looking right through me. It's an eerie feeling.

"This pack is very interesting." Ister is digging through the pack, talking to no one in particular. "Two uniforms that appear more appropriate for the *Italian* army and the papers are written in Italian – I cannot make out the barbaric language. So," Ister says as he turns back to face us, "there is one Italian pack and one Italian among you. There are three German packs, and yet there are five Germans here, training to be *boxers*. The packs contain army uniforms, not boxing uniforms …. It seems that the Jew was not being truthful with me. So, now, I will ask you one more time –"

The front door to the gym pushes open and this draws Ister's attention away from us … *thankfully*. Four more German soldiers enter. Two are carrying boxes of files and papers. The other two are carrying the assortment of German guns we use for weapons training.

"What have we here?" Ister waves for the men to come to him, "Auf dem tisch."

The men place the items on the table as Ister commanded.

"Einstein?" Ister asks.

"Nein," the first soldier says.

"Jemand anderes?" Ister asks about anyone else being here.

"Zwei Wachen. Beide tot." They killed the other security guards.

Ister flips rapidly through the files and hands that box to one of the soldiers. The papers in the second box hold his attention much longer. He pulls out several documents and drawings to study, and I can see what they are … descriptions and drawings of the equipment necessary to build an atomic bomb. Einstein used them in the lab to teach us what we would need to find and destroy once we were in Germany.

"Herr Ister?" The captain seems to be growing anxious as Ister continues to study the drawings for several minutes.

"Captain, I believe your men have found what we need. Our scientists will find these to be quite useful."

Ister then turns to face us. "Which of you is Kirk?"

None of us says anything, but Kirk visibly stiffened at the sound of his name.

Ister saw this, too, and walks over to face Kirk.

"Just as I thought," he says. "Your file was on top of the rest ... There is no need for you German boys to worry. I recognize some of your family names. We're going to bring you home ... give you some proper training. Conveniently, some of you already have uniforms that fit .... Von Becker!"

Ister turns and faces me. His eyes bore into mine. His breath is somehow fouler than his face. I should be afraid, but for some reason I'm not. This man intends to kill me. I sense that much, but there's no fear. Smith had no fear. Maybe I learned that last lesson. Maybe he meant the lesson specifically for me. Ister holds out his hand and Von Becker places the Luger in it.

"Maximo Medici. That file must belong to you ... Medici? It is quite a famous family name in Italy. Your ancestors have a long and entertaining history. We will not, however, be requiring your presence on our voyage." Ister raises the Luger, aims at my face, and –

"STOPPEN!" It's the woman. She rushes forward to Ister's side.

Ister looks irritated, yet doesn't lower the gun. "What is it, Lady Zelda?"

"This boy is Maximo Medici?" Whereas Ister pronounced my name incorrectly, this Lady Zelda gets it right.

"Yes, what of it?"

"I have seen his face in my dreams ... heard his name. Maximo Medici ... I have seen that he is important – nein – he is *necessary* for you to achieve your goals." She is tugging at his arm while speaking.

"He is not Aryan! He is not even German!" Ister's irritation grows deeper, into anger. I can see it in his face ... he yearns to pull the trigger.

"Do what you will, Herr Ister. But, if you kill this boy, your plans are doomed to fail." She turns from me to face him. Her blonde hair is in several large braided knots, yet it still extends halfway down her back.

Looking at her face now, Ister's anger subsides. He lowers the gun, and then hands it to Von Becker.

"Fine," he says, "Take them all."

Chapter 18

TREY TYSON
WASHINGTON, DC, USA
MARCH 25, 2014

Max and I sit on a bench in the lobby of the Smithsonian Museum of Natural History, facing a life-size elephant partially blocking a huge IMAX sign. A small tour group gathers in the lobby, several of them complaining that their guide hasn't shown up yet.

We're waiting to meet someone here, but when Max asked for her at the information desk, they told us to have a seat because she's a very busy person. Aren't we very busy people, too?

Max hasn't exactly spelled out the reason we're here, but he's never been one to give away too many details until it's absolutely necessary. Thinking back to what led us to be here, I can pretty much figure out his motive.

It all started last night when I told Max what Nostradamus had seen – a vision of Max and I using a crystal skull to *both* communicate with him – he couldn't wait until the next day. No. He insisted we get his crystal skull and try it immediately.

I tried to talk him out of it, but he was so excited that he didn't notice or care how exhausted I was.

We set the crystal skull next to the brass tripod and tried to make the connection with Nostradamus, but it didn't work. Oh, there was a strange connection between Max and me when we both touched the skull. It emanated some sort of energy that flowed through us … connecting us in a way. I could hear some of his thoughts and he could hear some of mine. That was a really cool new psychic experience, but I couldn't connect with Nostradamus while touching the skull.

Max isn't one to show disappointment, but this time it was visible. He had huge hope and our failed attempt crushed that hope.

I tried to look for a reason … for a way to help … and mentioned that Nostradamus said the skull in his vision was white.

While I thought it would take Max some time to get over the disappointment of not being able to communicate with Nostradamus, his mood improved immediately.

He said he knew where we could find the white skull – not *a* white one, *the* white one – and we immediately rushed to my laptop to buy airline tickets to DC for the following morning. Since we couldn't get a flight back until the day after, we got a reservation for adjoining rooms at the JW Marriott. Max also set up a meeting with Samantha, Bruce, and the president for tomorrow morning so we can all discuss this changing history problem … the problem that I caused.

Max never ceases to amaze me, so I shouldn't be surprised that he could make a phone call and get a meeting with the President of the United States of America on such short notice.

The drive from the airport was a bit of an adventure. Snow, at this time of year in DC is uncommon, and the drivers proved they weren't accustomed to it. Reminds me of the first snowfall of every winter in my days living in Michigan. Even though we all had long winters of driving in snow, ice, and slush – drivers treated every first snowfall like they had never seen the stuff before. Everyone driving way too slowly, yet there would still be multiple accidents on most major roads.

Not Max, though. He insisted on driving, and he was in a hurry – trying to pass cars every chance he could.

Parking was rough, too. We couldn't get any closer to the Mall of Museums than our hotel. Max knows DC like the back of his hand and decided we were best off to park at the Marriott where we are staying. It's close enough to the White House, I suppose, and not terribly far from the Mall. Still, the distance forced us to walk through the flurries. The snow was coming at us almost sideways.

We're cold and wet, but we made it.

Yawning, I say, "We should have waited one more day."

"Why wait?" Max slept on the flight here this morning, gently snoring, and now seems rested and alert.

"Jessica is over eight months pregnant. I don't like leaving her alone."

"She's the one who told us to leave. Trey, she's a doctor. She knows her own body and knows whether it would be risky to be on her own …. And, it's only one night. Her parents will be there by tomorrow."

"You have no idea how much she hates being alone."

"There have been nights when you've been gone," Max says, "and she's asked me to stay in one of your spare bedrooms in the main house. So, I've seen that in her, but I've never understood why she feels that way."

"It's from when she was a little girl," I explain, briefly reflecting on just how amazing it is that events from our childhood affect us so deeply for the rest of our lives. "Her parents went on vacation for a week and left Jessica with her grandmother in Detroit. The power went out on the second night, and her grandmother lit a candle and went into the basement to change the fuse. The lights came back on for a moment, and then Jessica heard a loud pop and a thud.

"In pitch black, she went downstairs to check on her grandmother. With only the flickering candlelight to guide her, she found her grandmother on the floor … dead … with blackened fingers. Jess has told me more than once that this is what motivated her to go into medicine in the first place. So she'd be able to help the next person she found in an emergency like that. On top of the trauma of finding her grandmother dead in the basement … electrocuted … it left Jessica alone and in the dark for the rest of the week before her parents came back and found her."

Max raises his eyebrows in surprise and concern. "I had no idea. How old was she when this happened?" he asks.

"Four."

"Oh, my dear God. She wouldn't know how to use a telephone. Probably too afraid to go outside. She had to wait all that time … alone … in the dark. How terrible for her."

"So, for Jess to tell us to go ahead to DC and that she'll be fine – you can imagine how hard that was for her."

"I can, Trey, at least now. We had to make this trip together, but from now on, when you travel, I'll stay with her."

"I appreciate that and I know she will, too. I just wish we could have found a flight back today, or that her parents could have gotten there. I'm worried, Max, about tonight. She hasn't been alone all night since I've met her."

"I'm sure she'll be –" Before Max can finish his sentence, we hear the chime of an elevator stopping at the main floor. An echoing set of high heels on slate tile approaches us from behind the elephant exhibit. A woman steps into view, walking with a sense of urgency. We stand as she approaches, and I see she's nearly my height. In her sixties, with an air of authority. She reminds me of someone … but whom?

Walking right past me, she extends a hand to Max.

"You must be, mmm, Mr. Medici," she says, somewhat reverently, with a thick British accent. How is it that everyone seems to know Max? He was in the *Secret* Service … on *secret* missions. I'm his son and I barely know any of his past.

Max shakes her hand, but seems dumbstruck for a moment, unable to speak.

The woman raises her eyebrows and then smiles as she finally seems to notice me.

"I'm the Associate Director of Science with the Smithsonian's National Museum of Natural History," she removes her hand awkwardly from Max's and extends it to me.

"Dr. Victoria Cromwell," Max finally finds his voice. "This is my son, Trey Tyson."

"Mmmm. Please call me Tori," she says, not taking her eyes off Max.

"Thanks Tori, I'm –" but she cuts me off.

"You've come at a busy time of year for us. The piece you're interested in is … mmmm, it's not something that many people care much to see. At least not enough as to schedule a visit. Not that I mind taking the time for you, mmmm, Mr. Medici."

"Can we see it?" asks Max.

"Of course," Tori says, turning to lead us back to the elevators.

We end up in her office, which reminds me of the way Max keeps his office. Books, documents, notes, half-finished projects all strewn about the office in a seemingly random fashion. I asked Max once why he kept his office like that, and he said he had so many things he was reading, researching, and working on that he had to find a way to keep them all visible all the time. As soon as a book or object was buried by something else, it fell off of his radar and might never be finished.

Tori carefully lifts a stack of documents from each of the two guest chairs in front of her desk. She looks at her tall bookshelf first, then her desk, then a short bookshelf to the side of her desk. Not an empty spot anywhere … except the floor, where she reluctantly places the documents.

After waiting for Tori to sit first, Max looks around the office and asks, "Is it here? I'd really like to see it."

"They're bringing it back from the labs any moment now. The carbon dating has taken *all* morning." She says this with a bit of exasperation on her voice.

If Max senses it, he's ignoring it. "I can't believe you haven't dated it before now. You've had it since 1992."

"Carbon dating, mmm … it didn't make any sense," Tori replies, now her British accent with more of a condescending tone. "It came in from an anonymous donor who claimed in a letter that it's from Mexico and originated with the Mayan culture. But, we know it's not, mmm, pre-Columbian."

"How can you possibly know that without carbon dating it?" Max is giving her a bit of attitude right back.

"Because," Tori smiles confidently, "it's made of, mmm … milky white quartz. We found it difficult to believe an ancient civilization could shape and carve it to the level of detail it has. So, to examine how it was made, we used, mmmm … scanning electron microscopy on it first."

"And?"

"And it showed that it had been shaped with a high-speed rotary tool … probably diamond-tipped … mmmm … *electric* …." She let that word sit there for a moment.

"So, you never carbon dated it." Max isn't letting that go.

"Carbon dating doesn't work on quartz, obviously. And … it was most likely made in the 20th Century – probably right before it was sent to us, meaning, mmmmm … it's a fake. Your idea from our telephone conversation this morning – to carbon date any material we can find in the fissures of the quartz. We never thought that was necessary."

"What?" I ask. "What are you two talking about?"

A knock at Tori's door keeps them from answering my question. A young man walks right in, not waiting for any acknowledgement from Tori. He's carrying a box that's a little larger than a cubic foot and looks for a place to put it, but quickly gives up and just hands it to her.

Tori opens the box without ceremony, or even caution. She pulls out a milky white crystal skull and finds a flat pile of papers on her desk to put it.

"A crystal skull," I say. "A white one. A little bigger than the one you –"

Max coughs loudly and then glares at me for a moment, as if I just revealed some deep, dark family secret.

"Mr. Medici, mmmmm … I don't want you or your son here to get too excited about the results we're about to hear. The accuracy of carbon dating is often to the nearest century, and I don't think this skull is even *one* century old. What," Tori turns her attention to the young man who brought in the crystal skull, "did you find?"

The young man shrugs, "It's the weirdest thing …."

Tori stands, all patience gone, "How old is the skull?"

"Between five thousand and six thousand years," he says.

"That's, mmm, simply not possible," Tori hasn't lost much of her confidence. "It's an anomaly. You took a bad sample."

"We took three separate samples from within three different fissures on the skull. All the results matched."

"Are you trying to tell me the early Maya, mmmmm … five thousand years ago … had high speed cutting tools and *electricity*?"

"All I'm telling you – what the lab results are telling you – is that this crystal skull is from the time of the earliest known Maya … from *at least* five thousand years ago."

I should be accustomed to this by now – accustomed to Max not telling me everything he knows – but I'm not.

"What," I ask directly to Max, who had quietly placed his hand on the crystal skull, "does the age of this crystal skull have to do with anything?"

He doesn't respond, eyes closed, and I'm not sure he even hears me.

Tori and her colleague stop their debate about the age of the skull and notice Max as well.

A full ten seconds go by.

"Max, are you alright?" I ask.

He removes his hand from the skull, blinks a few times, and then seems to regain his composure.

"This is no fake," he says.

Max then turns to Tori, "This is a much larger crystal skull than any other I've seen."

"There are rumored to be, mmm, thirteen of them, according to the few Mayan priests alive today who will even discuss the topic," replies Tori. "Not all of them are accounted for, but of the known crystal skulls, this is by far the largest."

"Thank you, Tori, for running the test, and for allowing us to see the crystal skull. Please … keep it safe," says Max.

"*Everything* at the Smithsonian is kept quite safe," replies Tori, her condescending tone in full force.

Max never answered my question in front of Tori, so as we're walking back to our hotel, I take it up again. "Why is the age of this crystal skull important?"

"Based on what you told me last night about your training with Nostradamus, I believe you're going to find that out while you're following me in 1945. There's a reason Nostradamus is showing you events in the order he's choosing and I think we have to trust in his intentions."

"That answer is getting to be frustrating to hear all the time."

"Patience, Trey. We knew we'd be stuck here tonight, so I packed the brass tripod."

I roll my eyes, but with the snow, he doesn't even see it.

Chapter 19

MAX MEDICI
ATLANTIC OCEAN
MARCH 29, 1945

We Boys and Men … no, we graduates and trainees … no, the six of *us*. We're not separate groups any more. Smith is dead. Jones and Einstein are back in Princeton. We're all that's left and we're all in this together now. Maybe we always have been. The six of us are in a narrow hallway in a U-boat. Erik, Kirk, Dieter, Bernie, Sebastian, and then me. All in a line, facing the gray steel wall of the hallway, each of us is handcuffed to the higher of two metal pipes of nearly a foot in diameter that stretch across the entire length of the hallway and beyond in both directions. The height of this pipe allows us to stand comfortably. We can lean against the two pipes, but sitting isn't possible. Our arms aren't long enough for that. Apparently, they want us to stay awake. At least for now.

German crewmen walk by on occasion. Some of them I recognize as the soldiers who took us from our camp. They say nothing to us. They've given us a little water, but no food. They take us, one at a time, to use the toilet. I think it's been about a full day since we boarded at gunpoint, but it's hard to tell, completely enclosed like this.

About once every hour, when no Germans are around, Kirk tries to break the pipe. He lifts himself with the handcuff chain against the pipe, places his feet against the lower pipe and heaves. The pipes never move.

He seems ready to try again. Kirk looks down both ends of the hall, sees no one, and then turns to face the pipe.

"Hold on," Dieter says. "You know what the professor always says. Trying the same thing over and over again, and expecting different results is the definition of insanity. Why don't we all try this together?"

"*Finally*," Kirk says. "Someone is willing to help. Let's do it."

Kirk and Dieter jump up and both have their feet pressed against the lower pipe in no time. The rest of us do the same, except Bernie, who climbs up the wall one step at a time instead of jumping. His one bootlace is still untied.

Kirk glares at Bernie for a moment, then says, "Ready … Pull!"

Six of us, working together, our chains scraping and tugging on the pipe.

I'm pushing with my legs and pulling with my arms with all my might. The strain of the handcuffs on my wrists is causing the metal to dig into my skin. The pipe doesn't budge, but no one wants to be the first to give up. We … the six of *us* … we keep pulling. A very slight creak emerges from the pipe, but it comes from the end of the hall.

"Harder," Kirk almost yells, and I let out a groan from the exertion.

We give it our all, but the one creak from the pipe is all we achieve.

Finally, Ian gives up and his feet drop to the floor. Then, Erik and Bernie also drop down. Dieter is next. Kirk and I don't give in yet, but it's just the two of us. He looks my way and then he drops to the floor as well.

My legs feel fine, but my arms are done. I let my feet fall, exhausted.

All of us are panting from the effort.

Ian is the first to speak. "It may be that you Men have already considered this, but what were we going to do if we broke free? The Germans outnumber us and they have the guns."

Dieter just raises his eyebrows at this, giving away nothing of what he's thinking.

Ian continues, "And, what if the pipe is filled with water? The whole compartment could flood."

Kirk jumps up, and tries to get past Dieter and Bernie in a wild, flailing attempt to kick Ian, but he falls well short and ends up hanging by his arms on the pipe.

After getting to his feet, Kirk is about to say something when we hear someone walking down the hall from my end of the pipe. All conversation stops and we turn in that direction.

Slow footsteps. I hope it's simply a crewman walking by. Hope it's not ….

"Little brother!" comes his voice. Booming. Resonating. Excited to see me, yet sinister. It's Rolf Barbie, and this is the third time since we've boarded that he's come to visit me. He completely ignores the others. They don't even exist to him.

There's a scraping sound as he slowly approaches, and I know it's the leather-bound rod sliding against the same pipe I'm handcuffed to. When I first saw him in Princeton, the only German soldier with black hair, I somehow knew he was trouble. I had no idea just how much, though.

He's still ten steps away. I wonder if I can reason with him, before he ....

"Why do you call me that?" I ask in as calm a voice as I can muster.

Barbie nearly sprints the last few steps and whips the rod against my ribs. *The pain* ....

"I did not give you permission to speak to me, little brother." Barbie smiles gleefully.

"May," I wheeze more than say, "I speak to you?"

The question seems to make him think. "Sure. You may speak." His English is nearly flawless. Better than Ister's ... much better than Professor Einstein's.

"Why do you call me little brother?"

"That is a reasonable question, little brother. Herr Ister told you my name. Correct?"

I nod.

"Have you not heard of my older brother, Klaus Barbie?"

I shake my head.

"Ah," he says. "Klaus is somewhat famous in Germany and now in France, and I thought perhaps you Americans would have heard of him. The French call him the Butcher of Lyon. The way Klaus treats the prisoners has made him famous. It is he who taught me the use of this." Rolf whips the rod to the other side of my ribs and I can't help but let out a yelp in pain.

"But," he continues, "that does not answer your question yet, does it? Klaus used one of these on me for most of my childhood. It leaves no permanent injury, but hurts like hell, doesn't it?" He whips my ribs again. "All he ever called me was little brother. When I asked him why he did this to me, he only said that one day when I have a little brother of my own that I would understand. Unfortunately, my parents didn't have any more children after me. I've waited my whole life to have a little brother, and now here you are. Like Klaus predicted, I *do* understand." He whips my thigh. This doesn't hurt nearly as much as my ribs.

I glare at him, remembering my father. Knowing what he did to me ... to my mother. I can't avenge my mother, because my father is gone, but this bastard is here. I have no emotions left in me except pure anger now.

I look straight into his cold eyes. "When I get free. When you least expect it. I will take that rod of yours, and I will kill you with it."

Rolf lifts the rod high, trying to find a path past my arms to my head, but before he can swing again a voice yells, "Stoppen!"

It's the huge, muscular man they call Von Becker, and he must have come from the other end of the hall. I can barely see past him, but it looks like there are two crewmen following him. I would guess the hallway ceiling height is about six feet, six inches. None of us, except Kirk, has had to worry about hitting our heads on it. Von Becker has to walk with his head angled down, and it gives him an ominous look as he approaches us.

"Herr Ister wants to see you now," says Von Becker in German.

The gleeful smile fades from Rolf's face. He lowers the rod and strides angrily past Von Becker.

Von Becker never makes eye contact with Rolf. He simply walks up to Erik, stops behind him, and places his thick hand around Erik's neck.

"You will talk," Von Becker says, more of a matter of fact than a question. His English is obviously not as well developed as either Ister's or Rolf's.

Erik, who has never been one to say much, only replies with two words, and in English. "Fuck you."

Still holding the back of his neck, Von Becker pulls Erik's whole body back about two feet, then thrusts him forward, and bashes his head against the pipe. There's no scream. There's no blood. The pipe that the six of us couldn't budge vibrates with the impact. By the force of the blow, and then the way Erik's body hangs after Von Becker releases him, I know he's dead.

Von Becker calmly pulls a key from his pocket and unlocks Erik's handcuffs. The body crumples to the floor with little noise.

"Rear Torpedo tube two," Von Becker says to the two crewmen, who don't hesitate for a moment to pick up Erik's body and haul him past the rest of us and down my end of the hall.

I get a glimpse of Erik's crushed-in forehead as they go by. Bernie gags and audibly fights off an urge to vomit.

Von Becker takes two steps, moving casually, almost as if he's a factory worker just about to pick up the next part on a conveyor line. He's behind Kirk now and grabs him firmly by the back of the neck. It's an odd picture, as Kirk is nearly as tall as Von Becker. They have the same dark blonde hair, with similar facial features and physiques, although Kirk isn't nearly as muscular. Kirk could pass for Von Becker's younger brother, at least if the circumstances were different.

"You will talk." It's the same tone and cadence as the first time Von Becker said the words to Erik.

Kirk's eyes are nearly bulging out of his head in fear. He coughs, and I'm not sure if it's because of the stranglehold around his neck or if he's trying to stall for a moment to think. Von Becker has left no doubt in my mind that he will simply work his way down the line of us, one by one, until we are all dead … or one of us talks.

I'm the last in line. Is it better? I don't know. I think we're all going to die one way or another, but then I remember that Ister brought our packs with the uniforms on the U-boat. *Why?* Just to give us hope? To make us think we have a chance to live … but *only* if we cooperate?

Von Becker pulls Kirk's head back away from the pipe, pauses for a moment, and repeats, "You will talk?" This time it's more of a question.

Kirk closes his eyes, sweat starting to soak through his shirt. He doesn't say anything, but nods his head a few times.

"Good." Von Becker unlocks Kirk's handcuffs and points down the hall in the direction from which he came. Kirk walks down the hall, never once looking back at the rest of us, and Von Becker follows, staying one step behind.

Four, maybe five hours go by. We haven't bothered trying to break the pipe anymore, and no crewmen have been down our hall. I'm exhausted, and would like nothing more than to sit and fall asleep. Bernie tried to hang from his handcuffs and sleep, but he never managed it. Ian is leaning up against the pipe, eyes closed, breathing deeply. He may have figured it out, but I can't get comfortable enough that way.

Just when I start to revisit the idea of leaning and sleeping like Ian, I hear footsteps coming toward us again.

It's Kirk in the lead this time. He's cleaned up and wearing his German army uniform. He refuses to make eye contact with any of us as Von Becker handcuffs him, about six or seven feet away from Dieter, and on the *lower* pipe. Kirk is able to stretch out on the floor. He closes his eyes and is either asleep instantly, or trying to make it seem that way.

Von Becker walks up to Dieter, pauses, and says, "I will be back for you."

He then walks past the others and stops behind me. Placing his hand around the back of my neck, the strength he possesses is instantly obvious. He could probably snap my neck just by twisting with the one hand. The pressure he exerts is measured. I can breathe, but I think he could stop that at any moment he chooses with just a slightly stronger squeeze.

"You will talk?" Again, it's leaning more toward a question than a command.

I can't imagine what I will say ... what Kirk may have said already ... if our stories will match ... what being questioned by Ister will be like ... how I will endure it. I can't imagine any of it. *Imagination* ... The professor told me to remember *everything* he taught me. *Everything*. One of those things was to *live* to fight another day. I find myself nodding.

"Good." Von Becker is a model of consistency, it seems. He unlocks my cuffs and the relief of my arms actually dropping to the side of my body is nothing short of glorious.

I know the way and start walking. I do make eye contact with Ian, who woke as soon as Kirk came down the hall. His eyes say so much to me. Be strong. Be careful. Stay safe. I silently try to convey the same messages to him.

The way is straight except for one area where we have to bend away from the middle of the U-boat all the way to the side, and then the hallway bends back to what seems to be the middle of the starboard hull. I noticed the large hump near the center of the strange, double hull U-boat when we boarded it, and it seems this bending hallway goes around the hump.

Is this the U-boat I imagined the Germans might build? The hump could easily be where they house a rocket, maybe the same rocket they launched at New York.

The professor said the rocket was not atomic. The Germans haven't figured out that piece to the puzzle yet.

They were seeking Einstein at the camp – not us. Maybe it was his knowledge they needed. They found his science lab drawings, though. Will that be enough for them to make their rockets atomic?

"Halt," Von Becker commands. I'm next to a door, and Von Becker raps on it a few times. This is it. Time to face Hagan Ister. Time to face death.

When the door swings open, it's not Ister's hideous face I see, but the beautiful face of the woman who saved my life ... Lady Zelda.

I enter and Von Becker follows me in, pausing to close the door behind him.

"Please sit, Maximo." Zelda says in a gentle, high-pitched voice.

I take the seat that Von Becker points to. He stands behind me – a silent, grim expression on his face. His presence is both easy to ignore and impossible to forget.

Lady Zelda opens one of the storage lockers in the cabin and removes something. It's round and wrapped in a black velvet bag. She takes a seat at the table, removing what turns out to be a large crystal skull from the velvet bag.

She places the clear, nearly life size crystal skull on the table, facing directly at me. Then, to my surprise, she asks, "May I see your scar?"

How could she know about the scar I got from the fight with Kirk? I've always combed my hair down in front, which easily covers the scar. I don't remember when it may have been visible to Zelda.

"Yes," I say, seeing no harm in it.

She lifts my hair and sees the scar over my right eye. She hesitantly touches it, pauses for a moment, and then she touches the smooth skin over my left eye.

"Your name is Maximo, right? Maximo Medici."

I don't say a word or give away anything with an expression.

"Let me tell you how this is going to go," she says, with sudden firmness in her voice. "Hagan Ister wants to know what you and your friends were doing in that camp. He wants to know everything you know about Professor Einstein. I was able to convince him to spare your life back at the camp and I was able to convince him to allow me to question you. You can answer my questions, or you can answer the same questions from Herr Ister. You will end up talking to one of us, and trust me ... you will find it much better to talk to me."

I believe her. I don't know why, but she seems to be looking out for me. *Why?*

Still, I refuse to answer her.

"Listen," she says, with more kindness in her voice. "Your friend, Kirk, already told us most everything Herr Ister wants to know. We know Einstein was there. We know he was training you. We know he fell ill and was taken to the hospital before we arrived. We know about your mission to destroy any German facilities for producing atomic weapons. We know the three packs were for Kirk, Dieter, and Erik ... and that Sebastian and Bernard were not ready for the mission yet."

My eyes close, astounded that they were able to break Kirk so quickly ... so easily.

"We know all that," she continues. "But what we don't know is what *you* were going to do. Why there was a different pack, with an Italian uniform, that could only be for you. It's obvious that Kirk does not know your purpose – he would have told us. So, what is it? Where were you going? What were you going to do?"

Opening my eyes, I don't speak. I don't even acknowledge that she has spoken.

She stares at me for a long time, sadness in her eyes. "I may be the only person on this U-boat you can trust, Maximo."

Von Becker grabs my neck from behind again, this time with enough pressure that I can't breathe. This may be the end for me, but I'm not talking. I'm not giving up.

"Ulrich, no," she says. The giant man obeys her and releases me.

"You are risking your future by not talking with me, Maximo. That much I have seen. I can tell you more of your future if you'll place your hand on the crystal skull."

She's almost pleading with me, and it seems like she's pleading for me to live. To make this one concession. This one small compromise. To touch the crystal skull.

Lady Zelda places her hand on the back of the skull, palm down, and waits for me.

Touch the crystal skull – can I give her that much? This strange woman who saved my life?

I reach out and touch it, gingerly at first, with just my fingertips. I expected it to be cold, but it emanates warmth. I don't sense any harm from it, so I place my entire hand on the face of the skull, palming it the way Zelda is palming the back of it.

More warmth. A calmness overcomes me. Visions of my past flit through my mind – so quickly, too quickly – the visions dominate my thoughts and I have to close my eyes. My childhood ... many of my favorite books ... my mother ... my father ... their deaths ... Ian and his family ... training with Johnny Fox ... training for Project Spear ... Professor Einstein ... *STOP!*

"It is alright, young Maximo, you can trust your thoughts to me." It's Zelda's voice in my head. Can she see my visions? Can she hear my thoughts?

"How do I know that?" I'm projecting my thoughts – not speaking. I don't have to wonder if the communication is working very long before she answers my question.

"I am not here of my own free will any more than you are, Maximo. I believe I can trust Ulrich – the man you know as Von Becker – to protect me, but I do not know if that protection will extend to you. This is the only way for us to communicate in private."

"You're not in chains or handcuffs," I point out.

"I am a mother, and Herr Ister keeps my baby hostage in Berlin. There are no stronger chains that would bind me to him."

"But you're helping the Nazis. They just launched a rocket at New York. We hear about what they do to the Jews. You saw what happened to my sergeant, and this Ulrich Von Becker friend of yours just killed one of my friends only hours ago. How can you help them? How can you help Ister?"

"Maximo, these things ... these terrible events would happen with or without me. Ister has to believe I am helping him. I have to give him some of the truth from what I see of the future ... enough for him to believe me. You need to know that what he is planning is far worse than what they have done already. I cannot stop them alone. I need your help, Maximo. I have seen you in my dreams. I think you can help me."

"What? What are they planning?"

"I can't tell you that. If Ister decides to question you himself ... if he ever found out I shared his plans with you ... we would both be dead. And your friends. And my baby."

Can this be true? Is any of this really possible? These thoughts I keep to myself.

"What is this skull?" I ask her.

"I will answer your question, but I need your promise to give me something in return. Something that will keep us both alive. Agreed?"

"I won't betray my country."

"There are small truths we can tell Ister that won't betray your country – but, something more than just that you love books."

"As long as I don't have to betray my friends or my country, then we have a deal." I don't know if I trust Zelda, but my instincts tell me I don't have a choice.

"What I tell you now, I tell you because we need to trust each other, Maximo. We are in this together, you and me, more than you can possibly know. This crystal skull, as you must know now, is extremely powerful."

"I see that, yes, but where does it come from?"

"From long before my time ... long before the sisterhood of the Oracle."

"The Oracle? Like the Oracle of Delphi? I've read about that."

"Yes, I saw. You have read about a great many things in your young life. The sisterhood of the Oracle extended beyond Delphi, but you are correct in the connection.

I am a descendant of the sisterhood, and I possess the psychic abilities that run down my family line."

"Psychic abilities?"

"Yes, Maximo, and you have similar abilities."

"Me? Psychic?"

"Yes. Otherwise, this could only be a one-way conversation. You must have some experiences in your past where you suspected this already. Dreams of the past or the future? Waking visions?"

"Perhaps." I'm not sure how much I should say, or if it matters. Zelda seems to know everything already. "But, what of the crystal skull?"

"You now know as much about its power as I do. It enhances my abilities when I touch it. You can see that it allows for our connection."

"How did you get it?"

"Herr Ister found it. He is the head of the Thule society. Have you heard of this?"

"No."

"The Thules believe the Germans, at least the pure ones, descend from an ancient lost civilization of people known as the Aryans. This Aryan race of people existed long before the Romans, before the Greeks ... even long before the Egyptians and other earliest known civilizations. Thousands of years ago, they were far advanced of the tribes of people that populated most of the world. Ister believes they were far advanced of even our society today. He believes the Thules, powered by the German armies are destined to rule the world ... to reestablish their civilization. The Thules are ever searching for signs of the lost civilization ... ever searching for artifacts the Aryans left behind. This skull is one such artifact and the Thules have others."

"How is it I've never heard of the Thules or even the Aryans or their lost civilization?" I ask.

"You have heard of them. Ister believes the Aryans come from Atlantis."

"Atlantis? The island that sank? I thought that was a fable."

"Fables all start from at least some bit of truth. Otherwise, they would not survive the millennia."

"Then how do the Thules think it's possible they are descendants of this lost civilization?"

"They believe some of their people — perhaps the ones who managed their servant tribes — escaped whatever cataclysm struck their city."

"Servant tribes?" I ask.

"Yes, the Aryans kept some of the tribes of the ancient peoples as servants. Someone, after all, had to do all the hard labor of keeping their civilization functioning. The Thules have found Aryan artifacts among far less advanced tribes of people. Ister has concluded these people must have been servants to the Aryans."

"So where does this all leave us? What does he intend to do?"

"I can't tell you everything, but you know part of their plan already. The atomic bomb is his immediate goal. Ister suspects that Atlantis was lost, to be sure. But sunk? No, he suspects they discovered the power of the atom, and not being able to control it was the cause of their demise. An accident, perhaps, but he believes their city was obliterated by an atomic bomb. What he wants most of all is to succeed where Atlantis failed."

"Zelda, I cannot give him that power. Even if I could, I never would."

"That's not what I need from you. I need a little of the truth. Ister already deduced that your training from Einstein was designed to help you identify the production equipment needed for atomic weapons. Your friend Kirk confirmed that he was supposed to find and destroy the equipment. He told Ister about the training you had, how you all speak German, and that your purpose was different from the others. Kirk, however, does not know your purpose. What is it?"

Fuck you, Kirk. This thought I keep to myself. Same with the realization that I don't need to pretend I don't understand German.

"If everything you say is true and my instincts tell me it is, then you've been more open with me than I could ever expect. I don't think I have a choice but to trust you. My purpose is to ... it's ... I'm supposed to kill Hitler ... assassinate him."

"You were planning to assassinate Adolf Hitler ... kill the Fuhrer? ... But you are so young. What was your plan?"

"I intended to portray myself as a messenger from Mussolini." The simplistic nature of the plan is embarrassing.

"With a private message from one dictator to another? In that case, looking like a young and innocent Italian boy does make some sense. It may have actually worked. What were you going to do if you did get close to Hitler?"

"As I said ... kill him."

"That would be a suicide mission, Maximo. Is that what you are prepared to do? Give up your life in exchange for Hitler's?"

"If it came to that, yes."

"My dear boy. Let us both hope it does not come to that .... This is the exact truth that Ister will want to hear. It's so absurd that it's believable. Remember, reveal nothing of our conversation to Ister. He is a very intelligent man. One small mistake would mean the end of us both. Understand?"

"I do." However, I'm not sure I really do.

"I don't know if or when we may get to have a conversation like this again, Maximo. I sense events in your future that are very important. Great deeds of great good. I will do my best to protect you. And, you must do your best to survive."

With that, Zelda removes her hand from the crystal skull, severing the connection instantly.

She looks up to Von Becker and says in a firm tone, "Ulrich, ask Herr Ister to join us."

Von Becker glances at me, then back to her. "I cannot leave you alone with him."

"The table is secured to the wall. You can handcuff him to the table."

Von Becker seems to find this to be an acceptable solution and does just that.

Waiting for Ister, I decide, is worse than waiting for Von Becker. Zelda is right in that Ister is very intelligent, but that's not the only reason. There's something inherently evil about the man.

It's not long of a wait. Two sets of footsteps, one far heavier than the other, make their way down the hall outside the open door.

Ister steps in first, with Von Becker right behind him.

"Von Becker tells me you have something to share with me, Lady Zelda. It has not taken you nearly as long as I expected. What is it?" There's a creepy maligned grin on Ister's face. It's even worse looking than when he's upset.

"You were right to suspect this Italian boy was up to something different from the rest, Herr Ister. I have discovered his plan. This boy was to be sent to kill the Fuhrer."

Ister almost instantly bursts into laughter. It's a high-pitched cackle, mixed with hisses. Von Becker, who has been nothing less than stoic, joins him. The two are so caught up in what they see as a ridiculous plan that even Zelda can't help but smile.

Was it that outrageous?

Is it so impossible to believe that I could succeed?

Maybe they're right. Maybe this was a dumb idea from the start.

Ister takes a while to stop laughing and catch his breath, then asks, "How, Medici?" The way he says my last name is wrong, though. He pronounces it Ma-di-see.

"My name is Ma-dee-chee," I say, mad at being mocked, and no longer worried if they know my name.

The backhand to my face is swift and stinging. Ister seemed prepared to deliver the blow at the slightest provocation. It reminds me of something my father would do, and the hatred I feel for this man is fueled by the years of hatred for my father.

"How, Medici?" Ister repeats, with the same mispronunciation.

I say nothing.

Ister's gloved hand makes a fist and he's about to punch me when Zelda places a hand on his shoulder – quickly and gently.

"Please, Herr Ister," she says. "I already have your answer. The boy intended to portray himself as a messenger from Mussolini with a private message meant for Hitler's eyes only."

"So *that* is the reason for the Italian uniform. I suspected as much." Ister turns to face me again. "All these fine German boys and the Americans decide to send you. What makes you so special? What makes you think you can kill Adolf Hitler?"

I still say nothing and just glare at him.

"You may yet get your chance, Medici." Ister shrugs off Zelda's hand and delivers a punch to my jaw. It stings worse than the backhand, but in a weird way I feel fortunate. It could have been Von Becker throwing the punch.

Ister turns to the giant and says, "Take him back and bring me the next one."

Chapter 20

JESSICA TYSON
LONGBOAT KEY, FL, USA
MARCH 25, 2014

I love our house, but it's much bigger than we need. Now, when I'm the only one here, it feels cavernous. I had just made a hot cup of chamomile tea before dialing Mom and it's already cold before taking my first sip. The scent of the lemon I squeezed into the tea is still there, but barely. Have we been talking that long?

"Did both boarding passes print okay?" I ask Mom. She and Dad don't fly much. They would normally just go to the airport and wait in line to get their boarding passes. I had to talk them through getting on the airline's website and printing their passes. It's a small thing that will probably save them a half an hour tomorrow. Of course, we've been on the phone for over an hour to accomplish this. It's been a blessing – distracting me from being alone.

"Aye, we have them both now, dear." Mom's Irish accent hasn't changed much after all these years in America. Trey says it always rubs off on me when I talk with her for a while. "Thank you for your help. I wish we could have gotten there today somehow. Are you sure you're going to be okay tonight?"

"I'll be fine, Mom. I just wish Trey could be here to massage my back. This baby's getting big ... and heavy."

"Dad saw the last picture you sent. He says you look like you're at nine months already and he thinks you're going to have twins."

"Tell him thanks for calling me fat." We both laugh. "I can't imagine having one baby, Mom. The thought of twins is ... daunting."

"You'll be fine enough. Don't worry," she says and *sometimes* I think she may be right.

"It's getting late. You and Dad must be tired." Am I? Am I going to be fine? I don't let that concern enter my voice. The last thing Mom needs is a reminder of how afraid I get.

"Is there a friend you can call to come visit? Maybe stay at a hotel?" she asks.

"It's one night, Mom. I can manage."

"Aye, sweetheart. Maybe put on the TV, but nothing scary," she says.

"I will. Call me before you get on the plane. I want to know when you get to the airport safe …. Goodnight, Mom."

"Goodnight, Jessica. Get some good sleep."

"You, too, Mom. Love you."

"Love you, too."

"Bye."

"Bye, honey."

I reluctantly end the call. It was hard enough, knowing she would let me stay on the phone all night if I needed it.

As I'm about to dial Trey, I see my phone needs to charge. Damn. Maybe a little TV while it charges will do me some good. After plugging my phone into the charger in the kitchen, I waddle over to the living room couch and, sadly, hear it creak as I sit. Only then do I realize the remote is nowhere to be seen and this means I have to stand again … and the creaking this time might come from my back instead of the couch.

I dig through the cushions … nothing. Look over the side tables … nope. Check back in the kitchen, as I've been known to carry it around with me and leave it there sometimes … not this time. Where? As a last resort, I check next to the TV. It's where Trey likes to leave it. Why someone would leave the TV remote next to the TV, I don't get. The whole point is to be able to control the TV from a distance. Ah, there it is. Dumb jock. Thanks!

Maybe a little CNN tonight. Trey loves Fox News. He's like a living billboard for the show, preaching how they're fair and balanced. It's not for me, though. I can't get enough of AC360. Anderson – Mr. Adorable – Cooper. If CNN is spewing lies, as Trey says, let them be spewed by Anderson Cooper!

The couch creaks again as I sit. Dammit.

Just as I hit the power button on the remote, the TV flashes for a moment then all the power in the house goes out.

No.

Not tonight. Please, no.

This happens sometimes, I tell myself. Living on an island has some disadvantages. Traffic is one. The threat of hurricanes. Too many tourists in the winter months. Low water pressure. And, a faulty power grid. Usually, a surge will knock out our circuit breakers. Sometimes the whole island goes dark, but why tonight?

Blackness.

It takes a few seconds before I can even move. I slowly stand, keeping a hand on the arm of the couch so I keep my bearings.

My phone! Trey taught me how to use it as a flashlight.

I will my legs to take the steps, ever so carefully, in the direction of the kitchen where I left my phone to charge.

Feeling around with my hands and gingerly slide stepping, the last thing I want to do this late in a pregnancy is to take a bad fall.

My hand lingers on the soft back edge of the couch. The kitchen is the next room, and it's an open space with no obstacles.

Ouch – my toe! Someone left one of the stools around the eating area a little further out than it should have been.

Found the counter. Feeling my way around the edge to where we leave our chargers.

Ah, here it is. Only 4% of a charge, with a red battery to remind me. Still, I don't have a choice. We have a flashlight in our bedroom and there's another one in the garage. I just have to make it to one or the other … the garage … that's where the circuit breakers are. Trey showed me where, so I would know in case of an emergency. I remember telling him he had better make sure I never have to worry about it. I told him about my Grandma. Told him I don't even want to know how the circuit breakers work.

Why tonight?

Dad will be here tomorrow … I … but I can't wait that long. Not alone. Not in the dark. Not again.

Just as I'm about to turn on the flashlight app on my phone, I see a flickering light coming from outside the back of the house.

Hold on … it's moving … then a crash … someone yelling … an answer … two men.

Move, Jessica.

I hear a window break … sounds like it's from the guesthouse Max uses. That glass is hurricane proof. About the only things I can imagine that would break it would be a sledgehammer or a bullet.

Time to get out of her and find some help. Right next to the phone charger is my car key. That will have power ... and lights.

Turning my phone away from me, I use the light coming from the face of the phone. It's just enough for me to see my way, bu not so much to draw any attention from outside.

Past the dining room.

Hallway.

Past the laundry room.

The door to the garage.

What if someone's already in the garage?

I was in the kitchen – why didn't I grab a knife?

The noises were out back and the garage is in the front of the house. Holding my breath, I open the door slowly. Silently.

More blackness, but it's quiet.

Peering down the stairs that lead to the garage, I can't stop the memory of Grandma's house. She was in the basement, checking on the power, when she was electrocuted.

Then another window shatters ... loud ... from inside the house ... our bedroom. Someone broke into the main house.

Terrified ... frozen, with one foot on the first step to the garage and the other in the house.

Voices ... muffled, but definitely men.

Move!

The ER doctor in me takes over. I try to view the situation as if it's a patient in emergency.

The patient is bleeding. If I don't do something to stop it ... if I don't act ... the patient dies.

I silently step all the way into the garage and close the door behind me, holding the knob turned so it doesn't click when the door closes. I ease the knob back into position and tiptoe down the steps and toward my car.

Thinking about the extra weight I'm carrying from my pregnancy, I pray the stairs don't creak the way the couch did.

Thankfully, I make it to the bottom of the stairs without a sound.

There's a sudden pain in my stomach. I almost fall to the ground, but I reach for the hood of my car. Gritting my teeth, I bend over and have to lean on the front of the car. The pain is intense.

Breathe!

I tell the patient ... myself ... to breathe.

The pain subsides.

I stand upright again and make it around the car to the driver's door.

Opening the door, a plan emerges in my thoughts.

I can't close the car door or start the car without any noise. I can't open the garage without making noise.

At least two men have broken into our house. I can get away, but I have to time it right.

One finger on the garage door opener attached to my visor.

One hand on the car door handle.

I'll press the button and close the car door just as the garage door is opening. Then I'll quickly start the car and take off. By the time the men inside hear me, I'll be speeding away.

Ready ... and ... I press the button and slam the car door closed.

As I try to jam the car key in the ignition, I notice the garage light didn't come on.

Whenever the garage door opens, the garage light comes on.

My foot is on the brake, and the red light illuminates the garage door behind me. The red flashes every time my foot presses the pedal, like it's a warning beacon. Move!

But the garage door is not opening. It doesn't have power! How *stupid* of me.

See the patient. Stop the bleeding.

I know I only have seconds and I'm trapped in my garage.

I do my best for a pregnant woman at hopping out of my car, while holding the trunk open button on my key fob. It pops open. Something works!

With more of a rolling motion, I almost fall into the trunk, get a fingertip grip on the lid, and close it. Quickly and quietly, but enough firmness to make sure the latch catches.

Now what? I press the lock button on my key fob ... thinking ... finally ... they can't get to me in here. My baby or me.

The door from the house bursts open. Voices. They're in the garage.

"Mmmmph." Biting my tongue, the pain from my stomach is so intense I nearly scream out.

Silence! I don't think they heard me groan. However, they must have heard a noise from the garage. It will be only moments before they figure out where I am ... before they figure out a way into the trunk.

My phone.

In the trunk, they won't see any light.

I dial 911 and press Call. One ring ... two ... an answer.

The little red battery light only has a sliver of power left. I turn the volume to minimum, but still hear a mumble coming from the 911 operator.

I don't dare say a word, praying they can figure out where I am from my cell phone number on their caller ID.

The voices in the garage are speaking and close enough for me to understand them.

"Who are we looking for?" says a man's soft nasally voice.

"It's not who, but what," says the other. This is much deeper and authoritative. Both men have an accent. Hard to tell, but maybe Eastern European.

"Are the cars all here?" asks the deep voice.

"Might be useful if we knew how many they had to start with," says the other, his voice starting to sound both nasally and irritated.

My thoughts drift to Trey … then to my baby inside.

Another wave of pain.

I nearly black out from this one.

No!

The wetness running along my legs tells me – or the ER doctor part of me that's still able to function – that bleeding … that self-built metaphor for losing *my* life is no longer my only concern.

My water just broke.

Chapter 21

MAX MEDICI
Washington, DC, USA
March 25, 2014

Trey is practicing the deep breathing techniques I taught him so many years ago – the same techniques my mentor Johnny Fox taught me.

We're in Trey's hotel room with the lights out, the curtains drawn closed, and a towel shoved into the small opening at the bottom of the door to keep out both light and noise from the hallway.

First, I light the candle in the tripod and then the peace pipe Johnny gave me. The history of this particular peace pipe is nothing short of amazing. It was once the property of the most famous Shawnee in history – Chief Tecumseh, the founder of the Presidential Curse, a key player in the war of 1812, and the ancestor of Johnny Fox ... as well as Samantha Fox.

Sam, as Trey likes to call her, is Johnny's niece.

Trey brought her back. As much as I let him have it for breaking the laws of nature, at least the laws as I understood them, I'm glad he did it. Sam's death was as much my fault as anyone's. What I owe her uncle – it was his training that kept me alive in some of the most difficult situations of my life – well, I feel like we've repaid that debt somehow. Samantha was dead, but now she's alive. History can be changed. History *has* been changed. Hard to fathom, but true.

Hell ... we just saw her yesterday in Florida, and now we have a meeting with her tomorrow morning at the White House.

Trey quickly eases into a trance state, and I can hear his breathing slow to the point of nearly stopping. He chose the reddish chaise that allows him to lay nearly horizontally, yet still see the flame in the tripod. That left me the tan desk chair. It's a little too upright for this old man's back. I imagine there's a lever or button that would allow the chair to recline or rock, but I can't figure the damn thing out.

It's a good thing I brought the tripod. At least he can continue his training tonight, and maybe it will distract him from worrying about Jessica for a little while. Trey badgered me for a good hour while we had dinner tonight about the meaning of the crystal skull. He kept asking why it was so important that we had to leave Jessica alone. One night, was my answer. She's been pregnant for over eight months and she'll be alone for one night. Really, what are the odds of something going wrong on this one night?

Yet, something may be wrong, regardless of the odds.

Trey's face suddenly contorts. His jaw quivers.

He never told me much about his training when he was viewing his own history, but Trey has been updating me on his progress viewing my history with Nostradamus. I believe he's watching me in 1945 on a U-boat, learning about the crystal skull and Lady Zelda.

Trey doesn't typically move during his sessions. His breathing fluctuates often. Sometimes his facial expression shifts and I imagine he's seeing something tense when that happens. He doesn't usually speak, but he'll occasionally blurt out an incoherent comment. The sessions usually end with Trey coming back to the present slowly … like waking from a long night of deep sleep.

Tonight is different. He moans and it sounds like he's in severe pain.

Now, he's clutching his abdomen.

I move to his side just in time to catch him as he leans over. Easing him to the floor, Trey contracts into a fetal position.

He punches the air, just missing my head.

Still moaning.

I don't know if I should wake him, but I can't let him go on like this.

"She's in so much pain!" Trey blurts out, still unconscious. "She can't breathe. She's … dying."

Suddenly, his eyes open wide.

"JESSICA!" he shouts.

Chapter 22

Sir Archie
Longboat Key, FL, USA
March 25, 2014

Even though I didn't give a shit, Nicanor insisted on telling me the plan from the Oracle. It was about some crystal skull. Something the Oracle could put to use … something quite powerful.

The Oracle had a vision that I … not Nicanor … not we … that *I* would return to Pytho Island with a clear crystal skull. I guess that's why she was looking at me so intently in the council chambers.

She had seen that the skull was in Florida, on the Gulf Coast, and even was able to provide an address.

Could the grunt have found the place – even with an address? I think not. Yet, they made him the Alpha and he's been telling me what to do since we left Pytho.

Pack food for the trip, Archie … Carry my bag, Archie … Find the house, Archie … Get us a boat in Florida, Archie …

For some idiotic reason, the grunt wanted to approach the house by boat instead of by car. Wouldn't give me an explanation. So, instead of a simple car rental, we had to find a boat that was close, but not too close to our target. The fact that we're coming to the house at night in waters neither of us have ever seen didn't matter to Nicanor … stupid grunt.

The Oracle drew us a basic diagram of the house with two guesthouses. She even drew an x where she thought the crystal skull would be and she was dead on.

We had the power and phone lines cut easily enough. Found the skull easily enough. Then the grunt saw movement in the main house right when he cut the power – a momentary flash of a big screen TV that shone easily through the window and out back where we were – and he couldn't just leave well enough alone.

He insisted we break into the main house as well.

All is quiet and Nicanor is just about to give up when we hear movement from behind a door.

Cautiously, we open the door and I point my flashlight into the blackness.

It's a staircase leading down to a garage.

Then we hear a car door close, followed by the closing of a car's trunk. Nicanor rushes down the stairs and I follow.

It doesn't take us long to figure out where she is. The problem is getting her out of the trunk without a key. Nicanor does what any grunt would do … apply brute force. He finds a brick paver in the corner of the garage and smashes the driver side window. It's safety glass, so the brick leaves a nearly rectangular hole in the middle of the window. He quickly finds a button to pop the trunk and there she is. Moaning. Soaked in sweat and amniotic fluid.

Nicanor rips a strip of cloth off his shirt and ties it around her head, stuffing part of it into her mouth to gag her. With another two strips, he first reveals his six-pack abs, then ties the woman's hands and legs. Even though she's pregnant, he easily lifts her out of the trunk and onto the garage floor.

On her knees, she's glaring at me … pleading with her eyes. With her red hair matted to the side of her head, her makeup smeared down from her eyes, her tears flow silently down her face. She knows this is the end for her, perhaps resigned to her fate. I wonder what she would say if we removed the gag. Would she beg for her life? I guess it doesn't matter now.

Nicanor, in his stupid metallic voice says, "We have to kill her."

"But we already have the skull."

"She's seen our faces. You know what must be done." Nicanor really gets off on being the Alpha … stupid grunt.

"The only reason she's seen our faces is because you came looking for her. Trust me … she'll never see us again."

"Is that what Karl taught you all those years as his Beta?" he sneers. "That leaving loose ends is acceptable? You're a Knight of the First Order, Archie – time to act like one."

"Look … I don't have any problem with killing someone, but this is wrong. She's pregnant." The last time I saw my sister, she was pregnant. Her child – I have no idea if she had a girl or a boy – would be nearly Nicanor's age.

"I don't like this any more than you, but we can't leave a witness alive. There's too much at stake, and … the Oracle will know. If we don't do this right, it'll be us at the wrong end of a gun when we get back." He grabs my hand and slams his gun into it.

"Why don't *you* just do it?" I sound nasally again and it annoys me more than I dare let on.

"The council needs to know …. *I* need to know that you can be counted on."

I look at the gun in my hand. I've held and shot guns just like this before, but only in training. Never with a person at the other end.

Karl never chose me for my bravery … never chose me because I can handle a gun, or because I'm good with my fists. He chose me because of my brain. I'm just not cut out for this kind of thing.

"Look, lady," Nicanor says to her, but I think the message is meant more for me. "You made two tragic mistakes. First, you kept something in your guesthouse there that belongs in a museum. Second, you should have invested in a better security system. All we had to do was cut your phone and power lines … all too easy."

"So we just shoot her and toss her into the ocean?" I ask, thinking this is probably why he wanted to come here by boat. He was expecting some conflict … expecting to kill someone … probably hoping for it.

"Sounds like a plan to me," he says. "Now, are you going to be a Beta your whole life, or are you going to be a man? You have a lot to prove. To me. To the council. To yourself."

A lot to prove. Become an Alpha. All I have to do is kill someone, but I've never killed anyone. I've never even aimed a gun at someone. What would Karl do if he were in my situation? He wouldn't hesitate. I just want to make sure it's a quick kill … for the memory of my sister … as quick as possible. I check the safety, aim for the heart, and pull the trigger.

Chapter 23

TREY TYSON

SARASOTA, FL, USA
MARCH 26, 2014

Using my wallet and Max's connections, we were able to hire a private jet and fly directly into Sarasota, Florida – just a few miles from home. It's a smaller local airport and they normally don't allow flights after midnight, but one call from Max solved it. We approached Sarasota just after 1:30am, and found the runway lit up and waiting for us.

I called our local police before we boarded the jet, frantically begging them to send a car to my house to make sure Jessica was okay. They refused at first, saying there was no alarm signal or even a phone call from the house. They thought I was nuts for telling them that something was wrong – without any proof – and calling them from DC. Max played the Secret Service card again, and the dispatcher finally promised she would send a car.

That left over two hours of flying with no news and no way to help.

I have little confidence the dispatcher even sent a car, so don't know what to expect. Yet, as soon as we disembark, a deputy sheriff is waiting for us with an electric luggage cart at his side.

"What happened?"

As we're all climbing into the cart, he says, "We have to get you to the hospital immediately."

He takes off, and I have to hold Max's arm so he doesn't go flying off the back.

"Why? What happened? Is she okay?"

"Mr. Tyson, I'm Deputy McAlpine. I know you're worried about your wife, but the hospital will not release her status over the phone."

This is immediately aggravating. Jessica has worked in the ER for years, so I know the policy, but the policy sucks when you're on this end of it.

"Tell me what you know … why is she in the hospital?"

"Shortly after your call to our dispatcher, we received another call. This one came from a cell phone registered to your address. Whoever called never said a word. Our dispatcher just heard breathing and then the line went dead. The dispatcher sent a car to your house. The deputies found that someone smashed some of the windows and the power was out. They went to the garage to check the circuit breakers and saw a pool of blood, with a trail heading out behind the house. Following the trail, the deputies found your wife on the beach and brought her to the hospital. I don't have any status on her – other than she is in the ER."

We bolt through the empty airport, out the main entrance, and find his squad car waiting just outside the door.

While the deputy drives us from the airport to the hospital, sirens blaring, I call the hospital.

After seven rings, a woman answers the phone and mechanically says, "Memorial Hospital."

"Yes, this is Trey Tyson. My wife is in the ER. Doctor Jessica Tyson. I need to know if she's okay."

The woman on the line says, "Sorry, Mister Tyson, but we don't provide status updates over the phone. All I can tell you is …" There's a several second delay while I hear keys clicking on a computer keyboard … "Doctor Jessica Tyson has been admitted and …" More seconds and more key clicking … "she is in the emergency room currently."

"Let me speak to your supervisor." As I say this, Deputy McAlpine swerves to avoid a man crossing the road on a red light. We have the green light, so the deputy honks. The man pauses for the briefest of moments to flip us the bird.

"Sorry, Mister Tyson. It's almost 2:00am. I am the highest ranking person in hospital administration available at the moment. If you want to speak to a supervisor, please call back after 9:00am."

"Is Doctor Kinderman available?" Jessica hasn't worked midnights since we've been in Florida. I doubt any of her colleagues I know are in at this time. Still, it's worth a shot.

"No, sorry."

"Doctor Khazanchi?"

"No."

"Doctor Quartermaine?"

"Sorry, no."

"Just fucking tell me if she's alive or not!"

The deputy hears my frustration and speeds up, using a shoulder of the road to pass a car 95 mph.

"I'm sorry, Mister Tyson. Let me connect you with a nurse in ER ... maybe they can help."

After 11 rings with no answer, I'm transferred to another line that starts ringing. Eventually, I hear the same woman with the mechanical voice say, "Memorial Hospital."

"Not you again!"

"Mister Tyson?"

"Who else would it be?"

The deputy says, "Mister Tyson, we're only two minutes out from the hospital."

I look at the speedometer and now it reads 105 mph. Ending my call, I say, "Thanks Deputy."

He screeches to a halt just outside the ER door and I jump out of the car.

Is she alive? What about our baby?

Someone's exiting the ER treatment area and into the lobby, leaving the normally locked door open just long enough for me to slide in past the lobby people who would want to waste time gathering my information.

I'm racing down a hallway. Max can't keep up, but I can't wait for him.

I pass a group of small rooms with only movable curtain walls separating several patients in various states of emergency, but Jessica's not here. My heart races; emotions are going off the charts. I don't know what to expect when I see her. How hurt will she be? Is she even conscious? Will I get to speak to her again ... ever? Our baby – what about our baby?

I keep going, finally finding an area where the rooms have real walls.

Flinging open the door to the first room, I see a young boy with a new cast on his leg.

Hands shaking, I run to the second room ... an elderly woman.

Finally, in the third room, I find her!

She's pale, lying flat on her back. Her eyes are closed, mascara smeared down her to her cheeks, red cropped hair matted flat against her head. Several tubes and wires snake up her arms and into machines. I look up and her vitals are flashing on a screen. *She's breathing!* Her heart is beating! *She's alive!*

Reaching her side, I place my hand on her forehead. It's warm.

My eyes move to her abdomen. It's covered by her hospital gown and the sheet pulled over her, but it's nearly flat.

No! I want to scream.

Tears stream down my face as I bend over and kiss her.

I take her hand in mine and give it a gentle squeeze.

She squeezes it back!

Her eyes flutter, then peek open.

"Trey," she says my name mingled with a groan of pain. My heart nearly breaks at the sound of it.

"What happened?"

"Men … they broke into the house." Her eyes close and she takes a deep breath. "I hid in the car trunk. Power and phones were dead … water broke. I was having trouble breathing. Then … then they found me. I thought they were going to kill me. They talked about it. Then the gun. And … one of the men shot the other. He dragged the dead man out of the garage. Told me to stay put. I did for a long time. Then I finally got the nerve up to try to find some help. I … I thought I'd find someone on the beach, but I collapsed …. Police found me." She stops, and her breathing slows.

"Rest, Jessica. I'm here now. Everything is going to be okay."

"Have you …." Jessica's eyes flutter open again. She's exhausted, on the verge of passing out.

"Close your eyes, sweetheart. You can relax now. I'll take care of you."

"Have you seen …." Jessica's eyes are open and they move to the doorway where a doctor has just entered.

She's holding a baby … *our* baby.

"Would you like to meet your daughter?" the doctor asks.

"Our daughter?" I say. "She's okay?"

The doctor answers, "It wasn't the ideal circumstances for a birth, but, yes, they're okay."

The doctor is someone I recognize. A petite blonde with a face younger than her years and a kind smile. Jessica works at the hospital on occasion if one of her patients gets admitted here, but I haven't met many of the staff and I can't remember her name.

"Doctor?"

"Pamela," she replies. "I work with moms and babies, so I try to keep it informal. You can call me Doctor Pamela if you want."

"Doctor Pamela, thank you."

I stand and meet the doctor halfway, and she hands me my daughter … my girl. She's the most beautiful thing I've ever seen. The Italian in my family genes has shown through in her full head of dark brown hair, dark complexion, and golden brown eyes. The depths of my broken heart from the fear of losing my baby are more than matched by the sun rising in my heart now. It's a dawn that overcomes me … a warm red dawn … an amber dawn. This is true love. Pure. Unconditional.

"So beautiful," I say. Looking to Jessica, I see her tears start to well.

Trying to lift her head, Jessica asks in a weak voice, "What will we name her?"

The name flows from me without thought, "Amber Dawn."

"Aye. It's a beautiful name for a beautiful girl. Amber Dawn Tyson. Let me hold her," Jessica says, "You're going to need your hands free."

I don't pretend to understand her meaning, but I gently place our daughter on Jessica's chest, and she wraps her hands carefully around the bundled girl.

In walks Max and a nurse, each is carrying another baby.

It takes me a full second to realize what this means.

Doctor Pamela seems to revel in the moment, letting me come to grips with it, before saying, "These are your two sons."

My daughter … and my two sons … *triplets* … I certainly didn't see this coming, and start to wonder what good these abilities I've inherited from Nostradamus are if I can't see something like my own triplets coming into the world.

"You may want to sit for this," the doctor says and I don't hesitate to sit in the one chair in the room.

First, the nurse hands me one of the boys and I cradle him in my right arm.

Max then comes up and places the second boy carefully in my left arm. He's reluctant to remove his hands from the baby, until he's sure I have them both securely held, but I'm not going to let them fall – not ever.

"Congratulations," Max says with a mixture of pride and warmth, nodding in approval, and blinking rapidly to prevent his own tears from starting.

The boys look like a mix of both Jessica and me. My dark hair and large round eyes, but their skin isn't quite as dark as mine is. One boy has my blue eyes, the other has Jessica's green. The love I feel for them pours from my soul. My three babies. So small and fragile. So beautiful. So precious.

"You name the boys," I say to Jessica.

"It's my family tradition," she begins, drawing strength from holding our daughter, "to give baby boys their own first name, but a middle name from one of their grandfathers. I would name them Zachary Thomas and Jacob Maximo."

"Then that's what we'll name them." We had debated between Zachary and Jacob for a boy's name should we have one, and now we don't have to decide, other than which boy gets which name. For that, I let fate decide. "This," I nod to my son in my left arm – the blue-eyed boy Max brought to me, "is Jacob Maximo. And this is Zachary Thomas." Another stroke of fate, perhaps, is that Jessica's father's name is Thomas, the same given name as the man who raised me, Thomas Tyson.

"I'm sorry, but I have to take them back," says Doctor Pamela.

"But they just …." I don't know what to say. After the trip I took. After the vision I had. Not knowing if Jessica or the babies were even alive. "You can't take them yet."

"I'm truly sorry, Mister Tyson, but they were born three weeks early. Their lungs aren't fully developed yet. They'll have to be on oxygen and antibiotics for a few days at least."

The doctor cautiously takes Jacob from me and the nurse picks Amber up from Jessica's chest.

"Go with them," says Jessica. "See that they're safe."

I carry Zachary, and follow the doctor and nurse, leaving Max with Jessica.

We make our way to the maternity ward. There, we find a room full of plastic cradles, some with pink blankets, and others with light blue. Several have a bubble top with oxygen lines feeding into them. It's these where we take my three babies, each gently lowered into a bubble cradle.

A glass wall outside the nursery allows new parents to keep an eye on their newborns. As I'm watching my triplets, Doctor Pamela stays with me to answer the questions she knows will be coming.

"What happened?" is all I can ask at first.

"I don't know what happened before Jessica was brought here, but it was touch and go for a while. We had to do an emergency C-section. With some rest and time, they will all be fine."

"Thank you. I can't thank you enough. I should have never gone on that trip." This is more than the doctor wants to hear, but I still feel the need to say it.

She places a hand kindly on my shoulder. "They are all going to be fine. You're here now."

"When can Jessica be moved into this ward?"

"In a few hours. I want to make sure she's stable first."

I drop my head, relieved.

"I have to get back to ER. Are you okay?" she asks me.

"Yes ... never better. Please tell my father to stay with Jessica until she is transferred here. She'll want me to stay with the babies."

"Of course."

Two men broke into my house and nearly killed my family. That thought creeps into my mind as I stare, unable to blink, at my babies. From now on, I need to be more cautious ... more diligent ... allowing nothing and no one to harm my family.

Chapter 24

SIR ARCHIE
PYTHO ISLAND
MARCH 26, 2014

Coming before the inner council can be daunting enough on its own, and even more so after traveling through the night to get back to Pytho. I'm exhausted.

Our task in Florida had gone according to plan. Mostly, at least. Other than Nicanor ending up dead and having his body left floating in the Gulf of Mexico as shark bait.

I don't think I could have killed the pregnant woman, but killing Nicanor didn't seem so bad. He made it clear that murder was my way to becoming an Alpha. He planted the seed. After some quick reflection, I deduced he was right. Murder was my quickest path to becoming an Alpha, but not the way Nicanor suggested.

If I had killed the woman, I would have impressed Nicanor, sure. He may have put in a good report on me, and Athena and Zeus may have been impressed as well. I may have proven to them my worth as an Alpha, but I thought it more likely that I would have proven that I was an effective Beta with Nicanor as my Alpha. That thought – the council considering me an effective Beta to a grunt – was the thought that woke me up from my despair. There was a way out. I only needed to have the balls to take it.

"Where is Nicanor?" asks Zeus.

It's not the entire council this time. Just Zeus, Athena, and the Oracle.

"He didn't make it."

"Didn't make it … as in dead?" Athena asks with a real sense of concern in her voice.

"Yes, as in dead. He was shot while we were searching the house. The home owner wasn't exactly happy to see us break into their house."

Not the truth, certainly, but not lies. I may need to backpedal out of this story if the Oracle has some way of really seeing what happened.

"He has it," says the Oracle, staring intently at me.

"Yes," I do my best to meet her gaze. "I have it."

I open my duffle and produce the crystal skull.

"One Knight's life is a small price to pay for this," says the Oracle. "Bring it to me. I must feel its power."

"Bring it forward," Zeus commands.

I hand the crystal skull to Zeus. He wraps his hand around it and closes his eyes. After a few moments, apparently gaining nothing from the experience, Zeus shrugs and hands it over to the Oracle.

The Oracle has a very different reaction when she touches the skull. She inhales suddenly and deeply, and then releases a slow, quivering breath. A minute of silence follows where Zeus, Athena, and I all stare at her, afraid to make a noise. The Oracle's free hand clenches and unclenches, then trembles. Another deep breath and she finally opens her eyes.

"Will this do?" asks Zeus.

The Oracle's eyes flutter for a moment before she answers in a tired voice, "It's not the largest or most powerful of the crystal skulls, but it will do for now."

"I've risked my life for this and lost an Alpha. I think I've earned the right to know what purpose this skull will serve," I say.

The Oracle doesn't defer to Zeus, as I thought she might, answering, "Over the many centuries of our existence, the sisterhood of the Oracle has discovered objects of power that can enhance the abilities of psychics. They fall into categories. Organic objects such as wood help tie the psychic's abilities to nature and make psychics more aware of our surroundings. Stone acts as a shield, hiding the psychic from prying visions. Fire acts as a light to help the psychic see more clearly. Some metals act as conduits, and thus can enhance the strength and projection of one's ability. Some crystals, like this skull, act to align different frequencies, and thus can enable the joining or communication between psychics. Across great distances ... even across the great divide of *time*."

"Enough," says Zeus. "I don't like that Sir Archie has now lost two Alphas. That just doesn't happen."

"Sir Archimedes is ready," says the Oracle. "He is the one I want. I want him to lead the team."

Does she know what happened? Nicanor thought she would see if we failed. Yet, she wants me to lead some team.

"What team?" I ask.

"He's not ready," Athena says, scowling.

"He is," says the Oracle. Confident. Steadfast. Both women – the young, pretty Oracle and the seasoned, gritty Athena – glare at Zeus, awaiting his decision.

Zeus is thinking. First, he looks to Athena, and she shakes her head. Then to the Oracle.

"Sir Archimedes brought us back the crystal skull. He's proven he can do it, and he's the Knight I want," the Oracle makes her case, for some reason a supporter of mine. Does she know, though?

"The team," begins Zeus, "is a new group of Knights within the First Order. Knights of History. You are going to choose your Beta, and work directly with the Oracle. With this crystal skull, she will be able to show you our history … and, perhaps, train you to influence it. You, Sir Archie, will become an Alpha, and you and your Beta will be the inaugural Knights of History for the First Order.

I bow as gracefully as I can, hoping I've hidden my gleeful smile.

An Alpha! Finally! All I had to do was murder a stupid grunt.

Chapter 25

MAX MEDICI
SARASOTA, FL, USA
MARCH 26, 2014

Trey would never leave Jessica and the babies at the hospital alone, so it was up to me to go check out the house and figure out what had happened there. The police had the house and the beach behind it all taped off. They've started their investigation, but based on what Jessica shared with us – that the First Order was behind this – I highly doubt the police will find anything of value.

Deputy Craig McAlpine toured the house with me, and his professionalism shone through both during the crisis and after. Samantha and I discussed hiring someone in local law enforcement to work with the Secret Service to help protect Trey's family. McAlpine has a few things going for him. He's professional, yet seems to understand when he should or shouldn't break the rules. Furthermore, he lives on the island, so will be close by if needed. I passed his name on to Samantha for a thorough Secret Service background check. My instincts tell me he's the right person for the job.

Here at the hospital, Jessica's been moved to a private room on the maternity ward. Her mother and father are with her, each holding a boy while Jessica nurses Amber.

"Welcome back, Grandpa!" Jessica says, seeming rested,, and glowing with happiness.

There's not nearly as much activity here in Maternity as there was in the ER. The beeps and blips don't go off nearly as often. Every once in a while a lullaby starts playing over the sound system. One of the nurses told me they play the lullaby every time a new baby is born in the hospital. If there are people in the hallway, I usually hear at least one of them say *aaaawww* when the lullaby goes off.

Being called Grandpa reminds me of my age, but this is what family is all about. This has been missing most of my long years. Maybe it's not too late for me. I have my son in my life, and now Trey and Jessica have three beautiful babies … my grandkids.

"It is good to see you all here … together," I say. "Tom, Irene, how was your flight?"

"The flight was fine enough. We were just worried when we couldn't reach Jessica this morning," says Tom. A rotund man of average height, Tom's silver hair has thinned out quite a bit since the last time I saw him. Irene is the vision of how her daughter, Jessica, will look when she reaches that age. Tall, thin, perfect posture, bright green eyes, and fiery red hair that hints at her fiery personality. Tom and Irene O'Neill had emigrated from Ireland when Jessica was still a baby, and their Irish accents are still strong after all these years.

"We tried Trey's number when we landed and found out they were here at the hospital," says Irene, not taking her eyes off Zachary in her arms. "So, we drove straight here from the airport. Aren't they just the most beautiful of babies?"

"They are the most beautiful I've ever seen," I agree.

I need to figure out if Trey and Jessica have told her parents any of the details of the events of last night. "Trey … with the, um, construction at the house it may be best if Tom and Irene stay at a hotel for the next few days."

Tom and Irene share a quick glance, and then look to Trey.

"Uh … yes … that *would* be best," Trey agrees.

"Construction?" asks Irene.

Trey can't lie to save his life, so I take this one on, "Yes. Having triplets was a bit of a surprise. As big as their house is, it wasn't designed with this many children in mind. We're converting the den into another bedroom. With the babies stuck here at the hospital for the next few days, we thought it would be the perfect opportunity to get the project done and the dust cleared before they all come home."

Jessica looks at me quizzically at first, but then nods in understanding.

"Max, let's have a quick conversation about the project," says Trey, gesturing for me to follow him out of the room. Once out of earshot, he asks, "What was the situation at the house?"

My Secret Service training takes over and I look around to make sure no one is listening to us before answering, "Someone knew what they were after. They cut the phone line, probably first, because most security systems – like the one you have – dial out on the land line if there's a breach. Then they cut the power. My office was ransacked. Then, they must have gone after Jessica in the main house."

"A robbery?" he asks.

"Apparently. Yes."

"What did they take? Jewelry? Electronics?"

"No. That's all still there, as near as I can tell."

"Then what did they take?" Trey asks.

"Only one thing. My crystal skull. I've been in touch with Samantha … told her about the First Order and the missing skull, and that was enough for her to get involved."

"Sam? Why is she getting involved?" Trey asks, seeming strangely uncomfortable to have Samantha around the house.

"This is serious, Trey. Jessica said the men mentioned being Knights of the First Order … right before they were going to kill her. It's a miracle she's still alive. Now, the fact that the First Order went after a crystal skull tells me they know about the breach in time you created. They know someone changed the past and *now* they will try to do the same thing. We're very fortunate that they didn't find you there, too. You're the only person who can stop them. Your safety is paramount. Samantha gets it. So, it seems your humble little mansion has now fallen under the protection of the United States Secret Service."

Trey rolls his eyes before saying, "What does that mean?"

"That means you're getting some modifications put in, and the timing couldn't be better to have you all stuck in the hospital for a few days … that's about how long it will all take."

"What are they doing?" he asks.

A nurse walks by, so we both look at each other for a moment, waiting, not wanting this conversation to be overheard.

"The biggest change is that they're putting in underground bunkers between the main house and each guest house." Trey's eyes display the shock he feels as I start there, but he's not complaining … yet. "There will be a generator with enough power to keep everything running for a week, in each of the bunkers. A weapons locker in each bunker." At this, he looks more concerned than shocked … still not complaining. "Battery backup for your garage door openers, deep underground wiring for communications and internet, with cellular backup. The hurricane proof cinder block construction is great, but they're upgrading all the glass to be bulletproof. A security and surveillance system that rivals the one used at the White House – and any alerts will go to both the local sheriff and the Secret Service. Plus, we'll stock each bunker with a week's worth of preserved food and water."

"Impressive," he says.

"Oh, and I *am* having them convert one of your dens to a bedroom. That way you can explain the construction away if you want to … not to mention that you're going to need it with triplets."

Trey takes a deep breath and slowly exhales, looking down then up, contemplating. I can't tell if he thinks I went too far, maybe he's even angry with me.

"It's not too late to stop all of this," I say. "If that's what you want."

"No." He shakes his head and places a hand on my shoulder. "I don't ever want Jessica at risk again … *ever*. Not her. Not the babies. I … I can't thank you enough … I think you and Sam have covered all the bases."

"We do have a little experience in the protection business," I say – glad he's going to allow the project to move forward.

Chapter 26

TREY TYSON

LONGBOAT KEY, FL, USA
APRIL 2, 2014

Walking through my own front door has never felt like such an adventure. I haven't been here since before the break in, and haven't seen any of the changes Max and Sam arranged while we were in the hospital. It's only 7pm, but it's been a long day already. Hell, it's been a long week. My back aches from spending six nights sleeping in a chair.

Yet, for the entire ordeal ... thinking I lost Jessica ... I've never been happier. We're coming home with our three babies. They were born three weeks early, and it took a full week in the hospital in and out of their oxygen bubble cribs for their lungs to finish developing, but we're home. Jessica is safe. The babies are healthy. Tom, Irene, and Max are all here to help us figure out how to manage with newborn triplets.

The dining room is near the entrance, and I notice the large circular table is set for dinner.

"You're doing?" I ask Max.

"I'm guessing you're all tired of hospital food and take out," says Max, smiling.

"Right, you are, Max. I'm starving," Tom says, eyeing the table while pouring himself a cocktail. He's always had a voracious appetite for both food and whiskey.

"Aye," says Irene, "but let's get these little ones into their cribs first."

Jessica hasn't said a word for a while. When Max came to get us from the hospital, pulling up in our new minivan – a vehicle I swore I'd never own – she just smiled. Tears formed in her eyes, but they never came out.

I told her I had Max trade in one of our cars for the minivan – the car where she hid from the men who broke into our house. I figured it wouldn't hurt to get rid of the reminder of her witnessing a murder and nearly dying. And, with three infant car seats strapped in, I can't imagine getting around without the minivan.

Now that we're home, she's looking around, smiling … thinking.

"Jess," I say quietly, "you okay?"

She nods without answering, still smiling, embracing Zachary. I have Amber and Irene is holding Jacob.

"The babies are all sleeping, so why don't I show you the nursery," says Max, breaking the silence.

The main level of the house sits on top of two side-turned garages and an open lower level set up for entertaining and storage. It's modern code for any region susceptible to hurricanes to have the main living areas well above sea level. Two sets of winding stone steps lead from the driveway to the main entrance. Beyond the entry, a parlor has a large glass sliding door – now bulletproof – that opens to the pool and patio. To the right is a library, then a door to a hall that leads to our bedroom, the nursery, and a door that opens to stairs down to one of the garages.

Just left of the entry leads to the dining room, a butler's pantry, the kitchen and a family room. Through the butler's pantry is a hallway to a guest suite, den, laundry room, and two other doors. One leads upstairs to another guest suite and a conservatory. The other leads down to the garage – the one where Jess nearly died. Knowing what she went through, the thought makes me shudder. In the dark, in fear for her life, water broken, two men with guns, one demanding she be shot. I can only imagine the terror she felt, and it angers me to no end.

Jess nods to Max, and he takes the lead to the right and the nursery.

Walking in, I see Max has chosen a vibrant green paint. I make a mental note to compare it to the green used by Notre Dame. Jess and I have a long-standing debate about whether her alma mater, Notre Dame, or my alma mater, Michigan, has the best football team and tradition. Tom, Irene, and Jess all went to Notre Dame University, and although Max chose their green for the nursery, at least he tossed me a small bone. There are two cribs that are the exact Michigan blue, and the third is maize – assuming my somewhat colorblind eyes aren't deceiving me.

Against the wall nearest the door stand a fully stocked changing table and two dressers. In the closet hangs a variety of boy and girl baby outfits.

Max thought of everything. Every wall socket has a safety cover. Twenty stuffed animals look somehow organized on the floor, as though he brought in a professional designer just for that small task. Sitting in an open toy chest is an assortment of plush toy blocks, each bearing a letter of the alphabet. Picking one up, I notice Max has had them customized with a simple letter on one side of each block, while each of the other sides has a symbol from the periodic table with the name of the element embroidered below each symbol. Love it!

An enlarged picture from the hospital of all of us with the babies adorns one wall. I remember Max asking Doctor Pamela to take the shot, but didn't know at the time what he had planned for it. On a second wall hangs the framed sketch Jess and I had made when I asked her to marry me in Paris. I have to stifle a laugh, seeing the crossed eyes the artist drew for me. What was it he said after Jess had asked him if he could fix it? "No fix! His eyes see many things at once."

I gently place my dear sleeping Amber into the maize crib, and watch as Irene and Jess lay the boys in the blue cribs. Jess is hesitant, not wanting to let go just yet.

"It's brilliant," I whisper.

"Just so." Jess now lets the tears flow, nodding her agreement.

Max turns on a night light that also acts as a baby monitor, grabs one of the receivers, and gestures for us all to follow him.

Once outside the room, with the door closed, he turns to face us and puts his index finger to his mouth in a signal for us all to be quiet. He turns the volume up on the receiver and holds it up so we can hear.

"Breathing," whispers Jess with a huge smile. "I can hear them breathing."

Max nods, also smiling, hands the receiver to Jess, and heads down the hall.

We follow him, and he takes us to the stairs that lead down to the garage.

Once down the stairs, we all seem to simultaneously remember that we no longer need to be quiet.

"The nursery, Max," says Jess, no longer whispering. "It's beautiful."

"Aye, Max," says Irene. "Did you hire an interior decorator?"

"No," he shakes his head. "I've always wanted to do this kind of thing for my family. It was especially fun after Trey told me not to worry about a budget. The nursery is just the beginning, though."

Max stands next to a line of tall storage cabinets along our garage wall. "We'll need to head down some more stairs to see the other changes," he says.

"In here?" I ask. I knew the construction crew was going to put in a couple of bunkers. I guess I didn't realize that they would hide the entrances. Makes sense, though. Max and I initially were going to keep the bunkers a secret from Jessica's parents. Then we talked it through and realized they will be watching the babies on their own at some point. It only makes sense that Tom and Irene know about all of the security features in the house. Max sold it as a way to make sure Jessica never has to be alone in the dark again.

Max opens the cabinet doors where I once had stored two sets of golf clubs, my shoes, and about a year's worth of my favorite golf balls. The inside is empty now, save for a door handle protruding from the back wall. He steps into the cabinet, turns the handle, and pushes inward to open a door – a door that had never been there before.

"A secret passage?" asks Jessica.

"The exact same setup is in the other garage as well," says Max.

"One question," I say.

"Yes?"

"Where's my golf gear?"

"Don't worry, Trey. I told Sam how important that was to you. She had the crew add some more storage in the other garage." Max winks, heading into the passage.

I let the others follow Max before me. As I pass through the cabinet, I see it leads to a staircase just below the stairs that head down from the house. At the bottom, a steel door leads to steel grated stairs that wind tightly around a pole and through a large concrete pipe. At the bottom of the winding steps is another steel door. This one has a keypad lock on it.

"What's the code," I ask?

"2828," says Max.

Jess looks up to me, "Your football number, again?"

I was able to keep 28 as my jersey number throughout my high school, college, and professional career. We've used 2828 for almost every code or PIN that requires four digits.

Smiling, I punch in the code, and the locking mechanism audibly opens. I swing open the door to see a bunker. It's a 25-foot long concrete pipe with at least a 15-foot diameter. Six suspended bunks hang high in the pipe, with just enough headroom below to walk through upright. The rest of the bunker is a mini kitchen area, tiny toilet and sink, a little steel desk with a laptop computer, and a drop down table with six folding chairs. The far end of the bunker has a mirror image of the steel door we just walked through.

"Impressive," I say. "What's through the other door?"

"It leads to another spiral staircase that heads up to the garage below my guest house," says Max. "Both of these doors and the two doors in the other bunker have the same access code. The computers have full Internet access, and can monitor the security system and cameras. Through that phone, you have high priority communications channels to both the Secret Service and local authorities. In those cabinets, we've stored enough food and water to last a week for eight people. There's a generator behind that cabinet powerful enough to run everything in the bunker and the main house. It's powered by natural gas and can run indefinitely."

"The whole house?" Jessica asks.

"The whole house," Max confirms. "It will kick in the instant the main power goes off – automatically."

There seems to be a cloud that lifts off Jessica's expression. Her smile is on the edge of exuberant. "No more darkness."

I put my arm around her and say, "No more darkness, my love."

Jess puts the baby monitor to her ear, and says, "I can still hear them breathing."

"The monitor has been upgraded with some Secret Service components. It'll work for 20 miles – underwater, underground, you name it. It's a military frequency with the latest encryption." Max is beaming; he loves talking about his high tech Secret Service toys.

"Amazing," I say. "It seems like you covered everything."

"With Samantha's help," Max says. "She lined up a crew that is dedicated to … government projects."

"It's all wonderful enough, Max," says Jessica. "I know I'll sleep better at night. But, can we head back up now? I don't like being this far from the babies."

Once we made it back upstairs and Jessica had a chance to check on the babies, Max took Jessica's parents on a tour of the other bunker. Jess led me into our bedroom and closed the door.

"Thank you." After putting her arms around me, the kiss she gives me is deep and lasting.

"For what?" I ask after catching my breath. "Max did all the work."

"Max told me about your vision while you were in DC. I don't think the babies and I would have survived if you hadn't come back when you did. If you hadn't gotten through to the sheriff."

"I'm just glad you're all safe."

"Aye – all of us! I never expected triplets. You might have warned me."

"I never knew," I say. "The babies have the same ability I have, apparently. Something passed down from Katarina. Visionaries and psychics can't sense them … not even me."

"There are going to be a lot of changes around here."

"With triplets? *Nah*, I'm sure it'll be just like before," I joke.

Jess takes a deep breath, her green eyes glimmering brighter than ever. "I've decided to sell my practice and stay home."

I raise my eyebrows, not sure what to say to this.

"I had time enough to think while we were in the hospital," she continues. "I get it now. There's nothing more important than your training … nothing more important than what you can do to protect us and to protect everyone else. You haven't trained in over a week, so get back to it tonight. I'm staying home to raise our babies and to support you."

"Really?"

"Really. I'm going to support you any way I can."

"*Any* way?" I wink.

"Aye. Soon enough, my dear man, soon enough."

I hug her gently and she pulls me in tightly, less afraid of hurting herself than I am of hurting her.

"Did you think when I asked you to marry me, that we'd be in this position by now?"

"You mean," she says, "with three babies and retired at the age of 40?"

"You're 40. I'll be 50 soon."

"Aye, an *old* dumb jock … one that I love more than anything."

"I love you, too."

Chapter 27

MAX MEDICI

EUROPE
APRIL 16, 1945

"I think we st … st … I think we st … " I've been speaking exclusively in English since the Germans first showed up at our camp back in Princeton, not wanting to let on that I speak German. Now, I stick with English because I don't want to betray my private conversation with Zelda.

"Relax, Max," says Ian. "We can tell that we stopped."

We've been traveling under water for at least a couple of days, and the fresh air now circulating through the U-boat is a huge relief. Between the hideous scent permeating throughout the U-boat and lousy food, Bernie has been sick to his stomach since we boarded. He's been heaving up what little food they've given us, and has probably lost a good ten pounds on the voyage.

We haven't seen Kirk and Dieter the last few days, and don't know if they're dead or alive. Every few hours a German crewman checks on us, but they say nothing. Ian asked once for news about Kirk and Dieter, but the crewman punched him on the side of the head, never saying a word.

"Do you think they're going to kill us?" asks Bernie.

"They killed Erik," says Ian. "If they wanted us dead, I think they would have done it already."

"Where do you think we are?" asks Bernie. Now that we've stopped, he seems a little better.

"We're in Italy," I say. "On the Adriatic, somewhere in the northern part of the country."

"How in hell's name do you know that?" It's Kirk. Somehow, he and a German crewman made it down the hall without us hearing them. Kirk is wearing his German uniform, and it fits him a little too well.

The truth of the matter is that there's no way we'd be traveling below water that long unless we were in waters the Germans consider dangerous. I initially thought we would head to northern Germany, but the latest war reports in Princeton showed that while the Germans were losing ground quickly from both the east and west, they still controlled the waters to the north. The fact that we stayed submerged for so long tells me we took a different route.

Is Kirk the traitor? He looks much too comfortable in that German uniform, even proud. I don't intend to answer his question truthfully, but he's just glaring at me.

"It was something Iss … Iss … Ister mentioned the last time we were chatting."

Kirk and the crewman exchange awkward glances.

"What's with the uniform, Kirk? Did you switch sides?" Ian has never been one to let go of an unanswered question.

"Switch sides?" Kirk says, smirking. "I was born German. So were you, Dieter, and Bernie. Max is the only one who wasn't … the only one who doesn't fit in. He's so st, st, stupid that he'll never fit in."

The crewman aims a gun at us while Kirk unlocks the handcuffs on Bernie and Ian. Then, reluctantly, he unlocks mine as well.

Kirk leads us through the U-boat, not speaking. The crewman follows, never lowering his gun. I'm beginning to feel uneasy. Is Kirk with us still? He's not carrying a gun, but he's also not in handcuffs.

We climb the metal ladder in an orderly line following Kirk up through the conning tower. Bernie and Ian climb outside first, each with an audible gasp. What do they see that's so shocking?

I quickly discover that it's not what they see, but the blinding light of the sun. So long in the dim, sunless light and our eyes adjusted to the darkness. Kirk must have been outside already, because he seems unaffected. The three of us are like three blind mice, not wanting to take a step for fear of falling.

Someone grabs my arm.

"Hold on," I say.

"I am holding on." It's Bernie.

"Come on, already." Kirk's voice is below us. Apparently, his vision is fine.

For some reason, searching for his voice with my eyes allows them to adjust more quickly. Colors other than blinding white start to come into view. Then shapes. Then the landscape.

We're at a group of piers customized for U-boats. Next to Ister's U-797, is a twin U-boat to the one we're on, U-796 painted on the side. Both have double hulls and look more than twice as large as their standard U-boats. Three standard U-boats dock to the left of U-797. The two massive vessels to the right of U-796 appear capable of carrying quite a bit of cargo, with twin cylindrical hulls and a huge central storage bay. Each has a built-in loader extending well above the deck. Yet, the whole vessel looks as though it could close up and be submersible. The designations, U-891 and U-892, give away their capability – they do travel underwater. It's hard to imagine they would stay upright with the huge cargo bay, but the twin hulls must be the part of the design that allows them to function. As far as I know, we don't have anything to compare to these in our submarine fleet.

"How do you think we made it through the Straits of Gibraltar?" Ian whispers to me.

It's a damn good question. The intelligence we had in the US was that the British held Gibraltar and the narrow waterway between Spain in Europe and Morocco in Africa. They would naturally be on the lookout for U-boats and cover the waterway in sonar.

"Something odd about all of these U-boats, now that I can see them in daylight, is that they're all black. Not a shiny metallic shell, but each seems coated with a dull rubbery substance. That may be how we went unnoticed by Allied sonar. Perhaps they absorb the sonar waves."

Ian raises an eyebrow and nods.

The crewman waves his gun at us, yelling for us to move, and we make our way down some steps that extend from the harbor.

Even after we're on firm ground, my whole body feels like the Earth is rocking to the rhythmic beat of waves. If we get out of this …. If I ever get back to the States, I will NOT be joining the Navy. This much, I know.

They don't give us any time to gain our bearings as Kirk puts handcuffs on each of us again. At least he leaves our arms in front of our bodies. This makes us more of a threat should any of us decide to try to escape. I'm left wondering if that's what Kirk wants, or is it simply that he knows how much our arms are aching from all the time chained up to the pipe?

The harbor is alive with activity as Kirk and the crewman march us a few hundred feet away from the sea. German crewmen are spilling out of the U-boats and going in every direction. Some head to the two cargo vessels. Some to a group of buildings to our north. Trucks come and go, some bringing crewmen, and others bringing cargo.

The wind is calm and the sky is clear. The latest reports we heard in Princeton were that the Allies were forcing the Germans to retreat back deeper into their own borders. America and the British had successfully stormed Normandy, liberated France, and had even fought their way into the northwest of Germany. The British were constantly launching bombing raids from the north. The Russians were approaching from the east. The Allies had long ago taken Sicily and southern Italy. Yet, this part of northern Italy seems completely unscathed by the war. The buildings are intact. There's a small airfield to the northeast that's functioning. Farmland borders the west, and it looks green and lush.

Approaching a junction where a road from the northwest ends at another road going east and west, my eyesight has adjusted just well enough to make out Dieter standing with two German soldiers. The soldiers have different uniforms from the crewmen coming and going from the U-boats. Dieter, wearing his German uniform, gives me a barely perceptible nod, and I don't think anyone else notices.

There are signs in Italian, and one gives away our specific location … Monfalcone, Italy. On the Adriatic, as I suspected.

The road from the northwest cuts between the airfield and farmland. Two large transport trucks rumble toward us from the east. They stop next to us.

Behind, I hear people coming our way. With my eyes still not fully functioning, and the evening sun behind them to the southwest, all I can see are their silhouettes. However, it's not difficult to figure out who they are. On the left, walk petite Zelda and the hulking figure that can only be Ulrich Von Becker, with three average sized men behind them. In the middle, walking with the authoritative gait of someone who thinks he owns the entire world, is Hagan Ister. To his right, as they come closer, I can make out Rolf Barbie and three more crewmen with submachine guns.

I haven't seen Ister in days, but his questioning of the others continued sporadically during our voyage. Not knowing if they were monitoring us secretly, Ian, Bernie, and I never talked about Ister's questioning or our answers. It was something Smith had taught us – just in case we were ever captured in Germany.

None of us ever guessed we'd be captured in New Jersey.

When Ister's group reaches ours, I ask, "Where are you taking us?"

Ister had been about to speak. He pauses for a moment, perhaps dismayed that I had cut him off. Looking directly at Kirk, he tilts his head toward me.

Kirk hesitates for just the briefest of moments. Then, his backhand to the side of my head is firm, not meant to knock me down so much as a reminder that I'm not the one who should be asking any questions. The fact that it was Kirk who delivered the blow instead of Von Becker or Barbie isn't lost on any of us, as both Ian and Bernie look more stunned than I feel.

A forklift carrying a crate from the U-boat turns toward us just as one of the soldiers opens the back of the second truck. Each truck has a driver and passenger up front, and a large enclosed back that seems fit for transporting troops or cargo. The forklift loads the crate in the second truck and the two soldiers push it to one side.

Out of the back of the first truck, emerge two men, both in military uniforms. One appears to be a high-ranking officer and the other carries a large, yet portable radio. Only when he sees Ister does the officer perk up.

"Heil Hitler," he says as he energetically performs the familiar German salute with an open hand facing out.

Ister's salute is less energetic, as if he's done it too often. His arm points out, barely making it to parallel with the ground, and he lets it drop almost instantly.

"Reports, Major Schmidt" Ister commands, in German.

Schmidt looks at me and asks, "In front of the prisoner?"

"Yes ... reports," Ister's ire rises, along with the pitch of his voice.

The major takes a deep breath and begins, "Let me start with the good news. The American president, Roosevelt, has died."

President Roosevelt is dead. I immediately feel sick to my stomach. I just saw the man before we left ... only two weeks ago.

A smile forms on Ister's face, but his voice hints at anger when he asks, "Why wasn't I informed while in transit?"

"He died just two days ago. You and your U-boat have been under radio silence the entire time since his death."

"How?" Ister is almost yelling. "How did he die?"

"Apparently of natural causes .... The reports are that he was in the middle of having his portrait done and he was with his *mistress*. Harry Truman is now their president." The major raises his eyebrows, probably concerned with how Ister will react to this news.

Ister places his hand on the shoulder of one his men … the one wearing an officer's uniform with a gold medical rod pinned to his collar.

"Dr. Brandt … I have outlasted the crippled fool," Ister says.

"You have a long and fulfilling life in front of you still," the doctor reassures him.

Ister addresses the major again, "What of our war efforts?"

"On the east, the Russians broke through our outer defenses. They have five times the men we have, five times more tanks, and seventeen times more planes. The secondary lines are holding, for now, at the Oder and Neisse rivers, but all three of our eastern army groups are insisting that they need reinforcements to hold their positions."

Ister nods, but commits nothing.

Major Schmidt continues, "On the west, our lines had reformed at the Rhine. The Americans were taking their time, seeming content to let the Russians –"

"I don't want your speculation," Ister hisses. "Just the reports."

"Yes … of course. Then, two weeks ago, the Americans began a new offensive, pushing suddenly past the Rhine and all the way to the Elbe and Hamburg. They did not even pause at the Elbe to catch their breath, and have flooded ever deeper into Germany. The Fuhrer has some … *speculation* … as to why the Americans have become so aggressive."

Seems like the major is referring to the rocket launch on New York, throwing a little blame at Ister, and dropping his connection to Hitler at the same time.

"The north, you say?" Ister ignores Schmidt's reference to Hitler. "We don't need to stop the Americans … just to slow them down."

"Just slow them down?" The major can't hide his incredulity. "At this pace, they will reach Berlin in two weeks. The Fuhrer is sending half of the reserves to help hold our western borders."

"He what?" Now it's Ister's turn to be incredulous. "We shall see about that."

The major seems undaunted by the affront to Hitler and continues, "To the south, the Allies still hold Sicily and southern Italy. Half the Italians have switched sides, but Field Marshall Kesserling has multiple lines of our defense still intact. We have not been able to retake southern Italy, but the front lines are stable."

This is the first report that doesn't seem to be terrible news for Germany and for some reason it has Ister scowling. Taking suddenly heavy breaths, Ister dips his head and his shoulders curl forward. His left hand starts to shake. "Doctor Brandt!" he yells, on the verge of falling over.

"Take it easy, Herr Ister, you are long overdue for your medicine," says the doctor, who points to Rolf and Von Becker. "Hold him up."

Ister's two guards support him while the doctor retrieves a prepared syringe from his medical bag, and injects Ister with it. This buoys Ister quickly, and he nods to his guards to release him.

Directing his attention back to Major Schmidt, Ister says, "The Allies must not be allowed to establish any air bases in northern Italy. Not now. Get a message to the Fuhrer to send Kesserling any reinforcements he requests."

The major shrugs, shaking his head, before arguing, "But, he has not requested any reinforcements. There is no immediate threat to our southern border."

Ister glares at Schmidt a full minute before facing the radioman. "You," he says. "What is your name?"

The radioman glances to the major, but quickly returns his focus to Ister. "Lutz," he replies with a small crack in his voice.

"You operate the radio?"

Lutz moves his mouth, but nothing comes out at first. Ister is this terrifying to his own people? Eventually, Lutz mutters, "Yes."

"And," Ister continues, "you are capable of both coding and decoding the messages?"

Again, Lutz squeaks out a "Yes."

Ister pulls the revolver from his holster and unceremoniously shoots Major Schmidt in the chest. The major's face reveals a stream of emotions from shock, to hurt feelings, to realizing his mortality. He drops to his knees, then slumps to the ground.

Lutz reaches for his fallen commander, but backs off quickly and returns his attention to Ister.

Ister starts bellowing orders to Lutz, completely ignoring Schmidt's dying whimpers. "Send a coded message to the Fuhrer. Make sure he understands it is from me. I want him to send the reserves he was going to send north to the south instead. Have them assemble at Nuremberg to assist Kesserling. We must hold the south."

Lutz just stares at Ister for a moment, then mumbles, "Herr Ister?"

"What is it, Lutz?" Ister asks, impatiently.

"The major did not mention it, but the Americans have an army to the west of Nuremberg now. They are poised to attack the city."

Ister's face scrunches, yet eyes bulge. "Then, we must go there now!"

Lutz nods solemnly. "Yes, Herr Ister."

Ister points to the crewman next to Kirk and says, "You will take the crates and these fine young German men to Heisenberg. See if he can put them to good use."

Heisenberg … Werner Heisenberg is one of the names Professor Einstein mentioned to me. He's the man most responsible for development of the German atomic bomb, and he's about to get all of Einstein's notes and drawings.

The crewman looks at Kirk for a moment, then says, "Come," before boarding the second truck.

"In the truck," says Kirk, gesturing for the rest of us to board the second truck. He's speaking in English, which is so damn confusing. If he were truly with the Germans, wouldn't he have told them that we all speak fluent German? Or maybe he truly is the traitor, but wants us to think he isn't?

I'm following in line with Dieter, Kirk, Ian, and Bernie when Ister points at me. "No. The other truck for you, Medici."

I pause as the others climb in the second truck. Singled out. Why? Are they going to kill me … now?

A soldier opens the back of the first truck. Maybe they don't intend to kill me – at least not yet.

Climbing into the first truck as best I can with the handcuffs binding my wrists together, Von Becker follows right behind me, with Ister, Lutz, Barbie, Zelda, and Dr. Brandt. Ister quickly sits, choosing the front right corner of the wooden bench bolted to the floor in front of the three walls of the truck bed. Von Becker sits to Ister's right and Zelda to his left. Lutz takes a seat on the left side bench, seeming more comfortable with a little distance between him and Ister. Then, the soldier from the outside shuts the rear truck door.

The doctor and Barbie sit next to Lutz, and Von Becker pulls me down into a sitting position next to him, just as the truck surges forward. We turn to the northeast and I can hear the second truck following behind us. We eventually turn into a small airport. We board one plane and everyone from the second truck boards another.

"Take us to Nuremberg," Ister commands the pilot.

Once in the air, Ister orders Rolf to remove my handcuffs, then he hands me the bag Professor Einstein had made for me. It still has the Italian flag embroidered on it and inside are two Italian military uniforms – both my size – and papers with a falsified message from Italian dictator Mussolini to German dictator Hitler.

"You, Medici," Ister turns his attention to me, pointing to the bag, "will change into your uniform."

I wonder why, but don't ask. They leave the handcuffs off, and let me keep the bag with the spare uniform and papers.

Heading over the Alps, the roads in Italy and southern Germany looked unscathed, but it was a different view as we approached Nuremberg. I could see the metal carcasses of destroyed German tanks and transports with several smoldering craters from recent bombings along the road from Munich to Nuremberg. The British bombers have obviously stretched their range deep into Germany. Another functional transport awaited our arrival at the Nuremberg airport, and the driver of our truck deftly swerves to avoid the potholes and stones most of the time, but we occasionally take a dip or bounce so suddenly that we are all jarred against the walls of the truck and each other. After a long U-boat journey, followed by the flight into Germany, everyone looks tired and disheveled. Only Von Becker seems unaffected.

We eventually stop and Barbie opens the back door. We step out of the truck and it takes a minute to adjust to the bright sunlight, but nothing compared to when I exited the U-boat. The driver tells Ister that we've reached our destination. I could tell from the hazardous drive from the airport that the city must have undergone British bombing raids, but that doesn't lessen the surprise at the amount of damage to the buildings and streets of Nuremberg.

This road looks centuries old and then the sign I read behind the truck tells me that it is. Blacksmith's Alley in Nuremberg can only mean one thing. I lean around the side of the truck and see Nuremberg Castle, with its spires still standing tall above us. The castle has appeared in pictures in the newspapers. It's what many consider the historic hub of leadership for all of Europe. It's also where Adolf Hitler so proudly and prominently displayed the German military forces in full dress uniform and formation to the rest of the world at the start of the war. That was long ago and the tides of war have turned dramatically against the Germans since then. The Allies will win this war, no matter what happens to me. At least so long as the Germans don't finish the atomic bomb.

I don't have any illusions about surviving the war, not in this situation. Not while I'm in Ister's grasp. Yet, I have to stop them. I can't let them finish the bomb. It's really all I have left. *Oh*, I remind myself, besides stopping the Germans from creating an atomic bomb, I have to find Adolf Hitler, kill him, find the traitor, and maybe kill him, too. These thoughts make me understand why Ister and Von Becker laughed at me. I may not be handcuffed, but Germans surround me. Von Becker, on his own, would be more than enough to stop me. How, in God's name am I supposed to accomplish any part of my mission? The situation is ludicrous. I am ludicrous. A laugh escapes me and I can't stop it.

A hand grabs my shoulder and turns me around.

"You think this is humorous? The destruction of a great German city amuses you?" asks Rolf Barbie. Glaring at me, he quickly pulls out his favorite whipping rod. Instead of caning me with it though, he uses it more like a staff, and jams it into my abdomen.

The air evacuates my lungs in a long, painful groan. My legs buckle, and I try to curl up as I crash to the stone cobbled road. I'm able to break my fall with my arms only because my hands are no longer cuffed. I silently thank Ister for that small favor.

I'm in no hurry to try to stand again, but a large hand – Von Becker's – grabs the back of my neck and effortlessly hauls me to my feet.

The sound of loud footsteps coming in our direction is the only thing that prevents Rolf from striking me again.

I'm still gasping, trying to refill my lungs, when the rest of our group all turn to face a short, stout man with dark, thinning hair who appears to be in his early sixties.

"Welcome, Herr Ister. Heil Hitler!" he says, extending his hand in the typical salute to their Fuhrer. He shoots a quick glance in my direction, but seems unfazed to see Ister with me in my Italian uniform. Of course, with this group of misfits, I probably don't stand out a bit.

"Mayor Liebel," Ister replies. "Nuremberg is in rubbles."

"Yes," the mayor, gloomy, head down, says, "The British pilots no longer have much opposition in the air and now the Americans are flying over from French bases. We try to shoot them down from the ground," he shrugs, "but with little success. The reports I get say –"

"Don't worry about the reports," Ister interrupts him. "We have what we need to complete the wonder weapons."

Mayor Liebel instantly perks up. "The wonder weapons … they are ready?"

"They will be soon," says Ister. "You must hold the city together. Fight to the last man. We will still win this war."

Ister believes what he is saying and the mayor believes him, too. Even with one of their most prized cities hit so hard ... even with American, British, and Russian armies in Germany and closing in on Berlin ... they still believe they can win. Finishing the atomic bomb is the *only* way that can happen. One bomb could wipe out an entire army. Can Einstein's notes really be enough for them – really provide the last piece of the puzzle?

"You are here for the artifacts?" asks Mayor Liebel.

"Yes," says Ister, "we need to get into the bunker."

The mayor leads us down the alley to a large padlocked garage door guarded by two men wearing black SS uniforms. The guards let the mayor proceed without complaint. Once the garage door is unlocked and open, we see double steel doors that require a different key on the mayor's keychain. Above the steel doors is a sign that reads, "Antiques New and Old."

The bunker opens to a loading dock, from which a long arched tunnel stretches slowly downward and under a building near the castle. At the end of the tunnel, we find several large chambers, which I estimate are actually positioned under the castle. The air down here is clean and cool, with the yeasty aroma of beer. This may have served as the castle's brewery, or at least as storage for beer.

Once the lights are on, we see a small room that seems to serve as quarters for the two guards stationed outside currently. The room is sparse, with only a picture of Adolf Hitler on the wall. A corridor leads past a room housing ventilation equipment and then we come to five locked steel vaults. The first four vault doors on the side of the corridor are large and the fifth, at the farthest end from the bunker entrance, is even larger. The mayor enters a numeric code into a keypad to open the foot thick vault door, which reveals an inner door of steel bars that requires two more keys from the mayor's keychain.

Whatever they have in this vault must be damn important.

Inside, lined up against one wall, are 20 large crates. Each crate has markings signifying where the crate originated and a number.

Mayor Liebel locates an inventory list and starts reading, "Are you looking for the true artifacts, or the replicas?"

"Have you seen the American army outside your city?" asks Ister, rhetorically. "The real ones."

"There are four crates that contain sets of the artifacts," says the mayor. "One –"

A sudden commotion from behind us interrupts him. Footsteps of at least a half dozen people head in our direction. When they arrive at the vault door, it turns out to be thirteen men, all wearing black SS uniforms. These, we learned in our training back in Princeton, are the special services troops formed for Hitler's protection. They also act as the Nazi secret police and are considered the most brutal of all the German forces. These are the men Smith told us to avoid at any cost.

"Heinrich Himmler," says Ister, only a little surprised to see the leader of the SS.

"Hagan Ister," replies Himmler. He's an average sized man, probably in his forties, with thin hair and a round face. His distinctive mustache is almost as silly as Hitler's. "What business does the Thule Society have in Nuremberg?"

"I am on a mission directly from the Fuhrer," says Ister. "What are *you* doing here?"

"Mayor Liebel," Himmler turns his attention to the mayor, "I hope you have not offered Herr Ister the Holy Roman Relics? My men and I are here to collect them."

"Herr Himmler," begins the mayor. "As I was just about to explain to Herr Ister … it was a mere six months ago when the Fuhrer last visited Nuremberg. He foresaw this day, and said that either of you two men might come to collect the relics, although I had not as yet met or even heard of Herr Ister."

The mayor bows slightly to Ister, and then continues, "He instructed me to keep the true relics and the three sets of replicas each in their original shipping crate – the four crates at the end." Mayor Liebel retrieves a crowbar, and hands it to Von Becker. "Would you mind opening the four crates?"

Von Becker nods and starts to do so.

"Within each of the crates are multiple artifacts, to be sure. But each also contains the Holy Roman crown, sword, and coronation cloak," says the mayor. "The originals were made for the first Holy Roman Emperor – Charlemagne – and they have been used for the coronation of every Holy Roman Emperor since. Oh, and another item in the set is the Holy Lance."

Dr. Brandt steps forward, "The Holy Lance? Are you talking about the Spear of Destiny?"

"One and the same," replies the mayor. "It is known also as the Longinus Lance. Used by a Roman legionnaire by the name of Longinus to finally put an end to the crucifixion of Jesus Christ. It is called the Spear of Destiny because –"

Ister cuts him off, "Because no man can be killed while carrying the spear."

The mayor nods, "It is stained with the last living blood of Christ and has mystical powers to protect the person who carries it. The story goes that Longinus was nearly blind … Legionnaires, if they were injured or too old for battle, were sometimes relegated to the less challenging duty of making sure anyone who had been on the cross for more than a day was actually dead. Most who were crucified died in hours, but some lingered on. A legionnaire, such as Longinus, would be charged to spear them in their sides to make sure they died.

When Longinus speared the side of Jesus, the Christ blood spilled over the spearhead, and splashed into the eyes of Longinus. The healing powers of the blood completely restored his vision, and converted Longinus into one of the staunchest believers in that Jesus Christ was in fact the son of God. He carried his spear on a lifelong quest to spread the word of God … the word of Christianity."

"Christianity," Himmler spits, "is nothing more than an evolutionary step for the Jews."

"Come now, Himmler," says Ister, "our Italian friend here is almost certainly a Christian. So many of them are."

"So what?" says Himmler. "I'm sure I have room at one of my concentration camps for a Christian." Heinrich Himmler, we learned early on at Project Spear, is not only the head of the SS, but the person in charge of the German concentration camps. He may be the one person whose evil actually rivals that of Adolf Hitler. Himmler glances my way, then back to Ister. "What is he doing with you, anyway?"

"He has a personal message from Mussolini to the Fuhrer," replies Ister. "We are escorting him. But, first, we are here to secure the Holy Roman Relics."

"*I* am here to secure the relics," Himmler insists. His men instinctively raise their guns as though he had commanded them to do so. Both Von Becker and Rolf raise their guns, as well.

"No!" yells the mayor. "The Fuhrer was very clear on this matter. You are each free to take with you *one* set of the Holy Roman Relics. It is his intention to keep the originals secure and to send the Allies looking for the replicas should they take the city. I will keep one set of replicas here and send another set away, leaving a trail the Allies can follow. One of you must choose the real relics and keep them secure.

The other of you is destined to be another decoy for the Allies. Herr Ister was here first, so he shall choose the set he wants first."

Himmler lifts his gun and shakes it at the mayor. "Those are my men guarding this bunker. They are *my* SS, so I was here first. I will accept taking just one set, but it will be the set I choose first."

Ister's anger rises, but looking around, he sees that he is greatly outgunned should this turn into a real fight. "Fine," he finally hisses, "choose your set and be on your way. The Americans will be here soon."

Himmler stops waving his gun and aims it at the mayor's face, "Which crate contains the real relics."

The mayor is amazingly calm. "The Fuhrer was certain one or both of you might try to coerce me into revealing that. You can shoot me if you must, but I cannot tell you which set is real, because even I don't know which set is real. They are truly identical replicas."

Himmler's face is pale, but a slight shade of red emerges, reminding me of Sergeant Smith. He seethes, "No man can be considered the legitimate leader of the empire unless he has the Holy Roman Relics. The Spear of Destiny is the spear that delivered the deathblow to Christ. It killed the embodiment of all of Christianity. For that reason alone, it should be regarded among the most cherished of relics! Beyond that – legend has it that he who holds the spear cannot be defeated … he is invincible. *You* were entrusted with the only keys to this bunker. The relics are in one of these four crates and you don't know which one?"

"That is correct," replies the mayor, a slight tremor appears in his voice.

Himmler follows with, "The outside of each box tells where it came from. Is that accurate?"

"Yes," says the mayor. "As you can see. The crates come from Vienna, Paris, Florence, and Vatican City."

Himmler smiles. "Then the choice is easy. Any true German knows that the real relics resided here in Nuremberg for centuries. When Napoleon went on his quest to conquer Europe and then the world, the real relics were quietly sent to Vienna for safekeeping. It was Vienna where Adolf Hitler, as a young boy, first saw them and vowed to bring them back to Nuremberg. Men … take the crate from Vienna."

Himmler turns to Ister as four of his men lift the crate onto a cart, and Ister shows no sign that he is either happy or upset with the choice.

"Until the next time we meet, Herr Ister," says Himmler, trying to sound sincere.

Ister responds, "I do not think there will be an occasion where we meet again."

"I suspect you are right," says Himmler as he follows his men back to the entrance of the bunker.

Ister waits to be certain Himmler and his men are out of range to hear him and then says, "That fool had part of the story right. In the 8th Century, Pope Leo III crowned Charlemagne as the first Holy Roman Emperor. To legitimize Charlemagne, he gave him the Spear of Destiny to carry into battle. Hold the spear and you are invincible, the pope told him. Drop it and you are not. Charlemagne won 47 straight battles carrying the spear, never getting so much as a scratch. Then, while hunting, it slipped from his hands and dropped to the ground. Charlemagne died shortly after that.

"Himmler was right that the relics resided here in Nuremberg for centuries. Before Napoleon came looking for them, they were sent to Vienna. At least the most convincing *replicas* were sent to Vienna." He smiles his most sinister smile, and even coughs out a twisted laugh. "The replicas were sent to Vienna; with just enough of a trail of evidence for Napoleon to chase after them should he have found the first false clue."

Ister looks over to Lady Zelda. "The real relics were sent somewhere else. Lady Zelda ... you are confident this Medici has some of your abilities?"

Zelda's face takes on a look of fear for just an instant before she can regain her composure. "Some ability, yes, but I don't know to what extent. I don't know if he will be able to identify the real relics."

"Now then," says Ister, turning his gaze to me, "let us find out .... You Americans like to make deals, right? Here is your deal, Medici. If you can identify the real relics, you will prove that you have some potential value to me. If not ... well ... we won't need you any longer. And, I'm not going to be turning you over to the Americans alive."

Rolf puts his hand on his gun again, excited at the opportunity to shoot me, but Zelda walks between us. Calmly. Gracefully. Looking to Ister, she says, "He will need to examine the contents of each crate ... to touch the relics to truly know."

Ister nods, "Naturally, but Barbie will be at his side. Not you. Just in case he tries anything stupid."

Zelda looks deeply into my eyes, willing me to understand the importance of this choice. I don't need her to help me get it, though. Choose the right relics or die. It's as simple as that. How, on Earth, will

I know the right relics? I have no idea. I can only hope there will be some sense I get, something like when I touched the crystal skull.

I walk over to the Paris crate first. It doesn't seem logical to me for someone to send the real relics to Paris if they were trying to keep them away from Napoleon. I'm hoping I can quickly rule out this crate.

The crates are each a little over three feet tall. I can easily see the top contents, and can reach the back of the crate and thereby touch most of the contents without having to dig around too much.

At first glance, I see the cloak, crown, and sword on the right side of the crate. These items are in a lined inner box, designed specifically to hold the relics safely and securely. In the middle of the crate is another inner box, also lined, that holds nothing but a spearhead. There is a wooden staff along the front of the crate that looks as though it would fit the spearhead. However, I'm not sure they go together because the spearhead looks ancient, while the staff looks nearly brand new.

Intricately encircled numerous times by a long silver wire and sheathed in gold, the spearhead has Latin words engraved within the gold. LANCEA ET CLAWS DOMINI. The spear and nail of our lord. The spear that killed Jesus and one of the nails that bound him to the cross … together in this one mystical relic.

What other contents within this crate deserve to share a place with this?

The left side of the crate has several paintings. I can't see the actual works of art, just the top edge of each frame. The frames look expensive, so I guess that the works are as well. At the furthest left corner is a large inner box containing thousands of small, glittering gold nuggets. No. Not nuggets. I'm appalled as I look closer, seeing that these are actually teeth. Thousands of gold teeth taken from Paris … but from whom? Did the Nazis kill thousands of Jews just for their gold teeth? No, I silently stew, seeing the bigger picture. They stole their art, their jewels, their possessions, and then when nothing else was left to take, they took the gold teeth from their mouths and killed them. It's evil. It's nothing short of pure evil.

The spear that killed Christ and the possessions of thousands of murdered Jews … together in a crate. Adolf Hitler is an Antichrist. If there were ever anyone who could be called that, it's Hitler.

Touching the crown, I feel nothing. At least nothing more than utter disgust. Then I touch the sword and the cloak. Still nothing. No warmth. No chill. I don't know what I'm supposed to feel, but I get nothing. The feeling I felt from the crystal skull may have had nothing to do with me. It may have come from Zelda. She believes there's some ability I have. Professor Einstein felt the same way. What is it? If it is there, how do I use it?

The spearhead looks so ancient and real. It would have to be almost two thousand years old if it's real. Sliding my fingertips carefully along the edge, it's dulled, but that makes sense. Who would sharpen the spearhead stained by Christ's blood?

I move on to the crate from Florence. The right side and center of the crate are identical to the Paris crate. Not only are the cloak, sword, crown, and spearhead indistinguishable from the Paris crate, even the inner boxes and lining are the same. I touch them all, feeling nothing.

Now I'm worried. I didn't expect the Paris crate contents to be real, and relying purely on logic, I think it would have made most sense to hide the Holy Roman relics at the Vatican. Now that there's only the one crate left, I'm feeling pressured. I don't have to look back to Rolf. He's breathing down my neck, eager to kill me.

"What's the matter, little brother?" he whispers in my ear. "Having trouble making a decision?"

The Vatican crate has art works on the left side, much like the Paris crate. Instead of gold teeth, it has gold plated cups and plates in it. I very slowly, very meticulously touch every Holy Roman Relic, willing a sensation to come from them. Nothing. I pick up and examine the spearhead. Again, nothing. Sweat starts to form under my arms and on my forehead. Rolf takes a half step closer.

"Well, Medici," says Ister. "Which crate is it?"

I don't know, I think, but don't dare voice the words. None of the relics gave me any sensation whatsoever.

"Make your choice, little brother," says Rolf.

"Ju, Ju, Ju … Just give me a moment," I say, not knowing if they really will give me a moment.

I step back to the Florence crate and look to the left side for any clues at all that might help. There are a few works of art. Several ancient looking books and a strange oval metal object with a thin chain attached to it. Looks like an amulet. I've never seen the type of metal used to make it before. The faint light in the room glitters off the amulet, and the color is ever shifting from chrome to bronze and back. It has some writing etched into it, but it's too dark to make out what it says. An instinct guides my hand and I grasp the amulet. Warmth. Power. My knees actually buckle from the feeling, and I slump uncontrollably to the ground. *This* is what I expected from the relics. A sign of some sort.

"What's going on?" Ister demands. "Stand up, you fool."

Struggling to my feet, I still don't know what to say. I had no sense that the relics in the Florence crate were real. The amulet is emanating something, but that doesn't mean the relics, just because they occupy the same crate, are real. This is not enough evidence to bet my life on the decision. I suddenly realize I haven't actually touched the spearhead from Florence. With nothing emanating from the relics, I moved on the first time here. Reaching for the spearhead, a spark suddenly arcs from the tip of the spear to my finger. It illuminates the inside of the crate and then disappears.

Only Rolf is close enough to see the spark and he yells, "Christus!"

This barely registers with me, because my hand goes numb, and the loss of feeling spreads from there to my arm and then the rest of my body. I fall to the ground, trying desperately to cling to consciousness, yet knowing I am losing the battle.

The last thing I hear is Ister saying, "Bring the crate from Florence."

Chapter 28

SIR ARCHIE
PYTHO ISLAND
APRIL 2, 2014

What a whirlwind. I truly had no idea how things would turn out when I came back to Pytho without Nicanor. Yet here I am at a place no one from Pytho – other than the Oracle, her sisterhood, and the council member Apollo – are allowed to visit. I'm actually within the Temple of Apollo … at the top of a pyramid … on the highest Plateau within Pytho. The entry is heavily guarded and only reachable by secret passageways hidden in the volcano wall. Among the clouds, the only place positioned higher than the temple is the helipad.

Hovering in the air around the temple is the sweet smell of burning incense, but there's an acrid tinge to the aroma. We're much too high to hear the sounds of the city on the main plateau, but the noisily chirping birds make up for it. Two blackbirds chase off a hawk. Just as the hawk disappears, four mocking birds chase off the blackbirds. Strange that the smaller birds seem to win each aerial battle.

I grew up, along with everyone else in Pytho, gazing up at the pyramid and the temple from the main plateau. Veiled by the clouds, I always wondered what they do here. Wondered about the Oracle. We've all heard that she can see the future.

The Oracle is a young pretty girl, around sixteen, with a slight build, auburn hair, fair skin, and silvery-blue eyes. If she were among the main population on Pytho, she'd be nothing more than a typical schoolgirl. As the Oracle, there's nothing typical about her. Everyone knows of her. Everyone reveres her. Even the council respects her every word. It's the power to see the future that forces this respect. She knows what will happen before it happens. She sees things from the future … from the past … from a distance. It's a gift within the Oracle's bloodline. A gift that has served our people, and kept us alive and safe when others wanted to hunt us down and kill us all … to eradicate our very existence.

The Oracle met me at the entrance, and introduced me to a former Oracle, known simply as Mother. Did she mean Mother of the Sisterhood? Or did she mean her own mother … or both? I don't know, but I quickly gathered that I'm to call her Mother as well.

"Let's sit down and chat," says Mother.

She walks in between the Oracle and me, and leads us to a small chamber room at the top of the pyramid. The view through a large passageway reveals the open air, columned part of the temple. Centered in the room is a small round stone top table with stone benches around it. Not comfortable, but certainly durable. For all I know the table and benches have been here since the construction of the pyramid.

Two young women, similar enough looking to the Oracle to be her older sisters, bring us trays of fruit and biscuits that are still steaming and smell divine. A pitcher of water and three cups – all made of wood – are also set on the stone table.

I can't wait, and help myself to a biscuit. Moist, buttery, hot, slightly undercooked – just the way I love them.

The two women leave us to talk. Both are older than the Oracle, probably in their twenties. As they walk toward the lit passage to the open part of the temple, sunlight shines through their sheer white clothing, revealing a silhouette of each of their figures. My eyes linger on the view even as Mother sits right next to me.

She's an elderly well-weathered woman. The few strands of her hair that have any pigment to them are a similar shade of auburn to the Oracle's hair. Her skin is more creased than wrinkled, and so far beyond pale that it appears to be translucent. Her eyes are tired, more gray than blue. Mother's a little shorter than the Oracle, but she's so bent over with age and wear that she may well have been taller at one point. The only thing that really indicates that Mother may not be the Oracle's birth mother is her age. She'd be more like her grandmother or even her great grandmother by my estimation.

Mid-chew, Mother gently places her dry, wrinkly hand on mine, then proceeds to squeeze.

"What you need to know first, Sir Archimedes, is that the bloodline of the Sisterhood of the Oracle is not just paramount within the Temple of Apollo … not only paramount on Pytho Island … it's the most important treasure in the history of the world. Proper mating pairs are planned decades – sometimes even generations – in advance. You are the first man who will be staying here on a long-term basis. If you ever and I mean *ever* try to fuck any of the girls here at the temple, I will cut off your balls and shove them down your throat until you choke to death. Is that perfectly clear?"

I can't help but glance at the Oracle, but she won't make eye contact with me.

Mother continues, "Only a virgin may be Oracle. Only a virgin can see the prophecies. No description of pain will do justice to what will become of you should you try to fuck the Oracle."

I'm not a particularly attractive man. At 42, I'm old to be a Beta Knight. Tall, but too skinny. Thinning dark hair. Eyes a little too small and too close to each other, and a long, crooked nose. I've never had anyone worry about women wanting to have sex with me.

Mother's squeeze intensifies as I try to swallow the bite of biscuit. It catches briefly in my esophagus, and I nearly choke, forcing it down with a drink of water before answering her.

"I'm here to protect the Oracle, not to have sex with her."

Mother points to a guard at the entrance to the room, and says, "We don't have need of further protection. You will be performing a very different service for the Oracle."

What the hell have I gotten myself into?

"I don't understand."

"Of course you don't," Mother says to me as though she's speaking with a child. "You've been in the dark since you were born."

"What are you talking about?" This is starting to piss me off. I'm starting to think I was better off as a Beta.

"It's not your fault," her voice is less condescending ... a little. "The council keeps the people of Pytho in the dark intentionally. They think they are the only ones worthy of our secrets, but they don't even know the full truth of our history."

I don't doubt this, having wondered why more hasn't leaked from the council to the people over the centuries. Karl couldn't keep a secret from me, at least not for too long.

"Why are you telling me this?"

"Because you are now the first Knight of History. You will need to be educated in our *real* history."

"Why?"

"Because," the young Oracle says with a much softer tone, "you are going to be seeing it."

"Seeing it ... like you do?"

Her eyes light up, "Yes ... *exactly* like I do!"

"How?"

Mother squeezes my hand tighter, making sure she has my attention, and I'm not paying too much attention to the pretty young Oracle. "The better question would have been why," she says.

Shrugging, I say, "Okay ... why?"

"*Seeing*," Mother says this word through a clenched jaw, as though it is the most incredibly powerful act anyone can do, "takes quite a toll on the Oracle. It can be ... difficult ... to come back from the vision and be able to relay the details of what is seen to others. In the past, we've always had someone with an ear close to the Oracle during her visions. This interpreter would listen to the Oracle for any whisperings, and attempt to find meaning from the Oracle's clouded message. Just as when different languages are interpreted, many times, the translation would not be fully accurate."

"What prevents the Oracle," I turn and face the young girl, "you ... from relaying the vision accurately yourself?"

Again, Mother squeezes my hand tighter, drawing my attention, "Two things. First, during the vision, the Oracle is in an induced state to help her stay focused on the vision ... to help her stay within a trance state even during the most difficult of visions. The induced state is indescribable if you haven't experienced it, but most men would look at it as a state of *ecstasy*."

Mother's voice is much younger sounding than her appearance, and the breathy way she says *ecstasy* almost causes an arousal within me, but her bent, ancient visage quickly squashes that feeling.

She continues, "And, second, the recent change in history has shown the Oracle that changes in the past *can* be made, and she has also seen *how* it is to be accomplished. Changing history will be no small feat. It requires the Oracle to be in a battle of wills, and this, too, will strain her greatly during her visions."

"A battle of wills – against whom?"

"The stray sisters," Mother answers as though I should know what the hell a stray sister is.

"I don't know what a stray sister is."

"Of course you don't," Mother's condescending tone is back in full force. "The stray sisters are women who share the bloodline of the Oracle, but who left the fold and are living in the outside world. Throughout history, they have caused more problems for the First Order than any man ever could. Yet, they may be our best chance to correct the great wrongs that we have had to endure. With the crystal skull you have retrieved, the Oracle will be able to connect with stray sisters in our past. The connection will be trying, to say the least, but nothing compared to the ensuing battle of wills. The Oracle will need an independent presence to observe and relay what has happened. To let us know if the change has worked."

"Okay, the why part makes a little sense, but the how part still confuses me. I don't have the Oracle's ability. How am I to see the visions as she does?"

"That is another part of the power of the crystal skull," and with this, Mother relaxes her grip on my hand significantly. She even tries to smile, although it comes across as more of a smirk. "The skull aligns brain waves, and the Oracle has seen that she will be able to align with you during her visions. You'll be able to see what she sees … see the connection to a stray sister … and see what unfolds. Now that we know it is possible to change history, it is imperative that we have a clear and unbiased view into that history. Your view."

"Why me? Can't she align with you or one of the other women here? Why have I been chosen?"

Shaking her head at me like I'm an idiot, she answers, "It's something within our bloodline. We can't see anyone who shares the bloodline of the Oracle in our visions. The crystal skull will allow us to connect with a stray sister from the past, but an alignment between us in the present is still impossible. We need someone from outside the sisterhood to do this. As to why *you* have been chosen – the Oracle has seen that you will do whatever is necessary to advance our cause … that you don't fear or even respect the council … more importantly, that you don't have the false morals that might prevent you from relaying the truth of what you'll see."

Not exactly a compliment. Apparently, the Oracle *has* seen what happened … what I did to Nicanor. Yet, she chose me. Not in spite of the fact that I'm a murderer … no … because I am. Because I pulled the trigger.

"Okay," I nod, starting to like where this is going.

The Oracle smiles at my acceptance and Mother's smirk grows wider.

"You'll need a history lesson," says Mother.

"My ascension ceremony is tomorrow. Shouldn't we hold the history lesson until my Beta is here to hear it?"

"Your Beta will not be here to do what you do," replies Mother.

"Then what will he be here for?"

"Your beta will not be a man."

I don't know if I should argue this point. I didn't choose Nicanor, but that ended up working out well. Perhaps the Oracle has seen the best choice for me. "Then what will *she* be here for?"

"You are to choose a female beta that you find *physically appealing*," Mother says in her younger breathy voice again.

"Why?"

"When the Oracle is in her state of ecstasy … the way she moves … the sounds she makes … throughout our history, this has been very difficult for men to resist if they are present to witness a vision. It's why we no longer allow men to be interpreters or even to stay in the temple. The Oracle doesn't have the ability or the *desire* to fend off a man while she's in this state. She is vulnerable. If you are not strong enough to fight off your own urges, she cannot fight you off. That is where your Beta will come in. Your Beta's role will be to ensure you don't act on your temptation with the Oracle in her state of ecstasy. Your Beta will be protecting her from you … and you from yourself."

"How?"

"Any way she must."

I try to stay calm, and pretend I'm in one of my business meetings from the outside world. "Um, okay. So, let's hear the real history of our people."

"Let me start by saying I know you're going to have questions when I tell you this history. Just shut up and listen. I'm going to tell you what I want you to know and nothing more."

She's an ornery old bitch, yet I find myself liking her anyway. I just nod.

"In the early days of what many know as Ancient Greece, the Oracle of Delphi was the center of civilization. Greece may have been split into many city-states … be it Athens, Corinth, Thebes, Sparta … even our own Delphi. None of the independent city-states ever made a major decision without consulting the Oracle.

"Word of our ability to see the future quickly spread beyond Greece, and leaders around the known world made the often dangerous journey to Delphi to seek our advice. For a millennium, the sisterhood of the Oracle influenced and often controlled the world. And … we were paid large sums of gold for our visions.

"We certainly knew of the prophet from Nazareth, but there have been many prophets throughout history … many with similar abilities to the Oracle. We never thought of Jesus as a threat. Truth be told, he never was a threat to us on his own. It was the Romans ... Constantine, in particular, during the 4th Century. They bastardized history ... converted to Christianity ... and began the first pagan witch hunts.

Mother downs much of her cup of water, dribbling some of it down her chin and not even bothering to wipe it off.

"Fortunately, we saw the coming calamity. The Romans sent forces to destroy the Oracle and her sisterhood ... along with any followers. When they got to Delphi, however, all they found was an empty city. They were too late.

"The Greeks weren't strong enough to fend off the Romans. That much we knew. Our ancestors packed up all we could carry with us and became a nomadic tribe. Most of us went to what is now known in the outside world as Germany. The barbarian hordes there *were* strong enough to fight the Romans, and we knew – with a little guidance from the Oracle of that age – they would eventually defeat the Romans."

Mother looks squarely at me, reading my face and my thoughts, and says, "Don't ask! I will tell you about the smaller group that did not go to Germany – because you need to know about them. The smaller group went in a different direction. They went to what is now known as Russia. A place so far out of the Roman Empire where the group hid, trying to stay out of the fight altogether. The *stray sisters*, we called them. The First Order didn't want them to go, but the Oracle saw that the stray sisters might prove useful in the future, so they were allowed to part ways with the main group.

"The First Order joined with the Germanic tribes and over the course of a century of battles, finally sacked Rome and put an end to the Roman Empire in the 5th Century.

"Our hopes ... our dreams ... our visions ... all hinged on defeating the Romans. Unfortunately, we were too late. The war took too long. Christianity had spread throughout the Empire and beyond. We defeated the Roman Empire, but the Roman Catholic Church endured. People tossed aside the Greek gods in favor of the one God ... and his son ... the prophet who was converted to deity ... Jesus Christ.

"Our ancestors spent the next few centuries trying to hide in plain sight. We had long established the first banks in the world, and with guidance, we became a financial power ... yet still a nomadic tribe with no home to call our own.

"Then, in the 12th Century, the Roman Catholic Church started looking for what they call heresy – anyone with a different view than the one God and his son. The Inquisitions soon followed. It was the year 1229 that the Oracle of that age saw a new doom. The Inquisitors would find us, and soon. We had to leave Europe all together if we were to survive. We thought of heading to Russia … maybe to join up again with the stray sisters. But, the Oracle had seen another option. An island where our small tribe could stay hidden … forever. We'd have our banks out in the world, growing our wealth, but we'd be safe. She guided the First Order and a small group of followers on what must have seemed like a suicide mission at the time … on a voyage to the middle of the Atlantic Ocean … to Pytho Island."

I've heard some of this history from my father when I was a boy, but never to this level of detail. I have so many questions, but bite my tongue, and can only hope Mother will tell me what I want to know.

"He wants to ask you about the death rays," the Oracle says to Mother.

Mother nods, "Yes, I'm getting there. You, Sir Archie – now that Sir Karl has passed – have more experience in the outside world than any of our knights. Have you seen anything like the death rays out there?"

Shaking my head, I answer, "No … I'm frankly surprised our Knights of Science were able to invent them."

Both Mother and the Oracle laugh.

"Think about it," says Mother. "Our Knights of Science would have trouble inventing fire if left alone on a deserted island. This technology is far more advanced than anything the outside world has, and it's been here for centuries … since before our ancestors ever found Pytho."

"I don't understand."

Mother nods. "Have you ever heard of the lost city of Atlantis?"

My eyes go wide, realizing instantly what she's saying. "This is it?"

"Yes," she says as though it's a simple little fact. "This technology was here when we arrived in the year 1229. Electricity … the death rays … they were all here. So much more as well, but the island was barren of people."

"Where did they go?" I ask.

"We don't know for certain. Rumors were that the island had sunk … or that a volcano or earthquake had swallowed the civilization whole. Yet the buildings were intact when our ancestors arrived. All the technology we found was intact and working. Our only guess is they had some major mishap with the science behind the death ray … something that vaporized all the people, yet left everything else unharmed. Regardless … they are gone, and we are here. It took our ancestors quite a while, but they learned to use most of the technology, and it has kept our people secret and safe. We can do what we need to do."

"What is that?" I ask, knowing I'm violating her rule about questions.

Mother smiles, almost warmly. "The First Order and the Oracle should still be at the center of the world … should still be able to influence and control what happens. However, the population of the outside world has grown beyond our ability to control it, and it keeps growing at an ever-increasing rate. There have been a few rare opportunities in history where someone in the outside world has been in a position to change all that.

"The most recent was Luis Khan. With Sir Karl's assistance, he came very close to transforming the world into a place where we could control it."

"So nearly a success," says the Oracle.

Mother nods, patting the young girl's arm. "We may have failed there, but there are two other opportunities from our past … two men who could have also set the world in its proper place. With your time spent on the outside, Sir Archie, you are one of the few of our people who would have even heard of their names … Napoleon Bonaparte and Adolf Hitler. It just so happens that each of these men had a stray sister near them when they were in the height of their power. And … they each had access to a crystal skull."

Karl recruited me because of my intelligence, and I'm starting to see the big picture … finally. "The crystal skulls were made by the people of Atlantis, weren't they?"

"Yes," Mother answers. "We believe the highly advanced civilization of Atlantis used some of the ancient civilizations of Africa and the Americas as both slave labor and foot soldiers. They had handlers based in pyramids such as this one, and needed to communicate with them across great distances. The crystal helps align brainwaves and enabled that communication. With the Oracle's ability – and your help – we will put the skulls to use in a far greater way."

Chapter 29

JESSICA TYSON
LONGBOAT KEY, FL, USA
APRIL 16, 2014

Mom and Dad went back home earlier today. Being a first time mother – with triplets – I couldn't have handled coming home from the hospital without their help.

We've only been home for a couple of weeks, but it feels like we're finally settling into a bit of a routine. Sleep is the only real problem. God didn't design the human body to nurse three babies, and they seem to be hungry all the time … especially at night. It's 6pm and even though the timing might be bad, they're down for a nap. I turned the baby monitor on and decided to clean out the dirty diaper container.

Sometimes the simplest of tasks can be so difficult.

It's just in my head, though. Nothing to be afraid of … not with the new security system Max had installed … especially now that we have backup generators that automatically kick in when the power goes out!

Still … this is my first time heading down the stairs to the garage or even being in the garage on my own since … since … a tear forms, and I angrily wipe it away with my free hand.

My other hand can barely lift the bag full of dirty diapers. *Holy cripes!* Who knew how many diapers triplets could soil?

Trey usually takes out the trash, but he's helping Max make dinner. I didn't want to bother him and maybe I just need to prove to myself that I can do this.

I only have to take a few steps down the stairs to where the trash containers are in the garage.

Simple enough. Just take a few more steps.

You put one foot in front of the other, and soon you'll be walkin' down the stairs – this plays in my head to the tune of a song I remember from a Christmas cartoon. I can't remember if it's from *Rudolf the Red-Nosed Reindeer* or *Santa Claus is Comin' to Town*.

I'm sure I'll know in a few years when the triplets start watching Christmas specials. Either way, the tune helps me get my feet moving.

Trey parked the new minivan in the closer spot to the stairs, so I have to walk around it to get to the trash containers.

This, sadly enough, leaves the spot where the murder took place in plain sight.

Max had the entire garage floors resurfaced so there are no signs of the ordeal I went through … no signs of the murder that took place.

The tall, thin man named Archie with the large, hooked nose could have easily chosen to kill me instead of the other man. I'd be dead … and my three babies would all be dead if it weren't for some strange twist of fate. Something caused that man to make that decision. What was it? I suppose I'll never find out.

The police looked everywhere for fingerprints, some remnant hair, or other DNA sample, but found nothing for Archie. The muscular, younger man – the one who's dead now instead of me – left enough blood on the garage floor and in the sand of the beach for plenty of DNA samples, but there wasn't a match in any record anywhere in the United States or through Interpol.

I even worked with a police sketch artist and had a good likeness drawn of each man, but no computer matches there either. It's as though the two men came from another world.

When I told Trey and Max that the muscular man mentioned the Oracle, the First Order, and even Karl's name, they both nearly flipped out. That man never thought I'd live, so never worried about sharing a few details I might hear. It's just too bad he didn't say where they came from.

They came by boat and all they took was some crystal skull that Max had from one of his adventures. Archie apparently dragged the muscular man all the way to the Gulf and got him in the boat somehow. However, no one saw the men except for me and no one saw the boat.

Now that I'm here, I'm having a hard time with the simple task of tossing this bag in the trash container and heading back upstairs. The memory of the murder is so clear in my mind. The trunk popped open and the muscular man stood over me with my water broken. I tried to punch him, but he easily avoided it, and I hit nothing but the top of the trunk, scraping two of my knuckles. He had me gagged and tied up in a matter of seconds. Then, he tried to get Archie to kill me.

Archie didn't want to do it. He knew I was pregnant … knew my water had broken, and that I was about to give birth … knew just how wrong it would have been to take innocent lives away so unnecessarily. He wasn't a good man, but he wasn't purely a bad man either. Somewhere in between. He killed his partner, yet he spared my life.

The doorbell rings and it finally spurs me to do the simple task I came here to do.

When I get back upstairs, I see Bruce Cullens from the AI division of the Secret Service standing in our foyer. With him is a woman carrying a Styrofoam box. Bruce is wearing a black suit, white shirt, and black and silver striped tie. He's on duty. The woman is a little taller than I am, thin, and wearing a crisp white blouse with a form fitting red skirt.

Max and Trey are standing to the right of the woman. Max is wearing a green polo shirt with navy slacks.

Then there's my husband. A billionaire who dresses as if he's worth no more than 50 bucks. A beat up orange Detroit Tigers t-shirt and burgundy fleece cut-off shorts with half of the Tampa Bay Buc's logo still visible. I close my eyes and shake my head slowly from side to side for just a second, hoping that when I open them, Trey will be wearing something that at least matches. Nope. My eyes weren't playing tricks on me. He really is dressed that way. *Function over form*, he often says. Apparently, he's out to prove his point again today.

Max steps forward and says, "Doctor Jessica Tyson, you know Bruce. Let me introduce you to Doctor Tori Cromwell. She's from the Smithsonian."

"Hello," I say, shaking Doctor Cromwell's hand. I give Bruce a hug. Although we've only met a few times, we all went through the 2012 crisis and ended up sharing our stories. Bruce has become a close friend with our family.

"Mmmm, why hello Doctor Tyson. Please … call me Tori."

Max politely reaches to take the large box from Tori, but she ignores the gesture.

"Fair enough, as long as you'll call me Jessica."

Tori nods with a curt smile.

Trey moves to stand next to me and says, "We were just about to have dinner and we have plenty. Why don't you join us?"

Bruce says, "Thanks, but I can't stay. I just flew in with Tori. She's here to deliver the crystal skull, and I'm here to make sure neither she nor the skull come to any harm." In his mid-20s, Bruce has a boyish charm and an easy laugh.

Tori, who I would guess to be in her mid-60s, shoots a quick glance at Max, who is wearing a sheepish grin on his face.

Apparently, that was the reaction she was hoping for, as she nods and says, "I'd like that. I'd like that very much. Thank you."

Max asks, "Can I carry the box for you?"

"Mmmmm, not, I'm afraid, until after we complete the transfer paperwork. Bruce, perhaps we should get that out of the way prior to sitting down for dinner?"

Bruce opens a rich brown leather messenger bag he has comfortably strapped to his shoulder, and removes a manila file with a document in it. "Samantha told me to get you to sign this, Max, before Tori can give you the box."

"We're glad you're here, Bruce," says Trey, "but why didn't Sam bring it herself?"

"Oh, she wanted to," says Bruce. "But, the president is traveling outside the country, and that almost always means that Sam is traveling with her."

Ugh. Why Trey has to have a woman for a best friend – especially one as attractive as Samantha Fox – I'll never understand. I'm just glad Bruce is here instead of her.

Bruce hands the document to Max, who quickly reads it before signing the bottom.

Tori then signs the document as well, and returns it to Bruce.

"One crystal skull. Under executive order from the, mmmm, President of the United States, this crystal skull is not to leave these premises without prior written approval from myself or, in my absence, from Director Johnson.

She very formally turns and extends the box to Max. There's a barely perceptible pause when Max's hand makes contact with Tori's hand.

Oh my. He likes her. And she likes him right back. Max hasn't had a love interest since Katarina. As long as I've known him, he's never made his own happiness a priority.

Max carefully places the box on the entry hall table, opens it, and removes a large white crystal skull.

After staring in awe at it for a few seconds, Trey finally breaks the silence, "Was it difficult to get approval to bring it here?"

"Mmm, no," says Tori. "Your father is quite persuasive, and the president assured all of us at the museum that your home is quite up to date now with security measures."

"Please come in," Trey says. "Now that we have the necessary paperwork done, would anyone like a glass of wine before dinner?"

"I'm afraid I can't stay," says Bruce. Max gives him a sideways glance, though and Bruce backpedals quickly. "Um … now that the transfer has been made … I guess I'm off duty, right?" Bruce looks alternately between Max and Tori after asking the question.

Tori answers first, "Your duty was to get both me and the skull here safely, and that's been done. I know you have a flight to catch, young man."

"You're not going back together?" asks Max.

"Mmm, no. This is my first time in Florida, so I took a bit of a holiday. I just realized, however, that I rode in with Bruce. I'm afraid I won't be able to accept your invitation for dinner, after all."

Bruce adjusts the shoulder strap of his bag and asks, "Can I give you a ride to your hotel, Tori?"

Max steps closer to her, "It's okay, Bruce. I can ride her after dinner."

To Bruce's credit, he manages to fight off the urge to laugh at the unintended innuendo from Max. The way he raises his eyebrows and slowly blinks twice, though, is too much for me to take. I have to turn and pretend to cough.

Trey caught it, too, with a grin so wide his face must be hurting.

Bruce quickly says his goodbyes and Trey heads down to our wine cellar to pick out a bottle.

"Please come into the dining room and have a seat," I say.

Trey often likes to give new visitors a tour of the house and I know he's proud of it, but I've never been fond of the idea. Now that we've experienced a break in, robbery, and murder in our house, he's letting that go, thankfully. The dining room is just off the foyer, so we don't have to go far. While Trey designed the layout, he left almost all of the interior design decisions to me.

Many of our friends in Florida seem to decorate with bright colors – orange or salmon being popular choices. However, I've always preferred the warm earth tones, like the sand dollar color we used on most of our main level.

After we sit at the table Max and Trey have set already, Tori says, "Lovely home, Jessica."

We exchange a few pleasantries until Trey returns with the wine.

He pours three glasses, aware that I'm still nursing the babies. I notice he chose a Corton-Charlemagne Chardonnay. My man may not dress well, but he sure knows his wine.

"I hope you like chicken parmesan," says Max as he circles the table, serving each of us individually. Again, it's not terribly obvious, but he lingers a little longer while serving Tori.

Trey pulls out his iPhone, and in a few seconds, the high-tech sound system he installed throughout the house kicks in softly with a Beatles song …. I think both McCartney and Lennon are singing …. She loves you, yeah, yeah, yeah ….

No, he didn't.

Yes … he did.

"Trey … just because Tori is British doesn't mean she likes the Beatles." Especially not that song. He's trying to be funny, but I don't want him to mess up the one time Max has shown an interest in a woman since Katarina.

"Mmmm, actually, the Queen Mum has often decreed that all Brits must, in fact, like the Beatles," she says, smiling.

We all laugh – Max, loudest of all.

He needs this. He deserves this. It's so good to see him laugh.

Chapter 30

SIR ARCHIE
PYTHO ISLAND
APRIL 16, 2014

Very different today, walking to the council chambers *with* the Oracle ... *from* the Temple of Apollo ... *through* the hidden passages within the volcano wall ... accompanied by four of her temple guards, each a woman displaying at least some family resemblance to the Oracle. We pass private offices for the council leaders. Then, we come up to a dining hall.

"Let's have a snack before the ceremony," says the Oracle.

It's so odd to have this teenager in a position of such power. She looks and talks like most any teenager I've seen in Pytho or the outer world.

In the dining hall are two women and a man. My vision's not the best from a distance, but as we approach, I recognize council members Artemis, Hestia, and Dionysus. Several trays of meats, cheeses, fruit, and biscuits are arranged on the large table along with pitchers of water and juice and a few bottles of wine.

Dionysus is the first to see us and immediately stands to greet us, "Oracle ... Sir Archie ... welcome."

In a much more forceful voice than I thought she could possess, the Oracle says, "He prefers Sir Archimedes!"

Dionysus bows, dramatically, and says, "Sorry. Sir Archimedes, please have a glass of wine ... it's a fine vintage." A short, bald, and rotund man with more chins than I can count, Dionysus pours wine into an ornate goblet and offers it to me.

I think back to the last time I was supposed to have an ascension ceremony and wonder how it would have gone if I had had a couple glasses of wine prior ... not well.

"Thank you." I accept the goblet to avoid being rude, but only sip from it.

"Can I speak with you a moment," the Oracle says to Dionysus. He nods and they walk off to the other side of the dining hall.

"So, how was it at the temple?" asks Artemis. The goddess of wild animals and hunting, her primary responsibility on Pytho is to make sure the animal life on the island stays balanced – not too many predators, yet enough to keep the other species in check.

Knights of War for the First Order are sometimes tasked with bringing animals to or from the island to achieve that balance. I've heard them complain about it, but I don't think the grunts understand the importance. Artemis also organizes hunting parties should a species grow out of control, and this is where the grunts are rewarded for their efforts. The reward they crave … they get to kill something.

During all my time with Karl and my recent conversations with Mother and the Oracle, I've come to see that there is and perhaps always has been a power struggle between the Oracle and the council leaders. They need each other – that much they all know – but when it comes time to make a decision, the struggle begins in earnest. As the first Knight of the First Order to spend any time at the temple, I imagine both parties view me more as a pawn than a knight in their power games.

"It's fine," I answer.

Hestia, goddess of hearth and architecture, turns to join our conversation. She's responsible for city planning … making sure Pytho has the infrastructure necessary to support our population growth. Both women are brunettes, but while Artemis is rather plain, Hestia is absolutely gorgeous. With a thin build, high cheekbones, and a high level of energy, she reminds me of an actress from some of the older movies in the outside world … can't remember her name though.

Placing her hand on my arm, Hestia asks in a voice just above a whisper, "What did you think of Mother?"

I glance to see if the Oracle is paying attention to our conversation and notice Dionysus passing her a small orange container that she quickly hides in her robes.

Returning my attention to Hestia, I say, "Quite a strong personality that one has."

The two goddesses look to each other for a moment, both smiling and nodding.

Hestia says, "I understand you're to choose between three Beta candidates today?"

"You probably know more about it than I do."

She winks. Leaning in, warm breath in my ear, she whispers, "When I heard about the Beta's role, I volunteered to step down from the council to be one of your choices."

Shocked, I lean back and ask, "Are you serious?"

She nods, sincerely, and says, "Zeus refused to accept it, unfortunately. Still, I –"

Before Hestia can finish her point, the Oracle walks up and says, "It's time, Sir Archimedes."

Having gone through the blustering opening statements from both Zeus and Athena, I stand with my new red clasp, facing the council leaders. Between us are three women, all Beta candidates, all facing me awaiting my next words. The council chambers are eerily quiet as I replace my black clasp with the red.

The Oracle walks over from her place next to Zeus, hops off the dais, and comes to stand next to me.

I whisper in her ear, "Oracle, do you know which one I should choose?"

Thinking she will whisper an answer to me, she instead announces to all, "Sir Archimedes ... the first Knight of History ... he, who was Beta to the great Knight of Economics, Sir Karl ... he, who is tasked with the most important mission ever for a knight of the First Order ... he, who is now an Alpha has asked for my advice in choosing his Beta."

The three women, who until the Oracle had spoken, were looking at me with indifference ... at best. The Oracle's words have dramatically changed the way they look at me now. At the very least, I sense a feeling of respect from each of them.

The Oracle glares at the three women. None of them has been allowed to share their names or their histories, as I will be giving the chosen one her Beta Knight name, and she must forget her life from the past.

On the left is a brunette, who looks much like Hestia, perhaps even her younger sister. She's around 30, so relaxed, and I sense a free-flowing spirit from her. Audrey Hepburn! That's the actress's name. Both Hestia and this woman remind me of Audrey Hepburn.

In the middle is an attractive blonde, about 35, who is much more serious. She's looking at the Oracle with curiosity, but when her gaze returns to me, the look doesn't change. No fear. No excitement. Neither longing nor disdain. Just curiosity.

On the right is a redhead, around 25. She also looks back and forth between the Oracle and me. I get no sense of emotions from her when she looks at me, but when she looks at the Oracle … sparks fly. Her lips curl, eyes flutter. She tilts her head, arching her back ever so slightly.

This is so fucked up. I'm choosing a woman to be my Beta *and* she's to be my mate. How long will this last? Is it supposed to be for our lifetimes? All three women are physically appealing, but that's not enough. I don't know a damn thing about any of them.

I have their basic Beta testing results in my hands, but what do these really mean? Three files that tell me the brunette is highly intelligent and was headed down the path of a Knight of Economics. The blonde is bright and highly influential. She was planning to be a Knight of Leadership. The redhead, although smaller in stature, has great muscle tone and is quite skilled with weapons. She's been planning to be a Knight of War.

I'm to choose one to be my Beta Knight of History. Will she be an ally? A foe? Aligned with the Oracle and Mother? A spy for the council?

I decide, just then, to rule out whomever the Oracle advises me to choose. I want my Beta to be *my* Beta, not hers.

The Oracle turns to me and whispers, "The brunette sees herself as your equal. The blonde sees herself as your superior. The redhead will do whatever you ask of her, whenever you ask it … a natural Beta to you as the Alpha. She's the easy and clear choice."

The easy and clear choice. I think the Oracle used the word *easy* on purpose.

"I have made a choice." I walk up to the redhead, clasp her hand in mine and say, "You will not be my Beta."

The dismay in the redhead's face only lasts a moment before it shifts into fury. She not only wants to hit me, I think, if given the opportunity, she'd kill me right now. Oh yeah, I'm feeling good about that decision.

Not looking at the Oracle for fear of seeing her disappointment, I step past the blonde, and face the brunette. Clasping her hand, I feel a slight tremor from her … something that tells me she's afraid I'm about to tell her she will not be my choice either.

"I bestow upon thee the honor of the title of knighthood, and dub thee, Dame Audrey … the first Beta Knight of History."

The Oracle didn't mean to, but she made this choice for me. I don't want someone telling me what to do for the rest of my life like the blonde would have. I don't want some simple follower – especially a psychopathic one – like the redhead would have been. I want a true partner in life. Not just some sexual plaything. Someone intellectual I can talk to. Share things. Grow together.

As I place the black clasp in her hand, Audrey's hand squeezes mine. She's gazing deeply into my eyes, smiling warmly.

Chapter 31

TREY TYSON
LONGBOAT KEY, FL, USA
APRIL 16, 2014

"What a great night," says Jessica while sitting in the lounge chair Max usually chooses for my training sessions with Nostradamus. She turns up the volume on the baby monitor to the point where we can hear them breathing. The sun set a few minutes ago and we held hands as we watched it together. Heat still rises from the brick pavers where the sun shone most of the day.

"I haven't laughed like that in months."

"Yeah, I know," she says. "You crack yourself up, don't you?"

"I may have picked the Beatles station on Pandora, but I had nothing to do with the song choice. That was purely fate."

"I'm surprised Tori didn't get up and leave … right then," she says.

"Why would she? She really likes Max. You should have seen the way she was checking him out when we met her in DC."

Jessica smiles, shaking her head, and says, "I hope this turns into something real for Max …. He's been lonely for a long time – at least since I've known him."

"The old man isn't wired like the rest of us. He's happy saving presidents … saving the world … so long as he can fly under the radar and protect everyone. He's fine."

"Tori sure thinks so." Jess stretches back a bit. "So, this is what you two boys do out here every night? Just sit and stare at the Gulf?"

"Don't forget the flame. I stare at the flame, too. It's grueling work, but someone has to do it."

"Oh, please."

"And, Max has to smoke his peace pipe. Think of the toll that's taking on his 85-year-old body."

As if on cue, Max emerges from the back of his guesthouse and says, "This 85-year-old body works just fine, thank you."

"Not if you're back this quickly," I can't help but jest. "I thought you were going to ride Tori for a while?"

Jessica stands and punches my arm. "That's quite enough out of you tonight, Trey."

Max nearly falls over laughing, though, and Jess soon joins him.

After catching his breath, he says, "That was a bit of a slip of the tongue there, wasn't it?"

I look at Jessica and wink.

She whispers, "Don't you dare go there."

I decide to let that joke go unsaid.

She turns to Max and says, "I really like her."

"I enjoyed her company, too," says Max.

"Are you going to see her again?" asks Jess.

"As a matter of fact, I'm picking Tori up tomorrow to show her around the area."

"A date?" I ask. "When's the last time you've had one of those?"

"I'm not sure I'd call it a date," says Max.

"Where are you going to take her?" asks Jess.

"I thought we'd start with a visit to Mote Marine Lab and Aquarium in the morning to see some of the local sea life, a nice lunch, and then I might take her sailing."

"On Tinef?"

"That *is* my sailboat," says Max, ready to defend the little boat to the end.

"Sounds like a lovely enough day to me, Max," says Jessica.

The baby monitor crackles and then emits a noise that sounds like one of them is rustling around. Most likely, it's Amber. Born first, she usually wakes first and wants to eat first as well.

"That's my signal," says Jessica. "Time to feed the little ones. You two enjoy your training."

I stand to kiss and hug my beautiful wife. "Love you."

"Love you, too. Good night boys."

The rustling noise increases and Jess heads back into the house.

"Are you ready for this?" I don't need to ask, because Max has already placed the white crystal skull next to the brass tripod, lit the candle, and is lighting his peace pipe, too.

"Ready as I'll ever be," he says. "You ready?"

"Let's do it."

We both position the backs of our adjustable lounge chairs to be more vertical so we can reach the skull and stay relaxed.

Max places his palm on the back of the skull. This is the first time I've seen the skull in the dark, and as soon as his hand touches it, the eye sockets begin to glow eerily. This causes me to pause for just a moment, but Max glares at me, so I slowly put my palm on the skull as well. The blue glow intensifies and the brightness competes with the flame coming from the candle in the tripod. Warmth emanates through my palm all the way up my arm. My pulse quickens.

"Do you hear me?" asks Max, but his lips never move.

We experienced a jumbled sense of hearing some of each other's thoughts when we both touched the clear crystal skull, but now with this larger white one, Max's voice comes through loud and clear.

"I sure do … pretty cool!"

"I hear you, too. This is just like when Zelda and I first communicated on the U-boat." The excitement in Max's projected voice is just as noticeable as if we were speaking aloud.

"I was able to see that connection take place, but I couldn't hear what you and Zelda were saying to each other. What was it?"

"Well," starts Max, *"I suppose since that already took place in your training, it's okay to tell you. She told me she wasn't there of her own free will … that Hagan Ister was holding her baby hostage to keep her and her abilities in his service. Zelda was trying to build some trust between us, so she gave me some information I'm certain she wouldn't have given if Ister could hear us. She explained that Ister was the head of the Thule Society and that he thought the Thules had descended from the Aryan race."*

"Really? What else?"

"I don't know what proof Ister had. I only know that he believed this and Zelda believed him …. He was convinced the Aryans were from the lost civilization of Atlantis."

"The island that sank?"

"That's the legend and what I thought, too," says Max. *"But, Ister was convinced the island hadn't sunk. He thought the people of Atlantis had discovered the power of the atom thousands of years ago. And, they had some sort of atomic blast that wiped out their society."*

"Did Zelda ever say how Ister knew all this?"

"No, but she did say the Thules spent years collecting Aryan artifacts. They may well have discovered something that indicated the fate of Atlantis. Knowing that these crystal skulls were shaped by electric tools and are thousands of years old at least gives some credence to the theories."

"Wow … anything else?"

"Yes. Lady Zelda said she descended from the line of the Oracle of Delphi."

"What? Did you end up killing her?"

"Trey, you know I'm not going to tell you something Nostradamus hasn't shown you yet."

We still maintain eye contact and I let him see me roll my eyes in disgust.

"Fine," I say. *"Let's summon the old prophet and see what he wants to say to you."*

Max asks, *"How do we do that?"*

"I have to enter a trance state first and then call out his name a few times. It doesn't always work, but almost every time. It's like he's back in the 16th Century just waiting for my call …. Although, when I think about it, he most likely knows exactly when I'm going to reach out to him."

"What do I do?"

"Hey, this is my first time traveling with a hitchhiker. I'm not sure, but I think you just have to relax and stay in contact with the skull."

Max takes a few deep drags from the pipe, keeping one hand on the skull. A hint of cherry in the tobacco that I've never noticed before tells me the old man probable bought a special vintage for tonight.

I position a seat cushion under my arm to keep it relaxed and in contact with the skull, then turn my focus to the flame in the tripod.

Slowly and deeply I inhale, then exhale. I see the flame, but everything else in my vision begins to fade. The only thing beyond the sight of the flame that I allow into my consciousness is the scent of cherry pipe smoke.

My breathing slows even more. The flame starts to shrink in my expanding vision. Soon, it's gone.

Then, my awareness shifts and my focus is beyond the here and now … expanding ever further.

"Nostradamus … Nostradamus … Nostradamus … Nostradamus …"

I sense his presence, but it takes him a few moments before he speaks.

"I am honored to finally be able to speak with you, Maximo Medici … my son of many sons." It's a tone of reverence from Nostradamus directed at my father … a tone I've never heard from him before.

A long few seconds go by before Max responds, *"The honor … it is all mine."*

Apparently, I'm just a wire here … just a conduit for these two to praise each other.

"You have far exceeded your gifts and your expectations, Maximo. To have stopped two Antichrists yourself, I owe you … history owes you a great debt of gratitude."

"None of the Antichrists could have been stopped without your grand design," says Max. *"And, I could have never managed the last one without Trey."*

Way to go, old man! A two-time MVP superstar Holy Warrior *and* a class act – way to stand up for your boy!

"That may be true," says Nostradamus, his voice much more sullen than usual, *"but he has created an enormous dilemma by changing history. What was done may now be undone and the First Order knows this."*

"They stole the clear crystal skull … is that what they need to change the past?" asks Max.

"While the abilities of the Oracle's family line and my family line are similar, they are not the same. I do not know how they will use the crystal skull. The timing, however, seems to indicate a need for it to accomplish their goals."

"Does this mean everything I went through in 1945 could be for nothing?" asks Max.

"That remains to be seen. The past is now malleable. There must be multiple different realities where you failed instead of succeeded in your 1945 mission. If the First Order can do what Trey did … change the past so our reality merges with another one … then any potential outcome is possible."

"Look," I say, *"I know I screwed up … made a colossal mistake. I'm willing to do what it takes to make this right. I just need to know how."*

"That is why I wanted to speak with your father, Trey. Without his help in your time, I believe you are doomed to fail." More than a hint of anger radiates from Nostradamus.

"Hasn't he done enough for this world? Max … my father … has spent his entire life protecting everyone else. He's only been in love the one time with Katarina and we all know how that turned out. Can you do something … anything to make sure he can relax and have some fun from now on?"

Nostradamus assumes a more reasonable tone, *"Trying to influence the future is not something that should be taken so lightly. Think about what might have happened if I had been able to speak with Maximo before he met Katarina and warned him about her. You would not exist. The third Antichrist may have been successful. I'm afraid that is not a promise I can make."*

Exasperated, I say, *"What about this Tori Cromwell woman. She's not a spy, too, is she? At least tell us that much."*

"What I can tell you is that I have seen the English woman's path from your time forward is to follow closely with both of yours."

"Really? That's all you're going to say? Might as well write a cryptic quatrain about it." It's my turn to be angry. *"Max has done enough. It's not fair to ask any more from him."*

"Trey," says Max in a warm, fatherly tone, *"I can help .... I want to help. There's no way I can let the mission from 1945 get unraveled and do nothing about it. What can I do?"*

Nostradamus takes a moment before replying, *"Let us examine what we know .... We know the First Order wants Adolf Hitler to be successful in his attempt to dominate the world. We know Maximo in 1945 was able to stop Hitler. We know the First Order stole the clear crystal skull from your home in your time, and we know the stray sister – this Lady Zelda – had the same crystal skull in her possession while she was advising Hitler in 1945. While I cannot see the Oracle or what she will do, we can at least apply logic to try to deduce what she might do."*

Max says, *"You think they are going to try to kill me in 1945, don't you?"*

Nostradamus answers, *"That is what I would do if I shared their situation and goals ... yes."*

"And, you think they're going to use Zelda?"

"That is, I believe, the only way they can get to you in 1945."

"We can't let that happen," I say, *"What can we do to stop the Oracle?"*

Again, a few moments pass before Nostradamus replies, *"As concerned as I am about what the Oracle may do, I am more concerned about you and your actions. Why I want your father to join you on the rest of your visits to 1945 is so that he can provide a steadying influence on your choices and actions."*

Steadying influence? He wants Max to keep me in check. We have the Oracle of Delphi trying to kill my father in the past and wipe out my existence, along with the entire future for my family ... and Nostradamus is worried about what I might do. My anger builds, but at the same time, I caused all of this. As much as I want to strike out at Nostradamus, he and Max have been right all along. I should have never tried to save Sam ... should have never opened this door to changing history. Hearing I need a steadying influence may be challenging, but maybe it's for the best. Max has always had my back. Always been there to guide and mentor me. He knows his own history better than anyone and he knows me. Even with the mistakes I've made ... all the way back to childhood ... Max has always been there to help me.

Finally, I say, *"If my father is okay with it, so am I."*

"Of course I'm okay with it," says Max. *"But, what will my role be?"*

Nostradamus doesn't hesitate this time, *"You know better than anyone what happened in 1945 ... what the key people did ... what their motivations were ... and, what you finally did to end it all. Trey may see something he thinks is wrong that is meant to happen. He may think his interference will help when it will not. I want you to help me guide him for the rest of this journey."*

Max answers, *"Anything I can do … I will do."*

Chapter 32

MAX MEDICI

EUROPE
APRIL 17, 1945

Votan places the bloodstained crystal skull on the red jaguar throne facing the entrance to the inner chamber. The skull seems to be grinning a red, bloody grin.

The vision in my dream blurs, briefly, and then regains clarity. Empty air appears where Votan just stood. Still in the stone temple atop the pyramid, my focus shifts to the green-eyed jaguar. Much like my previous dreams, dirt and moss coat the room now and a layer of dust covers the jaguar. I know when I turn I'll see a large blood-red swastika on the wall. I turn anyway.

Sudden sharp pain flairs in my shoulder.

"Wake up, little brother."

Another flash of pain, this time on my neck.

"*Little brother* ..." The melodic voice is familiar.

It takes me a moment, but I soon realize the pain and the voice are outside of my dream.

My eyes flutter and my dream ends, but I'm not ready to wake up yet.

Pain ... the shoulder again. I'm going to –

"You've had a lovely nap, but it's time to go."

As I gain my bearings, I find I'm on a plane in a seat pressed against a small window. My temple hurts. Pressing my fingers to it, I feel an indentation in the shape of the window edge. Not knowing how I got from the bunker in Nuremburg to the plane, I imagine Ister had Von Becker carry me. He probably tossed me into this seat and that's when my head hit the window.

My window faces east and the sun hovers just below the horizon. Small buildings dot the edge of the runway centered by a small control tower.

Ister sits with Zelda in the two seats across the aisle from Rolf, who's next to me. Von Becker is behind us, taking two seats on his own. Lutz, the radioman, and Dr. Brandt sit behind Ister, and the U-boat crewmen sit in the rearmost seats.

The pilot walks to us from the cockpit and Rolf turns away from me to hear what she has to say.

Looking out his window, Ister asks the pilot, "Captain Uhse – why did we land here?"

She removes her hat, letting her medium length blonde hair fall to her shoulders. "If you want to make it into Berlin alive, the airport here at Gatow was our best choice. The Russians have Berlin nearly surrounded and are shelling the city with their artillery. Gatow is outside of the Russian circle of troops. The Hitlerjugend are on their way to escort you to the city."

Rolf says, "Women pilots and Hitler Youth ... where are all the men?"

Anger sparks in the pilot's eyes and in her voice, "You have been away for too long, perhaps, and don't know ... the men are all dead. The British have shot down all our male pilots ... including my husband. You are stuck with the Hitlerjugend and with me."

Ister stands and says, "You have done well, Captain. This airport – Gatow – we will use it to get what we need back to the U-boats in Italy."

"The supplies from Dr. Heisenberg?" she asks.

"Yes, why?"

"That will take quite a few trips to Italy and back. We only have four functioning cargo planes with pilots." She looks down for a moment, calculating. "I believe we will need at least three weeks to transport everything Heisenberg wants to take."

"You saw for yourself, Captain," says Ister. "The Russians have set siege to the city, cutting off supplies. I doubt we have three weeks to work with. I will have Heisenberg send back the first crates immediately."

"What will happen if the Russians take Berlin?" she asks.

Ister sneers, "I was there when we invaded Russia – flew in several times during our long and bloody siege of Leningrad. In fact, that is how I found Lady Zelda. With what we did in Russia, I am certain they will be looking for revenge …. You do not want to be in the city when they take it."

We exit the plane just as the sun peeks through the buildings to the east. Not far from us, we hear the repeating combination of a small explosion, then the whistling of a flying artillery shell, and then a larger explosion. Dust, exhaust fumes, and burning oil pervade the air around us. Between the rising sun and us, several plumes of smoke slowly rise above Berlin.

A small squad approaches us of eight SS troops in a perfect two-by-four formation with every step synchronized. Each wears his black SS uniform and carries a submachine gun. As they get closer, I see they are in fact youths … all about my age. While I expect to see fear in them, or at least some doubt about their futures, all I see in their expressions is seriousness … with a dose of anger. I can't imagine the training they've gone through to be this way when their families are gone or in danger; their city under siege; their capture or death imminent.

One boy steps toward Ister, raises his hand forward, and yells, "Blood and honor! Heil Hitler!"

The seven others do the same in perfect unison.

Ister asks the leader of the boys, "You can get us into the city safely?"

"Yes, sir. This way." He rejoins the others in formation, and they turn around in unison and begin walking briskly to a small storage facility next to the control tower. We follow, with Rolf at my side every step of the way.

Once in the building, we pass through double doors, head down a wide ramp into an underground bunker. Another set of doors open to a tunnel. We take a group of carts that appear to be powered by electricity instead of gasoline and make our way through a labyrinth of dimly lit tunnels. Driving for miles, we often pass single or double doors, or open caverns. I'm doing my best to remember the way … hoping that knowing the right path to take will be useful.

Finally stopping outside a set of double doors, a small light barely illuminates the sign above them.

Institut für Physik … Department of Physics.

Past the doors is a massive cavern, too perfectly shaped to be anything other than man-made. Men and women in white lab jackets move about in all directions … just short of chaos.

A thin man wearing a gray suit and black tie emerges from the center aisle of the cavern, and comes to greet Ister. He's the only person in the cavern not wearing a lab coat.

"Welcome back, Herr Ister."

"Dr. Heisenberg. What is your status?"

Dr. Werner Heisenberg ... the scientist Professor Einstein told me is leading the Nazi effort to build the atomic bomb ... the scientist I can't trust.

"The papers from Einstein do provide some answers as we had hoped. The key to the chain reaction ... to exploding the bomb is rather simple, now that we know what to do. It's just a matter of imploding the uranium instead of exploding –"

A flash of light bursts from the back of the cavern behind Heisenberg. In the next instant, the floor shakes and the explosion knocks the physicist to the ground.

The confusion that follows the explosion provides a perfect opportunity for me to escape. Both Von Becker and Rolf quickly move to protect Ister. The SS youth form a human shield between the cavern doors and the rest of us. I could make a dash for the cart, but I don't even try.

There's a reason Ister has me in my Italian uniform – a reason why I'm in Berlin and why he's let me live this long. Thinking back to what he told Himmler ... that I am here to deliver a message from Mussolini to Hitler, and they are escorting me to the Fuhrer. It may be insane, but I'm starting to wonder if Ister *wants* me to kill Hitler. The war has become a disaster for Germany. Maybe Ister wants it to end as much as we do. As sadistic as Ister seems to be, he may be my best opportunity to get to Hitler.

One of the three U-boat crewmen still with us helps Heisenberg back to his feet. He seems uninjured.

Through the doors, men in lab coats grab gas masks and fire extinguishers, and run toward the back of the cavern.

Heisenberg looks through the door, checks in all directions, and then starts walking briskly in the direction of the explosion. Ister follows him and we all follow Ister.

Making our way through the cavern, I start to recognize some of the materials and equipment Professor Einstein taught us would be necessary to build an atomic bomb. Heisenberg is nearly running, so we pass each department quickly. Metal working ... wire harnesses ... detonators ... dynamite ... rocketry ... testing. What I don't see yet –

perhaps the most critical component to the atomic bomb – the enrichment equipment. Less than 1% of natural uranium consists of the 235 isotope, which is suitable to be used in a bomb. Enriching the uranium to increase the percentage of the 235 isotope is required to achieve the necessary chain reaction of atom splitting.

"NO!" yells Heisenberg. "Not that."

The sign next to the door where he stands reads, "Uranium Enrichment."

Smoke billows from the room. Just as Heisenberg is about to enter, two men emerge wearing gas masks and carrying a third man. They try to move past us … to get the man away from the smoke and to some medical attention.

Heisenberg holds up his hand and says, "Wait! This is Dr. Toch. Is he alive?"

Toch … that's the scientist who has been writing Professor Einstein. He's a friend of the professor's.

Dr. Toch blinks a few times and coughs. His left hand and arm are horribly burnt … red and blistered in some areas and crisped black in others. I almost vomit from the smell of his burnt flesh.

"Dr. Toch … Abraham … what happened?" asks Heisenberg, gripping the burnt man's jacket so the men carrying him can't move him.

Toch coughs again. "Sabotage … the American boy …." His voice is hoarse, barely audible.

Ister's personal physician, Dr. Brandt, steps forward and yells, "Bring him over here." He points to a table on the other side of the cavern … away from the smoke.

The two men in gas masks follow the doctor and lay Toch on the table. As Brandt begins his examination, more men emerge from the billowing smoke.

First, is another man in a gas mask supporting a scientist. The scientist is coughing and limping, but otherwise seems fine.

Emerging next are two more men in gas masks carrying another person. Again, Heisenberg stops them so he can identify the injured scientist. Peering over Rolf's shoulder, I see it isn't a scientist at all. It's Dieter. His left arm and part of his torso are gone. The rest of his torso is burnt. Dieter's not blinking … not coughing … not alive. I shake my head in disgust and dismay.

Did Dr. Toch help Dieter as the professor thought he might? Did he cause the explosion? Did he sacrifice his life to take out the Nazi's ability to enrich uranium? My pride in Dieter soon overshadows the sadness of his death. Everything I see points to his sacrifice. He's a true hero. I only hope I can someday share the news with Professor Einstein – and maybe even Dieter's family. That hope quickly fades when I assess my situation. If the Germans don't kill me, the British bombing raids or Russian artillery shells probably will. Or, I may end up in a position like Dieter to sacrifice myself for the cause.

Where are the others? Where are they keeping Ian, Bernie, and Kirk?

Heisenberg finds a gas mask at one of the stations outside the enrichment room.

"I suggest you wait in the testing lab," he says to Ister just before donning the mask. "I will see what happened."

Ister yells to the rest of us, "Come with me!"

Walking quickly with Rolf at his side and Von Becker one step behind, he leads us to the testing lab where we find many empty stations and empty chairs for us to sit and wait for Heisenberg. With the time, and no one paying too much attention to me, I'm able to assess the testing equipment the Germans are using. Several oscilloscopes show flat lines currently ... a few Geiger-Muller counters to detect ionizing radiation ... gaseous ionization detectors ... ammeters ... voltmeters ... wattmeters ... ohmmeters. The German scientists seem to have everything they need down here in the tunnels and caverns below Berlin.

Yet, until Ister arrived, they seemed content to keep working on the atomic bomb instead of evacuating. The British are bombing them daily and the Russians have surrounded Berlin. Can they truly be so close to completion of the bomb that they decided to stay?

The Germans started working on the atomic bomb before America even entered the war. The only thing they haven't yet solved was the concept of imploding the uranium core instead of exploding it, and that's not a terribly difficult concept. Something's not right. They should have figured this out long ago. The Germans should already have the atomic bomb in their arsenal.

Maybe Hitler never believed in it and withheld resources ... maybe something else prevented the scientists from completing the bomb.

It's not long before Heisenberg walks into the testing lab and removes his gas mask. He reeks of smoke and ash. His hands are black from silt, but he doesn't appear injured.

"I am sorry to report, Herr Ister, that Dr. Toch is dead. Your Dr. Brandt couldn't save him, but he stayed behind to treat others with injuries. Dr. Toch was correct in reporting the sabotage of the enrichment equipment. Someone built a small explosive device – probably from our supply of dynamite – and set it off in the lab. The damage to the equipment is beyond our ability to repair it."

Smiling, I remember Dieter always performed the best of our group in building explosives. I quickly hide the smile just before Rolf turns my way.

Ister stands and asks, "Is the supply of enriched uranium still safe?"

"Yes," answers Heisenberg.

"How much do we have?"

"Enough for three bombs."

My brief glee from thinking Dieter had successfully accomplished our mission immediately dissolves. Three atomic bombs present the potential destruction of three cities ... the potential deaths of millions of people ... the potential to reverse the tides of this war in favor of the Nazis.

Ister, resigned to his situation, follows with, "Then that will have to do for now. Start getting everything crated and over to Gatow."

Heisenberg blinks a few times and looks to the others before returning his attention to Ister. "But Herr Ister. We need some time ... at least four weeks."

"We don't have four weeks," Ister's voice rises in anger. "The Hitlerjugend will help .... Get it done in two weeks."

Heisenberg's only response is the Nazi salute and, "Heil Hitler!"

Chapter 33

TREY TYSON
LONGBOAT KEY, FL, USA
APRIL 17, 2014

Max and I have just watched the sun set over the calm Gulf waters. He's brought and set up the usual tripod, candle, and peace pipe. Yesterday we added the white crystal skull into the mix so Max could communicate with Nostradamus and help guide my visions into his past.

Today, he's also brought a glass of what appears to be his favorite adult beverage – amaretto on ice. The sweet almond aroma of the amaretto blends well with the salty breeze coming from the Gulf. He pours a glass to commemorate special days. Max never tells me what he's commemorating, but I think I know some of the reasons.

The most recent – every 30th of March – that's the day President Reagan survived an assassination attempt back in 1981. Max was in his prime back then, and heading up the AI division of the Secret Service. Knowing Max, he probably blames himself for the fact that Reagan took a bullet … ignoring the more important fact that Reagan survived and Max most likely had a lot to do with that.

Some days he'll pour a glass and I have no idea why; like the 21st of every December and every June – the winter and summer solstices. The 26th of every May is another one.

Other amaretto days include every Christmas, Easter Sundays, my birthdays, the day we took out Karl and stopped the third Antichrist, and every 22nd of November – the anniversary of Kennedy's assassination in 1963.

Every 30th of April is another … I think I'm going to understand that meaning much better soon.

And today – must have been one hell of a date with Tori!

"How did Tinef hold up to all the rocking today?" I ask him, tongue firmly in cheek.

"Hmmm? The seas were quite calm," he says, blissfully unaware of my attempt at humor.

"Don't you ever wonder why Einstein left you that sailboat in his will?"

"He knew I enjoyed my time sailing with him," Max replies. "Still, I do wonder ... quite often, actually. His only explanation in his will was similar to something Nostradamus would have written. Einstein wrote that he knew I was religious and he hoped I would someday find God and myself in unification on Tinef. I tried to guess his meaning. Maybe the professor had some prophetic abilities .... It was a fantastic day with Tori, especially sailing the Gulf."

"I'm glad to hear it, Max. She seems pretty special and you deserve nothing less."

Max takes a hearty swig from the snifter of amaretto, places it down, and lights the peace pipe. The cherry smoke perfectly complements the sweet almond and salty sea air ... olfactory heaven!

A relaxed smile forming, Max says, "Nostradamus told us tonight is the night we're going to go back and see the day I met Adolf Hitler."

"Yes, April 20, 1945. We'll have a gap of three days that you spent with the German physicists before meeting Hitler. Did you find out about your other friends?"

"Almost immediately. I ran into Bernie, and he told me the Germans questioned them in depth and then put them to work under direction of the Hitler Youth. Bernie was shocked when I told him what happened to Dieter."

"Sorry, Max. I can't imagine what you must have gone through. From what I've witnessed, Dieter seemed like a really good guy."

"He certainly was." Max raises his snifter in the air to salute his lost friend and then takes another large gulp.

"Anything else I need to know about what happened in those three days?"

"Not that I can think of. The Nazis spent the time getting as much information as they could out of me and my remaining friends ... and packing up what they needed from the caverns and tunnels to continue working on the bomb at another location."

"Where?"

"In due time, Trey. In due time."

"I know you don't fully trust me to do what needs to be done when it needs to be done. I know Nostradamus feels the same way. I've made some mistakes, so I understand why you feel that way. I sense I'm going to need that trust, though, and soon. We're coming to a crux point in time … I can feel it. You don't have the same abilities I have. Not even Nostradamus has the same abilities I have. I need you both to trust that I will do what I have to do to protect our past … not to mention our present and future."

Max says, "We all need to trust each other. You need to trust that Nostradamus is showing you what you need to see and when you need to see it. Nostradamus, on the other hand, must trust in your abilities. I think he does trust you, though, Trey. Otherwise, we wouldn't be doing this at all."

As Max takes a long drag from the peace pipe, I start to focus on the flame in the tripod. We both place a hand on the crystal skull.

With the comforting knowledge that Max will be along for the ride for the rest of my visits to his past, I inhale the deep, rich cherry pipe smoke. Focusing on the flame, everything else in my vision begins to fade. My breathing slows, and the flame shrinks. As my awareness expands I feel this new connection to Max tethering part of my consciousness to the present.

"Nostradamus … Nostradamus … Nostradamus …"

Something about this crystal skull enhances my abilities in a different way than my amulet. I can sense and actually visualize the connection to Max and the new connection to Nostradamus as he joins us. In this strange triangle of communication and time travel, I am both the conduit and the hub.

Nostradamus says, *"My sons of many sons. Are you prepared to return to 1945?"*

Max eagerly answers before I can, *"Yes."*

"Trey," says Nostradamus, with less disappointment in his voice than usual. *"Our next journey will be to the 20th of April in 1945 to see your father in Berlin, Germany."*

"Keep your hands and feet inside the vehicle for the entire duration of the ride," I say, knowing Nostradamus won't get the joke. Come to think of it, I can't imagine Max has ever been to DisneyWorld, Universal Studios, or even a park like Cedar Point where he might have heard a ride operator say that. Oh well. My humor is lost on these two.

Maximo Medici … Berlin, Germany … April 20, 1945 … Maximo Medici … Berlin, Germany … April 20, 1945 … Maximo Medici … Berlin, Germany

… April 20, 1945 … Maximo Medici … Berlin, Germany … April 20, 1945 …

A swirl of space suddenly forms around us. Stars emerge, and they circle counterclockwise. The dance of stars gains enough speed as to blur into a long, circling spiral of light with a mix of an electric blue hue and a flame red hue. This time, a full third of the spiral consists of the red hue. We're flying through space-time.

The spiral of light slows to the point where I can make out individual stars. Slower still, the stars fade and go dark.

Max quietly utters one word, *"Whoa."*

MAX MEDICI
BERLIN, GERMANY
APRIL 20, 1945

In the dimly lit caverns beneath Berlin, I've watched Kirk make the surprisingly rapid transition from American spy training to destroy the German atomic weapons program to a German SS leader of a squad of Hitler Youth. He traded in the gray uniform provided for him in Princeton for the all black of the SS after a long and private conversation with Ister.

Ian and Bernie also wear the black SS uniforms, and are among the 11 boys reporting to Kirk. Hitler Youth, ranging from as old as 18 to as young as 12, are all that remain of the German troops to defend Berlin.

Still in my Italian uniform, I get many strange looks from the Hitler Youth, but word has spread that I carry a message for the Fuhrer. Ister made it clear I'm to stay with Rolf Barbie every moment of every day, which means I'm also always near Ister. Rolf seems frustrated, but so far has obeyed Ister's orders to not kill me … unless I try to escape. He's even refrained from whipping me with the baton anymore for fear of ruining this charade … a charade I was supposed to create. Now, I'm just a puppet in Ister's plans.

He wants me to kill Hitler. It's the only way any of this charade makes sense. For my part, I'll let Ister pull the strings as long as I get to achieve my goal. Strange … Hagan Ister and I teaming up to kill Adolf Hitler. Apparently, Ister wants this war to end as much as I do. His reasoning might be that ending the war would spare the lives of countless Germans, but I doubt it. Something else drives him ... motivating him to remove Hitler from the top of the Nazi Reich.

Kirk's squad has been instrumental in getting the atomic weapon equipment and supplies packed and sent to Gatow airfield. With the airfield so close to the Russian circle of troops around Berlin, the British bombing raids have moved on to other targets. This leaves the few German pilots still alive the opportunity to make the necessary transport flights to Italy. The German scientists seem to be gaining confidence in their ability to meet the two-week deadline Ister has ordered.

Confidence and hope. I can feel it in the way some of the Germans speak to each other ... the way they go about their business. Remnants of both confidence and hope linger. Still. Not for all the Germans, to be sure. Some seem to be mentally defeated. Living underground for weeks at a time would naturally cause despair and depression. At the peak of Nazi domination, the Germans held most of Europe along with parts of Africa and Asia. Now, the Allies have them cornered in Germany with most of their leaders hiding underground. Everyone in the world knows Germany is about to lose this war except Ister and the Hitler Youth. *Why?*

What basis can they possibly have for hope? Hope that the war will end soon, perhaps, even if it ends in defeat ... even if it ends in death.

While we're hiding in these gray concrete underground caverns, tunnels, and bunkers, tens of thousands of Hitler Youth defend Berlin at the cost of many of their lives. I've overheard the reports coming in to Ister and it's been a bloody, horrific battle. The Russians slowly tighten their noose around the city, shelling Berlin with a nearly constant barrage of artillery, but the Hitler Youth make them fight for every step toward the city center.

Ister almost immediately arranged for an office to be set up close to the scientists. Small and dark, a concrete cube similar to all the rooms here beneath Berlin, he's ordered ornate walnut furniture brought in and artwork hung to provide some semblance of normalcy. He spends much of his time reading copies of reports from all reaches of the German military, and the rest of the time he applies pressure to ensure the atomic weapons equipment is being shipped on his schedule.

Rolf stays in the office with Ister, which means I do as well. Stationed outside Ister's door, Von Becker decides who gets in to see the leader of the Thule Society. Mostly messengers come with status reports, along with frequent visits from Dr. Brandt and Lady Zelda — the only two people Ister seems to respect enough to hear their advice.

Dr. Brandt's visits often include examinations, vitamins, medications, shots, and treatment for the wounds around Ister's face and neck … wounds that apparently aren't able to heal fully. The doctor seems to be Ister's only true friend and confidant, and Ister's mood lifts every time Brandt arrives.

When Lady Zelda visits, Ister insists on Rolf removing me from his office. As much as I'd like to hear what she has to say, I have to admit it feels like a vacation just being away from Ister. It's almost as though there's a high-pressure weather system hovering around the strange man at all times. Lightning might strike at any moment. People are uptight around him and he clearly enjoys it that way.

Many of the reports Ister received our first day here came via a telephone in his office, but the Nazi communications system became one of the many casualties of the Russian artillery yesterday. Now, all reports come via messenger, and I've learned so much more by hearing both ends of Ister's conversations. A man named Artur Axmann leads the Hitler Youth, and he's stationed in the Fuhrerbunker with Hitler.

Hagan Ister not only heads up the Thule Society, but he also leads an elite group of Hitler Youth known for their pure Aryan heritage. These young soldiers share a special emblem sewn over their heart on their black SS uniforms … a rounded swastika with a spearhead in front of it, and the spearhead shares the same golden sheath I saw on each of the spearheads crated in Nuremberg. What evil mind would combine a swastika with the Spear of Destiny?

Ister dismisses one messenger just as another arrives. Von Becker lets this one in without hesitation.

"Herr Ister," says Von Becker. "A messenger from the Fuhrer …"

"Enter," says Ister.

I wonder if Ister will order Rolf to remove me from his office, but he doesn't.

"The Fuhrer's birthday celebration will be held in the Chancellery Garden immediately."

Ister stops reading the report in his hand and gives the messenger his full attention. "I know the Fuhrer always celebrates his birthday with a ceremony for the troops, but outside? With the Russians shelling the city?"

"The Fuhrer has ordered General Steiner to attack the Russians with the SS from the north, and General Weildling to attack with the

9th Army from the south. The enemy knows we will break their siege from the outside, so the shells aimed into Berlin have stopped. The Fuhrer expects a delegation of your Hitlerjugend for the celebration at once."

Ister stands for a few seconds, at a complete loss for words. The reports he's heard have offered no hope for a reprieve from the Russian assault. One messenger from earlier today reported General Weildling's army had been decimated by the Russians at the Oder River. Another messenger reported all attempts to contact General Steiner had failed. Ister must at least doubt the validity of this report. Yet, an energetic "Heil Hitler!" is his response.

"Heil Hitler," says the messenger before briskly leaving Ister's office.

"Barbie," says Ister. "Go get two squads of my Hitlerjugend. Bring Medici with you …. It is time he meets the Fuhrer."

"Come, little brother," commands Rolf.

We proceed to find Kirk and another squad leader. Not all of the squad's boys are available with no notice, but Rolf is able to gather 19 Hitler Youth, along with the squad leaders and myself. Rolf leads our Hitler birthday celebration partygoers, which strangely includes Kirk, Ian, Bernie, and me, on a fast and orderly march for over a mile down a tunnel I haven't even seen until now.

Plans start to form in my mind. I'm unarmed, as are Ian and Bernie. A squad leader sets the pace for us, and carries a submachine gun. I'm second in line, and Rolf is right behind me, carrying both his baton and a luger. Ian and Bernie keep pace near the middle of the pack. Kirk is last in line, and also carries a submachine gun. Is the damned thing loaded? Has he completely switched sides?

I envision tripping the squad leader in front of me and taking his submachine gun, but I decide to wait until we're near Hitler before I try anything.

At the end of the tunnel stand four adult guards dressed in SS black and behind them are thick, blast resistant doors with large sliding metal latches at both the top and bottom. These may be the last few adult male soldiers in Berlin; it makes sense they would be guarding the path to Hitler.

"Reporting for the Fuhrer's celebration," announces the squad leader in front of me.

One of the guards says, "We're expecting you. Through this door, then the second door on your left, and then up a flight of stairs. You'll be in the Reich Chancellery Garden. Get your squads in a line – the Fuhrer will be there shortly."

The squad leader starts to walk past the guard, but they stop him.

"No weapons of any kind past this point," says the guard, who firmly grasps the leader's submachine gun. The leader doesn't hesitate to hand it over to the guard.

The guards carefully pat him down from his neck to his boots, then let him pass.

"What the hell are *you* doing here?" the guard directs to me while pointing to my Italian uniform.

"He's with me," says Rolf, stepping forward, and handing the guard his luger. "Herr Ister escorted him from Italy. He has a message for the Fuhrer."

At hearing Ister's name, the guards take a quick moment to make eye contact with each other, but they don't try to stop me. They do, however, thoroughly check every possible place I might carry a weapon or bomb.

Rolf tries to pass them with his baton still attached to his belt, but they even take that.

After everyone passes the thorough search, we form a line in the tunnel just beyond the blast doors. Before heading up to the garden, Kirk addresses the two squads.

"It is very important to Herr Ister that we make a good impression with the Fuhrer," he says. One at a time, Kirk faces each of us, touches his hand to his swastika spear emblem over his heart, and yells, "Blood and honor!"

Each of the Hitler Youth touches his emblem, in turn, and yells, "Blood and honor!"

When he reaches me, Kirk refuses to make eye contact. With my Italian uniform, no one seems surprised when he steps past me and faces Rolf instead. Rolf's uniform doesn't have the emblem, but he goes through the motion of touching his heart, and even yells, "Blood and honor!"

The other squad leader repeats the salute and then Kirk takes his place at the back of the line again.

Carrying a submachine gun and not using it against the Nazis had me suspicious of Kirk's allegiance, but this blood and honor crap has me convinced he must be the traitor. Ister broke him much too quickly and too easily.

In an orderly line, we pass through the second door on our left and up a narrow flight of steel steps. Once through the door we emerge into the northwest corner of what the Germans call the Chancellery Garden. The constant barrage of artillery shells has paused, but I have trouble imagining the Russians inflicting more damage upon the Nazi headquarters.

Smoke and clouds meet above the fray to block out the sun and create an even grayer visage than the caverns beneath the city. Various structures encompass the vast central garden, and every window on every building has been shattered. Small fires burn without anyone bothering to put them out. Piles of rubble have spilled from buildings in every direction. Roughly 200 Hitler Youth stand perfectly lined up in front of the wall with the least visible damage, with 4 panzers aligned parallel to them. They may call it a garden, but it's a battlefield in reality.

As our squads join formation, a man with a video camera emerges from the rearmost panzer. The downward angle from the top of the panzer allows him to shoot video of the ceremony while only capturing the unfazed Hitler Youth and the undamaged bottom of the wall.

Taking in the destruction of the Reich Chancellery, I never noticed the small entourage of men at the other end of the Hitler Youth line. Two men with still cameras on the outside of the group snap photographs. Two other men flank the man in the center. They smile …. They shake hands with the Hitler Youth …. They take part in the conversations with each boy …. However, their true purpose is to guard the man in the center.

Adolf Hitler.

Wearing a white shirt and black tie with the collar of his gray dress uniform up to shield his neck from the cold April air, Hitler moves quickly down the line. Shaking hands with each boy first, he then touches their chest and says something I can't make out from this distance.

Do I try to kill him now? If not, when will I ever get the chance again?

As if reading my thoughts, Rolf leans over and whispers, "This is not the time for anything stupid, little brother. We are just here to meet the Fuhrer. Nothing more."

Nothing more. Rolf is a puppet as much as I am. His strings are just longer.

Hitler draws nearer.

Recalling the photographs President Roosevelt had Dr. Bush show me, I have to make sure this man is truly Adolf Hitler and not his double. The real Hitler's left hand will shake uncontrollably, and his valet, Heinz Linge, will be at his side.

A mere 17 boys away, Hitler shakes hands with Kirk. I can't hear what Hitler says, but Kirk's reply is, "An honor, my Fuhrer!"

With the entourage now in view, the two men closer to me are obviously not Heinz Linge.

Hitler keeps his left hand behind his back, shaking each boy's hand with his right. The real Hitler would do this to hide his ailment. A double might do this to hide his lack of an ailment.

Nine boys from me, Hitler greets Bernie with an audible, "Brave boy," and pats Bernie on the chest. I can now see that the guard following Hitler presents each boy with an iron cross as he greets them, and he is not Linge. The only man left to identify is the last man in the entourage. The camera constantly in front of his face prevents me from being certain.

Seven boys away and Hitler greets Ian with, "Well done," before tapping his chest. As much as I want to see Ian's reaction to this, I don't dare make eye contact with him and blow our cover.

Hitler's first photographer steps to just a few paces in front of me. No one has a weapon I can see, so I consider the possibility of grabbing the camera from this man and bashing Hitler's head in with it. I just need to know he's the real Hitler before sacrificing my life too soon.

Rolf is next to meet Hitler. The second photographer still hasn't lowered his camera.

Hitler pauses in front of Rolf, looks at him for a long moment, and says, "Rolf Barbie, what are you doing here?"

This distraction provides me the opportunity to execute my plan, but just as I'm about to leap at the first photographer, the second finally lowers his camera. With light brown hair visible beneath his cap, he is decidedly not Heinz Linge. The man about to step in front of me and possibly shake my hand is *not* the real Adolf Hitler.

As my nerves ease back from the precipice of potentially murdering the most evil man ever to walk the planet, Rolf looks my way and says, "My Fuhrer. Herr Ister has escorted this messenger of Mussolini here from Italy. He carries a private message for your eyes only."

Fake Hitler finally turns to face me, and I am certain I would have never known he was fake without the help from Dr. Bush and President Roosevelt.

With hunched shoulders, watery eyes, and a weak and scratchy voice he says, "Your name?"

"Maximo Medici." I see no reason to lie to this man.

He looks me over for a few seconds and then turns back to Rolf. "I will send for him when I am ready. Relay this to Herr Ister."

Not interested in my message, apparently, fake Hitler turns and walks quickly in the direction from which he came ... entourage in tow.

The man atop the panzer stops filming.

The squad leaders start barking orders for the Hitler Youth to march to their various assignments and stations.

A loud pop from the east is followed by the ever-increasing volume of a whistling artillery shell overhead.

While the panzers scatter, the Hitler Youth eerily maintain discipline as the shell explodes just past the barracks building to our west.

The Reich Chancellery is a prime Russian target and we sit well within their range.

TREY TYSON
LONGBOAT KEY, FL, USA
APRIL 17, 2014

"Time to go," says Nostradamus and the clockwise vortex opens, taking us back to the present.

Part of me wonders if I could prevent him from ending a vision if I wanted to. I brought us here. I'm the conduit and hub. Shouldn't I be the one who decides when we return? Another part of me recalls Max saying I need to trust the guidance from Nostradamus.

"What do you make of the red hue in the vortex?" I ask Nostradamus.

"The red hue is new to the vortex," he says. *"I don't know this for certain, but I believe it indicates the influence of the Oracle. I expect the next vision we experience will be the crux point of the battle to change history."*

"We're talking about going up against the First Order and the Oracle. Aren't their prophetic abilities the most powerful in history?" asks Max.

"Perhaps they are," says Nostradamus. *"We have Trey on our side, and their blood flows through him as well. Their abilities are also his to wield, improving our chances in the battle to come. Our next journey will be to the 30th of April in*

1945. In your time, it is the 17th of April. The Oracle may be more powerful, so we must leverage every advantage at our disposal. The close family connection to the past improves our position. Maximo is your father, so that will be to our advantage. The closer the geographic location, the stronger the connection to the past. The First Order, with their long presence in Germania, will possess the advantage here. We must synchronize your date with my date with the date from your father's past to align our respective orbital positions and offer our optimal chance at success. I will await your connection from the 30th of April in 1655 here in Salon, France. I want you to wait until your 30th of April before you reach out to me and we take our next journey."

"A vacation right before the battle?"

"A respite," says Nostradamus. *"Be well rested by the 30th. History depends upon you."*

With that said, Nostradamus severs the connection from his end.

Chapter 34

SIR ARCHIE
PYTHO ISLAND
APRIL 30, 2014

After all the years I've yearned for a red clasp, looking at it now, I wonder why I cared so much.

I've come to the conclusion that I bear the burden of having too much time in and too much knowledge of the outside world. Maybe someone with less time out there would find the past two weeks to feel more normal. The sisterhood set up chambers for Audrey and me within the second level of the pyramid. An endless stream of pretty women – of varying ages and all apparently related to the Oracle and Mother – serve us our meals, bring us wine, change our linens, asking and fulfilling any or our needs.

Without the constant distractions the outside world offers, Audrey and I have spent the last two weeks getting to know each other. While we both enjoy the view from the open air portion of the Temple of Apollo, we prefer the long walks we take along the rarely used path leading from the temple down to the teatro below. Kilometers of lush hills, sweet smelling flowers, and – most importantly – isolation have allowed us to bond … more so as a couple than colleagues.

It took only an hour after we returned from the Ascension Ceremony for us to break the First Order rule that knights not share anything from their past. We agreed that having the unique status of being a couple transcends the typical Alpha and Beta roles. I don't view Audrey as subservient to me in any way. It truth, I find myself hoping she sees me as her equal. The tales of our pasts became our way of getting to know each other, holding back nothing except our real names for fear of slipping and exposing our transgression in front of the Oracle or Mother.

After telling her about my mother and sister, she shared her experiences from her youth. Audrey grew up in an extremely conservative family. Her father had been a Knight of Economics before he passed while on a mission in the outer world, leaving an eight-year-old girl to be raised by a widowed mother. I did enough probing to realize my mentor Karl was not her father, but not so much as to discover her father's identity. Audrey's grandfather stepped in as the fatherly figure she so desperately missed. He, one of the many guards on Pytho, is well past retirement age, she explained, but refuses to give up his service to the council and our people.

Audrey's biggest dream, I've learned, was to follow her father into knighthood. Becoming one of the inaugural Knights of History must be something she would love to share with her family, but she'll never have contact with them again. Athena will tell her family that she has become a Beta Knight, and that is *all* she will say. They won't ever get news of Audrey again. Missions … trips to the outer world … successes … failures … even if she dies … her family will never know.

Maybe that will change if we help the Oracle succeed. Trying to change the past in such a way as to allow our society to rule again would also ensure the outer world would become aware of us. Maybe then, we could end all this damned secrecy.

Audrey's other dream, a family of her own, has always been mutually exclusive from her dream to be a knight. When the unique opportunity arose to be my Beta, some may have seen it as simply being a sex slave. Audrey saw it as an opportunity to be a knight *and* to have a family … representing the achievement of both of her dreams … making possible what had always been impossible. Arranged marriages are the norm in our society … this arrangement is just a little different from most.

I never imagined a family in my future, assuming I would be a Knight of Economics my entire life, but the thought offers a certain appeal. Much like the clouds blocking the evening sun, these thoughts of the future swirl through my mind as we start to climb the pyramid steps to the temple above. Our mission, however, is to change the past. How does the future matter one iota if we're about to change the past? Our very existence is at risk.

The curse of my intelligence strikes as I ponder the paradox of the cause and effect of my actions. If we change the past such that our society becomes the one true power in the world, what happens to me? Is there still a First Order? Do we still need knights? Do my parents still meet? Am I ever conceived? If I'm never born, can this mission where I am instrumental in changing the past ever even occur?

And what of Audrey? She's come to knighthood with the virtue of desiring nothing more than being able to help our people. She knows no tainting from the council or the outer world. She certainly hasn't had to murder someone to get to where she is in life, as I did. The beauty she radiates comes from within, pure of mind and heart. Holding hands as we ascend the pyramid, I feel the stirrings of love ... not the blind lust Mother expected me to feel. Am I worthy of her, though?

As we reach the top level among the variety of bird species that make the open-air section of the temple their home, several of the Oracle's personal guards greet us and direct us to the one passage into the closed section of the temple with a door. These women know both of us well now, having seen us walking all about the pyramid and surrounding grounds. Audrey's warmth has lessened the initial tension caused by my presence here.

One of the guards opens the door to the heart of the Temple of Apollo, and a waft of air flows out, saturated in the unmistakable aroma of hyacinths. The chamber's importance strikes me as we enter. This is where the Oracle experiences her prophecies ... where we will attempt to change history.

A roughly ten by six meter space with a high ceiling, frescos adorn each of the four walls. I don't think many of our people would recognize the depictions in the frescos ... maybe not even the Oracle. As one of the few of us alive today to travel to Delphi, I've stood atop the original Temple of Apollo. The landscapes have certainly changed over the millennia, but I believe these frescos depict the four directional views as though we were standing upon the original temple in Delphi over 2000 years ago. The mountains ... the lush hills ... the teatro below ... all in vivid color ... all in perfect perspective.

Our ancestors tried to model Pytho after Delphi, but topography and the pyramid made that effort almost futile. A woman, who looks identical to the Oracle except ten years older, stands just past the entrance carrying a basket of freshly cut hyacinths. After placing the basket beneath the fresco of the southern descent from the temple, she smiles warmly to us as she exits the temple chamber. These lands in Delphi, as well as painted beautifully in the fresco here, are covered in the bluish-purple flowers.

More salient than any fresco could be, a circular altar of thick white marble with a two-meter diameter dominates the room with three brass legs suspending it a meter above the floor. A massive winding serpent, its head poised to strike toward the center of the platform, forms each of the brass legs. I suspect the altar may once have been used for sacrifices, human or otherwise, but the white cushions on top tell me it serves another purpose now.

With her feet dangling off the edge, the Oracle sits atop the altar wearing a tan peplos covered by a crimson chlamys. Positioned carefully to her side sit trays of meats, cheeses, fruit, and biscuits. Next to the food, one of the girls of the sisterhood also places two pitchers of wine, a large brass bowl of water, and a brass tray holding nothing more than a laurel branch. Glaring at us with its empty eyes from the center of the altar sits the clear crystal skull.

Mother stands at the other side of the room with her arms folded across her chest and a dour expression. With her motionlessly glaring at us, Audrey and I walk to her. I get the sense she wants to speak, but is unwilling to come to us. I've seen Karl do the same thing in meetings with executives from our own or other companies. It's some sort of power play. Still, we make the short trek.

Standing in front of Mother, she maintains her dour look as she examines us closely, especially focused on Audrey.

Now shaking her head in utter contempt, she says, "You have not consummated this relationship. What in Apollo's name have you been doing for the last two weeks?"

"I *told* you I am *not* here to have sex with the Oracle." My words come out with more anger than I intend. While I don't mind Mother's probing my life, I'm not going to allow the same for Audrey.

"And I told you that you have no idea how erotic and enticing a vision can be for the Oracle. No man can withstand the lust she inspires."

"I can, and I will."

"Guards," yells Mother.

"Wait," says the Oracle in a calm tone intended for Mother as well as the three guards rushing toward us, drawing daggers from their belts. "All of this is as I have seen it. I do not know with any certainty that we will be successful. I do know, however, that without Sir Archimedes we are doomed to fail."

Mother closes her eyes for a moment, fuming mad, apparently weighing the Oracle's words against her desire to control the situation. Her eyes finally open, jaw jutting out, she says, "As you wish. While you explain what is about to transpire to Sir Archimedes, I need to have a word with Dame Audrey."

Slowly, yet firmly, Mother removes Audrey's hand from mine and leads her out of the temple chamber. One guard follows them, while the other two stay with the Oracle.

I'm about to intervene, when the Oracle says, "She will be fine, Sir Archimedes." Something about her tone inspires my trust and I relax ... a little.

With my height, and her sitting atop the altar, our eyes meet at nearly the same level as she begins to explain the process of prophecy.

"First, let me say that I trust your intentions. Mother's words may be harsh, but she was not wrong in that no man can withstand the temptation during a vision. The sisterhood of the Oracle has over 2000 years of experience with visions, and no man has ever shown enough self-control to overcome their lust in our entire history. That is why we have forbidden men from being present. We are going to change history, and I need you here with me, Sir Archimedes. Therefore, we must prepare for the ritual. Mother is preparing Dame Audrey for what she must do, as I prepare you for what you must not do."

Her silvery blue eyes shine with such intensity I have trouble maintaining eye contact, but I refuse to look away. This moment for our society may well change everything any of us has ever known. Mother wanted Audrey to sate my sexual appetite, hoping she would leave me with less desire remaining for the Oracle's ecstasy to come. I've never been out of control when it comes to women, though. And, this young girl is certainly beautiful, but she remains just that ... a young girl. I can't imagine anything she might say or do – even in her wildest state of ecstasy – that would change my view of her.

"I'm ready," I say.

"Alright, this is how it's going to go. I'm going to take a very special pill that Dionysus smuggles in from the outside world for me."

I try to look surprised.

She shakes her head, and says, "You don't need to pretend with me. I know you saw him give it to me before your Ascension Ceremony. It helps me enter a very deep trance state. Side effects, as you've heard, include my being somewhat unable to coherently relay what I see in my prophetic vision. But, *before* the trance state, I'll physically become aroused. I won't be able to focus on the vision until I ... well, you know."

I'm reminded again how young she is by her sheepishly admitting she needs to orgasm without being able to say the word.

"Mother is very clear about this." I say. "What am I supposed to do while you're ... aroused?"

She blushes. "This is the first time I'll be in this state of ecstasy with a man present. It will be just as difficult for me as it will be for you. Maybe more so. Because you have no psychic ability, we will need to connect with the crystal skull. Then, you will be able to see what I see ... hear what I hear. I'll be able to project thoughts and visions to you, but you will only be able to receive the messages. Nothing you want to say or project will come through to me or anyone else. And, not everything you see in the vision will really be happening. Some visions simply portray my desires ... potential outcomes. But, no matter what you see in the vision ... no matter what we're feeling ... we can't actually have sex. I must remain a virgin."

Shrugging off the concern, yet having a far more difficult time maintaining eye contact, I say, "I don't know how to say this. I don't mean it to be ... unflattering ... but, I don't have any interest in having sex with a girl so young as you."

"It won't be *your* desires we'll be fighting ... at least not at first."

I look to the two female guards and wonder what they must be thinking of this conversation ... what they'll report back to Mother.

"You seem to know everything else," I say. "You must know I'm developing feelings for Audrey."

The Oracle smiles, confirming her awareness.

"Then, how does Audrey fit into all of this?"

"Mother is preparing her for what she needs to do," she says. "I know you're concerned about her. Be assured that she won't be harmed in any way. She won't be forced to do anything she doesn't want to do. Once the ... the ... *ecstasy* diminishes, Dame Audrey will have no role to play. You, however, will bear witness to my effort to change history."

"You must know already – will we be successful?"

Looking down, she answers, "I can follow the location of a crystal skull once I know of its existence, and we have located written records of a woman with a crystal skull aiding a Nazi leader in 1945. I can't see any trace of the woman, though. So, she must be a stray sister. That's the only explanation that makes any sense. To answer your question ... no ... because I'm going to try to influence a stray sister, I cannot see how she will react. I am the most powerful of us within the sisterhood.

That's why I was chosen to be Oracle. But, I have no way to gauge the strength of this stray sister's abilities."

"What do you need this stray sister to do?"

"Prevent the person who kills the Nazi leader from doing so," she answers.

"The Nazi leader ... you must mean Adolf Hitler ... from the history of the outside world, it's my understanding that he committed suicide."

"True history often differs greatly from written history." The Oracle says this with the quiet confidence of someone with far more experience than she should possess at this age.

"Then who killed Hitler?"

"A young Roman boy. He will stand out as very different from anyone else we see in the vision." The Oracle calls him Roman, but I quickly guess she must mean Italian – different eras of reference.

"Do you know how to get the stray sister to stop the Roman boy?"

"The only way I see to stop him is to kill him." I expect to see an expression of regret from her with this revelation ... at least a hint of sadness ... but all I see in her is anticipation. It finally makes sense. This is why she chose me. She saw me murder Nicanor, and she *liked* it. As much as she wants to stop the death of Hitler, she *wants* to kill this Italian boy ... maybe more. And, she wants me at her side when she does it.

The Oracle shares so much more when Mother isn't around to control her. Hearing her openness ... seeing her natural expressions ... her honest feelings ... even though it involves murder, my tensions ease. I find myself nodding ... curious ... even looking forward to this. "What –"

Saying my sentence for me, she jumps in, "What purpose do all these items on the Altar serve?"

Exactly the words I was going to use. Freaky. "Um ... yes ... what?"

Her smile evolves into something less shy ... more friendly. "The wine is for all of us, but I don't suggest you have too much. A prophetic vision can last anywhere from a few minutes to a couple of hours. The food is here because we may be in dire need of nourishment afterward." She points to the brass bowl. "Stirring the bowl of water with the branch of laurel initiates the visions I see."

"Is that all I need to know?" As I ask this, Audrey demurely enters the temple chamber and joins us.

The Oracle answers, "You are as prepared as you can be."

Turning to Audrey, I ask, "Where's Mother?"

"She said she cannot bear to watch a vision, so she entrusted me with her instructions."

The Oracle removes a small item from some hidden pocket within her chlamys. As she does this, one of the guards fills three goblets with wine, and hands one to each of us.

Revealing the orange plastic pill container she clandestinely obtained from Dionysus, the Oracle removes a turquoise pill, pops it into her mouth, and washes it down with wine. About to place the pill container back in her pocket, she pauses, opens it again, and takes a second pill.

"This won't take long," she says while keeping her eyes closed. "You two had best climb up on the altar now. Have some wine … it will help."

I help Audrey up before climbing atop the altar. Wondering where we should position ourselves, I look to Audrey, silently seeking her advice, and she confidently sits on a cushion next to the Oracle. I choose the cushion next to Audrey, keeping her between the Oracle and me.

The Oracle rotates, placing the bowl of water next to the crystal skull. She gingerly removes two leaves from the laurel branch, places them in her mouth, and chews them like a child eating Brussel sprouts for the first time. Without opening her eyes, she snags the goblet on the first try, and washes the leaves down with a large gulp of wine.

Audrey rotates to face the center of the altar, and I follow her lead.

The Oracle utters, "Sir Archimedes, place your hand on the crystal skull."

Having found the crystal skull in Florida and carrying it all the way back to Pytho, I don't anticipate any strange power from the skull when I touch it. Reaching my left hand to it, the skull emits nothing … just as I expected. I reach for and hold Audrey's hand with my right.

Placing the end of the laurel branch in the bowl of water, the Oracle finally opens her eyes. To my horror, they are solid white orbs … no iris … no pupil … yet, she stares at the water as though she can see it.

In the same distant voice, she commands, "Close your eyes, Sir Archimedes."

Even with my eyes closed, I somehow sense her moving her hand to the skull. My arm quivers as she touches it, and warmth immediately emanates from her and through the skull.

A picture forms in my mind. I see Audrey ... I see myself ... just as we would look from the Oracle's position on the altar. The picture moves like a camera and focuses on the bowl of water. A hand that seems to come from me – but doesn't – splashes the water with the laurel branch, and ripples flow out from the center to the edges and back.

The view shifts back to Audrey ... except I don't see Audrey anymore ... I see the Oracle in all her young beauty ... sitting next to me ... holding my hand. Her body starts to writhe, back arching, hips slowly gyrating. Her head leans back, eyelids rapidly blinking, breathing deeply. Releasing my hand, she touches her breast, pinching her nipple. Slowly she exhales ... eyes now closed, arching her back more. She lets out a long rumbling moan that sounds like she's just tasted the most delicious dish of her life. The warmth from the skull becomes heat ... burning ... but I can't remove my hand from the skull. The view moves back to the water and the hand uses the branch to splash it again.

Beyond my control, much like everything else going on right now, my eyes close. When they open again, I'm back in my body. The Oracle is invisible ... or gone. I look to Audrey, and it's not her. A woman is sitting where Audrey sat, and she takes my hand. She looks like the Oracle, but is at least ten years older. Actually, she looks just like the woman with the basket of flowers from when we first entered the temple chamber. Leaning in, the intensity radiating from those silvery blue eyes bores right through my soul.

Some invisible force coerces my eyes shut again. Moisture builds between our hands as the temperature in the room seems rise a few degrees. Her nose nestles into my neck, and the smell of almonds competes with the basket of hyacinths as her tongue glides toward my ear.

Is this Audrey, the Oracle, or one of the many Oracle lookalikes roaming the pyramid and temple? I've never been more aroused in my life, but I have to fight this urge. Releasing her hand, I reach to push her away gently, but when my hand accidentally finds her bare breast, thoughts of pushing her away evaporate ... my will no longer my own.

The questions of how and when she became naked flit into my thoughts as I reach around her lower back to pull her closer. No chlamys ... no peplos ... just smooth, warm skin.

Her mouth finds mine, and when her hand touches my shoulder, I realize I have somehow become naked as well. With one hand on my shoulder for support, she keeps the other hand behind her. Two protruding nipples make contact with my bare chest as her legs wrap around me.

What follows is a hot, awkward entanglement of zealous lovers each unable to use an arm … each desperately needing the other … each moaning our climax at the same moment.

The heat from the crystal skull subsides to warmth. I hear the splash of water, and my vision returns – but from the Oracle's point of view. The hand that isn't mine still touches the clear crystal skull. I see me … naked … my hand also on the skull. Between us, Audrey lays sprawled across a couple of cushions, passed out, naked, and drenched in perspiration.

What just happened?

"Everything is fine, now," the Oracle's voice projects into my head. *"We can proceed with our mission."*

The other hand that isn't mine uses the laurel branch to stir the water in a slow counterclockwise whirlpool. As if on a broken dimmer switch, the light within the temple chamber fades in a jumpy, haphazard way. The eyes that aren't mine close again, and the Oracle starts to chant something … incomprehensible.

TREY TYSON
LONGBOAT KEY, FL, USA
APRIL 30, 2014

"You forgot the Marines," I say to both Max and Samantha. I wasn't sure if Max would take the precautions I requested, but I needed to know my family would be protected. With time to prepare for the battle against the Oracle, Max made sure Samantha understood the importance of today. She brought Bruce from AI and another seven Secret Service agents, who currently surround our property. Local authorities, coordinated by Deputy McAlpine, monitor the two bridges to the island.

For even greater safety, I asked Jessica to bring the babies and stay in one of the bunkers tonight, so she spent the day making sure they would have everything they need down there. Bruce is with them now to both monitor the security systems and act as the last line of defense for my family should all hell break loose.

Ignoring my comment, Max continues setting up the brass tripod as the sun sets more quickly than I would like. He sports his typical polo shirt and khakis. Samantha, Bruce, and the rest of the Secret Service agents are wearing black combat gear, including side holstered pistols and rifles strapped around their shoulders.

"Oh, we may not have Marines," Samantha says with her trademark swink. "But, the president had the Navy arrange for two AEGIS cruisers and three frigates to patrol the Gulf."

"That's good," I say, not really knowing how much water those five vessels can cover.

"She also had the Air Force station four F-22s at MacDill in Tampa to patrol the airspace. And, these aren't typical Secret Service agents. This is the counter assault team, or CAT unit … the most badass of all the agents in the service."

"Do you think we're physically in any danger here in Florida from the First Order?" I ask.

Max finally joins the conversation. "No," he says calmly. "This battle will most likely be waged in the past from within your vision. The First Order has stayed hidden for over 2000 years. I don't believe they have the equipment or even the desire to assault the United States of America. But, it sure as hell doesn't hurt to be prepared … just in case."

Deputy McAlpine walks up and says, "The island is quiet tonight. Nothing out of the ordinary at all."

"Thanks, Craig," says Samantha. "Let's hope it stays that way."

Hmmm. Since when did Samantha and Deputy McAlpine get to know each other on a first name basis?

She touches his arm, and then says, "The rest of our conversation is going to be classified."

"I get it, Sam," he says. "I'll monitor things from in front of the house, and let you know if we get any reports of trouble."

He calls her Sam?

As the deputy departs, Max turns back to setting up for tonight's vision.

I say softly to Sam, "Are you and *Craig* getting to know each other?"

She eyes me for a long second before a broad smile forms. "You're jealous?" she asks, almost gleefully.

"What do you know about him?"

Raising her eyebrows, she asks, "What the fuck do you think I *should* know about him?"

"Think about it, Sam. He's at least fifteen years younger than you. In Max's day, they'd call you Mrs. Robinson. What would they call you these days … a cougar?"

"So!" her volume increases significantly and Max turns our way. "What a fucking chauvinist! Your wife is ten years younger than you. What the hell is wrong with a woman dating a younger man?"

"You're dating him?"

Shaking her head, she says in exasperation, "I never said that."

"You haven't denied it, either."

"Look Trey. First, you had your chance … multiple chances … over decades. Second, you're happily married to a beautiful wife with three beautiful babies. Why do you care if I'm dating someone?"

"I'm just worried about you, Sam."

"Well don't. You're about to do battle with the First Order and the Oracle. The fate of the world rests in your hands. Don't get distracted … not now."

"I can't agree more," says Max. "This is not the time for you to lose focus. You've been training with Nostradamus for all this time … all the effort you've put in … all the sacrifices that have been made …." He throws a glance to Sam as he says sacrifices and that's what puts this all into perspective.

I saved Sam and to do so I broke the laws of physics … the very laws of nature. She's here and she's alive. I have an amazing family. My wife … my babies … my brother and sister … my mom … my friends … and Max. The Oracle is going to try to take it all away … to destroy everyone and everything I know and love.

I don't know who the Oracle is. I don't know where she is … what she looks like … how old she is … why she does what she does … I just know one thing.

"We have to stop the Oracle."

MAX MEDICI
BERLIN, GERMANY
APRIL 30, 1945

I don't know why Ister is keeping me here … why he doesn't simply kill me or assign me to the Hitler Youth – not that I would fit in with them. Ister wants me to meet Adolf Hitler, still playing up the whole messenger from Mussolini charade. The messengers returning from the Fuhrerbunker, however, have all come back with responses saying Hitler is too busy with the war to meet me.

That's hardly surprising. The reports coming in to Ister have been nothing short of devastating for the Germans, yet he hasn't shown any reaction out of the ordinary for him. Then again, he always seems angry.

The Russians have taken most of eastern Germany, with the Americans, British, Canadians, and French fighting together to take most of western Germany. To avoid confrontation between allies, the two forces maintain a healthy gap from Berlin south, and Ister has exploited that gap to fly his supplies to Italy. The German capital, Berlin, has been nearly overrun by the Russian Red Army. Only a tight circle of rampaging Hitler Youth keeps the Russians at arm's length from the Chancellery, our tunnel entrance, and the entrance to Hitler's bunker. The tunnels and caverns below the city have been repeatedly rocked by the constant barrage of artillery shells, but we still remain hidden from the Red Army.

Ister seems to be making most of the decisions for the German forces, and he's been focused on keeping the route open for the four remaining pilots to fly between the Gatow airfield and Italy.

Amazingly, the scientists have met Ister's deadline, dismantling and clearing out the atomic bomb equipment and supplies via plane to Italy. Without the two squads of Hitler Youth helping them – including Kirk's squad – I can't see how they could have succeeded.

Ister sent the scientists and the first of his two Hitler Youth squads to Italy with the equipment, and now only Kirk's squad remains. With the tunnels almost empty, Rolf has taken to his favorite hobby, beating me with his baton whenever no one is looking. While Ister's mood hasn't changed with the reports, Rolf takes out his fury and his desire to strike at the Allies on me. Only my face, neck, and hands have escaped the baton thus far, and only because Ister still thinks I'm going to meet Hitler at some point.

A quick knock on Ister's office door is followed by Von Becker entering with Kirk at his side. They both look pleased.

Kirk, still refusing to look at me, reports, "Herr Ister, the last of the shipments is on the way to Italy. Two of the planes are expected back in three hours."

"What of the other pilots and planes?" Ister asks sharply.

Losing what little courage he had, Kirk looks to Von Becker.

Rolling his eyes in disgust, Von Becker says, "Two of the four planes were shot down earlier today. The skies south over Munich were clear until the Americans established a small airfield near Buchenwald. Only Captains Hanna Reitsch and Beate Uhse have been able to evade the Americans."

Ister bows his head slightly, and says, "Both women are fine Germans, and even better pilots. They will make it back. It is time we said our farewells to the Fuhrer." Looking back to Von Becker, he screeches, "Find Dr. Brandt and Lady Zelda. Bring them and my youth squad to the tunnel entrance to the Fuhrerbunker."

Von Becker nods and departs with Kirk.

Addressing me for the first time in days, Ister says, "Medici …. Do you still want to deliver your message to the Fuhrer?"

I am now certain we share the same goal. We both want Adolf Hitler dead. "I do."

Eyeing me intently, Ister says, "Then come with us. Barbie … bring his messenger bag."

Waiting outside Ister's office is a convoy of the electric carts, making the trip to the tunnel leading to the Fuhrerbunker a fairly quick one. As we approach the tunnel, we find Von Becker is already there and arguing with the guards, who have their submachine guns drawn at the hulking man. Behind Von Becker, stand Dr. Brandt and Lady Zelda. Both Zelda and the doctor carry large shoulder bags. The doctor's contains the many medications, ointments, and other medical supplies he needs for Ister's scars that never seem to heal. I can't imagine what Lady Zelda carries in hers.

The first two electric carts screech to a halt, and Ister nearly jumps out to intercede in the ongoing argument, "What is the problem?"

Von Becker, red faced, turns to Ister and says, "They say they have orders to prevent anyone from entering the Fuhrerbunker … anyone!"

This news has no visible impact on Ister. He faces the lead guard and says, "Gentlemen … you have served the Fuhrer as best you can for as long as you can. Only your bravery and that of the Hitlerjugend have kept the Russians out of the Chancellery and out of these tunnels thus far. Even so, the city is on the verge of collapsing. The Red Army will be swarming through these bunkers and tunnels soon. It will be two days … at most. It may be tomorrow … perhaps even later today."

"That is not what we have been told by Joseph Goebbels from the Fuhrerbunker," the lead guard replies nervously.

"Goebbels is the Reich Minister of *Propaganda*." Ister lets them digest that statement for a few seconds before continuing, "I am telling you from the reports I have seen, you have to evacuate now … *if*, that is, you wish to avoid a confrontation with the Red Army."

The lead guard turns and whispers with the others, then turns back to Ister. "What is the best way to go, Herr Ister?"

Not hesitating, Ister answers, "Out into the Chancellery Garden. You will find many of our panzers patrolling the headquarters. I would stick with the panzers if I were you. They will offer you protection from the Russians."

The guard nods gratefully. "Thank you. Thank you, Herr Ister."

Pausing only to collect their helmets, the four guards run into the tunnel and take the second door on the left.

Once the guards are out of earshot, Dr. Brandt says, "The garden is safe at the moment, but they will never make it through the Russian circle of troops. Why didn't you send them the safe way … through the tunnels to Gatow?"

Ister sneers, "They are heavily armed, and there wouldn't be room on the planes for all of us. Plus, they wouldn't fit in at Station 215."

I'm not surprised that Ister sent the men to likely deaths, but I check the reactions of the others, wondering if any are concerned for their own wellbeing. Dr. Brandt and Rolf seem unfazed. Von Becker, however, wears a look of dismay, perhaps wondering if *he* fits in at this mysterious Station 215.

A quick glance to Ister and he also sees the look on Von Becker.

"Von Becker," Ister blurts. "I want you, Dr. Brandt, Lady Zelda, and our newest squad leader to accompany Medici and me to the Fuhrerbunker. Barbie … you stay with my youth squad. If we don't make it back in the next two hours, you come and get us."

Gradually, Ister has been changing how he addresses the two squads of young Aryan boys that serve him from Hitler Youth to *my* youth. I get the feeling they will soon be known as Ister Youth.

We take two of the electric carts, with Ister, Dr. Brandt, and Kirk in the lead cart. Von Becker, Lady Zelda, and I follow in the second cart, and we make the mile-long trip in a matter of minutes.

At the end of the tunnel are two steel vault doors, each with an electric keypad. Ister, hand poised to enter the code on one of the doors, turns to me and asks, "Are you ready to deliver your message to Adolf Hitler?"

Before I can answer, Ister's expression sours.

"Shit!" he yells. "Your bag is still with Barbie."

I surmise that Rolf was supposed to make this trip with us to the Fuhrerbunker, but when Ister saw Von Becker's wavering confidence, he wanted to keep the giant close to him. Yet, he forgot the bag was still with Rolf.

Von Becker says, "I'll get the bag … it will only take a few minutes."

"We are short on time, and Medici cannot enter the bunker without the bag." For the first time in the weeks I've been around him, Ister looks indecisive. He turns to Lady Zelda, and asks, "Have you seen … do you know what we should do?"

Nodding confidently, she says, "Yes. You must go into the bunker and pave the way for us. I will go back with Ulrich and Maximo. I can prepare Maximo for what he must do when we return."

Ister scowls, not liking this answer, but he doesn't have a better one of his own. "Fine. Von Becker knows the entry code. Do not delay."

We zip back to Rolf, and he hands Von Becker the bag. Ian and Bernie stand behind him, the only two of the boys in the squad who are unarmed. They both look to me for some hint as to what is to happen next. I don't dare make eye contact, though. Drawing Rolf's attention to them is the last thing I want to do.

Before we part ways, Rolf says, "Be brave, little brother. You can do this …. You will have what you need." Placing his hand on his baton, he follows with, "If you fail, I will be waiting for you."

I would find nothing more pleasing than to take Rolf's baton and shove it into his eye socket, but my top priority is still Hitler.

Lady Zelda places a hand on my shoulder, guiding me back to the cart, and we head back to the Fuhrerbunker. Von Becker drives, with Zelda riding next to him, and I'm in the back seat. About halfway back, Zelda and Von Becker start a conversation.

"This is the time, Ulrich," she says.

Driving the cart straight through the tunnel requires little of his attention, so he turns to face Zelda. "What time?"

"The time to decide if you are your own person."

He shrugs, "I am always my own person."

"Good," she says smugly. "Then I will tell you, that if you go into the Fuhrerbunker, you are doomed to die in the next 48 hours."

Stopping the cart, he turns fully to her. "What are you talking about? Where else can I go?"

Eyes pleading, she says, "You can come with me … leave Herr Ister to his plans … help me save my baby."

He looks away from Zelda, and they both ignore the fact that I'm even in the cart. Even if I had a weapon, I'd still want to see where this conversation leads.

"I doubt your baby is still in Berlin," he finally says.

"You're wrong," she immediately counters. "We both know Ister has stashed my baby away with a woman. The woman is under strict orders to stay in Berlin … to stay in her apartment until Ister returns. You know who the woman is. And, you know where her apartment is. Ister has no intention to allow me to retrieve my baby. We both know that."

Von Becker looks down, then back to Zelda. "Assuming the woman is too terrified to evacuate … assuming your baby is still in Berlin … what can we do?"

Seizing this as a hopeful response, she says, "You know the city's defenses. I can sense any danger along the way. Together, we can do this." Going for the close, she follows with, "I've seen it. If you stay, you die. If you come with me, you won't have an easy path … I can tell you that in all honesty … but, you will live."

As the clock ticks and he doesn't refuse her, I begin to believe Von Becker is going to accept Zelda's proposal. This leaves me wondering if they will feel the need to kill me before they go.

Not answering Zelda, Von Becker starts to drive again. She says nothing … letting him come to his own conclusions. We make it to the end of the tunnel and the two steel vault doors, and he still hasn't indicated what he will do.

Standing and facing her, he says, "I will help you."

Zelda bursts into tears of joy, and leaps from the cart to hug the giant man.

He gently pushes her back, an eye on me, and says, "What of the Medici boy?"

Collecting herself quickly, she says, "We must send him on to complete his mission. If we don't, Ister will come after us. With Maximo in the Fuhrerbunker, Ister won't have a choice but to continue with his plans."

Von Becker nods his agreement.

Zelda points to my bag that hangs from Von Becker's shoulder. She faces me while I exit the cart.

"Maximo …. In this bag is a revolver," she starts. "It only has one bullet. That was meant to be a surprise for you … to allow you to complete your mission, but to do no more damage."

"Why are you helping me?" I ask.

Smiling, she says, "I have told you that I see great deeds in your future. This is the first of those great deeds." Reaching into her own bag, she removes a book. "I have a couple of items from the crate in Nuremberg. These seemed somehow *connected* to you. The first is this book."

It's the tattered book from the crate. Zelda places it carefully into my bag.

"Then, there is this amulet." She places that into my bag as well. "It has something inscribed on it. Something I believe is meant for you to read … to understand."

"For me? How can that be?"

"This will go much faster if we can share our thoughts. Ulrich, you don't mind if we connect for a moment with the skull?"

The giant looks too dazed by what's happening to fight her will anymore. He just shrugs.

Zelda reaches into her bag and pulls out the clear crystal skull. Turning the skull toward me, its eye sockets suddenly glow red ….

SIR ARCHIE
PYTHO ISLAND
APRIL 30, 2014

"The stray sister has made contact with the skull!"

The counterclockwise flow of water seemed to glow red for a moment and the eyes that aren't mine closed for a long few seconds. They opened, revealing a vision playing before me like a movie.

Three figures stand in a dark corridor … no, looking around, it's more of a tunnel. A short, blonde woman holds a crystal skull aloft like a talisman, aiming the red glowing eyes at a teenaged boy … an Italian teenaged boy dressed in a military uniform. Next to the woman stands the largest, most muscular man I've ever seen – a massive figure dressed in a black uniform. He has a shoulder bag with an Italian flag embroidered upon its flap.

As the vision zooms in on the woman, her unblinking eyes blaze directly at the Italian boy. She reaches into the large man's shoulder bag, retrieving a gun.

Words come from the large man, "What are you doing?"

She doesn't register the words.

The woman slowly raises the gun, arm muscles quivering, and aims at the boy. The struggle within her is visible … the struggle between the stray sister and the will of the Oracle. The short woman's jaw clenches … both arms shaking, one with the crystal skull, the other with the gun. Tears flow from her still unblinking eyes. The red glow from within the skull flickers as her finger hovers over the gun's trigger.

Understanding dawns on the boy and he dives for the gun, knocking it away from the stray sister before she can shoot.

The massive man intercedes, easily shoving the boy to the ground. He draws his own gun and looks to the stray sister for some indication of what he should do.

One reaction comes from the stray sister and it isn't her own. The red glow from the skull steadies and then intensifies.

With the boy trying to sprawl to his feet, the large man fires three shots rapidly into his chest.

The boy's eyes bulge briefly as he's thrown back to the ground by the force of the shots. Blood pools quickly around him and his eyes go blank.

"Yesssss," the Oracle breathes.

TREY TYSON
LONGBOAT KEY, FL, USA
APRIL 30, 2014

Max and I settle in to our lounge chairs, both comfortably within reach of the white crystal skull, while Sam stands guard over us.

I made the connection to Nostradamus and the three of us have followed the 1945 version of Max from Ister's office to the Fuhrerbunker. A group of six went to the bunker, but only Max, Lady Zelda, and Ulrich Von Becker went back to pick up the Italian messenger bag. The three retraced their path back to the bunker, pausing briefly about halfway down the tunnel, and have now stopped near the two vault doors.

The huge man named Ulrich agrees to help Zelda find her baby, and she leaps to hug him. Max then stands to face the two of them.

Lady Zelda pulls an item from her shoulder bag and shows it to 1945 Max before placing it inside his messenger bag that currently hangs over Ulrich's shoulder. It's an extremely old book, riddled with wormholes, and I think I recognize it.

"Your copy of The Prophecies … the one that sits on your shelf now?" I ask 2014 Max – making sure my projected voice can only be heard by him.

"That is correct," he says.

Next from her bag, Zelda removes an amulet … no guesswork necessary here … it's obviously the same amulet 2014 Max is wearing right now.

"Then, there is this amulet." Lady Zelda says as she places it into the messenger bag. "It has something inscribed on it. Something I believe is meant for you to read … to understand."

"For me? How can that be?" asks 1945 Max.

Zelda turns to face Ulrich, saying, "This will go much faster if we can share our thoughts. Ulrich, you don't mind if we connect for a moment with the skull?"

The large man just shrugs.

Zelda reaches into her bag and pulls out the clear crystal skull. Turning the skull toward young Max, its eye sockets suddenly glow red.

"Why the …." The 2014 version of Max is about to say more, but he pauses.

Everything pauses. Time itself slows to a snail's pace. This has happened to me before … a few times. I'm about to see an event before it actually happens. I have my mother's eyes as Max often says, and he means the strength of my psychic abilities come from her.

Prescience.

Never releasing the red-eyed skull, Zelda reaches into the messenger bag Ulrich carries. From it, she draws a gun and slowly moves to aim at Max.

Ulrich utters, "What are you doing?"

Zelda doesn't see or hear him, though. She's focused on 1945 Max ... and nothing else.

Without blinking, looking possessed, she points the gun at Max. Something causes her to pause for a moment, tears flowing. The red glow from within the skull flickers as her finger hovers over the gun's trigger.

Max figures out he's about to be killed and he dives for the gun, knocking it clear of Zelda before she can pull the trigger.

Without hesitation, Ulrich shoves Max to the ground. He then draws his gun and looks to Zelda.

Still possessed, Zelda stands firm with the red-eyed skull burning brighter and held outstretched as though she's performing the Nazi salute.

Max tries to stand, but Ulrich shoots him in the chest, pulling the trigger three times.

The force of the shots throws Max to the ground. Blood pools quickly around him and his eyes go dead.

Noooo!

Where are my vision options? This can't be the only way this event can go. I always get vision options.

Think, dammit.

No ... *concentrate.* That's what Nostradamus would tell me if he could match my mental processing speed. He'd tell me to concentrate!

What just happened?

How?

How do I stop it if I don't know how it happens?

The First Order stole the clear crystal skull from this very house.

The same clear crystal skull Zelda holds in her hand in 1945.

The white crystal skull Tori brought us from the Smithsonian allows me to connect with Max when we couldn't otherwise.

Maybe the clear crystal skull allows the Oracle to connect with Zelda when she couldn't otherwise.

Screw waiting for a vision option – I have an idea.

Time's pace in the vision accelerates in increments back to normal.

The 2014 version of Max finishes his sentence, and it sounds like a cassette tape that just skipped a beat, "... *hell is it glowing red?*"

Never releasing the red-eyed skull, Zelda reaches into the messenger bag Ulrich carries. From it, she draws a gun and slowly moves to aim at Max.

Ulrich utters, "What are you doing?"

Zelda doesn't see or hear him, though. She's focused on 1945 Max … and nothing else.

Without blinking … looking possessed, she points the gun at Max. Something causes her to pause for a moment, tears flowing. The red glow from within the skull flickers as her finger hovers over the gun's trigger.

Concentrating as hard as I can, I yell, projecting with my full essence, *"HIT THE SKULL!"*

Expecting to be sucked immediately back into the vortex of space-time, I limited my message to three words. No swirling vortex opens, however.

The 1945 Max figures out he's about to be killed and he dives at Zelda. This time, though, he knocks the crystal skull out of Zelda's hand.

SIR ARCHIE
PYTHO ISLAND
APRIL 30, 2014

With the boy trying to sprawl to his feet, the large man fires three shots rapidly into his chest.

The boy's eyes bulge briefly as he's thrown back to the ground by the force of the shots. Blood pools quickly around him and his eyes go blank.

"Yesssss," the Oracle breathes.

The vision flickers for a moment, and then the whole scene starts to play out again. Only this time the Italian boy dives and knocks the glowing crystal skull out of the short blonde woman's hand.

Pure blackness dominates as the vision of the stray sister and the past is instantly severed.

The eyes that aren't mine glow as red as the crystal skull's sockets, then open to the temple chamber in 2014.

A long hissing wail bellows from my mouth – but it isn't my mouth.

Still connected, as the Oracle's glowing red eyes slowly close, she's losing consciousness. Through her falling point of view, I see the empty shell of myself topple over on top of Audrey. The Oracle and I fall unconscious ... simultaneously.

MAX MEDICI

BERLIN GERMANY
APRIL 30, 1945

A strange voice ... or thought ... whatever it is, it screams "HIT THE SKULL!"

I realize Zelda is about to shoot me. My instinct is to knock the gun out of her hand, but that strange voice was so ... adamant. I dive at Zelda and knock the crystal skull from her hand.

Zelda's finger squeezes the trigger, but the gun only makes a click.

Without hesitation, Von Becker shoves me to the ground. He then draws his gun and looks to Zelda.

"Stoppen!" she yells, eyes blinking ... no longer possessed.

Von Becker maintains his aim at me, but doesn't shoot.

Zelda drops to the ground with me, trying to hug me and help me up at the same time, yet failing miserably.

After holstering his gun, Von Becker helps us both to our feet.

"What the hell just happened?" Von Becker asks Zelda.

"There's no time to explain," she says. "If Max doesn't get in the bunker right now, Ister will know something's wrong."

Zelda spins the revolver's cylinder, looking closely and shaking her head in disbelief.

Handing it to me, she says, "It still only has one bullet, but now the bullet is lined up in front of the hammer."

Von Becker hands me the messenger bag, and after inspecting the gun, I place it in the bag.

Turning to the large man, she says, "Ulrich, please give the crystal skull to Max. Place it in his bag for me. I best not touch it ... not ever again."

Hugging Zelda, I ask, "Will you be okay?"

With a tear forming but held back, she answers, "It has been and will be a trying journey, but I have seen a way to save my baby. You need to get in there and do what you came here to do. Not now, but when time permits, you must read what is engraved upon the amulet."

Holding it away from his body as though radioactive, Von Becker quickly places the crystal skull into my messenger bag.

Then he faces me and says, "I believe you understand this, but I will tell you anyway. Herr Ister shares your goal. He, too, believes everything will get better once the Fuhrer is … no longer in power. I have spent much time in the Fuhrerbunker, and know it well. This is the back door to the bunker, meant as an escape for the Fuhrer should there be a fire or maybe when the Russians find the front door. Herr Ister's plan was to get the soldier who guards this door out of the way for you. When this door opens, though, there will be an alarm that goes off at the telephone switchboard. You will only have a few seconds to find the Fuhrer before guards come to find you."

Von Becker is the man who killed Sergeant Smith. He killed my friend Erik. Do I use my one bullet on fake Hitler … or on Von Becker?

Looking up into his eyes, I say, "How do I know the man in there is the *real* Adolf Hitler? I've been told he often uses a double, and the real Hitler might be in Austria. The only way I can be sure is if I see Heinz Linge is here – and I know what Linge looks like."

Ulrich takes no visible offense at my defiant tone, stating simply, "Your intelligence is correct. The Fuhrer has often used a double. He has ruled more often from his villa in Austria than here in Berlin. I tell you now, though, the real Adolf Hitler is in this bunker … right here … right now. I am certain Heinz Linge is there as well. But, don't go in there and ask stupid questions. People have tried to kill Hitler before, and they have all failed. Mostly, from making stupid mistakes. When you get the chance, you take it. Understand?"

He doesn't seem to be lying. Not in the least.

"How do I find him?"

"It is fortunate we are at the back door. This door opens directly into a conference room. You had better pray there isn't a meeting right now. The first door on the right is a closet. The second door is the map room. The third door is his office, and that's where you'll most likely find him. If he's not in the conference room, the map room, or his office, you should check the rooms behind his office … his private sitting room, his bedroom, and his bathroom."

"What do I say if anyone sees me before I find him?"

Ulrich looks down at me, shaking his head with disappointment. "Look at you. You do not exactly fit in with the Hitlerjugend. You cannot waste your one bullet on anyone other than Hitler, and you cannot afford to stop and have a conversation. You –"

I cut him off, "I better just find him and kill him."

Ulrich actually smiles. "Yes … are you ready?"

Zelda comes close and gives me one last hug before saying, "Stay safe, young Maximo Medici."

She's borrowed my line, proving once again that she has seen and knows much more than she lets on to anyone. Hugging her tightly back, I say, "I hope you find your baby, and I hope you stay safe, too."

Punching a code into the locking mechanism on the bunker door, Ulrich says to Zelda, "Once this door opens, we have to leave immediately. All bloody hell will be unleashed."

The door starts to swing open. Ulrich and Zelda quickly turn to the other door, leaving me to enter the Fuhrerbunker alone.

Chapter 35

MAX MEDICI

BERLIN, GERMANY
APRIL 30, 1945

In the half-second it takes the door to swing open, it dawns on me that I'm about to run face first into hell on Earth ... *intentionally*. The one true ally I thought I had in this mission – Lady Zelda – just tried to kill me. Something or someone seemed to possess her through the crystal skull. Breaking her contact with the skull broke the possession. She did what she could for me ... I know it in my heart ... she set in motion the circumstances that led to my running in through this door alone. It's the only chance I have.

Alone. Zelda is off to save her baby. Professor Einstein fell ill. Sergeant Smith is dead. Erik is dead. Dieter gave his life to stall the Nazi scientists. Bernie and Ian are captured, probably soon to be dead. Then there's Kirk.

Everything I've seen on this journey points to Kirk being the traitor. All the deaths that have happened ... all the deaths that will happen with three atomic bombs in Nazi hands ... they're most likely Kirk's fault. I may run into him before I find Hitler. Too bad I only have one bullet. If this is hell on Earth, Adolf Hitler is Satan incarnate ... a true Antichrist. This one bullet is for him and him alone.

Scared, but undaunted, I run into the Fuhrerbunker.

As soon as I enter the bunker's conference room, an alarm bell above my head begins a continuous and annoying ringing. Ister did his part. The room sits empty, other than a wood table, bench, and a few chairs. The concrete walls exude the same German practicality as the walls in the tunnels beyond the bunker – gray, with a few wires and pipes that run along the top of each wall. Overcompensating for the bare and lifeless walls, the Nazis have hung paintings that appear to be masterpieces … probably stolen from the countries and people they've conquered.

Not pausing to rip the wire out of the bell, as I would like, I instead dash for the third door on the right.

After ignoring the first door leading to the closet, I peek into the map room as I run by its open door.

Empty. Thank you, Hagan Ister!

The third entry – leading to Adolf Hitler's office – is blocked by a steel door. *Please*, don't let it be locked. I don't have any illusions about surviving past the next five minutes. Accepting that the cost of this bright idea of mine will be my life, I just don't want to waste it. I need to find the real Hitler and take him down before any guards can stop me.

I reach for the door handle and turn it … praying.

Not locked!

The sound of men running in this direction from the other side of the bunker draws my attention as I pivot and leap through the door, running right into a tall man dressed in the all black SS uniform. As we both tumble to the floor, the shock evident in the man's face doesn't hide his identity.

Heinz Linge, valet and personal guard to the *real* Adolf Hitler.

Linge is quicker to recover to his feet and draws a gun from a hip holster. On the ground with only an instant to think, I jam my foot into the side of his knee, causing his leg to buckle and a wince of pain in his expression. Another well-placed kick sends his gun flying into the conference room, and I scramble to my feet while Linge falls to his knees.

I can hear the running guards getting closer as I pull the revolver from my shoulder bag and aim it at Linge while slamming the steel door closed and locking the top latch.

"What do you want?" asks Linge, still on his knees.

Stepping behind him, I say, "I have a message for Hitler. Where is he?"

"You are too late," says Linge, not moving, perhaps assuming I'm going to kill him and resigned to that fate. "Mein Fuhrer –"

Clubbing him on the head with the butt of my gun prevents Linge from finishing his sentence and he crumples to the ground, unconscious. At least two men start pounding on the steel door, yelling something I can barely hear over the ringing of the alarm bell.

Only one way to go. The door at the back of the office. It leads to Hitler's private sitting room.

I hear a dog barking behind the door and approach it with trepidation. I only have one bullet, so I can't afford to waste it on the animal. The only advantage I possess is that Hitler won't know I only have the one bullet. The alarm has announced the danger I represent. They could be in there arming themselves right now.

Bursting through the door, I see something that will be burned into my memory for the rest of my life – as short as that will be.

Bent over the arm of a large blue and white couch is a very attractive and very naked blonde woman, still barking like a dog in a high pitch almost as annoying as the alarm ringing throughout the bunker. Behind her, wearing only long black socks and having just paused from his pumping away at her to stare dumbly at an intruder, is a stunned Adolf Hitler.

The intruder – me – stares equally dumbly at the Nazi dictator. My gun, with its single bullet, vibrates with the tremors from my arm as I aim at Hitler.

He blinks, and for some reason I don't instantly walk over and blast his brains out. The absurdity of this situation causes me to delay.

The woman shrieks and then blurts, "Is this part of the emergency drill?"

Perhaps wondering why I'm hesitating, Hitler blinks again, and then says, "No, my dear Eva. The alarm is not a drill this time. This is a messenger from Mussolini in Italy." Slowly raising his hands from her blindingly white hips, he says to me, "Allow us to dress before you deliver your message. This is quite … undignified."

Finding my voice, I say with as deep and steady a tone as I can muster, "No. Sit down. I will find something to cover you."

Strewn on a chair between us lay Hitler's dark gray uniform jacket and black pants, as well as a sleek black dress with embroidered pink roses. Eva's dress will work. While Hitler and Eva sit on the couch, I keep my eyes and gun on him and toss them the dress.

Stepping closer, I aim my gun at his head, when he pleads, "Wait! We were just about to take cyanide pills. The Red Army is upon us, and I'm ready to die, but I want it to be my choice and by my own hand. Whoever you are … allow us this dignity."

Other than his black socks, they each also wear a wedding ring and one more thing … a thin chain around their necks with a tiny metal container in the shape of a capsule soldered to it.

"What dignity do you deserve," I spit. "Millions have died because of *you* ... one man's evil desire to control the world."

I take two steps closer to make sure I don't miss.

Eva screams, "NO! My husband! Mein Fuhrer!" Ripping open the metal container on her chain, she shoves the pill it held into her mouth, swallows it, and stares at me defiantly.

In less than three seconds, her eyes bulge and her cheeks turn cherry red. Gasping, she puts her hands around her own neck. The air she pulls in won't feed oxygen to her blood ... the cyanide prevents that nearly instantly. Her eyes turn to Hitler, silently pleading for help he can't provide. White foam forms in her mouth, sliding down her chin, as she falls flat to the couch ... convulsing.

Hitler uses this distraction to yank the pill from his own container and shove it into his mouth.

"Oh no you don't," I say in German, jamming the muzzle of the gun against his temple. "With your last few moments before you descend to hell, you will understand that an *American* has ended your Reich. An American has ended you!"

Squeezing the trigger, Hitler's head jolts against the couch, as the blast echoes throughout the room and beyond. Blood spews from the hole in his head and quickly soaks into the couch. He lays there, dressed in only black socks, but covered by Eva's dress and his own blood ... dead.

Adolf Hitler is dead ... the Antichrist ... killed by my hands.

The room suddenly feels smaller, the gravity of the moment dropping me to my knees.

Ringing. The alarm still blares, dominating my senses. The empty revolver falls from my hand.

I never hear it hit the ground.

I never hear Linge rouse, get up, and unlatch the door to the conference room.

I never hear the group of Nazis rush through Hitler's office and into his sitting room.

I never hear the gasps of the men as they take in the visage of a naked and dead Fuhrer ... next to a naked and dead Eva Braun ... a young Italian boy, on his knees, the obvious assassin.

I never hear Linge reach for his gun, only to find his holster empty.

I never hear Linge pick up a chair behind me, poised to crush my head with it.

I do hear a high-pitched scratchy voice yell, "HALTEN!"

Recognizing the voice, I mistakenly believe the command is directed at me.

"Halt? It's much too late to halt … don't you see?" I mutter.

The scratchy voice says, "Wait, Linge. We need to question him."

Still lost in the fog of my inner world, I don't hear Linge curse or put down the chair.

Watching Dr. Brandt examine Hitler, a laugh escapes my lips.

"Too late, Doctor. There's a hole in the asshole's head. I doubt you have anything in your bag to heal *that.*" While not meaning to voice these thoughts, it becomes readily apparent that I did when a hideous, scarred face emerges into my view. I barely register the punch to the side of my head, teetering, but not falling over.

What the hell are they waiting for? Why am I still alive?

Hagan Ister … the owner of the hideous, scarred face yells, "Where are Von Becker and Lady Zelda?"

Looking up at him, no longer afraid, I say, "Idiot. You didn't see this coming? They are long gone."

Furiously picking up the revolver I dropped, he points it at my face, and squeezes the trigger.

Click.

Still on my knees … smiling, ready to die, I shake my head at his stupidity. He's the one who made sure I only had one bullet. *Dumbass.*

After the Nazis exchange accusations and angry curses, Heinz Linge is the first to say anything that makes sense, "You two stand guard outside the office. No one gets in, and not a word of this to anyone – understood?"

The two guards are about to exit, when Linge yells, "Wait. Get Bormann and Goebbels. Tell Bormann to bring the Fuhrer's briefcase. And get that alarm turned off! The Russians are only a few hundred meters away. They may hear it."

Both guards nod before running out of Hitler's sitting room.

Dr. Brandt examines Eva Braun and announces, "She's dead. Cyanide. I can smell the unmistakable bitter almond from her mouth."

Ister paces wildly while we wait for the others to arrive. When I try to stand, he knocks me over. On the floor, sitting with my back to a chair, I wait for one of these Nazis to decide to find a gun with a bullet in it.

The alarm ringing finally stops and the only sound remaining is Ister's heavy breathing. He doesn't know Von Becker confided his wish for Hitler's death to me. This passionate display of anger is either fantastic acting or the visual of Adolf Hitler with Eva Braun is truly disturbing to him. A thought creeps into my mind and I wonder if Ister's anger is about Hitler's death or more about the way they were found … the obvious act going on when I burst in on them.

The guards allow two men to enter. Ister stops pacing and faces them.

"Minister Goebbels and Chief Bormann." He nods to both men, but their eyes are locked on the bodies of Adolf Hitler and Eva Braun.

I've heard both men's names in reports while sitting in Ister's office. Joseph Goebbels is the Reich Minister of Propaganda. He has his wife and children all living in the upper level of the Fuhrerbunker. Martin Bormann heads the entire Nazi party. Bormann could be considered the second most powerful German while Hitler was alive. Although everyone seems to treat Ister with the same respect.

Goebbels is the first of the two to speak. In a smooth voice, he asks, "What has happened here?"

Linze looks to Ister before answering, gets a curt nod, and begins, "Mein Fuhrer planned to kill himself. He and Eva just married, and he wanted to … *consummate* the marriage before they took their cyanide pills. This boy broke into the private quarters and … and … got past me. This is how I found them."

Bormann asks, "How did he get into the Fuhrerbunker?"

Linge says, "I don't know. He was alone."

Ister speaks up, "It doesn't matter now. The Russians will be here very soon. We have to read Mein Fuhrer's will. You brought it, Bormann?"

"I brought them, yes," he answers.

"Them?" exclaims Goebbels.

"Yes," says Bormann. "He had two wills made, signed, and witnessed. The first, Hitler meant for our eyes only, and was witnessed by Herr Ister and myself. The second is for the rest of the world. Let us start with his first and most important wish upon his death." Turning to Linge, he says, "Mein Fuhrer does not want the Russians to find his body and mount it in a museum. He and Eva are to be burnt to ashes."

Linge raises his eyebrows, and asks, "Where?"

"The chancellery garden. Dress them first. And, no one can see him this way. Wrap him in this rug."

It takes Linge and three other guards nearly as long to perform their last service for Adolf Hitler as it takes Bormann to read the first will.

The focus of this will is Hagan Ister. He is to begin the Fourth Reich with his Aryan youth he's been separating from the rest of the German people and troops.

Station 215 – wherever that is – will be the center of power in the new world order.

Bormann reads Hitler's last paragraph in his first will just as Linge returns from his gruesome task, "Hagan Ister, holder of the Spear of Destiny, Chancellor of the German Fourth Reich, you will rain revenge upon our true enemy, the Americans. Without the help of the Americans, both the British and the Russians would have fallen to the German war machine. Because of the Americans, the war has come to our home. You, Hagan Ister, will take revenge. You will take the war to their home."

After bowing his head in a moment of silent respect, Ister holds his hand out firmly in the Nazi salute and yells, "Heil Hitler!"

Linge keeps his focus on me, as the others follow Ister's lead and salute their fallen leader … the leader I just killed.

"You are to keep this private will as testament to your new role of Chancellor of the Nazi Fourth Reich," Bormann says, handing the first will to Ister and retrieving the second from a briefcase. "And now for Hitler's public last will."

Ister interrupts him, "I cannot stay for this reading. I must get to Station 215."

"What of the assassin?" asks Linge.

"I need to question him still, so he will come with me," Ister replies while motioning with my empty gun for me to stand and follow him.

On wobbly knees, I stand, and turning, I see Kirk is one of the two guards standing near the door to Hitler's sitting room. A hint of a grin on his face, he finally makes eye contact with me … as he walks over and once again locks my wrists tightly in handcuffs.

Ister, Dr. Brandt, Kirk, and I exit the bunker through the same door we used to enter it, and take the carts back to where Rolf and the youth squad wait near the tunnel entrance. Only once we've all loaded into the carts and started back toward Gatow airfield does Ister explain the situation to Rolf. Hitler is dead … at my hands. Von Becker and Lady Zelda have disappeared.

From there, we all take the carts and head west toward Gatow. Almost immediately, explosions shake the tunnel, causing cracks to form and cement dust to rain upon us. Nearly halfway back to Gatow, an artillery shell explodes above the tunnel and it crumbles from the shockwave. Natural light blazes through the fissures and debris falls, taking out the last cart in our train and four Ister Youth with it. The tunnels ahead hold, and the explosions from there echo further and further behind our train of electric carts.

Emerging from the tunnel into the storage building at Gatow, we're greeted by Captain Uhse. She looks exhausted, bathed in sweat and grime.

"Herr Ister," she greets him first.

"Chancellor Ister," Rolf corrects her.

With a nod of approval, she starts again, "Chancellor Ister, my plane is here and refueled. Captain Reitsch should be here any moment."

"I'm glad to see you safe, Captain Uhse," says Ister. "Have –"

A sudden burst of gunfire outside the building interrupts Ister. The sound comes from a distance to the south and above us. We then hear what sounds like a roaring airplane engine coming right for us and the whistling sound that indicates something large is dropping quickly.

Ister yells "Bombing raid – take cover!"

He's the first to dive behind a large crate, but Dr. Brandt and Kirk are right behind him. The Ister Youth form a protective semicircle around Ister. Rolf, looks to the youth briefly, then joins Ister behind the crate.

Captain Uhse sprints for the door closest to the runway. "My plane!" she screams, running outside.

Holding my ground with no concern for my life, I see Ian and Bernie. Still the only members of the squad without weapons, they stand in the chain of boys forming the semicircle. While the others all face out, expecting danger to come crashing through the roof at any moment, these two friends of mine only look at me with kindness and concern in their eyes.

This looks to be the last chance I will ever have to speak with them, so I approach them, slowly and with my handcuffed arms outstretched so the rest of the youth will see I'm unarmed.

"Ian, my friend." I want to hug him … somehow relay just how much his friendship means to me. The handcuffs and situation don't allow it.

"Is what Ister said true – did you kill Hitler?" he asks.

"When you get back, let the professor know all the time he spent training us was worth it."

Shaking his head, he says, "You tell him yourself … when you get back."

The whistling sound gains volume as it gets closer.

"Is it the Americans bombing us?" asks Bernie.

"I don't know, Bernie, but if we live, you and Ian stay safe ... keep each other safe."

Something big hits the ground outside the building, but there's no explosion, at least not yet. An eerie scraping sound starts off quiet and distant, but quickly closes in on our location. The Ister Youth widen their stances, preparing for battle.

Captain Uhse comes sprinting in through the door she just left. "Back up!" she yells, and dives into the line of Ister Youth, forcing the two she can get her hands on to fall back. The others do so as well, including Ian and Bernie.

The scraping sound is on us, and the wall facing the runway suddenly crashes inward sending the wood beams and pieces of the aluminum wall and roof flying in all directions.

First through the wall is a huge propeller rumbling and aflame. The youths all scramble to get behind the crates where Ister hides. The huge cargo plane screeches against the aluminum walls of the building, prying itself inward, but finally stops just a few feet from the crates.

The door of the plane bursts open and a woman jumps down to the ground, followed by a blast of flames that would have engulfed her had she hesitated one instant. She rolls to the concrete floor, then spryly springs back up and checks her jumpsuit for any sections that might be on fire.

From about a mile to the south, we hear an explosion, and the few youths who hadn't hid behind the crates hit the ground and cover their heads with their arms and hands.

The two pilots and I are the only ones left standing.

Captain Uhse smiles to the other woman and says, "That was some landing, Hanna."

Hanna removes a flight cap, revealing a crop of short brown hair as she also reveals a broad and engaging smile. "Turned out better for me than the American pilot."

The women laugh and hug each other.

Ister emerges, hesitantly, from behind the crates and the others follow him.

Eying the flaming cargo plane, he says, "Captain Reitsch, you made it back, but your plane –"

She finishes his sentence, "has flown for the last time." Seeing his irritation at being interrupted, she quickly does the Nazi salute and says,

"Heil Hitler …. Sorry, Herr Ister. We can all fit into Beate's plane, though."

This doesn't lessen his irritation in the least. "The Fuhrer is dead and we need *two* planes."

"There is another plane," says Captain Beate Uhse. "It is the plane we have kept in reserve to fly the Fuhrer to Austria in case he needed to go there. It is small, though … only enough room for a pilot and three passengers."

Ister takes this in, calculating options, and soon comes to a decision. "Captain Uhse, you will fly the cargo plane to Italy with me, Barbie, Dr. Brandt, my youth squad, and the Medici boy. Captain Reitsch, you will fly the Fuhrer's plane with the other three Americans."

Hanna takes a step closer to Ister and asks with an assumptive tone, "I'm to fly to Italy as well?"

Shaking his head, Ister says, "No. You will fly to Buchenwald."

Her eyes widen in disbelief, "But, that is where the American airfield is."

"Yes," he hisses. "You will leave first and draw off any American fighters. Set your radio to their frequency and let one of the boys talk to them as you approach. Tell them you have Americans on your plane and you are surrendering to them."

"For what purpose?" she demands.

Ister reaches back, about to hit her, but stops himself. In as calm a tone as he can muster, he says, "After you land, the three American boys will tell the American leaders what they have seen and heard. It is *important* to my plans."

TREY TYSON
LONGBOAT KEY, FL, USA
APRIL 30, 2014

The clockwise swirl of stars signals our journey back to the present, apparently brought on by the will of Nostradamus again. With my growing abilities, my senses tell me he's still connected with Max and me. The stars – almost all blue now – slow, and then stop.

Exhausted, I fight to keep the connection with Nostradamus going. Still, it's hard to contain the excitement of seeing one of Max's greatest moments as it happened in the past.

"You did it, Max! You really did it. You killed Hitler! But, how the hell did you get away from Ister after all that?"

"What we saw … it didn't happen quite the way I remember it," projects Max. *"The two histories are both in my head, but in the original way it happened, Lady Zelda never tried to kill me. She gave me the crystal skull without ever being possessed. Zelda and Von Becker simply let me into the bunker and then they left to try to save her baby."*

Nostradamus speaks, his voice weaker than when we first started this session, *"That was the influence of the Oracle, I believe. From your time, she possessed this Zelda in 1945 and tried to kill Maximo."*

"I had no idea possession was even possible. Do you think I've inherited the ability from Katarina? And, how did we stay connected after I changed the past? I thought we'd disconnect immediately."

Nostradamus answers, *"You did not change the past this time. The Oracle did that, and along with the possession, I imagine the effort has taken quite a toll on her."*

"Did we win? I mean, is it over? What ever happened to the Fourth Reich? How does Max get away from Ister?"

"Calm down, Trey," says Max.

"Yes, you will need to recover before we finish this part of your father's history," says Nostradamus.

"Recover?" I want to fight his suggestion to wait, as curiosity is killing me, but I'm having trouble maintaining our connection. *"How long?"*

"Take two nights off. Be with your family. Rest. Then, on your third night, we will go back to 1945. Our next and final visit to this part of his history will be to May 26, 1945."

Chapter 36

TREY TYSON
LONGBOAT KEY, FL, USA
MAY 3, 2014

"We're keeping Red and the babies in the bunker again?" asks Sam.

"You know Jessica hates it when you call her that," I respond.

Sam just swinks at me.

As the sun sets over a Gulf so calm it appears almost glasslike, Max finishes setting up shop for what will be my last journey into his history with the second Antichrist, Adolf Hitler. Turning to us he says, "It's just a precaution. The Oracle and the First Order have failed to change history ... at least where it comes to the Nazis."

"Then why is Trey going back again?" asks Sam.

"First, Nostradamus has his reasons for continuing the training in this time period," I answer. "I've given up trying to guess what they are, but I know he has them."

"And second?"

"I need to see the rest of the story. Max doesn't share any of this shit with me."

Max smiles, "Would you believe me if I did?"

"Probably not," I laugh. "Still, there's going to be a pretty large gap. We left off on the 30th of April, and we're going to pick it up on the 26th of May. That's nearly a month. What happened in between?"

Max looks around to make sure it's just the three of us here. Bruce is in the bunker with my family. The security system has a video feed they could be watching, but no audio. "Well ... the two planes did get off the ground from Berlin. Ister sent the first plane with a pilot, Ian, Bernie, and Kirk out ahead of ours. They drew off the American fighters in the air as Ister had hoped. So, our flight to Italy was uneventful. We landed, boarded Ister's U-boat, and our pack of U-boats made it quietly through the Mediterranean to the Atlantic. America's naval efforts were focused on Japan and the Pacific at the time, so the U-boats never met any resistance in the Atlantic."

"Where did you go? Where is this Station 215 the Nazis kept mentioning?"

"You'll see in just a little while," Max smirks.

"Hold on," says Sam. "The last time you didn't trust me, I ended up dead. I think it's time to include me in these details."

Max faces her, thinking for a moment, and then says, "You know … you're right. I trust you to guard over us while connecting to Nostradamus and the past. I will trust you with the location of the Nazi Fourth Reich as well. It was Chichen Itza …."

MAX MEDICI
CHICHEN ITZA, MEXICO
MAY 26, 1945

Dressed in all black with an emblem of the Spear of Destiny joined with a red swastika embroidered to his chest, Hagan Ister stands atop the pyramid just outside the temple the Germans call El Castillo, using the name the Spanish have used since Cortez first found Chichen Itza in 1531. The local Maya call it by a different name. They know it as the Temple of Kukulkan.

The clear skies, warm temperatures, vivid colors, robust plant life, and lack of artillery shells blasting overhead are in stark contrast to what we left in Germany. When the sun rises over a pyramid, it's a spectacular view. I never imagined I'd see a pyramid in person, yet here I am, standing atop the same Mayan pyramid from my dreams.

Next to me stand three massive rockets, painted in a black and white checkerboard pattern, with their nose tips almost perfectly at my eye level. To the north of the rockets is a large, rotating metal dish. Listening to Ister brag, I've learned the new V3 rockets – at 90 feet – are twice as long as the older V2 model. They have a range of 2000 miles and an airspeed of roughly 3500 miles per hour. Each of the three rockets is armed with an atomic warhead.

Every morning, just before sunrise, Rolf puts me in handcuffs and escorts me up the pyramid steps. We stand on the small plateau atop the pyramid facing northeast, where Dr. Brandt joins us. At sunrise, Ister starts the day by addressing the Aryans, who have established the city of Chichen Itza as a Nazi base designated Station 215.

Staring up at him from the cleared land on the north side of the pyramid, stand 300 Aryan men and boys, all dressed in the same black uniforms with the same emblem as Ister. Some come from the ranks of the Hitler Youth we found in Berlin, but most are men Ister identified as pure Aryans and sent here to establish the base. The strict formation consists of three straight rows, each with 100 Aryans.

I was shocked when, two weeks ago, our pack of U-boats docked in Mexico. Even more shocked when we made the trek to Chichen Itza … finding out the Nazis have taken over the ancient city … seeing the pyramid from my nightmares … realizing there's obviously something or someone supernatural influencing my dreams.

I view it as a sign, reinforcing my belief in God. I've prayed for the strength to overcome my adversaries, but I stand alone amongst 300 blonde-haired, blue-eyed Aryan men.

Between the Aryans and the pyramid, approximately 900 Maya slaves begin their days by having their chains removed, and they are then forced to listen to Ister's speeches in German, which they don't understand. Every day the Nazis send out hunting parties, and every day they come back with more Maya – forcibly removed from villages in the area. Once here, the Nazis brand each of them with a swastika on the side of the neck and a unique number on the forearm. Old habits die hard and without Jews around, the Nazis needed an alternate slave labor force.

Scanning the crowd, I see the Mayan men and women look emaciated, with dark circles under their eyes, matted hair, and hollow cheeks. Some wear loin clothes, while others are naked. The 300 pale-skinned, blonde-haired, blue-eyed young Aryan men stand at attention facing Ister with submachine guns at their sides.

Replacing the Nazi salute to Hitler – now that he's dead – Ister raises the Spear of Destiny to the Aryans below, and they respond by pounding their fists to their emblems.

"Today marks the birth of the Fourth Reich!" Ister yells. "We come here as Germans and as Nazis … but we stand above the rest …. We are *Aryans* of pure blood!"

In nearly perfect unison, the Aryans yell, "Heil Ister!"

"We embark upon a new frontier today. German destiny. The Aryan destiny to rule the world. Thanks to you, we will soon have our wonder weapons!" Ister points to the three massive rockets that dominate the clearing to the west of the pyramid.

Again, the Aryans yell, "Heil Ister!"

"Many of our brothers have sacrificed their lives for this cause," Ister has to yell for his screechy voice to project to the men below. "Today, we justify those sacrifices. Today, the world will know our resolve!"

At this, each Aryan raises his right hand with thumb and first two fingers extended. As one, they yell, "I swear by God this sacred oath ... I will render unconditional obedience to Hagan Ister ... the fuhrer of the German Reich and people ... supreme commander of the armed forces ... and will be ready as a brave soldier to risk my life at any time for this oath."

Ister lowers the Spear of Destiny, and the Maya below know they will now be forced to watch something else they don't want to see before the Nazis herd them off to work as slaves. The Nazis have plenty of work for the Maya, between farming, reconstructing the ancient city, cleaning, and helping to build the launch platforms for three atomic rockets. With the pace Ister demands, the hunting parties are constantly pushed to find more slaves.

Six days ago, the Nazi hunting party brought back fifteen Mayan natives. As the new slaves were paraded in front of the pyramid for Ister to inspect them, it was quickly apparent that one of the women in the group was special to the Maya. They call her Mamah Hmen, which translates in my mind to mother shaman, and they all grow quiet and bow whenever they see her. The reverence they show this woman instantly angered Ister. He had one of the men from her group brought to the top of the pyramid. The Mayan man calmly climbed the pyramid steps and approached Ister with two Aryan guards shadowing his every move.

While ascending the top step, the man suddenly pulled a small obsidian blade he had hidden under his loin cloth. He slashed at the two guards, slicing a long red cut into the cheek of one of the Aryans. As they reeled, trying to maintain their balance on the steep pyramid steps, the Mayan man rushed at Ister.

I couldn't tell if Ister was surprised by the attack, because he smiled as he smoothly whipped the end of the Spear of Destiny around and lopped the warrior's head clean off his neck.

Ister got such a sick thrill from killing the man this way; he decided to start every morning by challenging one of the Maya to a battle to the death.

Today's combatant, a short dark man in his thirties, emerges from the temple – dragged by two soldiers to the edge of the stone plateau. The 900 Maya at the base of the pyramid now give their full attention to Ister.

"People, you *must* hear me!" Ister yells while moving to stand next to the Mayan man. "God demands something from us!"

One of the Aryan men from the crowd below yells, "Sacrifice!"

Another Aryan yells, "Yes, sacrifice!"

Then, the first man starts chanting, "Sacrifice … Sacrifice …"

The shaman woman, standing in the middle of a group of Maya near the jungle to the south, throws her hands in the air and screams, "Ma' kinsik!"

My mind quickly translates this to "No kill!"

Looking back to see what Ister will do, I realize he's standing in the exact spot Votan stood during my recurring dream of Chichen Itza and the Maya. Hagan Ister isn't holding the obsidian bladed club from my dream. Instead, he wields the rebuilt Spear of Destiny. The spear I identified from the Florence crate back in Nuremberg.

The 300 Aryans join the chant in sync, "Sacrifice … Sacrifice!"

Ister raises the spear as high as he can reach, his left arm vibrating with tremors, and then he waits. The crowd falls silent.

Sudden sharp pain flairs on the back of my thigh.

"Are you going to help us, little brother?"

Another flash of pain, this time on my neck.

"*Little brother …*" The sickly melodic voice belongs to Rolf Barbie.

Dr. Brandt, standing next to me, completely ignores the abuse Rolf unleashes on a daily basis. I'm not human to him. In fact, I'm not human to any of them. Only Aryans matter. Everyone else is meant to serve or be conquered.

Ister wants me to use my abilities to help Dr. Heisenberg finish the wonder weapons. While Ister always seems to push everyone to an extremely tight timeline, the intensity he's shown about having the atomic rockets available to use today exceeds anything I've seen from him yet.

He's threatened me. He's had Rolf beating me with his baton. They've tried depriving me of sleep, then food, and then even water. I just don't care.

Something turned inside me when I killed Hitler. I knew the task President Roosevelt set upon me was a suicide mission and even though my body still lives, I feel as though I'm dead in spirit. Not caring about my life provides an unusual sense of freedom. It's been easy for me to refuse to help the Nazis … at least until they started sacrificing the Maya. Even with Ister's history, seeing him chop off a man's head with the long blade of the Spear of Destiny startled me. The next day I pleaded with him to stop harming the Maya. He never answered me. Instead, he forced another Mayan man to do battle with him. His guards dragged the man to the top of the pyramid. They then let the man choose a Mayan weapon to use to face Ister from a knife, spear, machete, or club – each bladed with obsidian. The second Mayan man lost his head the same way as the first. After the man's head bounced to the ground next to the pyramid, Ister approached me and offered to stop killing the Maya … only *after* I proved useful with my abilities.

I still refused.

The three Maya killed after my refusal never knew I was to blame for their deaths … but I know.

This Mayan man … today's sacrifice … standing at the edge of the plateau atop the pyramid … waiting for the inevitable moment when he has to battle Ister and the Spear of Destiny … has no idea the Nazis will stop if I simply say I will help them.

But I know.

"You realize," I say to Rolf, "this situation is different from Germany."

Rolf snickers, "How so?"

"In Germany, you Nazis outnumbered the Jews. You were able to butcher them without fear for your own lives. However, here in Chichen Itza, the Maya already outnumber you Aryans three to one, and you keep bringing in more every day. People will only accept bullying for so long. When the Maya figure they have enough warriors here to stop you, they will."

After whacking my neck again with his baton, Rolf says, "The natives only have rocks and sticks to throw at us. Not much of a match for our submachine guns."

"You get enough of them together and get them mad enough, and then those rocks and sticks will become a real threat."

Rolf looks to Ister, demonstrably shaking his head.

"Let him choose his weapon," Ister hisses.

The guards release the man's arms, and point to the knife, spear, machete, and club laying near the man's feet. He chooses the club.

Ister swings the Spear of Destiny while the man is still bending to grab the club. It's the same way he killed yesterday's sacrifice. This Mayan man, however, anticipates the attack and thrusts the club up just in time to block the spear.

Short in stature, but heavily muscled, the man leaps toward Ister. I would make the same move, thinking you need to get close to take away the main advantage of the spear … length.

Ister deftly flips the spear over in his hand and jabs the shaft into the man's forehead, sending him to his knees. Drawing back the spear a couple feet, Ister thrusts the shaft into the man's head again. Blood spurts to the sides of his head while the cracking noise leaves little doubt this battle is over. The Mayan man's eyes close, yet somehow he manages to stay on his knees. Blood flows slowly from a gash in his forehead and his chest heaves up and down with labored breaths.

Ister sweeps the spear around in a long sloping arc. The Mayan man's head, much like Kukulkan's did in my dream, flies from his body and bounces down the pyramid steps to the ground below. Blood spews from his neck as his body slowly falls to the side.

Some of the Maya scream in horror. Some look away. Many others stare up at Ister with more hatred than fear in their eyes.

Awash in shame, I utter, "One of these warriors will kill him."

Dr. Brandt turns to me and says, "Chancellor Ister wields the Spear of Destiny. You of all people should respect the mystical qualities it possesses."

"Only a Nazi would take pride in holding the spear that ended the life of Jesus Christ."

"That's not true," reasons the doctor. "The Spear of Destiny has been held by some of the greatest leaders in history, starting with the first Holy Roman Emperor."

"You mean Charlemagne?"

"Yes," says the doctor, "He won 47 straight –"

"I know," I interrupt. "I remember from when we were in Nuremberg. Charlemagne won 47 straight battles while holding the Spear of Destiny. Only after he dropped it, did he die. Still … that can't be the entirety of the legend. Otherwise, wouldn't there be more examples like Charlemagne in history?"

Dr. Brandt looks at me as though I'm a stupid child he's indulging and says, "The examples begin with Emperor Constantine in the 4th

Century and span history through Napoleon's quest to find the spear. Some have died immediately after dropping the spear, such as Barbarossa. He dropped the spear while swimming across a river, and immediately drowned. Others have taken longer, such as Charlemagne."

"In all this time, not one person has died in battle while holding the spear?" I ask.

This gets a raised eyebrow from the doctor. "Actually … twice, in all of history, has someone been killed while holding the Spear of Destiny. Both times the weapon used had already been used to kill royalty. This part of the legend is rarely told. A weapon stained by royal blood is the only thing that can defeat the Spear of Destiny …. Luckily for Chancellor Ister, I highly doubt the sticks and stones these barbarians carry have ever taken a royal's life."

Taking a step toward the pyramid steps, Rolf tugs on my handcuffs to keep me in place.

"Not so fast, little brother. We're not done here."

"What do you mean?"

The answer to my question comes in the form of another Mayan man – dragged from the temple to where Ister stands.

Rolf steps to my side and says, "Dr. Heisenberg was supposed to have the wonder weapons ready by no later than yesterday. This morning, they still aren't ready. Chancellor Ister believes you can help him and he needs those rockets to launch today. He's going to kill a slave every hour until the rockets are ready to launch."

"Why today?" I ask.

"Well, little brother, I don't think there's any point in keeping you in the dark about this. The Fourth Reich begins today. We have 40,000 panzers and 300,000 men on a massive armada of ships waiting in the Atlantic just northeast of Miami. The reason Ister needs the rockets to launch today is that they are the spear we will thrust into America's belly. The first rocket will hit Miami, and it will act as the signal to our armada to begin the invasion. The other two rockets will hit Washington, DC and New York City."

"That's a stupid plan," I say. "There are over a hundred million people in America, and many of them are armed. Your invasion won't last a week."

"Think about it," Rolf counters. "Your American president, this Harry Truman, has been in office for barely a month. You have most of your fighting men in Europe. Your entire naval fleet is in the Pacific fighting Japan. You think you're safe in your own country with only Canada and Mexico on your borders? What do you have left to defend your people at home ... factory workers and farmers? Without leadership, your defenses will fall almost instantly. We'll have everything east of the Mississippi in a week, and the rest of your country will surrender soon after that."

"You're not making a good case for me to help you. Why would I value a few Mayan lives over the greatest country in the history of the world?"

With that, Rolf whips his baton across my face, nearly knocking me off my feet.

"The invasion will take place with or without your help. The worst-case scenario is we wait a day or two for Heisenberg to finish. It's only 24, maybe 48 of these barbarian's lives. As you said, why would you care about a few Mayan lives?" Rolf turns to Ister, shaking his head again.

Ister raises the Spear of Destiny, left arm quivering once more.

The Mayan man looks to me, somehow understanding his life is in my hands, even without understanding our words. In his eyes I see fear ... but I also see resolve.

"Wait!" I yell.

Ister had already begun the downward slice with the spear, but is able to halt before hurting the man.

Turning to face me, Ister asks, "Are you going to help Dr. Heisenberg?"

Before I can answer, the shaman woman screams from the clearing below, "BEORA!"

Looking down, I see a group of Mayan warriors turn in unison and break for the jungle. They merge in a strange formation that I can see clearly from up here. One warrior sprinting in front is followed closely by four rows of three warriors. The Aryans, all looking up at Ister, are caught off guard. Still, it doesn't take them long to turn south and start shooting at the warriors.

The closest three warriors fall almost instantly, but the other ten are unharmed and keep sprinting. The Aryans shoot another burst of submachine gun fire, and the second row of warriors is mowed down.

With a mere 20 yards between the lead warrior and the jungle, more Aryans turn and the submachine gun fire becomes continuous from an ever wider arc of shooters. The third row of warriors falls.

Ten more yards and only one row of defenders before the lead warrior makes it to the cover of jungle.

The right and left warriors fall almost simultaneously. The middle warrior of the last row leaps in the air as he's riddled with bullets. When he hits the ground, the lead warrior is gone. He made it.

The Aryans continue firing wildly into the jungle, hoping to hit the lead runner, but with no way to confirm it.

Ister yells, "Stoppen!"

With the roar of submachine guns blaring, it takes a full 30 seconds of various Aryan leaders yelling before the shooting stops.

Now quiet, Ister is able to issue his orders, "Form a hunting party. Don't come back until you find him. Bring back his body in pieces if need be."

In a move that seems far too quick for a man of Ister's age, he turns and slashes the Spear of Destiny, sending the head of the Mayan man flying off the pyramid. The head bounces to within a foot of the shaman woman at the base of the pyramid.

"Bring her up here," he yells. "She is next in line."

Turning to me, fury in his eyes and bloody mucus flowing again from the scars around his face, Ister screams, "You have one hour!"

Rolf shoves me toward the temple entrance and I stumble before regaining my feet.

"This is it, little brother. Time, once again, to prove your value or die. Only, this time, there's more than *your* life on the line."

His words ring true. My life doesn't matter to me anymore, but I have to think beyond myself. The Nazis are poised to launch an invasion into America, with millions of lives and the future of the free world at stake. These Maya are victims as well. Enslaved now, they will be killed as soon as the Nazis don't need them … just as the Jews were in Europe.

How can all of this rest in *my* hands? What can I do to stop this Nazi war machine, led by a complete lunatic?

Walking through the entrance to the temple, there are wires I have to step over that run from the three launch pads below all the way up the side of the pyramid and into the temple. Our path to Dr. Heisenberg follows the wires, which feed into a large metal box with several switches, buttons, and a television screen. Across from the metal box is a large wooden worktable cluttered with various books, maps, charts, and drawings. Painted on the wall behind the worktable is a large blood-red swastika … in the same place as in my dream.

Only Heisenberg, another scientist, and an armed Aryan guard are in the temple. As we walk by, Heisenberg looks at me with a perplexed expression, probably wondering how I can possibly help him ... the same thing I'm wondering.

They want me to use my abilities to help them solve whatever problem he's facing, but I don't have the slightest clue as to what my abilities are or how to use them.

Rolf shoves me again, this time toward the worktable. He reaches under the table and picks up my messenger bag with the Italian flag embroidered on it, and then plops the bag on top of the drawings on the table.

"Here," he spits, as he unlocks my handcuffs. "Chancellor Ister told me to give this to you. It's everything Lady Zelda left for you ... except, of course, for the gun. You best have an answer for us before the hour is up, or that crazy slave bitch is the next one to have her head bouncing down the pyramid steps."

"For me to succeed, I'm going to need her help," I say.

"The crazy slave bitch? Why?"

"Lady Zelda told me I have some abilities and I believe her, but mine aren't as strong as hers. I can't work the crystal skull without some help and I think that Mayan woman is a shaman."

"What the fuck is a shaman?" he asks.

"A seer ... someone with prophetic abilities. If she is what I think she is, then she may be able to open the door to the crystal skull. With her assistance, I may be able to see and solve whatever problem Dr. Heisenberg is having."

Glaring at me for a long moment, Rolf takes his time deciding if he should get the woman and bring her here. Finally, he says, "It's her life on the line." Turning to the guard as he walks toward the temple entrance, he orders, "Keep an eye on him."

The guard nods as he raises his submachine gun toward me.

"And you, Doctor Heisenberg, had best stop worrying about Medici and get back to work."

Heisenberg turns back to the metal box, as Rolf exits the temple.

The second scientist, a short, bald man with a monocle, stares intently at everything Heisenberg is doing.

Asking Rolf to bring the shaman woman serves two purposes. First, I truly hope she can unlock the crystal skull, and making her seem useful to Ister may just save her life. More important, however, are these few

313

minutes without Rolf looking over my shoulder. I'll be able to see – discreetly – what Lady Zelda wanted me to see.

My bag! Since the moment Lady Zelda told me to read whatever is engraved upon the amulet, I've been dying to find out what it says. Rolf took the bag in Germany, and this is the first time I've seen it again.

Digging into the bag, the first item my hand finds is the crystal skull. Fear suddenly grips me, as I remember Zelda touching the skull and something or someone possessing her. No such fate for me, apparently. No warmth … no power … no glowing eye sockets … nothing special happens when I touch the skull.

I have a very different experience as my hand finds the next item … the amulet. An immediate sensation of both warmth and power extend from my fingers through to my chest. My next breath is deeper … richer. My mind gains clarity and I quickly forget my lack of sleep, food, and water.

A thought pounds into my consciousness. The Spear of Destiny was in the same crate with this amulet and an ancient book. *This was no accident.* Someone made certain these items were packed together … that someone may have had prophetic abilities … perhaps that someone meant for me to find them.

Made of a strange shimmering metal, this is the first chance I've had to examine the amulet. A silver chain attaches to the oval amulet in two places. Inside a raised circle centered within the oval, is an engraved image of a two-headed eagle. When I hold the amulet up by the chain, the circle inside of the oval makes an eerie eye shape. It's a human eye … unblinking … all seeing.

Turning it over, I can barely make out the text engraved into the back of the amulet. Rubbing the thin layer of the dirt off reveals the message more clearly:

Mon fils de beaucoup de fils, le second Saint Bellator
MM 26 MAI 1945
C II Q 24
C V Q 29

I nearly drop the amulet after reading the second row. Today's date. This thing looks ancient, and *today's date* is engraved on it. This could be some sort of trick Ister is playing, but I don't think Lady Zelda would take part in it.

Then, there's the MM in front of the date. Does that mean MM as in Maximo Medici?

I'm starting to believe in the power of prophetic abilities. This amulet was packed in the same crate with the Spear of Destiny. It's made of some strange metal that warms to my touch. I was *meant* to find it ... meant to have it ... and ... *the book.*

Reaching back into the bag, I pull out the ancient book.

Written in French, Le Propheties by M. Michel Nostradamus was published in 1566. Is this his book? The Prophecies ... 1566 .... No wonder it's riddled with wormholes.

My father once told me Nostradamus had a daughter who married into the Medici family, and that we descend directly from the Medici-Nostradamus union. Some controversy stemmed from the marriage, though, and he said the woman's heritage was to be kept a secret within the family. Considering my father was completely drunk when he mentioned this, I wasn't sure if I could believe him. However, the first row of text may confirm what he said. *My son of many sons, the second Holy Warrior.* Is it possible the book *and* the amulet are from Nostradamus? Are these somehow *intended* for me?

If I'm truly a descendent of Nostradamus, that would explain why Professor Einstein and Lady Zelda think I have some sort of psychic ability.

Maybe I do. I just don't know how to use it.

Delicately opening the ancient book, I find a page with the heading, "Centurie II."

What follows on the page are seven poems in a mix of French and Latin, each consisting of four lines of verse.

Quatrains.

Each quatrain is numbered and this page holds quatrains 41 through 47. Carefully flipping through several more pages, I discover Nostradamus organized the quatrains into 10 centuries, each apparently consisting of 100 quatrains.

Looking back to the amulet, I quickly deduce rows three and four are pointing to specific quatrains in the ancient book written by Nostradamus. The first engraved quatrain, C II Q 24, points to the 24th quatrain in the 2nd Century. It only takes a moment to locate the quatrain:

La liberté ne sera recouvrée,
L'occupera noir fier vilain inique:

Quant la matiere du pont sera ouvrée,
D'Hister, Venise faschée la republique.
(Nostradamus, Michel. The Prophecies. C5:Q29)

My French and Latin may not be fluent, but my translation to English leaves my mind spinning:

Freedom will not be recovered,
while occupied by the wicked villain proudly in black.
The matter depends upon a bridge being crafted.
Like Venice, Hister wants fascism for the republic.

There's no denying the meaning of the quatrain, pointing to Ister as the wicked villain in black. Hister ... H. Ister ... Herr Ister ... Hagan Ister. All this time I've thought of Adolf Hitler as the second Antichrist, but Nostradamus aims this quatrain at Hagan Ister.

Unless Ister is Hitler!

Maybe Nostradamus is combining the names Hitler and Ister when he writes Hister.

Could the lunatic leading the Fourth Reich be the same man who led the Third Reich ... only disguised?

Clues stream visually from my memories.

In Princeton ... President Roosevelt and Dr. Bush telling me Hitler often uses a double to foil assassination plots. They also told me the real Hitler has a shaky left hand and wouldn't be found without Heinz Linge at his side.

Ister hiding his left hand when the Nazis showed up in Princeton to try to seize Professor Einstein and his work.

With his puffy face, scars, and oozing bloody mucus, Ister's true identity could be hiding behind a new face. Dr. Brandt's history of performing experiments on humans makes him the perfect fit as Hitler's personal physician.

Back in the bunker in Berlin ... Hitler having sex with Eva Braun. His raised left hand was as steady as a rock, even with me pointing a gun at him.

Seeing the deceased Hitler and Eva naked together made Ister jealous.

Then there was the conspiracy to kill Hitler. Ister *wanted* me to do it. He set the plan in motion and cleared the path for me in the bunker. He made sure Kirk was there to see what happened and then sent Kirk,

Ian, and Bernie flying back to the Americans. Why? Was it so they could tell the world that Hitler is dead?

If I'm right, Ister's diversion has been brilliantly executed. But, it means I killed the wrong man in Berlin …. It means I have to kill Hitler … *again.*

The first line in the quatrain speaks to freedom, and freedom is at the heart of the matter. Freedom from Nazi oppression. My freedom … freedom for the Maya … freedom for the republic of America … freedom from Ister and fascism … from slavery and death.

Venice is referenced in the fourth line, but in the 16th Century, governments were formed around city-states more than by countries. Nostradamus must mean northern Italy … where Mussolini forged a fascist dictatorship and aligned the Italians with the Germans. What Nostradamus is saying is that America is doomed to become a fascist state, just as Italy did.

The third line of the quatrain holds the key. The matter depends upon a bridge being crafted.

What bridge?

My eyes settle on the crystal skull. Is the skull the bridge? Bridge to what … or to whom?

Before I can flip to the page with the next quatrain, Ister walks into the temple holding the Spear of Destiny. Behind him are Rolf and the shaman woman.

To Heisenberg, Ister asks, "Doctor, have you identified the problem with my rockets yet?"

"I have it narrowed down to the control box, but not the specific problem," Heisenberg replies.

Ister pounds the shaft of the spear into the temple floor and yells, "My army is ready to invade. They await the signal of the first atomic explosion. The rockets have to launch today!"

Fury in his eyes, Ister turns to me, screaming, "And you, Medici, had best prove your value to me. Tell me. How can this woman help us?"

Adolf Hitler hides behind that hideous new face. With a new clarity of mind from contact with this amulet, I find it difficult to believe no one else has figured this out. Dr. Brandt surely knows. Did Von Becker know? What were his words before I rushed into the bunker? *I tell you now, though, the real Adolf Hitler is in this bunker … right here … right now.* He spoke the truth. I sensed as much. The real Adolf Hitler in his Ister disguise *was* in the bunker at the time.

Gathering myself, I reply, "I believe I can help solve the problem with your rockets. I need to connect with Dr. Heisenberg through the crystal skull, but my psychic abilities are not as strong as Lady Zelda's. The Maya have called this woman a shaman … or a seer. She may be able to bridge the gap between Dr. Heisenberg and me."

Glaring at me, Ister asks, "What do you need to do this?"

"I have to wear this amulet," I answer as I slowly put the silver chain around my neck. When the amulet makes contact with my chest, the power emanating from it intensifies. "Then, I need her to place her hand on the skull with me."

The woman stands all of 4' 6", but exudes strength … her stark features and stern eyes appear far more accustomed to commanding than obeying.

Assuming she can't understand any of the languages I speak, I gesture to the skull and demonstrably place my open palm on it.

Rolf pushes her toward me and raises his baton, threatening to beat her if she doesn't comply.

The woman begrudgingly takes the few steps necessary to join me. Staring directly into my eyes, she places her right hand on the skull. Almost instantly, the skull's eye sockets glow blue and I close my eyes.

"What is your name?" I project into her mind.

"I understand your thoughts. You are not new to me. I have seen your face in my dreams and I have seen this crystal skull. You are here to help us … I have seen it …. My people know me as Itzel. What do your people call you?" Her Mayan language thoughts translate in my mind easily.

"My name is Max. I am not with the others who have captured you and your people."

"That is clear. I have seen you in chains."

"The evil men are called Nazis, and I am sorry for what they are doing to your people."

"One of our warriors escaped to get help," she says. *"I have seen it. They will soon arrive from the river."*

"River? I have seen no river near here."

"The rivers connect the cenotes and flow underground. One flows directly beneath this pyramid."

"How will your warriors reach us if the river flows under the pyramid?"

"Our warriors will need your help," she projects into my mind. *"A secret chamber inside the pyramid can only be reached by a long underwater swim from the cenote. Only our strongest and bravest warriors can make it. Once in the chamber, they must climb steps inside the pyramid to reach a passage into the temple. The*

passage represents a sacred bond between the high priest and our people. It may only be crossed if both latches — within the temple and beneath the temple — are opened. You will have to open the hidden latch in the temple."

"The jaguar throne. I press the left emerald eye?"

A few seconds pass before she answers, *"How do you know this?"*

"I have seen it in my dreams. King Kukulkan's sacrifice ... his temple ... the jaguar throne."

"The bad men call this El Castillo," she says. *"The name was first used the last time bad men came here ... so long ago. The bad men hurt my people. They kill my people. I have seen you in my dreams. You have been sent here to save my people."*

"I hope you are right, but we don't have much time. The man with the spear is evil. He's going to kill us both if we don't help each other. He's going to kill your people and he's going to kill my people."

"That is also clear. You told the bad men you needed my help. What do you want me to do?"

"There is a man standing over there. I need to share my thoughts with him through this crystal skull. I need to see the events of his past and future. Can you do this?"

"Let us find out," she says.

Opening my eyes, I find Ister has taken a step closer, watching us intently.

"We are ready," I say to Ister. "Dr. Heisenberg needs to join us now."

Ister turns to Heisenberg and says, "Herr Doctor, come put your hand on the skull with Medici."

Heisenberg stares at Ister for a long moment, dumbfounded.

"That was not a request, Doctor," Ister points to the skull while glaring at Heisenberg.

Reluctantly, Heisenberg steps over to the worktable and places his open palm on the skull. The skull's glow shifts slightly from blue to violet.

"Dr. Heisenberg," I project to him. *"Nod slightly if you can hear my thoughts."*

His nod is barely perceptible.

Focusing on the connection, I try to ignore Ister, Rolf, and the other scientist as they take another step closer.

"Doctor, this woman is a shaman among the Maya. Her name is Itzel and her abilities allow us to communicate through the skull. We may be able to see your past and future. You can hear me, but I will not be able to hear anything you say or

think. If I ask you a question, however, nod for yes or shake your head for no. Understand?"

He nods.

"Itzel, can you look into this man's work on the rockets outside? These men call them wonder weapons."

As I close my eyes, she projects, "Wonder weapons." She inhales deeply and exhales in a low-pitched moan.

Sensing a flow of energy from Itzel through Heisenberg, visual memories begin to stream as though I were seeing them through his eyes.

Everything blurs for a moment. When focus returns, Heisenberg is meeting with Adolf Hitler and another physicist. They discuss the importance of finishing the wonder weapons before the Americans can build an atomic bomb.

Everything blurs again.

Even before visual focus returns, I hear a conversation with a physicist, who suggests to Heisenberg that their atomic bomb delays may be due to trying to explode the uranium. The physicist goes on to suggest they look at implosion instead.

The vision blurs and then Heisenberg reassigns the physicist with the implosion idea to Nazi Station 211 on Antarctica.

The vision blurs and then Heisenberg sits in a meeting with Abraham Toch. Toch says the tracking device he's mailing to Einstein will lead the Nazis right to the American spy camp.

The vision blurs, and then clarity reveals a place I recognize – the underground tunnels and caverns beneath Berlin. My friend Dieter speaks with Heisenberg. Heisenberg tells Dieter the most vulnerable position to place a stick of dynamite to damage the German uranium enrichment equipment.

The vision blurs and then Heisenberg opens a panel on the back of the large metal box connected to the three rockets here in Chichen Itza. Heisenberg loosens a small screw, disconnects a red wire, and then closes the panel.

The vision blurs – for much longer this time – and then the scientist with the monocle stands at the metal box with Ister, Rolf, the guard, and Heisenberg watching. "I figured out the problem," says the scientist as he opens the panel, reconnects the wire, and the television screen on the box comes to life. Ister turns to Heisenberg and says, "You have been delaying … on purpose!" Ister then plunges the Spear of Destiny into Heisenberg's abdomen.

The vision blurs and then the other scientist manipulates two levers on the control box while watching the television screen. Ister speaks to the group, but his message is for me, "You will like this, Medici. Our scientists have installed a camera in the nose of the rocket and it is transmitting the signal back to this box." The television shows a bright sky with thin wisps of clouds streaming by the camera at an alarming speed. At the bottom of the screen, choppy waves give way to beachfront and palm trees. On the horizon, tall buildings come into view. Ister says, "Wait until the rocket is directly over the city." The view shows the rocket approaching the city rapidly. "To the right!" Ister yells. "Aim for the center of the city." The scientist moves the right lever on the box to the right slightly, and the rocket responds by turning. "I will press the button to detonate," Ister says, with his hand poised over a large red button next to the control levers. As the rocket approaches Miami, a bustling downtown streams into view. Ister presses the button and the screen instantly changes to a static pattern.

The vision blurs and then a German naval captain on a large vessel at sea watches a mushroom shaped cloud form over a city. To an officer wearing a Nazi uniform next to him, he says, "Radio the fleet …. The rocket has hit and obliterated Miami. We invade America now!"

The vision blurs and stays blurred longer this time. The next vision reveals Itzel standing at the edge of the pyramid plateau looking down at her people. Her people have attacked the Germans from the jungle, but are being mowed down by submachine gun fire. Ister laughs as he swings the Spear of Destiny and sends her head flying down the pyramid steps.

All goes black.

Having witnessed visions of both the past and the future, I open my eyes to take in the view of now. Itzel has blood dripping from her nose. She keeps her eyes closed, but Heisenberg opens his and focuses on me.

The connection between the three of us is still intact, but Itzel seems distant. We have seen the future and it is bleak.

"Dr. Heisenberg, nod slightly if you have seen everything Itzel has shown us."
He does.

"Our intelligence is unaware of your efforts to delay Hitler and keep him from having the atomic bomb. We thought Toch was our friend and you were our enemy. If we make it out of this alive, I will make sure authorities in America learn the truth."
He nods again.

"*Itzel, you have seen that if your people attack before we can open this passageway in the temple, they will all be killed.*"

"*I have,*" she projects weakly. The blood from her nose streams down her neck.

"*We cannot let the future transpire the way you have shown it. I have an idea. It's risky, but I think it's our only chance. My plan is for Dr. Heisenberg to announce that Itzel and I have shown him an image of faulty wiring in the control box. Doctor ... you must be the one to find it and fix it, otherwise we all die. You must then actually launch the rocket. Ister will want to step outside to see the rocket lift off. That will provide the diversion I need to open this end of the secret passage for Itzel's warriors to storm the temple.*"

More hesitantly, he nods again.

"*Itzel, if your warriors survive the river and make it into the temple, you will need to let them know that Heisenberg and I are on your side.*"

"*Yes, I understand,*" she says. "*I cannot hold this any longer.*"

"*Then, we better do this now .... Ready?*"

Itzel utters, "*Yes.*"

Heisenberg nods.

Itzel opens her eyes, unable to prevent tears from forming.

Heisenberg stands, formally shakes my hand, and says, "Thank you both for your assistance."

Turning back to Ister, he says, "The boy and the woman have shown me the problem. With some cooperation, we can solve this quickly."

With a surprised look, Ister says, "Of course, Herr Doctor. What do you need?"

Heisenberg points to the other scientist and says, "To test my theory, I will need Professor Sprecht on the ground by the launch pad of the first rocket and someone outside the temple to relay messages between him and me."

Ister nods and issues the orders, "Sprecht, you heard him. Barbie, keep an eye on Medici. You," Ister says to the lone guard in the temple, "go out there and let us know when Sprecht is in place."

Smart! Just like that, Heisenberg has removed two of our adversaries. That leaves only Ister with the Spear of Destiny and Rolf with a pistol and his baton here in the temple with us.

As soon as Sprecht exits the temple, Heisenberg opens the control box panel. He's now able to repair the wiring without someone looking over his shoulder. From the vision, I'm sure the repair only requires a few seconds, but Heisenberg lingers at the panel opening to give Sprecht enough time to descend the pyramid steps.

Rolf, apparently bored waiting for the repair, decides to get my attention by whipping his baton across my shoulder. Smirking, he says, "If this works, little brother, I may let you have a cup of water as a reward ... maybe even some food."

His comment reminds me just how thirsty I am. My body must crave food, too, but it's been nearly two days since the Nazis last gave me water.

The guard leans into the temple entrance and announces, "Professor Sprecht is ready."

Heisenberg closes the panel and flips a switch to the on position. The television comes to life, showing a black and white image of the sky.

To Ister, Heisenberg says, "I will signal the first rocket to light the ignitor. If the connection is correct, Sprecht will be able to see it."

Ister yells to the guard, "Have Sprecht check the ignitor flame of the first rocket." To Heisenberg, he says, "Go ahead, Herr Doctor."

Peering past Rolf, I'm able to see three rows of four color-coded buttons. Each row has a black, yellow, green, and red button.

Heisenberg presses the top black button, and the television screen now has text across the top reading, "RAKETEN EINEM" or rocket one.

He then presses the top yellow button and yells, "Ask Sprecht if he sees the ignitor flame."

The guard yells the question down to Sprecht, who quickly responds with "Yes!"

Ister, nearly giddy, hisses, "My wonder weapons are finally ready .... Dr. Heisenberg, launch the first rocket as soon as possible."

With a hint of a smile, Heisenberg presses the top green button. A low rumbling noise outside, much like distant thunder is immediately followed by a man's high-pitched wail.

Ister flashes an angry look at Heisenberg, and then rushes out the temple entrance to watch his first rocket launch.

Rolf turns toward Heisenberg while taking his gun out of its holster and blurts, "Was that scream from Sprecht?"

Lunging for Rolf, I kick the gun from his hand and it flies toward the temple entrance. With a look of instant fury, he slashes the baton to knock me to the ground.

The amulet grows suddenly warmer against my chest, and my perception grows with its heat. I roll and pounce to my feet, just in time to see Rolf hurl himself at me. Whipping the baton around from a pointed staff position to a raised club, he slams it down toward the crown of my skull.

I'm able to twist to the side, diverting the main force of the strike to the side of my head. Slightly dazed, I punch his chest to buy a moment to regain my balance. He breathes an "oomph" and staggers back.

The low rumble of the rocket launch almost instantly evolves into a roar that shakes the pyramid. Itzel cowers into a fetal position next to the worktable, blood still flowing from her nose. Dr. Heisenberg marvels at the moving sky on the television screen.

Rolf yells, "Guard! Get in here!" However, we both know there's no way anyone outside the temple can hear him.

Sergeant Smith taught us to strike first and strike fast, but my combat training from Ian's Uncle Johnny always focused on patience and counterstrikes.

"You have no weapon, little brother," says Rolf. "I will beat you senseless with my baton."

"I'm going to take that from you and kill you with it."

He lunges again, this time with the baton pointed at my stomach, wielding it like a staff.

The attack reminds me of Kirk rushing like a bull at me in the boxing ring so long ago in Princeton. With my newly enhanced sense of perception, I feel like I have to wait several seconds for Rolf to reach me. I begin rolling back a fraction of a second before he hits me. Grabbing the baton with one hand and his shirt with the other, I roll back and take him with me. Kicking my feet into his groin as my back curls into a ball, I hurl him back over me.

When I did this to Kirk, I released him and sent him flying out of the ring. This time with Rolf, I don't let go. Shifting both hands to the baton, I rip it from his grip as Rolf starts to move his arms back to brace himself for the impact he must realize he's about to suffer.

Rolf's back smacks against the stone temple floor and our combined momentum has him skidding toward the entrance to the throne room. Climbing him as though I'm hopping on a surfboard at the crest of a wave, I jam one foot into his throat while I break his baton over my knee. The diagonal break leaves the inner ends of both halves of the baton as sharp as spearheads.

In the split second it takes Rolf to guess what I'm about to do, he only has enough time to open his eyes to the point of bulging before I jam the two baton halves into them so deeply I expect brain matter to ooze out of his ears.

The sadistic bastard convulses a few times and dies quickly. Too bad. If anyone ever deserved a slow and painful death, it's Rolf.

With the sound of the rocket quickly fading – meaning the rocket is well along its path to Miami – I rush over to the jaguar throne and push on the left green eye.

Nothing happens. It doesn't budge.

I saw Votan press this very eye in my dreams. It *has* to work!

Then again, it was a dream. Even if it really did happen, the last time this jaguar throne moved may have been nearly a thousand years ago.

I press harder ... and harder still ... no movement.

Ister yells something from outside the temple.

Running back to Rolf's body, I yank one of the baton halves from his eye and sprint back to the jaguar throne. Pressing the pointed broken end of the baton against the jaguar's eye, I slam my fist against the back of the baton.

Nothing.

I slam it again.

This time it works. The emerald eye grates against the stone socket, but it slides in.

Click. That's the same sound the throne made when Votan did this.

Heaving with all my weight behind me, I slowly push the jaguar back, revealing a carved stone compartment below the temple floor. I believe what I see, but at the same time, I don't. Lying alone in the compartment is just what I hoped would be there. I grab it ... staring in disbelief ... feeling the club with my hand is surreal. My dreams were real. Votan lived. He sacrificed King Kukulkan with this very club a thousand years ago.

The compartment must slide open as well, but only after someone opens the latch from *inside* the pyramid. Itzel's warriors aren't here yet ... or they are having trouble opening their door.

"Don't move!" Ister yells from behind me. I then hear the highly recognizable sound of someone pulling back a submachine gun's bolt handle.

Very slowly, I turn to face the evil bastard and the three Aryan guards with him.

Ister looks down at Rolf's body – and following his gaze, I see Itzel lying unconscious next to the worktable. Blood covers the shaman woman's face and chest.

Turning to Heisenberg, Ister asks, "What happened, Herr Doctor?"

Heisenberg shrugs, wide-eyed, and says, "I do not understand. I was watching the launch from the control box. The sound of the rocket was so loud; I never heard anything behind me."

"You," Ister thumps his finger into the chest of one of the guards, "get the slaves back from the fields. It looks like Medici has chosen his weapon and wants to fight me."

As the first guard runs out of the temple, another guard keeps his gun pointed at my chest while the remaining guard takes the club from my hand.

Ister walks toward the temple entrance, but pauses to address Heisenberg, "Herr Doctor, how long until the rocket hits Miami?"

Heisenberg glances at the control box and then at his watch. "The rocket is averaging 5629 kilometers per hour. It will reach Miami in … just over 10 minutes."

"Good!" says Ister. "Keep it on trajectory. This will not take long." To the guards, he says, "Bring out Medici when I tell you to do so."

Ister walks out of the temple confidently and begins issuing orders to his men about gathering the soldiers and the Mayan slaves quickly.

Where are Heisenberg's loyalties? From the visions with Itzel, it's apparent he delayed the atomic bomb development. The first rocket is flying at one of America's most populated cities and Heisenberg controls it. It will be his finger on the top red button when the rocket reaches Miami. *Will he press it?*

As though able to read my thoughts, Heisenberg announces to no one in particular, "The rocket will reach its target in 9 minutes. When Chancellor Ister returns, he will most likely want to detonate the atomic bomb himself."

That answers my question. I have to defeat Ister in combat, or the explosion will incinerate the people in Miami, followed closely by DC and New York, and then the Nazis invade America. Heisenberg will be powerless to stop it.

The two guards behind me never lower their submachine guns while the Aryans take nearly six minutes to gather the Mayan slaves around the pyramid to watch Ister's latest show. Heisenberg has been kind enough to announce the passing of each minute as it transpires.

"Three minutes," he says, eyes transfixed on the television. "I can see land in the distant view of the rocket's camera."

From outside the temple, Ister yells, "Bring Medici!"

As I walk out of the temple and into the bright midday sunlight, I'm forced to squint as I take in the view. Ister stands proudly at the pyramid edge with the Spear of Destiny in his right hand.

Dr. Brandt stands to the side to watch the battle. The rest of the Aryans watch from the ground below.

Passing near Brandt, I say, "This is *your* doing. *You* created this abomination."

His eyes don't meet mine. Instead, he only looks down.

This open plateau outside the temple appears to be 20 feet by 10 feet, or almost exactly half the size of the boxing ring we used for training back in Princeton. That seems like ages ago, yet it's only been a couple months.

Ister hisses, "You have outlived your usefulness, Medici," still pronouncing my name incorrectly.

"You may not be able to say my name right, but I can say yours ... *Adolf* .... I know that's you under that hideous new face. You're not fooling me."

Nodding, Ister – or *Hitler* – says, "Choose your weapon, Medici."

The Aryans at the base of the pyramid stand behind the Maya. They begin to chant, "Sacrifice! Sacrifice!"

Shrugging with as much nonchalance as I can muster, I point to Votan's club the guard next to me still carries and say, "I'll use this."

Hitler nods to the guard, who hands me the club and backs away with the other guard.

"You don't seem afraid, Medici," Hitler hisses. "Haven't you been watching? I've easily killed these slave warriors and they've been training their whole lives to fight with these primitive weapons. As long as I hold the Spear of Destiny, I *cannot* be defeated. You are about to die! Don't you care? Or ... are you just *stupid?*"

The amulet heats up instantly with my anger. *Stupido!* That's what my father used to call me. Sometimes he just used words ... sometimes he would beat me as well.

I want to lunge at Hitler and bash his brains in with this war club ... to make him pay for what he's done ... the people he's hurt ... the people he's killed. My arms tense, eyes squint, and I take a step forward.

In a flash, Hitler whirls the spear around and thrusts it at my groin. I've seen him attack one of the Mayan warriors this way and know he's feigning – trying to get me to lower my arms. What he wants … with the Aryans and the Maya all watching … the *only* acceptable way for me to die in his mind … is to behead me.

I twist my body to the side and raise the club to defend my neck.

The thrust was no feign. The spearhead tears into my hip. Searing pain roars through my side and I instinctively hobble a step back as blood pours down my left leg.

Breathe! I want to lunge at him still, but words from my past echo in my head; *an angry warrior is rarely a wise warrior.* The words belong to Johnny Fox … Ian's uncle … my mentor. I need to make the words my own.

Grinning, Hitler says, "That has to hurt."

From the temple, Heisenberg leans out and yells, "Two minutes!"

Closing my eyes, I take a deep breath and the heat from the amulet lessens.

"I'm afraid your time is up, Medici," says Hitler. "I don't blame you for not wanting to see this."

I open my eyes just in time to see Hitler step forward and slash the Spear of Destiny around … this time aiming for my neck.

The club feels balanced in my hands as I thrust it up to block his strike. Hitler whirls the spear over my head and slashes from the other side. Sensing this attack, I bend and roll forward, trying to close our gap and take away the main advantage of the spear. The pain in my hip prevents me from popping up to my feet as quickly as I thought I could and Hitler is able to strike my neck with the spear shaft.

I hit the ground hard as he quickly moves his grip up the spear to shorten its length.

Rolling back, I'm able to make him miss with his next slash, and move just beyond the spear's reach.

Feeling woozy from the blood loss, I at least remember to use my right leg to pop up from the ground this time.

An angry warrior is rarely a wise warrior.

With Hitler taking a moment to catch his breath, I say, "That double you had in Berlin sure did look like you."

Hitler purses his lips and nods, never taking his eyes off me.

"I really thought I was killing you when I shot him in the head."

Glaring at me, Hitler says, "I am *not* so sorry to disappoint you."

"You can't be too upset with me, though. I mean, after all, the double was fucking *your* girl when I found them. Was *that* part of your plan?"

Seething, Hitler tightens his grip on the spear, readying to thrust it at me again.

Heisenberg yells, "One minute!" Then he rushes back into the temple.

"Here's the point," I continue. "You and Eva were together for years. She had to know she was with your double ... and she *fucked* him anyway."

"Ayyyyyeeee!" Hitler screams gutturally as he thrusts the Spear of Destiny directly between my eyes.

Leaning my head to the right, I let the spear pass my ear before I grab the shaft with my left hand and swing the club around with my right. The club's obsidian blade splinters the spear shaft, leaving me with the spearhead in my left hand and the club still in my right.

I hear a gasp from Dr. Brandt and some major commotion from within the temple.

Hitler drops the shaft and reaches for his holstered pistol, but I'm on him before he can draw.

Burying the spearhead into Hitler's stomach, I say, "That has to hurt."

With Hitler buckling over, I swing Votan's war club down furiously and rip off his head as though he were a rag doll.

Blood spews from the dictator's neck as his body topples to the side.

Dr. Brandt and three Aryan guards still stand atop the pyramid with me.

The three guards raise their submachine guns at me in unison.

Thwang!

Again, in unison, the three guards drop to their knees before falling face down ... arrows in each of their backs.

Mayan warriors pour out of the temple. The Aryans on the ground start shooting the Mayan slaves in front of them, but quickly realize more Mayan warriors launch spears, sticks, and arrows at them from the jungle.

Confusion runs through the Aryans as arrows also fly at them from atop the pyramid, and they begin to fall quickly.

The Mayan slaves hurl themselves into the fray and start beating the Aryans to death with rocks, sticks, and anything else they can get their hands on.

Running toward the temple, I see Dr. Brandt with his hands up, pleading with Itzel and two of her warriors to spare him. Instead, they spear him. Once in the groin and once in the neck. He falls dead.

At Itzel's direction, the Mayan warriors allow me to pass them and enter the temple.

There, in front of the metal control box, stands Dr. Heisenberg, finger poised over the top red button.

The television screen shows the rocket hurtling through the air at an unimaginable speed toward a large metropolis filled with tall buildings and bustling with people.

Seeing me out of the corner of his eye, Heisenberg says, "Do you want to press the button … or should I?"

I sense no vitriol in his voice … no malevolence. Only kindness and redemption.

"Allow me," I answer.

He moves his hands to the levers and turns the rocket a little to the left as I take position next to him and ready my finger over the red button.

The television shows the rocket passing over Miami and zooming past a strip of barrier islands. The wide expanse of the Atlantic Ocean now dominates the screen, but a vast armada of vessels quickly comes into view.

Heisenberg turns the rocket a little more to the left, homing in on the center of the German fleet.

He counts down in English, "Five … four … three … two … one …. Now!"

I press the button and the screen flashes blinding white before instantly switching over to a static pattern.

The invasion is over before it begins, with 300,000 Nazi soldiers obliterated by their own wonder weapon.

From behind me, I hear a woman's voice yelling commands in Mayan.

Whipping around, I see Itzel. In her bloody hands are Votan's war club and the head of the Spear of Destiny.

The gunfire from outside has ended, meaning the Aryans have all been killed or they surrendered.

A new sound emerges from outside … from above the pyramid … a loud repeating thumping noise.

I rush outside to find a brightly painted helicopter circling above, looking for a place to land. It's mostly yellow, but I can make out a large white star within a blue circle and a couple of red and white stripes on its tail. It's American!

Behind me, emerge Itzel and Dr. Heisenberg.

To Itzel, I say, "Friends," hoping with our shared connection earlier that she can understand some of my language as I understand some of hers.

"Amigoo!" she yells to all the Maya around her as she points to the helicopter.

The Maya instinctively clear away, leaving a large patch of open ground for the helicopter to land.

I'm about to start the descent down the steep pyramid steps when Dr. Heisenberg asks, "Can I look at that?"

He's pointing at my hip, and I suddenly realize it doesn't hurt anymore.

Still wearing my Italian military uniform, the trousers are ripped and blood-soaked at my left hip. I pull apart the tear a bit as Heisenberg and Itzel step closer. Not only has the bleeding stopped, but the wound has closed and only a scar remains.

"You were pierced by the Spear of Destiny," says Heisenberg. "Your healing this quickly is nothing short of miraculous."

Itzel bows, offering me both the spearhead and Votan's war club.

I accept the spearhead, but tell her, "You keep this," pointing to the club. "It belongs with your people."

After watching Heisenberg quickly disable the rocket control box, I gather my few belongings in my messenger bag, and we descend the pyramid for the last time. We pass nearly 300 Aryan corpses on the way to meet the helicopter in the clearing near the remaining two rockets.

Bernie exits the helicopter first, nearly tripping over shoelaces that still dangle untied. He's followed by Kirk and then Ian.

Tears well up instantly, and even with Kirk there, I can't stop them from flowing.

"How the hell did you guys find me?" I manage to say.

Ian steps up, throws his arms around me in a bear hug, and says, "You have these two to thank for that!"

I shake my head ... not understanding what he means. "I thought Kirk was a traitor ... thought he was working with the Nazis."

"So did we," says Ian, stepping next to Kirk. "Turns out he was on a special mission from Sergeant Smith. He had to convince the Nazis he was a traitor, so he could learn their secrets. Had us all fooled. Once the Nazis trusted him, Kirk was able to find a map of all their secret bases around the world."

Floored by this new information, I say, "That still doesn't explain how you found me. Here in Chichen Itza."

"That was Bernie's doing," says Ian.

"It's a chicken," says Bernie. "It's a chicken …. It's a chicken. You kept on saying that while you were sleeping."

Ian follows with, "When we made it back to the American base near Nuremberg, it took Patton and Ike a while to trust us, but when Kirk produced the map, that got their attention. Eisenhower was reading off some of the cities where the Nazis had bases, and he saw the one here in Mexico … so close to America."

"It's a chicken," Bernie repeated.

Kirk finally speaks, "Chichen Itza. We couldn't get General Eisenhower or General Patton to agree to send any troops here, but after Sebastian unrelentingly harassed them for a few days, Ike finally agreed to requisition a cutter and a Coast Guard helicopter out of Key West and let us scout it out for ourselves."

"I st … I st … I st …." Dammit! I'm trying to say I still don't believe it, but can't get the words out.

With the first warm smile I've ever seen from him, Kirk extends his hand and says, "Max, I'm truly sorry for the way I treated you. I … I'm proud to say we're on the same team."

Shaking his hand, I say, "I still don't believe you found me, but I'm glad you did."

The Maya bring forth three Aryan soldiers. Apparently, these three surrendered to the warriors before being slaughtered like the rest of their comrades.

Dr. Heisenberg asks, "Do you want to bring them back and interrogate them?"

Pointing to the helicopter, Kirk says, "Bernie and I will stay with the missiles until reinforcements arrive. But, you still won't have room for them."

"I have a feeling Itzel and her warriors will dispense justice to these three in their own way."

The noise of the helicopter makes it nearly impossible to speak to my friends on the short flight back to the cutter waiting for us in the Gulf of Mexico, but I finally have a moment to read the second quatrain in the ancient book from Nostradamus.

Bestes farouches de faim fleuves tranner,
Plus part du champ encontre Hister sera,
En cage de fer le grand fera treisner,
Quand rien enfant Germain observera.
(Nostradamus, Michel. The Prophecies. C2:Q24)

Translating to English, I marvel at Nostradamus' ability to see and manipulate the future:

Beasts ferocious of hunger come from the river,
With the greater part of the battlefield against Hister.
Trapped by a great force, three will be feasted upon.
The German infancy will see no more time.

Thus ends the day old German Fourth Reich, along with Adolf Hitler … the second Antichrist.

TREY TYSON
LONGBOAT KEY, FL, USA
MAY 3, 2014

I wake to Sam shaking my shoulders and screaming in my face.

"Trey! Trey! You okay? Time to wake up."

My mouth moves, but no words come out.

"Shit, Trey. What's wrong?"

Stirring from where Max sits. Groggily, he says, "That was intense. Give him a minute, Samantha."

"He's never been like this before," the concern in her voice is palpable.

Max says, "To hold that connection for that long must have been excruciating for him. Give him some water."

A word finally escapes my lips, "Amaretto."

Chuckling, Max says, "Yes … of course … amaretto may soothe him. It is more appropriate."

Sam throws ice into three large snifters, and pours the amaretto so rapidly that she spills as much as makes it into the glasses.

"What happened?" She demands. Not waiting for us, she takes a swig from her glass.

"Max," I utter, "Tell her."

Max proceeds to bring Sam up to speed on everything I saw while visiting his past.

Sam blurts, "Holy shit! Max … you personally detonated the first atomic bomb in history."

Shaking his head with a sudden look of agony, he says, "That's not a moment of pride for me, it's … it's horrific."

"But, you wiped out 300,000 Nazi soldiers before they could invade America!"

"Again – not proud of it. You have to remember almost all of those soldiers were indoctrinated into the Nazi cause. It's my humble opinion that only Hitler and a few men in his inner circle were truly evil."

Having regained some of my energy, I add, "But, think of how many American lives you saved. Think about how many lives around the world you saved because America is still the bastion of freedom that we are. All of that could have been lost without you. On top of that, you killed Adolf Hitler … twice!"

That brings a slight smile to Max's face, "Okay, that does make me somewhat proud."

Sam's next question is the one that has been troubling me the most as well, "How did your hip heal so quickly?"

Max's answer is as revealing as most of his answers to my questions over the years, "I don't know."

"Dr. Heisenberg thought it was a miracle," I say. "For a physicist to think something is a miracle … beyond reasonable scientific explanation … well, I think that says a lot."

Max just shrugs.

"I'm not letting this go so easily," I continue. "The last time Jessica evaluated you, she said something that didn't make much sense at the time. Maybe it does make sense now."

"Red?" says Sam. "What did the good doctor say?"

I toss Sam a quick look of admonishment for calling my wife *Red* again. "Mind if I tell her, Max?"

He shrugs again.

"Jessica ran Max's lab results and said his physiology matches that of a healthy 50-year-old."

This time, Sam shrugs, "He's always looked young for his age, but so have you. I figured it was just good genes."

"It may be more than that," I counter. "He's 85, and Max doesn't look a day over 60. If we told a stranger he was 50, they'd probably believe us. Maybe ... just maybe, when he was cut by the Spear of Destiny, some remnants of Christ's blood found their way into Max."

"Holy fucking shit, Trey," Sam raises her eyebrows and blinks slowly. "Aren't you the one always finding a scientific answer any time someone points out some sort of miracle, or even if someone just talks about their faith. *You,* of all people, think the healing blood of Christ is keeping Max young?"

My turn to shrug and I down the rest of the amaretto in my glass.

Sam has always been thorough, and she hits on a key point, "Max, you obviously wear the amulet you found in 1945. You brought the crystal skull back with you. You gave the Mayan club to the shaman woman. Gotta ask you two questions .... Where was the Spear of Destiny before all of this? And, where is it now?"

Laughing, Max says, "You already know what I'm going to say. Nostradamus has his reasons for showing us history in the order he's choosing. We'll just have wait until he's ready to reveal those answers."

Epilogue

ULRICH VON BECKER
BERLIN, GERMANY
APRIL 30, 1945

Smoke and fire billow from half the buildings in the city. Amazingly, we were able to find Zelda's baby, but escaping the Red Army has not gone so well. We stand against a red brick wall with five Russian tanks surrounding us.

Turning to Zelda, I grab her by the arms, but not so roughly as to shake her baby. "I thought you said you could use your abilities to find a way out of this mess!"

Beautiful even now, with silt covering her cheeks, she answers in her sweet, high-pitched voice, "I am truly sorry, Ulrich. This is as I saw it. I spoke the truth to you. If you had stayed with Ister, you would have died. Tell the Russians who you are. Tell them you protected Hitler. They will want to question you. They will sometimes hurt you, but they will not kill you. It isn't a good life, but it is life."

"What of your daughter? What kind of life will she face, captured by the Russians?"

"That is not your concern," bellows a man as he emerges from the center tank. He wears an officer's uniform. Could be a general. As the man steps down from the tank, I see he is nearly my height. Following him is a boy of six or seven years.

"Who are you?" I demand of the Russian. Thoughts of rushing him enter my mind, but six Russian soldiers come from behind the line of tanks and stand with the first man.

Aiming a gun at me, he answers, "General Krostov. This is my son, Viktor. I find you, sir, standing in this god-forsaken city with my wife and a baby. Who the hell are you?"

I say nothing.

Zelda answers, "I will tell you, my husband. This is Ulrich Von Becker. He helped me rescue my baby from Hitler. He was Hitler's body guard. My baby ... her name is Katarina."

Rolling his eyes, General Krostov says, "I asked *him* the question. Not *you*. After you were taken from me in St. Petersburg, I thought I would never see you again. I find you in Berlin with a baby girl under the age of two. You were taken *four* years ago!" He removes the baby from Zelda's grip and hands her to one of his men. Turning to the boy, he orders, "Viktor, you can never let someone betray you. Keep your eyes open, son. This is important."

The boy obeys his father.

General Krostov studies me, especially noting my SS guard uniform, and says, "General Zhukov will want to speak with you."

The general nods to two of his soldiers, who put handcuffs on me, and walk me past the tanks and have me join a small group of German prisoners.

Behind me, I hear a single gunshot, and then the sound of a small body crumpling to the ground.

SIR ARCHIE
PYTHO ISLAND
APRIL 30, 1945

Waking from what feels like a week of sleep, I feel famished. But, my throat is so dry that I need to satisfy my thirst before eating.

Wearing a strange smile, Audrey hands me a goblet of wine.

Just rousing where the Oracle had been before I passed out, there's an older woman from the sisterhood. She looks like the woman who brought the basket of flowers ... just like the woman I had sex with during the Oracle's strange vision.

Finding my voice, I ask, "Where is the Oracle?"

The older sister says, "I'm right here. Don't you see me?"

"You may be related to the Oracle, but she's much younger than you," I answer.

"Oh no," her shoulders slump. "Attempting a possession is far more trying than a normal vision of the past or future. Making the attempt has taken the lives of several previous Oracles. If not life, itself, possessing another can take away many years. How much older do I look?"

Is this really her? Really the same young girl from before the vision?

"Did we have sex? Are you still a virgin?"

Shaking her head, the Oracle answers, "I was able to project my feelings ... and my image onto Dame Audrey ... and, I was able to feel what she felt ... her love for you served to enhance the, um ... *experience.*"

Audrey asks, "Did it work? Did you change history?"

"No," I say. "A split-second decision by a boy from 1945 prevented us from accomplishing our mission."

"It was not a wasted effort, though," says the older looking Oracle. "There are lessons we can take from the experience, and we will have at least one more opportunity for success."

"When do we try again?"

Rallying her strength, the Oracle sits taller and says, "I will need some time ... I don't know how long ... but, I must recover from this before we try again."

MAX MEDICI
PRINCETON, NJ, USA
JUNE 1, 1945

"It's mighty good to see you on your feet again, Professor Einstein!"

His office here at our camp in Princeton is just as cluttered as the last time I saw it, but the warmth of June and the glow of success reflecting on his face create an entirely new feel to the log cabin.

"It is quite good to see you as well, Maximo. I have so many questions for you. Unfortunately, our time is somewhat limited. President Truman is meeting with Kirk, Bernard, and Sebastian in *ze* gymnasium. He wants to meet with you next ... privately."

"Anything I need to worry about?"

"No, Maximo. I imagine he just wants to thank you."

"We lost some good men, Professor. Sergeant Smith ... Erik ... Dieter. They gave their lives to save our country ... to save the world."

The professor lowers his head and says, "That is my responsibility. My fault ... not yours."

"How could it be your fault?"

"I have read *ze* notes from your debriefing. We chased *ze* wrong people in our pursuit of *ze* traitor. I should have known that Toch was against us."

"How could you know? We have to trust our friends and trust our instincts. Sometimes, we'll be wrong. Sometimes, those closest to us will hurt us more than any stranger could. But, why bother living if you can't ever trust in people?"

With raised eyebrows, Professor Einstein says, "I hear *ze* wisdom in your words. You have matured, Maximo. Your assignment is officially over. *Ze* technology we have learned from *ze* rockets recovered in Mexico will shave years from our research."

"That's it? My assignment is over? Where does that leave me? There's no career path for a young spy ... at least not that I know of."

"Be patient, and opportunities may –"

A knock interrupts our conversation. Without waiting for a response, Secret Service agent Floyd enters the professor's office.

"President Truman is ready to meet with you, Maximo."

"Okay," I say. "I guess I'm ready to meet him, too."

"Look," says Floyd. "The president is a practical man and loyal. He knows what you've accomplished. He's going to offer you a job ... any job you want. The Secret Service could use a good man like you. You're young. Too young by our standards, but he'll bend the rules if you tell him that's what you want. You're a natural, kid. A perfect fit for the job of protecting the most important man in the world."

2ND HOLY WARRIOR

V. RAY

www.ingramcontent.com/pod-product-compliance
Lightning Source LLC
Chambersburg PA
CBHW070307280626
47159CB00017B/346